FROZEN REACTION
By Spencer Jacobson

Frozen Reaction

By Spencer Jacobson

A15 Publishing

5219 Monticello Avenue #5037

Williamsburg, VA 23188-9998

WWW.A15Publishing.com

To the man who edited, molded, and influenced my writing style through years of heavily edited research papers, speeches, and stories. I love you, Dad, and could not have done it without you.

CHAPTER ONE

Amanda Jorgenson was dead. Sheriff Erikson was sure of it, even without a body. The Sheriff's department was combing through her house just outside of town. Originally, Erikson was hoping that Amanda was simply tired of the brutal Minnesota winters and gone on a spur-of-the-moment vacation. Sitting in her kitchen drinking coffee and staring at the shattered, bloody mirror, however, he knew there was not much hope for her.

The deputies were searching the small two-bedroom house for clues while the lab technicians worked to identify and age the blood samples from the broken mirror. Erikson had been in law enforcement long enough to know how the mirror had been shattered. As the head lab technician—a short, stocky man named Thompson—approached him, the sheriff held up his hand.

"Let me guess, the impact in the hall mirror was caused by someone smashing someone else's head into it, probably last night or really early this morning." Erikson was staring at Amanda's table, spinning the white mug of cooling coffee in a lazy, absent-minded circle.

The lab technician furrowed his brow.

"You got it with the impact, boss. We won't know the time until we get some samples back to the lab, but from our initial analyses here on scene, I would have to say you are correct about that one as well."

Erikson stopped spinning the mug, meeting Thompson's gaze. Two men who had been doing this for much of their adult lives. Two men who didn't need the lab results to tell them that Amanda Jorgenson was dead. In a typical case, he'd follow protocol and chalk it up to another sick fuck taking out his anger on a love gone south. God knows he'd seen his fair share in this business. No, this had a feeling of somehow being a beginning rather than an end. End to poor Ms. Jorgenson that he'd easily surmise. The why's and who was another matter that the team would know soon enough.

He sighed and asked, "Anything else, Tom?"

"A few hair and fiber samples, nothing that really sticks out at this time. We'll run it all, just to be sure." Thompson turned to finish his collection.

"We're getting ready to head back. You need anything else from us, Gerry?" Erikson thought for a moment before responding.

2

Thompson's forensics team had been there for a few hours already and had combed through the small house as thoroughly as could be expected.

"No, take your guys back to the lab. I'll swing by the hospital after I get back to the office. Thanks, Tommy."

Thompson smiled weakly, then turned and directed his technicians out the front door, through the sub-zero temperatures, and back to their van. Erikson sat by himself in the quiet house. He had subconsciously resumed spinning the coffee mug. Taking another deep, measured breath, he pushed himself away from the table and stood up.

As he replaced the chair, Erikson looked around the small house. Three out of the five deputies were concluding their search of the bedrooms. The lead deputy shook his head as he removed his latex gloves. Nobody had found anything in the house, so Erikson did a final sweep through the short hallway to the garage.

It was actually the garage that had given Erikson hope when he'd first arrived. He'd received the call on his way home for lunch and, though he could've sent any of his dozen or so on-duty deputies to the site, he'd decided to swing by himself. He had radioed in and headed over to her house to check it out.

He pulled in the driveway and braced himself before getting out into the -10-degree wind-chill. Tugging the collar of his department-issued brown parka up around his face, he let his mind wander to the warm, sandy beaches of Maui, where he and Ellen had vacationed briefly last winter. *I desperately need some time away*, he thought as he rang the doorbell. *Hopefully his earlier assumption was just his stressed out, cop brain taking over.* He rang the bell again with another silent plea wishing that Lahaina Resort is where Ms. Jorgenson has gone off to.

Amanda Jorgenson's house was a typical size for a single, early-thirties cleaning lady. He rang the doorbell a second time, listening to its hollow buzz on the other side of the door. *Nothing.* Erikson scanned the outside of the house, his keen, bright eyes taking in every detail. The blinds were closed making it impossible for Erikson to see inside. There were no footprints in the snow in her yard. The driveway had been shoveled, so there wasn't much to see there. Erikson shivered as he stepped over to the side door that led into the garage. He tried the knob. *Locked.* Backing up a step, he raised his right leg and slammed his heavily booted foot into the door.

3

"DAMMIT!!!" he snarled as he felt his 36-year-old knee pop. *I'm getting too old for this shit,* he thought, smiling with gritted teeth at the cliché. *Thompson would be loving this,* the Sheriff thought through this shooting pain in his knee. Out of the two men, Thompson was far less likely to complain about his age, despite the decades more he had experienced. Erikson bent his knees, making sure they both still worked.

"Good enough," he sighed, and stepped into the slightly less cold garage. With the exception of some cleaning supplies and lawn care equipment, it was empty. No vehicle. Erikson quickly searched his memory for the dispatcher's description of Amanda's car. A gray, early 2000s Dodge minivan. The only trace of the van was the brown, icy sludge that drops from the bottom of cars in garages around Minnesota all winter long. Erikson had not been terribly concerned before, and now he was pretty sure that Amanda Jorgenson had simply decided to take a little vacation. While violent crimes had been on the rise across the state, his jurisdiction had, thankfully, been spared the worst of it so far. A few shootings here and there, mostly drug related, and only in ones and twos. His eyes scanned the far wall. A snow blower, a weed whacker, a mower, gas can. Typical things, nothing of note. As he turned around, though, his optimism dried up.

Upon closer inspection of the brown slush, he could make out two heavy sets of boot prints, walking side by side, leading from the house to the center of the garage. Between the boot prints, two drag marks.

Erikson froze. His eyes widened and his pupils dilated. His senses were heightened as he reached to his gun belt and quickly disengaged the retention strap and pulled out his pistol. He keyed his radio:

"Dispatch, this is Sheriff Erikson, I need backup and forensics here, *now.*" His breathing was so heavy he barely heard the reply. He slowly walked toward the door. Erikson turned down the volume of his radio and held his Glock 21 .45 caliber handgun just under the center of his narrowed field of vision. Heart racing, he reached out, pulled the door open and rushed inside. He moved through the house in a quick, practiced manner. Living room, *clear.* Kitchen, *clear.* Hallway and both bedrooms, *clear.* Bathrooms, *clear.*

He was only vaguely aware of the shattered mirror in the entryway until after he had finished his sweep. Certain that nobody else

4

was in the home, Sheriff Erikson spotted the unbrewed pot of coffee, flicked the maker on and sat down at the table. He could see the mirror, and he could see that Amanda Jorgenson was dead.

CHAPTER TWO

Thomas "Tommy" Thompson and his lab technicians were nearly back to the sheriff's department offices in downtown Alexandria when the all-points bulletin went out on the radio for Ms. Jorgenson's van. Early 2000s gray Dodge minivan, plate number 473 KZR, two or more suspects, probably male. Possible hostage with them, woman, early thirties, brown hair, 5'3", 155 pounds. Tommy grimaced. This kind of thing always felt so impersonal over the radio. Tommy had been at this a long time, at sixty-five, he had been serving the same community for nearly forty-three years, but he still had not quite got used to hearing the dry descriptions over the radio. Dry descriptions of people that made them sound something less than human.

He'd been a sheriff's deputy for twenty-five years. That job had cost him a marriage early on, but he had loved serving his community more than he had loved that jealous woman, so he didn't regret one second of it. Serving the community was a good start but he couldn't give up on the promise he'd made to his mother and went back to school. With the doctorate in criminal forensics he continued his work in the community and lead as chief of the forensics lab in the Douglas County Sheriff's Office. Having the knowledge to unearth tough crimes and protect the place he loved, gave him a deep sense of pride and purpose.

This was not his first kidnapping. They weren't common, but he had seen a few over the years. Usually they involved more blood, more destruction within the home. Drapes torn, glass broken, tables flipped. Something about this one made Tommy uneasy. With the exception of the hallway mirror, nothing was out of place. The whole thing felt off. Too cold, too clean. Almost professional. Tommy shuddered as he drove back into town, looking in the rearview mirror at his staff.

Tommy's team of crime scene investigators weren't allowed to openly carry sidearms, as they weren't law enforcement. But Tommy had been in this line of work for a long time and had been fired on more than once in the white panel van that said "Douglas County Forensics" on the side. He had petitioned the sheriff's department, but Sheriff

Erikson remained firm. This wasn't Hollywood, and the forensics team would not be allowed to carry weapons, not openly anyway.

As a compromise, Erikson had invested no small amount of his personal time teaching the forensics team members concealed carry laws and how to shoot a handgun. After two lengthy days of operative and tactical instruction, Erikson issued each of the six team members a conceal and carry license.

The forensics van was mostly quiet, each of the five sitting in the mobile lab with stony expressions on their faces as they reflected on the crime scene, and the investigation ahead. As Tommy turned the van from the county highway back on the main road to Alexandria, the radio crackled to life.

"Douglas Sheriff, this is Alexandria Police Dispatch."

"Go ahead, APD," said Sheriff Erikson through the radio. Judging from Erikson's gruff, weary voice, Tommy wondered if he was still at the crime scene. Tommy changed lanes to pass an elderly couple tooling along in their Cadillac.

"We— One of our patrolmen found Ms. Jorgenson."

"Roger APD, what is her status?"

"Deceased, sir. Single gunshot wound to the back of the head. Our patrolman says some kids found her in a dumpster next to Walmart."

The forensics van filled with quiet tension as they all digested the grisly news. Tommy could see one of his younger lab technicians shaking his head. He realized he had been holding his breath as Erikson started to speak again.

"Copy APD, anything else you can tell us?"

"Only that her wallet was left with her ID. No cards, no cash. Looks like a robbery."

It can't be, Tommy thought, even as Will, the forensic team's newest member blurted, "It can't be, sir. We saw the house; nothing was taken besides the car."

"Hang on, Will, I'm trying to hear," Tommy snapped, a little more forcefully than was warranted, and he turned the police radio back up to hear Erikson's response.

"Understood, APD. Should we come to you for pick-up, or can you bring her to us?"

Will started shaking his head. "Why is Erikson agreeing with them, it makes no sen—"

6

"Dammit, Will!" Tommy half-shouted, turning toward the co-pilot seat. "The sheriff just needs the information from the police. He doesn't need the approval of twenty-five-year-old know-it-alls."

Tommy turned back to the road. All of his staff were staring at him, mouths agape. None of them had heard him get anywhere near as worked up before.

Tommy started slowing the van down as he approached the city limits of Alexandria. The community was beginning to stretch the limits of its infrastructure, having grown from roughly 12,000 people to nearly 50,000 in just ten years. For Tommy, and anyone who'd lived their entire lives in small-town Alexandria, the growth felt like it had happened over night.

Crime was up, but it was mostly contained to the hastily erected lower income housing on the outskirts south of town, next to the new industrial park. Most of that crime consisted of petty things like theft or controlled substance busts. Occasionally something bigger, but even then, seldom violent.

The sheriff's office hadn't gotten a facelift in thirty-some years, as the rapid community expansion had necessitated that the Sheriff's Department put any available money into hiring and training more deputies rather than cosmetic changes, so they had co-located the forensics lab with the morgue at the hospital. As Tommy prepared to turn left off of 3rd Avenue and onto Broadway towards the hospital, he was temporarily blinded by the glare of the early afternoon sun bouncing off the glass and snow in the downtown area.

As Tommy rounded the corner, the glare lessened, and his eyes readjusted. He saw something that made his heart race: a gray Dodge minivan was waiting at the light at the end of the block. Before Tommy's aging eyes could make out the license plate, Will had already snatched the radio transmitter from the console.

"Uh, Sheriff, we see Ms. Jorgenson's van."

"Identify yourself please and explain how you're sure." Erikson's voice came back over the radio, a mixture of annoyance, excitement, and concern blending together through the static.

"Give me that!" Tommy wrenched the microphone from Will's hand. "Gerry, this is Tommy. We are at the intersection of 6th and Broadway, and we have in our sights a gray Dodge minivan, license plate 4-7-3, Kilo Victor Romeo. How copy?"

"Solid copy, Tommy. Standby for a patrol unit."

The light turned green, and the line of cars lurched ahead. Tommy could see an Alexandria Police Department SUV coming from the opposite direction.

"Good thing we're only a few blocks from the cop shop," Will remarked. "They got someone out here fast. Maybe we'll see these guys get rolled up."

Tommy gave a slight smile. "Let's hope so." The SUV's light bar and siren lit up and the forensics van grew quiet again, this time thick with excitement.

The gray minivan screeched to a halt as the police SUV slid in front of it, cutting it off. The forensics team watched as the patrolmen got out of their vehicle, rifles up. Will rolled down his window.

"Step out of the vehicle, slowly!"

"Put your hands in the air!"

"Holy shit, man, this is way more exciting than most days!" Will was hanging halfway out his window now, excitedly witnessing what most would only ever see in movies or on TV.

A dusty red Pontiac sedan eased out of line and pulled in front of the forensics van, blocking Will's view. Tommy reached for the radio, eyeing the sedan uneasily.

"Oh shit, Tommy!" Will shouted as he jerked himself back into the car. "That Pontiac is full of guys with guns!"

Tommy mashed the transmit button on the radio. "The gray van is a trap! Red Pontiac coming straight for you!" Too late. The Pontiac lurched towards the officers. They dove in opposite directions as the car slammed into the police SUV. Even while on the ground the officers staggered to their feet and opened fire on the car, but they were heavily outnumbered. Seven men in black hoods and body armor spilled out of Ms. Jorgenson's van. Quick bursts of automatic fire cut the officers down.

The forensics team watched, wide-eyed and speechless, as four men clambered out of the smashed Pontiac. For a moment, the eleven gunmen stood in a rough circle, facing each other. Suddenly, they turned and started firing into the cars and shops around them.

One of the gunmen walked towards the forensics van, stitching the hood and windshield with bullet holes. The team threw themselves to the floor as the van was perforated by bullets. A second gunman joined the first, firing into the side of the van. Tommy heard some of the guys screaming and crying out in pain. He closed his eyes and

8

prayed for it to be over quickly, and, after what felt like an eternity, the firing stopped.

It took him a moment to regain his senses, but he heard the slamming of car doors and the screeching of tires through the sounding nearby car horns. Then the smell hit him. The scent of blood and human excrement meant that someone on his team had to have been hit. He looked to his right. Will was okay. Clearly in shock, but physically okay. Will and Tommy had been protected from the frontal barrage by the engine block, and the second gunman appeared to have focused on the rear of the panel van.

As he turned, Tommy could hear a fresh round of gunfire start again off in the distance. *What the fuck? What the fuck? WHAT THE FUCK?* He took stock of the carnage in the back. Looking at the mangled mass of perforated metal, shattered glass, and torn bodies, he knew in an instant that he and Will were the only survivors.

The gunfire in the distance swelled, and so did Tommy's rage. This wasn't supposed to happen. Who the fuck were these asshats, and what the fuck did they think they were doing? He opened the back door with his handgun drawn. A small Smith & Wesson 9mm, it stood no chance against the automatic weapons the gunmen had been wielding, but he had an idea.

Tommy stepped out of the van into utter anarchy. People were lying all over the pavement, screaming for help or rolling over in the throes of death. The medics were just arriving on scene, bravely rushing into the chaos to help whoever they could. Keeping low, he sprinted to the police SUV, where the fallen officers lay in pools of steaming blood from visible head, shoulder, and stomach wounds. Stuffing his concealed carry piece back in its holster, he removed both of their gun belts, scooped up their rifles, and hustled back to the van. Will was sitting upright, staring hard at nothing in particular.

"Will, snap out of it," Tommy wheezed, out of breath from his sprint. "I need your help, Will." Will turned his head towards Tommy but seemed to be looking right through him. "Come on, Will, we gotta do something about these assholes," Tommy pleaded. He grabbed the kid's hand, and Will startled for a second, then his eyes focused on Tommy. "Come on. We gotta go." Will nodded his head, and slowly climbed out of the van. "You know how to use this?" Tommy held out one of the patrol rifles, a Bushmaster AR15. Will nodded numbly and reached out and took the rifle from Tommy. "What about this?"

Tommy held out the officer's pistol belt, with a Glock handgun and three spare mags. Again, Will nodded. He took the belt, snapping it on and tightening it around his waist. "Alright, Will, let's go get these fuckers."

CHAPTER THREE

As quick as they could, Tommy and Will hustled toward the sound of gunfire. As they grew nearer, they could tell that the fighting was coming from the sheriff's office. Taking short, painful breaths in the bitter air, Tommy and Will stopped about a half a block away and stood behind a thick maple tree as Tommy took stock of the situation.

The sheriff's office only had two entrances and exits: the front door and the garage. The garage door was closed, which was a good sign. It looked like a lot of cars had been shot up in the parking lot next to the garage door. Peeking out, Tommy could see the remaining gunmen taking cover behind the newly installed bollards in front of the main entrance they were focused on their attack of the sheriff's office and did not notice Tommy and Will hiding behind the Maple tree. Ms. Jorgenson's van was smashed against one of the furthest of the four-foot wide bollards.

Tommy counted seven gunmen still in the fight, with four lying in pools of freezing blood on the sidewalk. He could hear sirens approaching, but he had no way of knowing if it was more police, more medics, or a combination of both. Ducking back behind the tree, he addressed a clearly shell-shocked Will.

"Alright, Will, here's the deal, I count seven of these guys still up and breathing. You take the far side of the street, and I'll take this side. Lie down and start shooting at the furthest one down the street and work your rounds back this way. Don't get any closer unless you have to. If you run out of ammo in your rifle, drop it and use the pistol. Hopefully we can divert their attention long enough for the guys inside to make a few good hits." Will stared at him and nodded. Tommy continued, "It looks like they're wearing body armor. Headshots if you can." He grabbed Will's shoulders and locked eyes with him. "Let's do this."

Pushing out from the tree, Tommy and Will quietly sprinted towards their designated areas. Tommy lined up his sights on the closest gunman, then waited for Will to get across the street before squeezing the trigger.

Tommy's first shot dropped the gunman. Will was nowhere near as disciplined, ignoring his instructions and standing fully upright, firing wildly in the general direction of the gunmen. His magazine was empty within seconds, and as he threw his rifle down, the remaining six gunmen turned to fire on him. Tommy saw the first couple of rounds blow through Will, spraying blood across the snow. An ugly, guttural noise issued from Will's throat as he tried to draw his pistol.

Tommy focused on his sights, frantically trying to hit more of the gunmen before they could finish off Will. He struck one under the arm and the side of the head and another in the chest plate, causing the gunman to jerk in pain and fall to the ground. Five of the gunmen still managed to get their rifles trained on Will, still unaware that they were taking fire from Tommy's position. Tommy felt his rifle go empty. He drew his pistol and stood up to rush the gunmen. As he watched Will get struck by bullets from the five remaining gunmen, he was vaguely aware of more rifle fire coming from the sheriff's office. He emptied the first magazine without really aiming, drawing fire away from the building.

Tommy dove behind the first bollard as the rifle shots cracked and hissed above his head, making a sharp popping sound as they smacked into the bollard in front of him. He ducked his head to reload his pistol and saw the first of the sheriff's deputy cars pull in at the end of the street. As the flashing lights and sirens caught the attention of the gunmen, Tommy rose and renewed his frantic rush towards them.

The next bollard was only a few feet away, and that was as far as he wanted to go, but as he rose, he saw the closest gunman's head splash open onto the sidewalk as someone inside the office landed an effective headshot. Tommy seized the opportunity to close the distance as fast as his sixty-five-year-old legs would allow him.

The next gunman was crouched facing away from Tommy, evidently unaware that his accomplice was no longer backing him up. Tommy lined up the sights of his pistol and fired but pushed the shot low and struck the gunman in the rear plate of his body armor. This knocked the gunman forward, and he started to turn. Tommy emptied the last twelve rounds of his pistol into the gunman, striking him in the head and dumping his brains all over the sidewalk.

Down to three final gunmen. The closest one turned as Tommy tried to take cover behind the closest bollard to him. A flurry of fully automatic gunfire spit in Tommy's direction. The bullets blew through Tommy's thigh, nearly severing his leg at the knee. Tommy screamed in pain and struggled to reload his pistol as he dragged himself behind the bollard. He only had two magazines left, and he knew he was losing a lot of blood. Tommy looked down at his leg, saw the mangled mass of flesh and bone being held on by a loose flap of skin, and felt a rush of nausea.

Fighting down the urge to puke, he stuck his pistol around the bollard and emptied his magazine blindly. There was nothing more he could do. He was starting to black out as he inserted his last magazine into the pistol. As his vision blurred, he became vaguely aware of three shapes running across the street. He fought to bring his vision back into focus and recognized the three gunmen. Raising his pistol, he emptied his final magazine into the moving shapes, praying he'd strike anything.

The slide locked back on the empty magazine, and Tommy dropped the pistol. He knew that he should have been colder than he was. He stared straight ahead, unseeing but vaguely aware that of one of the three escapees was screaming in pain. A sudden chill gripped his body. *There's the cold,* he thought. *But at least I got that guy.* Tommy frowned as he was enveloped in darkness.

CHAPTER FOUR

Several hours after the carnage, Erikson was sitting in his office reading the preliminary reports. Sixteen civilians dead, thirty-four wounded in the initial slaughter on Broadway. The two APD patrolmen who had tried to confront the gunman-laden van on Broadway. Four of the six forensics team were killed on Broadway. Four deputies killed in their cars as they left the garage at the sheriff's office. One killed while firing from the second-story window as the gunmen tried to storm the front door. Tommy and Will, the last of the forensics team, killed while assisting the office standoff. Eight gunmen killed, four trying to charge the front door. One was even outfitted with an explosive vest that had failed to detonate. One gunman wounded, captured, and in stable condition with a SWAT team guarding him. Two escaped, gone without a trace. Total time from the APD SUV making contact to the surviving two gunmen escaping: fifteen minutes, thirty-eight seconds.

What Erikson wished was that Thompson and Will had not left the relative safety of their van to chase after these guys. Tommy was sixty-five for Christ's sake, and Will was a young, pudgy lab rat. Deep down, Erikson understood that it was probably some sense of duty, but right then, he was just grief stricken at losing his friend.

He couldn't stop watching the tapes. Security cameras all around the office and the surrounding buildings, one of the few infrastructure upgrades that the department had been able to afford; had captured every second of the killing spree. They figured out that the Pontiac had been reinforced with steel plating to make it more or less bullet-proof, which explained the ineffectiveness of the previous shots fired by the two officers who'd made initial contact.

Witnesses were saying that the shooting lasted for upwards of ten or fifteen minutes, but cameras don't suffer from shock. The tapes said three minutes and twenty-four seconds from first shots fired to the gunmen piling in their van. After the gunmen left, the tapes showed Tommy running over to the fallen officers, appropriating their gear, and taking off on foot with Will Schlitz in tow.

Two minutes and forty seconds later, the tapes showed four of the gunmen tumbling out of the still-moving van, setting up a skirmish line, and unloading on the deputies who were exiting via the garage. The four deputies who made it out before the garage was locked down were cut down in fifty-four seconds.

The remaining gunmen jumped out of the car, allowing it to smash into a bollard. Thirty-two seconds later, the gunmen regrouped in front of the office, firing controlled bursts at the windows and front door. Fourteen seconds later, there was a sharp increase in fire, as four gunmen rushed the front door while their comrades covered their advance by shooting at the front windows of the building. They were cut down in only ten seconds.

The standoff continued for three minutes and twenty-four seconds before Tommy and Will made their move. Tommy killed the nearest gunman with a clean shot to the head, but Will stood there like a maniac, firing blindly, and he was cut down for it, dead within seconds. Tommy managed to get closer and kill two or three more—the video wasn't conclusive on one of them and the state forensics team wouldn't arrive for a few more hours to replace the one Douglas County had lost. One minute and fifteen seconds after rushing the bollards, Tommy got hit in the leg, bad. Erikson grimaced. The medics said he took six rounds to the leg, nearly simultaneously, nearly cutting it off above the knee. They figured he had to have been losing consciousness around the time he emptied his last magazine, and Erikson reckoned it was a miracle that he'd even landed his rounds in the same zip code as the surviving gunmen, let alone clip one in the pelvic girdle. Two minutes, fifty-one seconds after Tommy got hit, he bled out, and the last two gunmen got away.

Fifteen minutes and thirty-eight seconds of pure terror had left Erikson with a decimated sheriff's department, zero forensic capabilities, and short one of the best friends he would ever have. Tommy had used his hard-won experience to guide the younger sheriff, and although Tommy was technically no longer a deputy, they had always looked out for each other. Erikson rubbed his eyes with his palms and started to cry.

His grief was interrupted by his personal cell phone buzzing. Swiping his eyes and nose with his forearm, he composed himself long enough to see that the call was coming through as a restricted number.

He picked up the phone and denied the call. He leaned back in his chair and started mentally replaying the tapes, thinking about what he could have done differently, or how he wished it could have been him instead of any one of the victims. He knew that the news crews were already in town, and that this would almost certainly be branded one of the largest terrorist attacks since the wars "ended."

15

Another restricted call lit up his cell phone, and again he denied the call. The caller tried again, this time on his work cell, and then his direct office line. Startled, Erikson picked up his office phone.

"This," Erikson swallowed hard to clear his throat, "this is Sheriff Erikson."

"Sheriff Erikson, this is James Gunderson. Do you remember me?"

"Gunderson…as in Judge Gunderson's son?" Sheriff Erikson replied.

There was a grim determination in the caller's voice. "That's the one." *What the hell does this guy want?* Erikson racked his mind for more memories of this Gunderson. Something clicked, but it didn't shed much light on why the man would be calling him now.

"Aren't you in the Army or something like that?" Erikson frowned into his handset as he tried to piece the puzzle together. His mind was already numb from the day's events.

"The Air Force, or at least I was. I left after the wars ended and the bases were getting shut down. But that's not why I called you." Gunderson's voice was oddly calm. "I work in the private sector now, run my own business actually, and I have something that will benefit both of us." Erikson's heart started racing. "If it has something to do with the shit show that occurred this morning, I suggest you tell me right now. I don't much feel like playing games." Erikson was as polite and forceful as he could, but even he could tell he was speaking sharply to the man on the other end of the phone call.

"I won't be doing that, Sheriff, not yet anyway, but I would like to meet with you at a mutual friend's house."

"First tell me something about what you know, and then I'll decide if we meet or not." Erikson needed to maintain control of the conversation, to assert himself in some way. As they spoke, he started to remember more. His father Samuel was a county judge in town. His mother Diane was a teacher at the community college. James joined the Air Force right after college. Upstanding guy, Erikson supposed, but there was still nothing that could connect him to this morning's killings.

"Fair enough, Sheriff. We have the two missing gunmen in our custody. We not only know the identities of all the men who were killed and captured this morning, we also know where they were trained, and how they entered the country." Erikson's eyes widened. The bit about the two escapees hadn't been released yet. Now Erikson was sure that Gunderson wasn't bluffing. "We believe that this is the first in a series of attacks, that the attackers are a new breed of revolutionary terrorist, and that you and your small force of deputies are going to be sorely outmatched within a couple of months."

Erikson took a few deep breaths. "Listen, Mr. Gunderson, if you're fucking with me—"

"Check your phone, Sheriff," Gunderson interrupted. Erikson looked down at his personal cell and it lit up with an incoming message. He unlocked the phone and let out an audible gasp. "So, you see the picture?" Gunderson asked intently.

"Yes," Erikson replied, "but how the hell did you get this?" The picture showed two men, handcuffed and on their knees with two more men holding rifles above them. Even without their masks, Erikson recognized the two terrorists from the security tapes. Same shirts, same body armor.

"Trade secrets, Sheriff," Gunderson replied. "The man on the right is Anwar al-Kobani, a radical militant who has popped up from time to time all over the Middle East. The man on the left is Jesús Longoria Reyes, a former narcotics trafficker and mid-level managerial thug for one of the cartels in Mexico, now a gun-for-hire and human trafficker."

Erikson thought for a minute. "When and where should I meet you?"

"7:00 tomorrow morning at the Severson manor." Gunderson replied. The sheriff looked at the clock on his wall. It was already 11:30 p.m. He had been at work for nearly twenty hours.

"I'll be there. Is this one of those 'come alone' type of deals, or can I bring a friend?" There was a slight pause on the line, as if Gunderson was composing his reply.

"Bring only who you can trust, Sheriff. It's going to get ugly out there."

CHAPTER FIVE

The next morning dawned bright and just as bitterly cold as every other day in the last several weeks. Erikson had arrived at the Severson mansion just as the sun was rising over the wind-blasted lake. He was early, as always, but he got the feeling that old judge Severson had expected that. Erikson was ushered into a posh study and invited to relax while they waited for Gunderson to arrive. One of Severson's security team had left a tray with a pot of coffee on a large wooden desk.

Although there were several large leather chairs, Erikson didn't feel like sitting. He was agitated, wired from too much caffeine and too little sleep. A half night's worth of searching Google had yielded only cursory information about Gunderson. Most of it was stuff he already knew. Old newspaper articles from Gunderson's athletic career as a high school student in Alexandria, volunteerism in the community, church articles, innocuous stuff.

Some of the more recent articles had covered his appointment to the Air Force Academy at the turn of the century. Various medals and achievements, citations for things in prestigious assignments in SOCOM and AFSOC, and then a sudden departure from the Air Force as a young major in 2010. After that, there was nothing. Not a single mention of James Gunderson anywhere. Erikson knew because he had looked. All night.

Taking a deep breath, the sheriff poured himself a mug of black coffee. The smell alone usually woke him up, but the stress of the last 24 hours was starting to wear on him. He let out a long sigh over the top lip of the mug, partly to cool the hot, dark liquid, and partly in an attempt to focus his mind on something other than how tired he was.

Erikson was lucky enough to have a team of highly capable deputies who were handling the grunt work of the investigation. He was also grateful that, despite the persistence of the media, he did not have to give any interviews. The mayor, Jennifer Stark had determined that only a select few were to talk to the media, and, for whatever reason, Erikson's name was not on that list. That suited him just fine.

Erikson's thoughts were interrupted by the sound of footsteps at the door. He was shortly met with the visage of the elderly Bob Severson. A former attorney and, later, district court judge, Bob had remained active in the community well into his 80s. At 93, his age was finally catching up to him, although he didn't appear to have much trouble walking himself around.

"Good morning, Sheriff." Severson stuck out a gnarled hand. "Mr. Gunderson and his associates will be with us momentarily." Erikson accepted the handshake, being careful not to squeeze too hard.

"I appreciate you facilitating this meeting," Erikson did his best to smile, "but I have to admit, I don't have any idea what Gunderson wants."

Severson smiled softly as he walked around his large oak wood desk. "I think you will be very interested in his proposition, but I am going to let him tell you about it." Severson sat down gingerly, placing his elbows on the desk and clasping his hands together in front of him. Erikson was about to respond when he heard the sound of a car crunching its way up the icy driveway. As he neared the window, a white Toyota SUV pulled up to the parking apron and slid to a stop next to Erikson's cruiser. Leaving the engine running to keep the truck warm, three men in heavy coats with collars turned up against the wind exited the car and walked briskly to the front door. Erikson heard the front door open, followed by the murmurs of the three men as they spoke with the security team, and their footsteps as they crossed the hall to the study.

There were three sharp, authoritative knocks on the study door, to which Mr. Severson cheerfully replied, "Come in! Door's open!" The heavy wooden door swung open, and three men in business casual strode into the room. The first Erikson recognized immediately as James Gunderson, looking almost exactly like he had nearly a decade ago, but with a trim beard and a smattering of gray hairs. Gunderson crossed the room and extended his hand.

"Sheriff Erikson, so nice to see you again." Gunderson shook hands quickly and firmly. "Shame it had to be under such tragic circumstances."

"I just want to know what is going on." Erikson sounded exasperated, even to himself, but Gunderson simply nodded. "Fair enough, Sheriff, but I advise you to sit down, as this is going to be a bit of a presentation."

Erikson took a seat in one of the large, leather chairs, and Gunderson started to speak. "Sheriff, I wish we could be meeting under better circumstances, but there is nothing we can do about that now except be ready for a potential follow-on attack. I am sure that you are aware of my military history, and equally sure that you are unaware of my activities since I left the military in 2010."

The sheriff nodded and Gunderson continued, "Shortly after I left the military, I started my own private security company. For this company, I manage the logistics, accounting, and other bean-counter type aspects. My vice president for operations and training is Mr. Anthony Dufraine, a former Marine Raider." Gunderson motioned to the man to his left, and Mr. Dufraine stepped forward to shake the sheriff's hand. "To my right, I have my VP of intelligence, surveillance and reconnaissance, Mr. Ajay Yale." Mr. Yale stepped forward in like manner, shook Erikson's hand, and stepped back. "Mr. Yale is a top-notch specialist in his field and comes from one of the many three-letter agencies in the federal government."

Erikson nodded. Despite not knowing what was going on just yet. He looked over at Severson, who looked on pensively, as Gunderson continued his spiel.

"For the past several years, our organization has been perfecting its craft in the southwest region of the country, assisting in the so-called war on drugs and with various border security operations. We are a small outfit, and we have recently relocated. Officially, what we are offering you is the opportunity to use us, free of charge I might add, in an advisory role as you train your deepening snatch and grab missions to round up suspected terrorists and revolutionary members in and around central Minnesota."

Erikson sat for a minute, processing what he had just heard. Gunderson and his associates stood silently, watching Erikson's mouth open and close partially before he found the words to speak.
"So, what you're saying is, that a bunch of *mercenaries*," the sheriff hissed through his teeth, "are going to be rounding up citizens in my jurisdiction without due process?" He looked wildly around the room. "And who the hell is paying for this bullshit if it's free of charge?"

"Sheriff, please." Gunderson held his hands out, palms up in an attempt to placate the man. "First of all, we're not mercenaries, although I can understand why you may think of us in this way. We are private security contractors, all of us loyal to the United States and her constitution." Gunderson paused and, seeing no change in Erikson's attitude, continued. "Second, we will most likely not be rounding up any innocent citizens of the United States. Our ISR capabilities are phenomenal under Mr. Yale's team of experts, and we are explicitly

20

here to capture known Islamic extremist and cartel connected terrorists. We also extend the offer of the best mass-casualty response training in the country, and again, this is all free of charge for you."

While calmer, Erikson was still uncomfortable with what he was hearing and was about to say so when Bob Severson spoke up softly from his desk. "Sheriff, I know it's difficult to understand, but these men are good at what they do. I've hired their personal security teams for years and have several that are with me on a permanent basis. I cannot recommend their professionalism any higher."

Erikson blinked and stared, dumbfounded, at Severson. "But Judge Severson, with all due respect, can we really have mercenaries running around town? Enforcing whatever laws they damn well please?"

Gunderson broke in again. "Sheriff, while we will be operating around Alexandria and Douglas Counties, it is highly unlikely that anybody besides the terrorists and criminals we hunt will notice our presence. We specialize in low-profile operations, and have a very specific, targeted mission to accomplish here. Further, we're not going away anytime soon. We've set up a permanent base of operations just outside of town and intend to stay there."

The sheriff shook his head and grumbled, "I don't believe this."

"It's okay, Sheriff," Severson soothed from across the desk. He paused. "I'm on my last legs, you know." That comment resulted in a sharp swing of the sheriff's head. "It's true," Severson said simply. "I'm ninety-three. I've lived a wonderful life, but I have no children, and no family to pass my fortune onto, so I am making one last contribution to the community that I've loved for so long."

Erikson had, of course, known on some level that a ninety-three -year-old man couldn't reasonably expect to live much longer, but he hadn't really thought about it. He also had heard the rumors that the old man in front of him was worth nearly half a billion dollars. "You're giving them your entire fortune?" he asked, incredulous.

"Good lord no," Severson laughed. "Not even close, the rest will go to various charities around the state."

"So that's…"

"So that's a lot of money you don't need to worry about." Severson smiled across the desk. Erikson nodded, still taking it all in.

Turning back to the three men, Erikson chose his words carefully. "So, besides answering to yourselves, who will you and your company answer to exactly? What if I say I don't want your help?"

"Actually, Sheriff," Gunderson said forcefully, yet politely, "you do not have a choice. The evidence indicates that a combination of foreign and domestic actors at play here, and we have been contracted to carry out investigative and enforcement operations that the federal government is no longer able to adequately conduct."

Gunderson shared a brief look with Mr. Dufraine. Dufraine smiled at Erikson and spoke for the first time since walking in the room. "Sheriff, we understand your concerns, but I assure you that our men answer to us. More than that, we are placing ourselves at your disposal…if you'll cooperate with us."
Dufraine paused and launched into his portion of the pitch.

"Our company has built a state-of-the-art facility with which to house, train, and deploy our men in what are proving to be rapidly evolving situations. Currently, we have twenty-four direct action team members, two squads of twelve containing two fireteams of six each. Separately, we employ two teams of expert marksman, for when situations require such precision. Additionally, we have two full-time medical trauma teams, including six medics, two ambulances, and one medevac chopper. Finally, we have eight of the highest quality weapons, tactics, and medical instructors that we could coax out of the public sector. And this is just on the operations side."

"That's right," Ajay Yale broke in enthusiastically. "We have a full staff of dedicated analysts, drone pilots, information assurance technicians—anything that you could possibly need in terms of intelligence, surveillance, and reconnaissance. We also have a number of team members who specialize in personal intelligence."

"And," Gunderson stepped in, , "we are in the process of standing up our air wing with two small cargo planes, two multi-purpose helicopters, two smaller helicopters, and four fixed-wing trainer aircraft, including two T-6 propeller driven aircraft and two T-38 jet trainers."

Erikson sat quietly for a minute, feeling utterly overwhelmed. As his mind tried to process the firehose of information, he began to see the benefits of what the three men had to offer. "You haven't won me over yet," he said begrudgingly. "Hell, I don't even know what you call yourselves."

22

"My apologies, Sheriff," Gunderson said with a look of genuine surprise. "It must have slipped my mind. We," he went on with a slight flourish of his hand, "are Norseman Consulting, specializing in all your training, security, and intelligence needs."

"Fine," Erikson grunted, "and did you say you already built your facility? Is this where you are keeping those two assholes?"

"Yes, Sheriff," Gunderson confirmed. "We'd like you to accompany us out to our headquarters, and we'll show you what we have in store."

CHAPTER SIX

The three men in the Land Cruiser sat in silence for a few minutes. Dufraine was driving, constantly checking the mirrors and scanning his surroundings. There was a palpable tension in the car, the natural state of three men who never really learned to relax after a lifetime of special operations, intelligence work, and security consulting. Two minutes in, Yale broke the silence.

"Do we really trust this Erikson guy?" he asked, staring out into the bleak, frozen landscape in front of them.

"To an extent, yes," Gunderson responded. "He's been serving the same community for years, without faltering. He's something of a local hero. Erikson is relatively young to be Sheriff, but he's old school. In his world there are clear lines between right and wrong, and he has always tried to stay on the side of right."

"So what?" Dufraine snapped. "What does his local reputation get us?"

"The man's dedicated to his community," Gunderson turned towards his partners, "and one of his best friends was just killed by these assholes."

"Yes, but," Yale broke in, "how much do you intend to let him in on?"

Gunderson took a deep breath and blew it out through his nose before answering. "Like we told the sheriff, we are here to help train his deputies and the police department. Additionally, we will be running a few low-profile snatch and grab missions."

"And the rest of it?" Dufraine glanced at Yale through the rear-view mirror before looking back to Gunderson, already anticipating his response.

"We're going to bring the hurt to these guys, and we're going to end it before it gets any worse," Gunderson almost whispered as the Land Cruiser pulled up the Norseman Consulting compound.

In the sheriff's SUV, Erikson's eyes widened. They hadn't driven for more than ten minutes from Mr. Severson's mansion, through a small suburb of Alexandria called Carlos, and into the woods on the northern end of Lake Carlos. The sheriff had heard rumors that there was a lot of building out here over the last year or so, but he was entirely unprepared for what he saw when he pulled up to the gate of Norseman Consulting.

A tall, chain-link fence with two small gatehouses flanked the entrance to the compound. There were cameras everywhere, and just to get through the gate required a large swing arm to be raised, which only happened after the four guards at the gate had checked the IDs of each vehicle's occupant. While the IDs were being checked, a bomb-sniffing canine cleared the vehicles and another guard rolled a mirror around, checking the undersides of the cars.

After the first gate was cleared, there was a second fence, with a pop-up barrier and an electric sliding gate. The whole experience reminded the sheriff of what he had seen in news footage of the entrances to military bases, a feeling that was only reinforced as they made their way up the long drive to the main building.

Off to the left, Erikson could see the airfield with six large hangars looming beyond and a control tower poking out above the trees. He couldn't see any of the aircraft, though. He gawked, his eyes scanning in every direction, trying to take in as much of the scenery as possible.

There was a simple network of roads that branched off of the main drive. Tracing the path of one off to the right, Erikson could make out a set of secluded one-story buildings and what appeared to be a large shooting range. He couldn't help but wonder how they managed to build it all so quickly and quietly.

Within a few minutes, the small convoy had reached another gate, this one manned by two security guards who waved them through without checking their cars or IDs. Erikson noticed the swinging gate was stowed in the upright position as they drove over the pop-up barrier into the compound. They made an immediate right and parked their vehicles in a covered parking lot.

Stepping out of the vehicle, Erikson looked around in disbelief. He was surrounded by one and two-story buildings, buildings that had not been there the last time Erikson had been in this area. Had it not been for the security measures and the covert airfield, the area would have been a fairly ordinary neighborhood. "Holy shit," Erikson muttered.

"Sheriff," Gunderson jerked his head in the direction of the nearest building, and Erikson followed him over to a single-story, gray building that resembled a sprawling ranch house. As the four men walked through the front door, they stepped into a modernly decorated foyer and reception area. The front desk was staffed by a tall, brunette wearing a tight fitting blouse in her mid-thirties, who stepped out from behind the desk as soon as the crew walked up to the desk.

"Good morning, gentlemen," the receptionist smiled. "May I take your coats?"

"Thank you, Ashley," Gunderson said as he shed his heavy winter coat and handed it to the woman, revealing a black pistol on his hip. "Has there been any news since we left?"

"Nothing for you and Mr. Dufraine, sir, but Mr. Yale's presence has been requested in The Brain as soon as possible."

"Thank you, Ashley," Mr. Yale said as he shucked his coat. "Gentlemen, I will see you in a few minutes." Mr. Yale headed off down a long hall, a pistol on his hip as well. In fact, Sheriff Erikson could now see that everyone standing in the foyer, including the receptionist, was carrying a weapon.

"This way, Sheriff," Gunderson said as he led the group down a short hallway. "I assume the firearms don't alarm you?" Erikson shrugged. Gunderson turned to Mr. Dufraine as they arrived at a door with JAMES GUNDERSON emblazoned on it at eye height. "Anthony, would you please run and grab Alex and Randall?" Gunderson opened the door and ushered the sheriff into the office. "I will entertain Sheriff Erikson with our sales pitch."

Gunderson's office was warmly decorated. Leather armchairs were situated around a coffee table with a few magazines and books spread across it, and a green Banker's lamp illuminated the desk. "Please, Sheriff, have a seat," Gunderson said, motioning to one of the leather chairs in the center of the office as he stepped around his desk to his own high-backed leather chair.

"Mr. Gunder—"

"Please, Gerry, dispense with the formalities, we are going to be working very closely together for a while. Call me Jim." Gunderson smiled and reclined in his chair.

"Fine, Jim." Erikson was growing increasingly impatient, "Can we just get on with this? How about you start by telling me where you're keeping the two suspects?"

Gunderson gave a sort of strained smile as he replied. "The two perpetrators are being kept here, where they are being questioned...vigorously." He held his hand up as Erikson started to protest. "Don't worry, Sheriff, they are not being tortured by any means. We have some of the most consummate professionals in the intelligence business plying them for information. Once we have finished interrogating them, they will be turned over to you for processing into the justice system. Now, tell me what the situation is with the third perpetrator your men managed to capture."

"He's been recovering at the hospital, kept under constant guard by the Douglas County Sheriff's Office and the Alexandria Police Department for the last twenty hours or so, but we don't know fuck-all about him. He didn't have any ID, and his weapons were totally sanitized—no serial numbers, no importation marks, nothing."

"Does the press know you have a man in your custody, and, more importantly, does anyone besides you know that we have the other two in our custody?" Erikson continued his questions. Gunderson's tone had grown cold, strictly professional.

"No," Erikson responded. "The first of the major news outlets only just started showing up this morning. Nobody even knows about these other two besides myself and some of my deputies who watched the security tapes. People will figure out that we have a guy in custody soon, though. It's hard to keep secrets in a small town and having a SWAT team hanging out at the hospital is sure to raise some eyebrows."

"That's fine." Gunderson said. "We really didn't expect to be able to keep it quiet. I grew up here, I know how it works."

Erikson nodded in agreement, and the phone on Gunderson's desk buzzed. Hitting the button, Gunderson said, "You got 'em?"

Dufraine's voice barked back through the speakerphone, "Yeah, we'll be there in just a few seconds."

"Roj," Gunderson said, and tapped the button again, terminating the call. "Anthony and two of our tactical team leaders will be here in just a few minutes. In the meantime, I will get the presentation spooled up." Gunderson lifted a remote off of his desk and turned on the large, flat-screen television on the left side of the office. He leaned over and wiggled the computer mouse on his desk.

"Presentation?" Erikson asked. "There's more?"

"Oh yes, Sheriff," Gunderson nodded. "Like I said, Anthony is bringing two of our team leaders to the office. They were actually the men on the ground who rolled the two assholes up yesterday." The television screen came to life, split into four parts. "Alex and Randall were out on a familiarity run, listening to the police scanner when everything kicked off."

"What am I looking at?" Erikson asked.

"Well the top two images are our two prisoners from the massacre yesterday." Gunderson circled the quadrants using a laser pointer embedded in his remote. The two men were sitting, handcuffed to tables, talking to two additional men who were facing away from the camera. "Those are our interrogators, and below that, bottom left," the laser moved down, "is the overhead video we took from one of our drones."

"Drones?" Erikson looked at Gunderson incredulously. "So, now you have predator drones circling Alexandria?"

"Good God, no!" Gunderson laughed. "Predators are much too expensive to maintain for us, not to mention too big to be covert. We don't want to startle the good citizens of Alexandria with a predator looming overhead. These are much smaller, basically remote-controlled planes that we fly from our headquarters here. Not to mention that they're unarmed."

"So, you just have drones up overhead, twenty-four hours a day, seven days a week? Just surveilling the citizens of Alexandria?"

"Yes, Sheriff," Gunderson responded. "They are a necessary evil at this point. Our drones only are able to record video, not conversations, and are being used to target people specifically related to the drug trade in and around the Alexandria area."

"Hrmph," Erikson grunted and was about to respond when he was interrupted by a heavy knock on the door.

"Come in!" Gunderson called, and the door swung open, revealing Dufraine and two men whom Erikson presumed were the team leaders, Alex and Randall.

"Sorry it took so long," Dufraine apologized as he took a seat in the chair next to Erikson. "We got rolled up in the bullpen." The two team leaders took positions on either side of the screen as Dufraine spoke. In contrast to the business casual slacks, loafers, and collared shirts that Gunderson, Dufraine, and Yale had been wearing, these two were dressed in blue jeans and navy-blue hooded sweatshirts, which were tucked behind the pistols on each man's hip.

"Take it away, gentlemen," Gunderson said as he tossed the remote to the man closest to him. The man caught the implement with barely a glance.

"Good morning, Sheriff. I am Alex, leader of team one here at NC." Erikson nodded, and the man on the right side of the screen added, "I'm Randall, team two leader." And with a nod from Erikson, Alex launched into his briefing.

CHAPTER SEVEN

"Sheriff, as you may know, the man on the left side of the screen," Alex gestured with his laser pointer, "is Anwar al Kobani, a freelance radical and thug for hire. Before yesterday, he had only ever been seen in the Middle East, typically kicking around Syria and Iraq with the Islamic State." Erikson had not heard of al Kobani before, but he nodded that he understood, prompting Alex to continue.

"This man here," a new dot started its slow orbit around the man in the top right quadrant of the screen, "is Jesús Longoria Reyes. Reyes is a Mexican Federale turned narco enforcer after he was caught taking bribes from a couple of the cartels down there. He was associated with the Sinaloa Cartel for the past several years but fell off the grid about a year ago. Our intelligence specialists presume that he made the journey to the US at that time and helped set up the new cartel drug operations in the Greater Minnesota area."

Erikson nodded again, and Randall took over. "Yesterday morning, Alex and I were driving around the Alexandria area, becoming acquainted with our new area of operations, when we heard the APB go out for Ms. Jorgenson's van. We didn't think much of it and stayed more toward the outside of town to finish our tour of that area.

"When the gunfire kicked off, we headed back into town to see what we could help with. It took us a while to get back, and when we rolled up to the police station, we saw these two guys jump into a Grand Cherokee and take off."

Alex spoke up again. "We figured the two guys running with Kalashnikovs were not the good guys in this instance." Erikson looked back at them blankly. The stress from the last couple days, compounded by the lack of sleep, was taking its toll.

Alex shrugged and resumed speaking. "So we tailed them for a bit until they cleared the major population center," the red dot traced a path on the roads leading south out of town, stopping at what appeared to be a cornfield near a pond, "then we performed a PIT maneuver on a patch of ice, flipped their Jeep, yanked 'em out, and brought 'em here."

There was a brief, awkward pause as Erikson processed what he had just been told. Looking back and forth between the four other men in the room, Erikson realized that they were waiting for him to say something, ask a question, or react in pretty much any way that indicated his comprehension. "So…" Erikson mumbled while rubbing his eyes, "now what?"

"Well the good news is that this guy," Gunderson circled Reyes with the laser pointer, "is singing like a canary in a coal mine. Al Kobani hasn't said a word, and probably won't."

"We'd be better off just putting a bullet in him and burying him behind the woodshed," Dufraine said gruffly. The way he said it, so straightforwardly, without any hint that he was joking was more than a little unsettling to the sheriff.

"You're not," he interjected, "actually going to do that, are you?"

"Unfortunately, no," Gunderson said coldly. "We will be turning him over to you after we have finished interviewing him. At which point the justice system will have to suffice."

Looking around the room, Erikson was greeted with blank, expressionless stares, indicating that the men standing around him were less eager to relegate the two captives to the justice system than Gunderson was. "What, uh," the sheriff stuttered, "what is the Mexican guy telling you?"

Gunderson frowned. "Unfortunately, Sheriff, he does not know as much as we would like." Making a small motion with his arm, the Norseman Consulting president indicated that his two team leaders should move forward with their briefing.

Alex clicked the slide forward. "We have marked on this map where Reyes says they brought their crew." Alex circled a blue "X" on the digital map that now occupied the entire screen.

"Arizona?"

Dufraine fielded the sheriff's question, shrugging his shoulders as he spoke. "Where they entered is of little concern to us. What we want to know is why."

"And that is what we are hoping to get out of al Kobani," Gunderson added. "But so far, all he has said is 'More are coming' or simply tried to spit on our interrogators' shoes."

"I don't suppose that Reyes knows the reasoning behind all this?" the sheriff asked.

"Reyes is just a hired gun," Dufraine explained. "Loyal to a paycheck, and nothing else. He doesn't know why, doesn't care. He just likes the money…and the violence."

Erikson's head was spinning. There had to be more to this attack than violence for violence's sake. Gunderson seemed to sense this and interrupted the sheriff's thought process. "Sheriff, I know this is a lot to take in, and I promise you, we will keep as open and transparent lines of communication as we can. What I can tell you right now is that we are on the same side, and we are going to get the guys who did this."

The sheriff nodded, although he was fairly certain that the Norseman Consulting contractors had wildly different ideas than he did about the order of law and due process. Right at that moment, though, all he wanted was for this nightmare of a day to be over. He needed sleep.

"I can see that you're tired, Sheriff," Gunderson said quietly. "Our briefing is done here. Go home and get some rest, and I'll have a training agreement sent to you for your review and signature tomorrow morning."

"Training agreement?" the Sheriff asked. "What training agreement?"

"It is our end of the bargain with Mr. Severson," Dufraine reminded him. "Most of the money he paid us went into building a law enforcement training facility, which we are to extend to your department, as well as the City of Alexandria Police Department, free of charge. We just need your signature, and that of the City Chief of Police, to make our agreement official. You'll both be getting a copy in the morning."

The sheriff nodded and rose to his feet. "So, that's it, then?"

"That's it, Sheriff." Gunderson walked around from behind his desk to shake Erikson's hand. "We'll be in touch."

As Randall escorted the sheriff to his SUV, Gunderson called over to his intelligence boss's office.

"Ajay, the sheriff is gone. I want to go over what we know."

Gunderson set the phone down, picked up the clicker from his desk, and pulled up a map of the outlying areas. The room was quiet, save for a faint humming in the background that was designed to inhibit listening devices or other electronic bugs. Dufraine was picking at his nails with a folding knife as he and Gunderson reviewed the map in front of them.

Within a few minutes, the pudgier frame of Ajay Yale strode into the office. He huffed and plopped down in one of the office chairs. "I have some good news."

"What do you have for us?" Dufraine asked. Dufraine found Yale to be a bit tedious, always thrusting his intellect around. To Dufraine, it felt like pulling teeth to get information out of Yale, and when he did get the information, it was never without a condescending tone.

"Well," Yale began, "my guys were able to get the location of the terrorist safe-house out of Reyes." The intelligence guru was grinning smugly, waiting for the other two to ask him to expound. Yale looked at his fingernails as if he was inspecting them while he waited for Dufraine's questions. Dufraine exhaled loudly through his nose, an agitated snort that barely concealed the disdain that he felt toward Yale's theatrics. Yale didn't really care what Dufraine thought about him. In fact, Yale barely even remembered that they worked together until they were in these face-to-face meetings. Yale mostly considered Dufraine and the rest of the operations side of Norseman Consulting to be a bunch of knuckle-dragging primates who were lost without his intelligence team.

Gunderson could see the annoyed look that had fully spread across Dufraine's face and broke in, "Oh hell, Ajay, spit it out already."

"I was getting to that." Ajay handed a note card to Gunderson. "Reyes gave us this address." Gunderson typed the address into the computer, causing the map to relocate. Prominently displayed on the screen was a small farm, south of the Alexandria area, with a long driveway leading to a large house and an even larger outbuilding. "We got this location out of Reyes. We still haven't gotten anything out of al Kobani." Yale frowned. "But I put up a constant rotation of surveillance drones over the farm."

"Good work, Ajay," Gunderson said. "When will we have drone coverage?"

"If you flip over a couple channels, you'll see we have coverage right now." Yale smirked.

Gunderson flipped over to the drone feed and started inputting his password while Dufraine questioned Yale. "What else do we know about the farm?" he asked, already started to put together an assault plan.

"Well, let's see." Yale started flipping through a small notebook he kept in his pocket. "Here we go. Farm is eighty acres. It was purchased by some corporate entity in an estate sale about three years ago. We looked into the company, but it's a shell corporation, and we haven't been able to get to the bottom of the money trail through all of the offshore and international holdings that were used as cut-outs."

"Give me layout details, Ajay," Dufraine huffed impatiently.

"Oh, right," Ajay nodded. "We have a two-story house with a basement, a rather large horse barn with a grove of trees behind it, and nothing between the road and the house but snow and ice for over a quarter mile."

As Yale finished his rundown of Norseman Consulting's newest target, Gunderson pulled up the drone feed. "Would you look at that," Dufraine muttered. "It's like a goddamned convention down there."

The drone feed showed the farmhouse from before in real time. The barren, white landscape was peppered with at least a dozen black specks milling about between a row of trucks and the barn.

"It looks like they're gearing up for something," Gunderson said. "Anthony, I want you to get a recon team as close as we can. Tonight." Dufraine nodded and stood up. "Ajay, I need you to get every last piece of information about that property to the operations teams, and I want to make sure we have 24/7 drone coverage."

"You got it," Yale said as he heaved himself out of the chair.

"Alright, we're going to recon this house tonight," Gunderson said, "and then we are going to hit these bastards tomorrow night."

34

CHAPTER EIGHT

Despite Gunderson's advice, Erikson did not head straight home for some rest. Travelling through town and back to his office, he figured, would help him gain some perspective on the last couple of days, or even shed some light on the events. He drove in silence, only the sound of the engine and the tires on the frozen pavement keeping him company as he wound his way through the frigid lake country back to the city limits.

Thoughts swirled through his head, confusion mingled with guilt, until rage and remorse took over. He didn't like that Norseman Consulting was here, conducting operations without legal oversight. There was something fishy about the whole thing. How had they set up such a large scale of operations so quickly? Most importantly, was Gunderson and his band of contractors hiding something from him?

Erikson wasn't stupid. He knew that Gunderson and his cronies were hiding something from him. He suspected the nature of their presence in Central Minnesota was a closely guarded secret, and he was anxious about having a powerful secret organization around in his backyard. Especially a powerful, private organization that might not have any accountability.

His thoughts were interrupted as he turned onto Broadway and noted that the carnage from the previous morning had been mostly cleaned up. Tarps were covering the shattered shop windows, wrecked cars and dead bodies had been hauled away, the wounded had been taken to the hospital, bloodstained snow had been shoveled away. He spotted a small crowd gathered in front of one of the shop windows.

The stoplight turned red, and as he pulled up next to the curb, he could make out the pictures of the victims taped to the window behind a few of the town's religious leaders. The crowd were holding candles, heads bowed.

The light turned green and Erikson drove away, tears gathering in the corners of his eyes.

As he neared his office, he could see rows of news vans gathering on the side streets. Reporters were already crowding the sidewalk in front of their cameras, doubtlessly putting together material for their evening broadcasts.

Erikson parked his SUV in his designated spot, climbed out numbly, and began climbing the stairs to his office. The normal hustle and bustle of the office was gone, replaced by an eerie, miserable quiet. He could hear somebody sniffling over the sounds of typing. He walked straight to his office, barely making eye contact with the few deputies still in the office.

At his desk, Erikson set himself down heavily in his chair, took a deep breath, and started typing. As he typed, he documented each of his failures that could possibly have led to the events of the previous day, and he realized he was writing his own resignation letter. He got to the bottom of the page, saved his draft, and opened the internet browser.

Determined to find something, anything, about Norseman Consulting, he began another vigorous search, which yielded only the company's innocuous homepage. Vague capabilities statements and references to past work that were difficult to decipher. Erikson's headache began to worsen, and he pressed his hands into his eyes. It was nearly 12:00. Erikson sighed, printed his letter, and left for home.

As he pulled into his driveway, he could see his wife, Ellen, standing in the front window. He wondered how long she had been standing there. He pulled his cell out of his pocket and wondered how long it had been dead.

Erikson opened the door and, without a word, walked across the room to his wife and hugged her.

"Where have you been, Gerry?" Ellen whispered. "I've been calling everywhere for you."

"It is a long story, and it's been a long day, Ellie." Erikson replied. He squeezed her tighter. "Let me sit down first."

Ellie nodded, kissed him softly, and they made their way into the living room. Erikson strode over to the cabinet on the far side of the room next to the TV and poured himself a glass of bourbon. He downed it.

"After yesterday's attacks, I got a weird phone call," Erikson began. He poured himself another glass and took a sip. "James Gunderson. Said had some information on the attacks."

"Judge Gunderson's kid?" Ellie looked at her husband quizzically.

"Yeah." Erikson took another sip from his glass as he sat down on the couch next to his wife. "He's back in town, and he runs this…private military company or something." Another sip. "I've been with him and his crew all day."

"What could they possibly have to do with all this?"

Erikson recounted his story, staring at the ceiling and swirling his glass absentmindedly. Suddenly, he began to weep. Small, silent tears at first, but then Ellie pulled his head into her and he began to release fully. Crying over his dead friend, his deputies, his own sense of helplessness, until at last he fell asleep on Ellie's lap.

CHAPTER NINE

"Archer One-One, Base," the radio crackled faintly in the headset, "is there any change to status? Over."

A faint rustling stirred in the small snow cave that had been dug the night before. One of the three men buried beneath the snow quietly clicked his radio once in response. *Negative.*

"Copy, Archer One-One," Dufraine's voice sounded over the headset. "Stand by for DA insertion, ETA thirty mikes."

Two clicks this time. *Affirmative.*

The rustling began anew as the man switched from his command channel to his operations channel.

"Archer Two-One, Archer One-One." Steam evaporated from the man's mouth, barely visible in the moonlight. "ETA to kickoff, thirty mikes."

Two clicks.

Shivering in their hide, one of the other two men whispered, shivering and barely audible, "Holy shit, dude. I did not figure in the cold when I took this job."

"Oh, come on, Hondo, what the hell did you expect, moving to the Great White North?" The third man in the hide did not take his eyes from the scope of his suppressed rifle as he spoke.

"Well fuck, Sam, I don't know," Alejandro said. "But I was not built for this shit, that I do know."

The first man rolled his eyes and, without moving his eyes from his own rifle, whispered softly, "Please, shut up. Sound carries when it's this cold."

"Aye, *Grandpa,*" Alejandro retorted as he picked up his binoculars and resumed scanning the objective. The other sniper, Sam, snorted his acknowledgement.

The two sniper teams had been buried in their snow caves for almost twenty-four hours at that point, having inserted the night before under cover of darkness. There was little moonlight, as the faint moon had only just started peeking through the clouds, but this was of no concern to the sniper teams, who had been equipped with top-of-the-line thermal and night vision optics. Darkness was their greatest ally. Even at four hundred yards, Melvin and his team could clearly make out the guards standing on the porch or, as most of them were doing at the moment, standing around watching a soccer game in the living room.

Melvin, unofficial code name "Grandpa," had joined Norseman Consulting after nearly twelve years in the Marine Corps, working as an infantryman and then as a scout sniper. At thirty-two, he was actually among the youngest of the contractors Norseman Consulting employed, but his mane of nearly snow-white gray hair and beard had made for an easy nickname.

The second sniper in the hide, Sam, was an Army veteran, who left the military and found himself doing border patrol work in south Texas. As he told it, that job was boring as fuck, so he moved into the private sector and the employment of Norseman Consulting when the opportunity knocked.

Alejandro was one of the few contractors who had the distinction of being younger than Melvin. At only twenty-eight, he had been a Marine Raider for several years, and had gotten out to try to salvage a failing marriage. His efforts had failed, and his now ex-wife had thrown him to the wind. Like many of the contractors in the company, he had been approached with a lucrative job offer, and he hadn't looked back.

Melvin was mentally rehearsing their plan. His team was situated near the road, facing one corner of the house, allowing them visibility of two sides of the house and one side of the barn. The other team was situated catty corner, allowing the two teams to cover all four sides of the objective.

He felt Sam moving slowly, laying out magazines for his rifle, using the snow to hold them in place. Melvin started to do the same.
The rifles they were using were heavy, bullpup bolt action rifles fitted with suppressors and chambered in one of the flattest shooting calibers Melvin had ever used. They made hits in excess of a thousand yards a breeze. Four hundred yards would be a cakewalk. *If only I'd had something like this in the Corps.* Melvin smirked to himself. It didn't really matter, he had one now.

Melvin could tell Alejandro was getting antsy. Hondo wasn't a sniper; he was an assaulter. But he'd been assigned to Melvin's team for added security. As such, he wasn't equipped with the high-end sniper rifle, but a 7.62 NATO battle rifle equipped with a medium-range variable scope and a suppressor. Melvin could tell Hondo was frustrated at not being in on the assault portion of the raid, but Dufraine had been insistent that the sniper teams each take an additional rifleman in case the snipers were discovered prematurely.

The radio crackled again, "Archer One-One, Base. Fifteen mikes."

Two clicks. *Affirmative.*

Barely ten miles away, at the Norseman Compound, Alex and Randall were gearing their teams up for the raid. Had it not been for the advanced weaponry, body armor, and communications gear hanging in the lockers, the team room could have been mistaken for a professional sports team locker room. There was a quiet, palpable tension in the room as the men checked and rechecked their equipment, thumbed rounds into rifle magazines, and cross checked their teammates' equipment. It was Axe team's turn to be the primary assault team, while the members of Sword team knew they were on tap to serve as the cordon and quick reaction force.

The door to the team room opened and Gunderson, Dufraine, and Yale strode in. "Gentlemen, gather round," Gunderson spoke. The twenty-four contractors formed a hasty semi-circle. The flat screen monitor at the head of the room was switched on, showing an overhead image of the objective house, with two red flags indicating the locations of the sniper teams.

"Alright gents," Dufraine spoke this time. "You know the drill, but quickly: Axe team will be the main assault force," Dufraine motioned to his left, where Alex and his team were clustered. "Sword team," he continued, motioning to Randall and his crew, "will be the QRF and cordon element."

Dufraine looked around the room, receiving quiet, intense stares in return. The men were ready, hyped up for the raid.

"Axe will drive to this location," Dufraine used a laser pointer to circle an area just past the driveway of the house, "and complete their infiltration to the barn on foot."

A few men nodded silently. He traced the red laser over to the image of the barn. "Once there, Axe is to sweep and clear the barn. From what we've been seeing, there is very little foot traffic between the barn and the house at night, so this should be a quick ordeal."
More nods.

"Once set, Axe will wait for Archer teams to initiate the raid," Dufraine slid the laser up to the house, "at which point, half of Axe will enter through the basement door here," the laser made a quick circle around a doorway, "and the other half will enter through the main level here."

"At this point, Sword, acting as the QRF, will be inserted on two different choppers, and set up a cordon in case of any squirters." Dufraine looked around the room. "Any questions?"

A hand raised towards the back of the Axe team huddle. "Yeah, Rob?"

"Two questions, sir. What are our rules of engagement, and what should we be looking for during our site exploitation?"

Gunderson fielded the questions with a fiery glare. "Guys, after the bloodbath on Broadway, I'm not inclined to give them any quarter, but as far as the ROE, we want at least one man alive. Other than that, if they have a weapon, they're fair game."

Grim nods and grunts accompanied smirks in the crowd. "As far as your SSE," Yale added, "bring everything and anything to me. We want to be able to build a target deck and figure out what these guys are up to."

"From what we're seeing," Dufraine went on, "these guys are amateurs. Our eyes in the sky and guys on the ground are reporting that they're sloppy and careless, armed mostly with shit-tier weaponry. Most of them appear to be packing garage-built submachine guns, but a few of them have Kalashnikovs and shotguns."

"Any word on how many?" This time, one of the Sword team members, a smaller man named Rafael inquired.

"Right now, intel points to between one and two dozen," Dufraine responded.

"As of twenty minutes ago," Yale said, "our overhead was picking up six guys on patrol around the house, although they're mostly just standing still on the porch trying to keep warm. There're another ten watching a soccer match."

"Any more questions?" Silence. "No? Alright, we are wheels up in five minutes. Get your gear square and let's go."

The contractors quickly fell to finishing off their final gear preparations. While each contractor had been allowed to pick their own plate carrier, load bearing equipment, and helmet, they did have some gear standardization that Gunderson had insisted on. For starters, they were all wearing snow-pattern camouflage, and they all had the same set of night vision devices securely fastened to their helmets.

Additionally, they were all outfitted with identical Swiss-made carbines.

The carbine was one of the few things that Gunderson and Dufraine had differed over. Dufraine had wanted to allow each of the direct-action team members to pick their own rifle, so long as it remained in a standard caliber. Gunderson had insisted on using a standardized rifle, as he postulated it would make them appear better organized, and therefore more appealing to prospective employers. In the end, Dufraine relented, and Gunderson had negotiated a deal with a Swiss firm.

Chambered in 300 Blackout, the rifles had short, stubby barrels, making them ideal for close-quarters situations. They were also outfitted with suppressors and loaded with sub-sonic rounds, making far less noise than standard carbines. They were expensive, but Gunderson anticipated that prospective contracts would subconsciously associate Swiss with quality and had used that to his advantage.

Along with the suppressed carbines, each contractor carried a sidearm. This was one area where Dufraine, along with his direct-action team leaders, Alex and Randall, had been able to convince Gunderson to allow for individuality. Each contractor carried their choice of handgun chambered in 9mm.

With gear checks complete, Alex and Randall and their teams made their way out the door, slapping each on the back or giving a fist-bump as they jogged to their vehicles.

Alex spoke into his radio. "Archer One-One, this is Axe One, Five minutes to kickoff."

Two clicks. *Affirmative.*

CHAPTER TEN

"Archer One-One, Axe One, we are set at the base of the barn." Two clicks sounded over the radio.

After ditching their vehicles a quarter mile from their objective, Alex and his team had slogged through the deep snow of the state-run wildlife area that was adjacent to the farm. It had taken them several minutes longer than anticipated, due to some serious inexperience with the snow, and now the raid was behind schedule by three minutes.

With his team gathered in the trees a scant ten yards away from the barn, Alex braced himself for confirmation from the sniper team leader. Axe team was still hyperventilating from the combination of adrenaline and sheer exertion of trudging through the snow in sub-freezing temperatures, and they fought to control their breathing before the raid was initiated.

"Axe, Archer One-One. We are set and ready," Melvin's voice whispered over the radio. "We will initiate on the house on your mark."

Alex keyed his radio twice, indicating his confirmation. With a quick hand wave, his first element dashed out of the trees, over to the back door of the barn. As soon as they were set, the element gently pushed the door in, surprised to find it unlocked, and rushed inside.

"Axe Two, barn clear," Alex's assistant team leader, Ted, called out over the radio. "Looks like a lot of drugs in here, though."

"Roger Axe Two, prepare to hit the house," Alex responded.

The plan was for Ted and his element to exit out the front door of the barn, while Alex and his element flowed around the side of the barn. Axe Two would take the basement, and Axe One the ground floor and the upstairs.

As Axe One made their way towards the side of the barn, there was a crash of breaking glass inside the barn.

"Axe One, HOLD," Melvin hissed forcefully over the radio. "Guy on the porch heard something, he's heading your way."

Fuck, Alex thought, keying his radio twice. He threw his fist up to let his element know to hunker down for a second. *This is not good.*

"All teams, prepare to initiate on my mark," Melvin called over the radio. Alex could hear the guy walking towards him, muttering to himself in a foreign language. *Wait, is that Russian?*

Inside the barn, Ted was fuming. One of his element had knocked over a tower of beakers and other scientific looking glassware. He could hear the guard from the house crunching and cursing his way through the snow toward the barn. The infiltration was probably blown, and there wasn't much left to do but adapt.

Ted and his team tensed as they heard the man grab the handle of the barn door. There was a wet slapping noise, followed by a muted, sharp crack. "Go! Go! Go!" Melvin's voice sounded out over the radio, and Axe team broke from the cover of the barn to begin their assault on the house.

As he threw open the opposite barn door, Ted had to step over the body of the man who had come within seconds of discovering the assault team. He sprinted to the basement door and caught a glimpse of Alex and Axe One making a break for the front door. Several more muted cracks sounded through the frozen night. A body fell off the balcony that ran across the top floor. Glass shattered, and confused shouts rang out from the house.

Ted slid to a stop at the basement door, feeling his team stack up behind him. He felt a tap on his shoulder. *Ready*. Ted keyed his radio, "Axe Two, set."

"Breach!"

Ted pushed his non-firing hand backwards, tapping his teammate behind him. As the tap was reciprocated down the line and back up again, Axe Two's breacher, a giant of a man by the name of Bryan, came forward and slammed his foot into the door, breaking it open, then stepped out of the way and brought his carbine up to provide cover for his teammates as they flowed down the stairs and into the basement.

Ted and his team rushed down the stairs, swinging into the basement, where they were met with four guys standing in front a row of computers. Three of the men sat in front of the computers frozen with fear. The fourth tried to bring his shotgun to bear.

Pft-pft pft-pft pft-pft. Three of the contractors hammered the shotgun-wielding thug, splashing blood against the far wall. The contractors moved quickly through the room, grabbing the three at the computers and throwing them to the floor, then binding their arms behind their back. With one contractor assigned to place a knee in the back of each tech support guy, Ted and the remaining two element members prepared to move to the main floor. "Basement clear," Axe One's leader called out over the radio.

As Ted, Bryan, and the third contractor, Elias, waited tensely at the bottom of the stairs, they could hear the muffled shots of Axe One working the floor above, and the sudden roar of the two helicopters depositing Sword One and Sword Two. From the basement, the members of Axe Two suddenly heard the full report of unsuppressed gunshots hammering above them.

The breach of the main floor had gone smoothly enough. Alex and his element had made it through the front door and cleared the living room. They'd only encountered three guys, albeit heavily armed, and easily dispatched them. Four of Axe One's six contractors had placed a pair of shots in each gunman, creating a bloody mess across the living room windows.

A couple of the gunmen had broken away from the soccer game early, two had gone upstairs to bed, and three were in the kitchen foraging for a snack. The muted sound of gunshots emanating from the basement and living room had been enough to tip off the gunmen in the kitchen.

As soon as Axe One's point man, a wiry thirty-five-year-old named Angelo, stepped through the door to the kitchen, one of the gunmen tackled him to the ground. The man following Angelo into the room, Robert rushed over and delivered a swift kick to the gunman, throwing him off Angelo. As Robert pushed the sights of his carbine over the sprawled gunman, two of the man's companions sprang out from behind the kitchen island, blasting away at Robert.

Robert took a half a dozen pistol rounds to his armored chest plate, knocking the wind out of him and sending him stumbling backwards through the door.

Still lying on his side, Angelo brought his carbine up and started ripping rounds into the standing gunmen. As soon as they hit the floor, Angelo turned his attention to the gunman who had tackled him. He was crawling away, spitting blood from the kick that Robert had delivered to his ribcage.

"Stop right there, motherfucker!" Angelo roared. The gunman half turned, firing a pistol wildly over Angelo's head.

Pftpftpftpft. Suppressed gunshots sounded above Angelo's head. It was Alex, who had just pushed through the door and had a clear shot at the gunman. The crawling man dropped to the floor and spasms wracked his body.

Angelo pushed himself off the floor. "I'm okay, I'm fine," he heaved to his teammates. Upstairs, the remaining gunmen were clamoring about.

Alex keyed his radio. "Archer teams, can you thin the herd upstairs? We're about to get a lot of heat."

Two clicks came over the radio, and muted cracks sounded above them, coinciding with breaking class and heavy thumps. The Norseman contractors could hear the gunmen yelling back and forth, occasional unsuppressed rifle shots punctuating the chaos.

Alex turned around to check on Robert. He was lying on his back, gasping for air while one of his teammates set about patching a hole in his trapezius muscle. "He going to be okay, Sean?"

Sean did not look up from his work. "Yeah he's going to be fine. Got the wind knocked out of him, but he took all but one in the plates." He packed gauze into the wound in Robert's shoulder. "One of the fuckers burned through his trap, though. And he's going to have a hard time breathing for a bit."

Alex nodded, and motioned for one of the remaining four Axe One members to stay put with Sean and Robert. The other three, led by Alex, set about clearing the ground floor while the sniper teams kept the gunmen upstairs at bay.

Axe One hurried through the remaining rooms on the ground floor. "Ground floor, clear," Alex called.

"Axe Two, coming up," Ted's voice sounded out over the radio, and he, Bryan, and Elias emerged from the basement.

As soon as Axe Two was in place, Alex keyed his radio again. "Archer teams, Axe is preparing to take the top floor, shift fire!"

"Shifting fire," Melvin's voice crackled through the radio.

Alex turned to the rest of Axe team and called, "Follow me!" and they pressed upstairs.

At the top of the stairs, Alex turned left, while his second guy turned right, and the rest of the team alternated directions until all six had peeled off into the two bedrooms. They were met with quite a sight. No fewer than six bodies were lying on the ground in a bloody heap, courtesy of Archer One. A quick scan of the room told Alex and his element that there was nothing more for them to do there. "Clear," he called.

In the other room, Ted and his element encountered four more bodies, the handiwork of Archer Two, along with three other gunmen, crouching in the corners. When the Norseman contractors crossed the threshold of the bedroom, a shotgun blast tore into the drywall behind Elias's head. Axe Two made quick work of the shooter. The other two froze, staring at the contractors in front of them.

"DROP IT!" Bryan screamed. "Drop it or I will shoot you!"

The two gunmen exchanged a look and simultaneously tried to bring their weapons up. Bryan splashed a half a dozen rounds across the first one's chest, and Elias blasted away at the other until his magazine was empty. The first gunman slid to the ground without as much as a twitch. The second went into a death spasm, but not before pulling the trigger on his homemade submachine gun, sending a ten-round burst through the floor and into the kitchen.

"FUCK!" Bryan shouted. "Clear."

A sudden crash of breaking glass sounded from across the hall and the contractors spun around.

"Axe, Raven One. You have a squirter," one of the orbiting helicopters called out over the radio.

"Copy that Raven. Sword, can you grab him?"

"Yeah, we see 'em."

A surviving gunman had jumped out of the bathroom window and was hobbling toward one of the parked cars in the driveway. Randall's Sword team had tightened their cordon during the raid, and one of the cordoning elements rushed forward to intercept the escapee.

"Stop!" Sword team's element formed a rough horseshoe around the man as he clambered into the SUV, "GET THE FUCK OUT THE CAR!"

Snarling curses at the contractors, the gunman opened up with his submachine gun, blowing holes in the door of the vehicle in front of him.

Calmly, precisely, the Sword team contractors returned fire, dropping the man's body into the snow.

"Squirter clear," the element leader said into the radio.

"Alright, let's wrap it up," Alex called. "All elements, collapse on the house. Let's get this show wrapped up."

As the Sword and Archer teams moved into the house to help with site exploitation and to wait for extraction by helicopter, Axe Two brought their prisoners upstairs. Robert was placed on a helicopter with the captured men, and the chopper headed back to the Norseman Consulting compound.

The rest of the contractors set about wrapping up the operation, a few working to run the dead men through a biometric database, scanning their irises, or if unavailable, their fingerprints. The rest set about gathering the tech equipment from the basement and loading it into their trucks to be brought back to the compound.

"Axe One, Sword One," Randall sounded over the radio. Alex could hear that something in the barn had excited him.

"Go ahead, Sword One," Alex responded.

"Get over here, man," Randall's voice sounded almost giddy. Alex quickly handed his site exploitation bag over to Bryan and jogged toward the barn.

"Over here, dude!" Randall was standing in one of the horse stalls.

As Alex rounded the corner to the stall, his eyes went wide. "Is that—"

"Fucking-a, it is, man," Randall laughed. "There's got to be close to ten mil in cash in here!"

Sitting in front of them in translucent green wrapping, were stacks of cash, and pallets of white powder. Bricks of heroin, or maybe cocaine, Alex presumed, but he didn't care about that.

"Alright people," Alex was grinning from ear-to-ear, "you know what Gunderson said. Let's leave what we're supposed to leave and take what we're supposed to take. We're outta here in five minutes."

Less than an hour later, Erikson was awakened by his wife, who was gently shaking his shoulder.

"Gerry, wake up," Ellie urged. "Your phone is ringing."
Snapping out of his slumber, he grabbed the phone.

"Erikson," he muttered, squinting at his clock. *3:30 in the morning? Are you fucking kidding me?*

"Hello, Sheriff." The voice on the phone was garbled, and Erikson recognized the sound of a voice modulator. "Do you have a pen and paper?"

"Uh, yes, yes I do," Erikson scrambled to grab the pen and paper he kept next to his bed.

"Write down this address," the voice on the other end of the call demanded, rattling off the address quickly, "and Sheriff?"

"What is this?" Erikson inquired.

"You're going to need a lot of body bags."

The call ended.

CHAPTER ELEVEN

In the predawn darkness, Sheriff Erikson and his team combed through the wreckage at the farmstead. Inside the barn, his deputies had discovered a massive stash of drugs, mostly heroin with smaller quantities of cocaine and weed. That alone was enough to make the farmstead a noteworthy discovery, but the scene inside the house and on the front lawn was unfathomable, even for the most jaded deputies.

In the basement, they found six desktop computers and laptops with their hard drives missing, several empty rifle cartridge casings scattered about on the floor, and a grisly mural of blood and brain matter decorating the far wall. The rest of the house was in similar shape. Bullet casings littered the ground floor, and the walls and floors were stained red. Laid out on the front lawn were twenty-four deceased men with a single page stapled to each of their chests. Dossiers with names, birthdates, nationalities, citizenships, even criminal rap sheets.

"Well, they certainly did some of our job for us," one of the deputies, a slightly overweight deputy named Johnson, remarked cynically.

Erikson was halfway through his inspection of each of the printouts on the corpses' chests. "Well," he said as he stood up from his stooped position, "this is a first for me."

Johnson spoke again, his voice shaking from the cold. "Shit, Sheriff, this is beyond bizarre."

Erikson turned to his deputy. "Has the state CSI team been called yet?"

"Yes, sir," Johnson replied. "They should be here in the next few minutes."

The sheriff nodded. His mind was racing. Doubtless the blood tests would match the bodies, but maybe they'd find some DNA evidence of whoever fired the shots. *Although*, Erikson thought, *the world would hardly miss this motley crew.* The dossiers detailed a violent and disturbing history. The mildest crimes included several counts of domestic violence and drug distribution. On other end of the spectrum there were two guys laid out side-by-side who were apparently jihadist mercenaries from Chechnya. One of the guys was labeled as a former Iranian special operations soldier. If all of the dossiers held true, and Erikson had an inkling that they would, they painted a concerning picture.

"Sheriff!" another deputy shouted as he strode out of the farmhouse and onto the lawn. "The forensics team is about five minutes out."

"Alright, thank you, Tyler," Erikson responded as he checked his watch. 5:30 in the morning. He and his team had been here for roughly ninety minutes, collecting evidence and combing through the house and barn. Taking a deep breath, Erikson turned back to Johnson.

"Johnson, I'm leaving you in charge, I gotta go into the office."

The deputy nodded. He started, then paused, then asked the question everyone but Sheriff Erikson was asking. "Who do you think did this?"

Erikson looked at him blankly. "I have no idea." He turned abruptly and walked to his car.

Just a few miles away, the Norseman Consulting leadership was wrapping up their after-action reports. The assault teams had finished their hot-wash of the assault itself, and the contractors had gone for some much-needed rest, but only after they'd swung past the hospital to give Robert a hard time about his apparent lack of agility.

Gunderson, Dufraine, and Yale were sitting in Gunderson's office, looking through the documents that had been hastily prepared by Yale's intelligence team. The computer hard drives they had filched from the tech center in the basement were still being analyzed, and the three captured "computer nerds"—as Dufraine was calling them—were undergoing interrogation. What they did have was a concerning set of dossiers on each of the two dozen men they had gunned down.

"What does this mean?" Gunderson asked Yale, agitation rising in his voice.

Yale looked up at his two partners, and exhaled sharply before answering, "I'm not sure yet, but the presence of the two Chechens and the one Iranian is a pretty strong indicator that our OGA contacts were correct about the presence of jihadis for hire in the U.S."

A few months prior to Norseman Consulting finishing up construction and moving into their new headquarters in central Minnesota, the company had been contracted to sort through a set of data for one of the federal government's intelligence agencies. A Special Forces raid in Yemen had yielded a huge haul of data and intelligence and Norseman Consulting had had prime access to all the drama.

"Yeah, but why?" Dufraine asked Yale. "What's the point?"

"Well, deniability mostly," Yale said, "but also misdirection."

Dufraine scowled at Yale, his frustration apparent, "On whose behalf, Yale?"

"Americans still tend to jump to the conclusion that everything is radical Islamic terrorism," Gunderson said. "So, whoever actually hired these guys wouldn't be looked at too closely."

Yale nodded. "Yeah, plus, targeting a quiet little area like Alexandria shows people that nobody is safe."

"Okay," Dufraine said, "that makes sense. But what about the drugs? And more than half the guys that we smoked today weren't jihadi mercenaries. They're just two-bit drug runners and gang members."

Yale paused for a moment before speaking. "My guess is just logistics. Most of these guys are from Minnesota, either Minneapolis or Alexandria. It's easier, and therefore cheaper, to hire local muscle than to sneak a bunch of mercs in from overseas."

"My guess is," Gunderson said as he rubbed his temples, "most of them didn't even know where the money was coming from. They were just told to meet up somewhere by their gang-boss who actually accepted the money."

The room got quiet for another moment as the three men stared at the documents on the desk.

"Go home," Gunderson finally spoke up. "Rest up. Hopefully, the intel we collected helps us answer a different question."

"Yeah," Dufraine grunted. "Where next?"

CHAPTER TWELVE

Three days after the "Farmhouse Massacre," as the media had started calling it, the Sheriff's Department didn't have much to go on. Conspiracy theories were in abundance, from government-sanctioned retaliation for the attack on Broadway to gang-on-gang violence all the way to the typical religious claiming that the men had been struck down by God for their sins.

What the state forensics team had been able to tell the Sheriff's Department was only slightly more concrete. According to the report, the majority of the men had been killed with single rounds from a high-powered rifle, likely fired from a considerable distance by four or more skilled marksmen, as indicated by the unique markings on a few of the slugs they had been able to recover. The rest had been killed at close-range with an intermediate cartridge. The team had been able to recover very few usable slugs from the bodies or the walls of the farmhouse, finding mostly mangled shards of copper jackets.

All but one of the blood samples matched the DNA of the twenty-four men who'd been laid out on the lawn, and the dossiers matched up. One blood sample had been found near the kitchen that didn't match any of the men, and the report read that the sample had been contaminated by some chemical compound that Erikson couldn't pronounce that made the sample unusable.

Erikson put the reports back down on his desk and rubbed his eyes. He was relatively certain that Gunderson and his crew were responsible for the attack on the farmhouse, but he had been unable to get a hold of anyone at Norseman Consulting. None of their contractors had been admitted to the hospital, and nothing concrete tied them to the events. Even if they were responsible, what could he do about it? And why would he want to? As far as most of the DCSO deputies and APD officers were concerned, whoever had whacked twenty-four scumbags at an abandoned farmhouse was doing the Lord's work.

Standing up to stretch his legs, Erikson turned his attention to the muted television in the corner of his office. Mayor Stark was featured prominently, with news crew microphones fastened to the podium in front of her. Sighing in an attempt to expel his frustration, Erikson turned the volume back on.

"...and I assure the good citizens of Alexandria, and the rest of Greater Minnesota, that we will get to the bottom of these heinous crimes," Mayor Stark made a hammering gesture with her left hand as she spoke, "and those responsible will be brought to justice."

Some light applause sounded through the television speakers. Erikson rolled his eyes. He was still banned from talking to any of the media, which was alright by him, but since the only person who was allowed to talk to the media seemed to be Mayor Stark, the information getting to the public had been inaccurate at best, political grandstanding at worst.

Grimacing, the sheriff muted the TV again and turned back to his work. It was no secret that Mayor Stark had aspirations of running for higher office. Last Erikson had heard, Stark was in talks with donors about running for the soon to be open senatorial position. Erikson was sure that being associated with the successful capture of those responsible for one of the deadliest terrorist attacks in the country's history, would be a nice feather in her cap as she entered another political race.

Shaking off his general dislike for Alexandria's mayor, Erikson turned his attention back to the three dossiers that bothered him the most. The two Chechen and one Iranian in the group were obvious outliers. The other twenty-one had all either been Hispanic or white, and they'd all been tied to one of the known gangs in Minnesota or, in one case, as a laborer on the rigs in the oil fields near Minot, North Dakota.

The dossiers indicated that these three outliers were guns-for-hire, mercenaries who used their religious affiliations as an excuse for violence. This was a mindset that Erikson could not fully wrap his mind around. The idea that men like this were running around his county made him shudder. Erikson's mind went to the men in the Norseman Consulting holding cells, Reyes and al Kobani. The connection was obvious, but he was the only person in the building who knew about it and, despite his gut feeling, Erikson was keeping that knowledge close to his vest. Erikson's instincts were telling him that he should really inform more people of his contact with Norseman Consulting, but he was letting it go for the time being.

The phone on his desk rang, breaking Erikson's concentration. The sheriff was somewhat disappointed to see that the number was not the masked number he was sure would eventually come from Norseman Consulting. It was from the front desk downstairs. He glanced at his watch as he moved to pick up the phone. *Probably just Ellie dropping off my lunch like she always does.*

"Sheriff Erikson."

"Sir, you might want to come down here right away," the front desk deputy responded animatedly.

"What's going on?" Erikson demanded, not in any sort of mood for guessing games.

"Tyler just brought some guys in. They're pretty doped up, but they claim they were at the farmhouse the night of the attack." That grabbed his attention. Erikson slammed the phone down and sprinted for the stairs. He ran to the first floor and slammed through the door to the cage behind the front desk at full tilt. "Where are they?" he demanded. The front desk attendant gave a wide berth for the Sheriff. Deputy Tyler stood wide-eyed when the sheriff barged through the door.

"They're in one of the empty holding cells," Tyler yelped.

Erikson's mind finally caught up to the adrenaline and he took a deep breath. "How can we be sure that they were at the farmhouse attack?"

"Well sir," Tyler started, "they have the same dossier printouts on them as the guys from the farmhouse."

"What do you mean 'on them'?" Erikson called over his shoulder as he walked down the hallway towards the cell. Tyler didn't respond, but he didn't need to.

Seated in the holding cell, hands cuffed in front of them, were three men. Two were propped up against the walls of the cell and the third was sitting upright, staring around the cell with a hollow look. All three were dressed in white boxers and white t-shirts with small blood stains emanating from a staple in each man's chest.

"Tyler! Erikson bellowed down the hall. "Get the fuck over here now!"

Rapid boot steps sounded. "Yes, sir?"

"How did you find these men?"

"Uh, well, I was getting a cup of coffee at that gas station on County 42," Tyler recounted, "and I came out from paying and they were just leaned up against my truck with handcuffs on them."

"Wait," Erikson turned back to the cell, "those aren't your handcuffs?"

"No, sir," the deputy said, tapping the handcuff pouch on his duty belt. "I still have mine right here."

"Thank you, Deputy," Erikson said. "I want you to finish your report of what happened and get it to me right away." Pushing past the deputy, Erikson hustled back up to his office. His mind was racing.

He ascended, slammed his office door behind him, and reached for his cell phone. In a flash, Erikson suddenly became aware that he was not the only person in the office.

Sitting in one of the chairs in the sheriff's office was James Gunderson.

"Oh, what the hell," Erikson moaned.

"I think I owe you an explanation," Gunderson said evenly, "and I prefer to do it in person."

"Yeah, no shit" Erikson snorted. "And you can start with where the fuck you get off conducting illegal interrogations, drugging and torturing prisoners, and killing two dozen men without due process!"

Meeting the sheriff's gaze, Gunderson responded in a quiet, level voice. "Sheriff, I felt that we were very upfront about our intentions."

"But—"

"But," Gunderson interrupted, "you weren't anticipating so much violence."

Erikson nodded sharply.

"The reason I am here today is to inform you, off every sort of record, that Norseman Consulting's activities have been officially sanctioned by certain three-letter agencies within the Federal Government. We chose not to tell you about this until now because we weren't sure how well you would play ball with us."

Gunderson held eye contact with the sheriff during an uncomfortably long silence. Erikson was just now realizing how unsettling Gunderson was. His seamless transition from charming and charismatic to cold-blooded and emotionless made the sheriff extremely uneasy.

Realizing the weight of Gunderson's last statement, Erikson nodded again.

"What this means," Gunderson continued, "is that the federal government has taken an interest in the events that are unfolding and have outsourced the investigative work to my firm. It is highly unlikely you will see any federal agencies poking around Alexandria."

"So, what does all of this mean for me and the sheriff's department?" Erikson finally asked.

"It means that I need your help," Gunderson responded simply. "The raid on the farmhouse yielded an absolute goldmine of information by way of the computer hard drives and the three men we captured."

"Well you seem to be capable to conducting this little operation all on your own," Erikson scoffed. "What the hell do you need me and my deputies for?"

"The information we gathered will allow us to build a target deck of several more safe houses, backup safe houses, dead-drop locations, transportation sites, etc. within the network of terrorists and petty criminals that we're up against," Gunderson explained. "While my teams are highly skilled, if we shut down all the locations ourselves, eventually it is going to get out that we're no longer looking at them as common drug dealers. They'll get spooked and move everything, making it more difficult for us to shut the operation down."

"So, we aren't just looking at this as a combination of terrorists and drug dealers?"

"No, Sheriff," Gunderson shook his head as he replied. "Among the more startling pieces of information we gleaned from the raid is that the drug trafficker–terrorist combo is nothing more than a front. What we, and our federal contacts, believe is that the operation is sanctioned by an unfriendly nation. These goons we've captured are working on their behalf."

Erikson could hardly believe his ears. If what Gunderson was saying was true, then some other country was conducting acts of war on American soil. "Well, fuck," Erikson exhaled sharply. "What else do I need to know?"

"I think the last piece of information that is pertinent in this case," Gunderson grimaced, "is that the mayor, or someone in her office, appears to be involved in the operation."

"What do you mean?" Erikson almost laughed. Jenny Stark might be a political opportunist and ruthlessly ambitious, but treasonous? This was highly doubtful in Erikson's opinion.

"We are not yet sure, but there are several references that tie her and her associates to the men at that farmhouse." Gunderson shifted in his chair. "We are still working through the details."

"Alright, Gunderson," Erikson said, resignedly. "What do you need from me?"

Gunderson stood and pulled on his coat as he spoke. "Sheriff, what I need is for you to send the DCSO Special Weapons and Tactics team to the Norseman Consulting compound for some training over the next few days." Gunderson stood in front of Erikson's desk. "After they're done, send over your patrol deputies. I'd suggest you take in some training from my men too. You'll find that they are highly qualified."

"And then?" Erikson asked as Gunderson finished buttoning his coat.

"And then, Sheriff," Gunderson replied, sticking his hand out for a handshake, "then we give these fuckers everything we got."

CHAPTER THIRTEEN

The weeks that followed felt like a blur. Erikson had sent his SWAT team out to the Norseman compound for training, but not without explicit instructions to observe and report everything they possibly could. His SWAT deputies were loyal and followed the additional command to observe and report back. After eight hours every day the deputies came back sweaty, exhausted, and trained, but with very little of consequence to report. This was partly due to the fact that the training compound was far removed from the main facilities.

What they could report was that Norseman Consulting had hired some of the sharpest, most difficult trainers his deputies had ever encountered, chief among them was an above-the-knee amputee who went by "Chuck."

Their rigorous training program encompassed everything from de-escalation techniques and non-lethal takedowns to close combat within and around vehicles and advanced building clearing methods. The instructors were relentless, pushing the DCSO deputies past their perceived personal limits for each training evolution. The experience was physically, mentally, and emotionally exhausting, but each of them had learned more in a week of training than they had throughout their entire careers.

After the SWAT team's week of training was over, Erikson sent his patrol deputies over in groups of four. Erikson was somewhat surprised to learn that his patrol deputies were joined by other law enforcement agencies, mostly from the small towns surrounding Alexandria, but also some guys from the state patrol and even out of state.

It had been four weeks since the surprise delivery of the three tech nerds from the farmhouse, and in that time, Erikson and his deputies had been heaped with praise for their "anti-crime" efforts; shutting down drug dealers and distribution centers and arresting many criminals along the way. The Alexandria City Police Department had also been credited with several successful busts. The mayor was on the news almost every day. At first, she appeared confident, gushing with praise for the men and women of the local law enforcement agencies. As the weeks wore on, the mayor grew more and more agitated, speaking sharply and quickly to reporters when questioned.

It was Monday morning and Erikson was sitting in his office barely listening to his deputies recount the final training evolution while he sipped his coffee and split his attention between the deputies' story and shooting quick glances over their heads at the muted television on the wall behind them. The closed captioning subtitles spelled out a cleanly written and delivered speech, congratulating the APD on yet another successful bust, but the mayor giving the speech was visibly agitated. Erikson noticed that the police chief standing behind her also looked a bit uncomfortable, in contrast to his categorically stoic nature.

"...and as soon as she wrapped into the second room," one of the deputies was animatedly talking with his hands, pointing to the lone female deputy in the sheriff's office, "WHAM!" He swung his hands across his body. "Fuckin' Chuck hits Chelsea right across the ballistic plates with a goddamned baseball bat!"

Sheriff Erikson smiled faintly. Each of the teams had been subjected to the same training model, and so the after-action reports bore a lot of similarities. Despite this, Erikson had insisted on sitting down with each of the teams in the vain hope that someone would have been able to collect more information about the comings and goings on the Norseman Consulting compound.

The deputies wrapped up their report, and Erikson ordered them out of his office so they could go home and rest. As the door clicked shut behind them, the sheriff slid into his high-backed chair behind his desk. Reaching into his pocket, he extracted a sparse ring of keys, and singled out a small, black key nestled between his car key fob and his house key. Clutching the small key between his fingers, Erikson reached down and unlocked the deep bottom drawer of his desk and removed a stack of manila folders.

He spread the folders across his desk and started rereading the reports that had been anonymously finding their way to his desk of late. The reports detailed the raids that had been conducted over the past four weeks, and it hadn't taken the sheriff long to notice a pattern.
While many of the raids had resulted in the capture of drug dealers and gang members, with relatively few casualties—and this is what the news was reporting—the later busts had resulted in more and more foreign nationals being killed or captured, and then dragged off. Most of these were Chechens or Middle Eastern and many of them had been labeled as mercenaries by the anonymous analysts that had put together

the dossiers. Erikson presumed that the news had not been reporting the mercenaries because the Norseman contractors had been whisking the bodies away and leaving the bodies of the druggies and gang bangers behind.

There had been more reports on Erikson's desk than there were news reports. Some of the raids had taken place as far away as the oil fields in western North Dakota, so they had not been connected to the violence in Alexandria and more than a couple were written off by the media as gang-on-gang violence. While the raids had been more than successful thus far, they had also been conducted exclusively by the Norseman contractors. The sheriff figured this was the reason for the mayor's discomfort: she didn't know who was conducting the raids, but she sure as hell knew it wasn't the APD.

Several of Erikson's deputies had been called out to investigate the aftermath of some of the closer raids, and all of them had reported roughly the same story: dead gang-bangers, some drugs and weapons, but never any foreign nationals or their bodies, no technology, no cash. After the dossiers started showing up in his mailbox, the sheriff figured out why the tech and communications devices were missing, and he could well imagine why there was never any cash.

Also of concern were reports from Erikson's patrol deputies that they were experiencing a whole new level of tension in the industrial housing area just outside the south of town. Notoriously crime-ridden, this lower income area had been the focal point for most of the sheriff's office callouts, but ever since the raids had started in earnest, the callouts had all but stopped.

The deputies were spooked, and from what Erikson was hearing from the APD, the city cops were feeling the same sense of uneasiness. The prevailing opinion amongst the patrol deputies was that the tension would culminate in some sort of violent clash, and that it would happen soon. Frowning, Erikson opened up the last folder on his desk. He'd read it several times already that morning, but the information it held still didn't feel real.

This folder contained not a raid report but a compilation of information on Mayor Stark's political ambitions and the means she was employing to achieve them—meetings, phone calls, and payments from someone claiming to want to help advance her political career. The file went on to show how the money was being funneled through multiple cut-outs and offshore accounts, all owned by shell companies.

Some of the notes inside the file indicated that the analyst compiling the report believed that the money was coming from a country in the Middle East. Erikson had always known that Mayor Stark's political aspirations did not stop at Alexandria City Hall, but he had never imagined that she would be willing to go so far in order to advance.

The sheriff thumbed over to the last page, tucked the report back in its manila folder, and stared down at a sticky note on the back of the folder. The small, orange note had two words written on it: Call me.

With a sense of foreboding, Sheriff Erikson picked up his phone.

Deputy Johnson was not exactly thrilled with the task that the sheriff had given him and his new partner. To be honest, Johnson wasn't exactly thrilled with his new partner, either. Most of the deputies in the sheriff's department had traditionally operated alone in the patrol cars in order to provide a wider net of coverage across the county. But recent swells in violence had inspired Sheriff Erikson to mandate a change in the system designed to ensure more support for his deputies. Johnson understood that, and could even get on board with it, but what he could not fathom was why the sheriff had paired him with Deputy Aaron Tyler.

Deputies Shaun Johnson and Aaron Tyler were completely different from each other in both demeanor and ambition. Johnson was one of the older deputies in the Douglas County Sheriff's Office, and it showed—from his semi-permanent scowl to the extra weight in his gut that dug uncomfortably into his gun-belt. Johnson was quiet, even stoic, and was looking forward to earning his retirement in the next couple of years. Where Johnson was old, salty, and overweight, Tyler was young, ambitious, and physically fit to the point of obsession.

Tyler's career had only commenced a few years earlier, after budget cuts had forcibly removed him from his Military Police job in Oklahoma. At only twenty-two, Tyler was among the youngest, most ambitious deputies, and would tell anyone who would sit still long enough of his great desire to join the DCSO SWAT team.

Johnson was now subject to Tyler's almost continual rambling for close to fourteen hours a day. Thankfully, the conversation had held a little more variety since Tyler had become a recent graduate of the Norseman Consulting training course.

Johnson had not yet been sent out for training; his course was coming up in two weeks and he was slated to go with three other deputies and four city cops. As Johnson guided the sheriff's patrol SUV through the light traffic of rural Minnesota, Tyler was espousing every last detail of what had been imparted to him the week prior. At the moment, he was discussing the finer points of fighting in and around vehicles.

"Man, you're gonna love it." Tyler was turned almost sideways in the passenger seat, looking around the neighborhood as Johnson drove on. "Chuck and his guys are super demanding, but it's totally worth it."

Johnson grunted in reply as he flicked the SUVs turn signal up and swung into a right-hand turn. They felt the SUV slide a bit as it hit a patch of ice in the middle of the intersection. Johnson smoothly corrected the slide before the SUVs electronic traction control system even registered there was a problem.

"Probably the most applicable training," Tyler continued, "for the average deputy, anyway, was the fighting in and around the vehicle." The younger deputy grinned a little bit as he turned to see if Johnson was still paying attention. He wasn't, but Tyler continued anyway.

"They took us out and started having us take shots into cars from different angles," Deputy Tyler had turned back to scanning the neighborhood. "Chuck even hobbled out with a goddamned fifty-cal. Freaking blew the engine block apart."

As Tyler was animatedly describing the effects of a .50 caliber sniper round on the average passenger sedan, the radio mounted to the SUV's dashboard squawked out, "Car two-two, are you out there?"

"Car two-two here, go ahead," Deputy Johnson spoke for the first time since getting into the SUV with his new partner that morning.

"Can you head to the Walmart out by the freeway?" The radio operator sounded bored. "The manager has a shoplifter in his office."

"We'll go check it out." Johnson set the handset back onto the dash and pressed the blinker down to signal a left turn.

"Aw man," Tyler spoke up, "this boring stuff drives me nuts."

"This isn't exciting enough for you?" Johnson could barely contain his annoyance. These new guys and their thirst for excitement drove him a little crazy.

"Naw, dude, all these calls are some punk-ass kid, made a bad mistake," Deputy Tyler gave a somewhat dismissive wave of his hand as he settled into his seat, "and now we gotta come in and take the dumbass statements and all sort of shit."

"Man, ain't you trying to get into SWAT?" Johnson snorted a little bit. He knew Tyler was. He had said so at least six times, and it was barely two hours into their shift.

"Yeah, so what?" Tyler huffed.

"You know they don't just take anyone, right?" Johnson stared ahead as he turned the SUV onto the country road heading to Walmart. "You gotta pay your dues, have a record of good police work."

Tyler grunted and fell silent for the rest of the trip. Deputy Johnson smiled the entire way to Walmart.

CHAPTER FOURTEEN

On Erikson's second visit to Norseman Consulting, he noticed a significant increase in security. The guards at the front were all openly carrying rifles that the sheriff could not identify, and even after he was cleared at the first gate, he was forced to stop again at the entry control point at the administrative compound and subjected to an additional search.

After finally being admitted to the compound and finding a parking spot in the covered lot, Erikson made his way into the office building, where he was immediately ushered back to Gunderson's office by the receptionist, Ashley.

"Good morning, Sheriff!" James Gunderson greeted Erikson warmly with a smile and a handshake.

"I don't understand why I had to drive all the way over here," Erikson responded gruffly. "Your note said to call you."

Gunderson laughed as he replied. "My apologies, Gerry, but it is a part of the tradecraft." Indicating the chairs in the center of the room in front of his large desk, Gunderson invited the sheriff to take a seat.

"Gerry, I think it's time we come fully level with you," Gunderson said as he leaned casually against his desk. "There's been a lot going on, and I regret that we have had to keep you out of the loop." Erikson raised his eyebrows. He had not expected any sort of transparency, and he was skeptical that he was going to get any at all.

"You have my attention, Mr. Gunderson," the sheriff said.

"Here's the deal, Sheriff." Gunderson circled back behind his desk and sat down, looking at the sheriff frankly. "Through the raids, we have been conducting, we have been able to obtain a lot of information. Much of it we have passed on to you."

Erikson nodded.

"Well," Gunderson continued, "as we have indicated in our reports, we believe that the organization behind the attacks is being run by a contingent of Iranians somewhere within the Greater Minnesota area, almost certainly within the Alexandria area."

The sheriff's eyes widened slightly, but he was not entirely surprised. The reports had been indicating the involvement of a foreign agency. He just hadn't been aware that the agents might be situated in the country, much less in his backyard.

"What we have been able to gather is that the Iranians have been taking advantage of the current failure of the American Security Apparatus and resulting communist and socialist sentiment brewing within the working class," Gunderson said. "And they have been paying both imported guns for hire, mostly from Chechnya, but also some home-grown gangsters and anti-establishment militia types."

Gunderson stopped for a minute to take a sip of water from the Nalgene bottle on his desk, allowing Erikson to chime in.

"What purpose does that serve them?" Erikson's inquiry was valid. After several straight presidential elections that promised to bring about significant change and return the country to her former glory, the country had slipped even further down the road to economic depression, resulting in, among other things, the once mighty American military being gutted and called home from their far-flung posts across the globe. The Iranians were running the Middle East, and the Russians were the dominant party in Europe and were fighting China for control over Asia. The sad truth was that the United States was no longer the dominant power. Many of the federal agencies besides the military had been gutted down to near nothing, and control had mostly slipped from the grasp of the federal government and into the hands of the state politicians. From Erikson's perspective, Iran—or anyone else for that matter—had no reason to interfere with America anymore.

"Well, Sheriff," Gunderson sighed, "even though American foreign policy no longer can project power as it once did, we still represent a threat to other powers, especially those that are rising."

"So? Why would that make the Iranians want to conduct these attacks?"

"The Iranians are running out of their own resources. They've been fighting the United States and other Western powers for control of the Middle East and Asia, and their reserves—even their oil reserves—are getting low." Gunderson took another sip of water. "It is the opinion of my crew, and my employer, that the Iranian security services are attempting to conduct a series of operations within our borders to destabilize what little sense of security we have left. We think they hope to keep us so busy at home that we end up crippled and don't return to the world stage when the depression is over."

Erikson looked at Gunderson. He didn't know how much of this he could believe, but Erikson didn't think Mr. Severson had been thinking about national security when he'd hired Gunderson and his team. "And that's why you're here."

"Correct again," Gunderson grinned a little bit more. Reaching into his desk drawer, Gunderson pulled out a sealed folder and tossed it to the sheriff. "Read it before you leave, then leave it on my desk."

Erikson opened the folder and started pulling out the documents. He paused and looked up. "I have another question."

"What is your question?" Gunderson asked, watching the sheriff organize the documents on the coffee table in the middle of the office floor.

"How does Mayor Stark fit into all this?"

Gunderson leaned back in his chair. "It is well known within her personal circle that she harbors a far-left leaning. Some of her close advisors and college mentors are known communists and sympathetic to the revolutionary cause. We think her ambitions got the best of her. She was approached a year ago by an unknown benefactor who offered her a ton of money for her political pursuits. The benefactor also promised her political victory, claiming she'd win it by being the woman who cleaned up drug trafficking in the city."

"Isn't that what you're here to do?" Erikson was looking down at the documents on the table while he listened to Gunderson.

"Well, I moved the company here due to the low population density and the ability to train my contractors in different environments based on the season. But yes, I told you our role out here was to clean up the drug and terrorism problem."

"But Mayor Stark doesn't know you're out here."

"Correct. And what we think is happening is that she was going to come up with a 'creative solution,'" Gunderson made air quotes with his fingers, "to solving the terrorist attack and drug trafficking ring. Looks like she intended to hire a foreign firm, one that has no apparent ties to Iran, to come in and solve the case, crack down on their competition. Theoretically, Mayor Stark would be in a good position to become Governor Stark, which would then allow her to cede the territory that the communist faction, Revolutionary Independence Front wants, or even impose far-left policies on the entire state."

"I'm not sure I understand it, but I guess I'm supposed to take your word for it?" Erikson was not well versed in international politics, but the line he was being fed from Gunderson sounded a bit far-fetched.

"Well take a look at the documents, and after you are done, I have to make a request of you." Gunderson sat forward in his chair.

"And what might that be?"

"I need you to participate in the next set of raids."

Deputies Johnson and Tyler had wrapped up their investigation of the shoplifting teenager, and it had gone almost exactly as Tyler had predicted. A young kid, thirteen, had tried stealing a couple Blu-ray disks by stuffing them under his threadbare winter coat. The deputies had felt bad for the kid, who they both empathized with, but they did their best to stay focused and took the police report.

A few minutes later, the two deputies were debating where they should go for lunch. Johnson argued for a burger at the McDonalds down the road. Fitness-obsessed Deputy Tyler argued just as persuasively for something a bit healthier and tried to convince his new partner to drive to Subway. In the end, Deputy Johnson was driving so the older man guided the car to the McDonald's drive-through.

"This shit will freakin' kill you, man," Tyler pouted from the passenger seat.

Johnson was grinning from ear to ear. After an entire morning of listening to the younger deputy flap his gums, he was relishing this opportunity to get under the kid's skin in return.

"It probably won't kill me any sooner than having to listen to you squawk all day," Johnson said as he turned to give his order to the drive-through kiosk.

"Aw fuck you, dude," Tyler responded as the drive-through attendant started taking Johnson's order for a quarter-pound cheeseburger. "And tell her to throw in a side salad!"

Within a few minutes, the two deputies were on their way back to the industrial housing neighborhood to continue their patrol. The pair drove in relative silence, scanning the area and eating their lunch.

There wasn't much activity in the area, but Tyler, who hadn't driven this route before, was fixated on the apparent poverty. Run-down, single-story houses and apartment complexes lined the streets, many of them boarded up. The younger deputy couldn't wrap his head around the discord between the almost idyllic downtown of Alexandria and the crushing poverty just outside the city limits. Johnson wasn't

68

apathetic to the plight of people living in extreme poverty, but his lifelong experience made him numbed to it.

Built shortly before the American economy had started its downward spiral, the industrial housing area was meant to house the employees of one of the larger manufacturing firms that had intended to set up shop in the district. The construction had been long and expensive, and when the economy caved, the building was halted, and the land sold off to a developer based out of Minneapolis.

The result was four square miles of squat buildings surrounding what was supposed to be called "the Spire," a twelve-story apartment and office building. Now, the locals referred to the hideous building as "the Finger," a reference to its ugly brown exterior, as well as the general feeling that the manufacturing firm had given them the proverbial finger by abandoning the project midway.

Many of the apartments and houses in the industrial housing area had remained empty for a few years, but as the economic situation worsened in the cities, more remote, rural areas like Alexandria had experienced mass immigration of workers seeking what little there was outside the cities. With much of the labor force leaving the towns, a couple of companies within the manufacturing industry had seen an opportunity and had followed the workforce back out to Alexandria's south side.

Now, two new manufacturing plants had started up, and much of the industrial housing complex was occupied by their workers. There was a slight boost to the economy, but the vast majority of the workers still lived in poverty. Many of the area's residents chose to supplement their income through illicit activities such as drug trafficking or prostitution. Others decided to spend their meager wages on the illegal goods their neighbors were selling.

Johnson and Tyler drove around for a few minutes, winding their way to the back of the complex. As they passed the Finger, Tyler broke the silence. "God, that thing is ugly. Who even lives there?"

"Low-income folks," Johnson grunted in reply. "A lot of the exodus from Minneapolis, St. Paul, and St. Cloud, and what-have-you ended up here due to how cheap it is to live in an unfinished apartment building."

"Who do you think those guys are?" Nodding over to the front doors as they passed, Tyler indicated to the two black Chevy SUVs parked on the curb in front of the Finger. Johnson turned his head slightly.

"Hell, if I know," Johnson turned his head back to the front. "Some jackasses who can't afford a real house but decided to buy a baller truck."

"Naw man," Tyler said as the older deputy pushed the patrol SUV down the street, away from the Finger. "Didn't you see how low they were sitting? Or the four guys hanging around outside the cars?"

Deputy Johnson grunted in reply. He had noticed; he just didn't care. Weird things were happening all the time out here, and all Johnson wanted to do was finish this patrol and go home.

"Those dudes were waiting for someone." Tyler had returned to scanning the passenger side as he spoke. "Had to be. Why else would they be standing outside with how cold it is?"

The dashboard thermometer indicated that the temperature outside was holding steady at thirteen degrees Fahrenheit, a temperature that Deputy Johnson had no intention of trekking out into.

"So, what?" Johnson asked. "What do you wanna do? Go ask 'em who they're waiting for?"

"Well…no," Tyler said. "I was thinking we could at least just watch 'em for a little bit."

"You want to set up a stakeout?" Johnson laughed. "In a large, marked, sheriff's department SUV?"

Tyler sank back into his seat, dejected. "No," he sighed.

"Come on." Johnson was shaking his head. "Let's just finish this patrol. You can tell me more about the random shit that one-legged dude taught you."

CHAPTER FIFTEEN

As the two deputies were winding their way around the streets of the industrial housing neighborhood, Erikson was following James Gunderson down a hallway in the Norseman Consulting office building. The information that Norseman Consulting' intelligence team had provided to him was mind-boggling. Erikson could not believe that Mayor Stark's ambitions would include foreign cooperation, but he also felt fairly sure she did not know who she was getting in bed with. From what he could see, it was about to get out of control. The files that had been given to him in Gunderson's office had been thrown in a shredder before they left the room, except for one manila folder containing a series of pictures. That folder was clutched in Erikson's left hand, and his head was spinning as they walked towards a windowless door at the end of the hallway.

Gunderson stopped as they arrived at the hallway door, reached into his shirt pocket, pulled out a keycard, and swiped the card through a reader mounted on the wall near the doorknob. As he swiped the card through the reader on the wall, he turned to Erikson.

"We are heading into the Brain and the Ops Room," Gunderson held the door open for the sheriff as they stepped through into a small room with yet another door. "Ajay and Tony have a plan for the next phase of the operation."

Erikson nodded as the first door swung shut behind him. The click of the first door reverberated around the small room, prompting Gunderson to swipe his card for the second door. He stepped through and held the door open for the sheriff. The two men had stepped into a stairwell, and Gunderson led the way down and into a dimly lit hallway. They walked silently, their shoes noticeably clicking on the tile floor.

Roughly halfway down the hallway, Gunderson turned to yet another windowless door, swiped his card a final time, opened the door, and stepped into a bustling room.

In a word, Sheriff Erikson was surprised. After all the security measures, he had expected the Brain to be a dimly lit command center, like they had in the movies, with dozens of people talking into headsets, frantically typing at computers, and staring at a full-wall video feed of satellite footage.

The room was brightly lit, and a half dozen people were sitting at their desks, facing the front of the room to Erikson's right as he entered the room. There were several large, high-definition televisions mounted to the walls on all sides, but most of them were turned off, and the few that were on were running a muted, closed-captioned showing of the twenty-four-hour news networks.

There was some significant bustle in the room, and the atmosphere of the Brain was somewhat tense. Erikson could feel it as his host turned to the left and brought the sheriff to the back of the large room, toward a series of glass-enclosed offices.

"What is everyone so excited about?" Erikson inquired as he and Gunderson made their way past the final desk on the main floor and reached one of the offices.

Gunderson slowed and turned to face the glass door to the office in front of him as he replied. "Our intel guys have sorted through a lot of data," Gunderson rapped on the glass door, "and I think we have identified two major players."

Erikson heard a light click, and Gunderson ushered him in.

"I think that Ajay will be best suited to fill you in from here." Ajay Yale had walked around his desk and greeted the two men as they entered his office.

"Greetings, Sheriff," Yale shook Erikson's hand as he crossed to the center of the room. "It's so good to see you again. Please—take a seat."

Erikson sat down heavily on the old sofa at the far side of Yale's office. He couldn't help but get the feeling the pudgy man sometimes slept on the couch. The cushions were well worn, and it had a slight smell that contrasted greatly with the sterile nature of the Brain. As Erikson pondered the quality of a light brown stain on the armrest, Yale turned the monitor of his computer around so that Erikson could see what was on the screen.

There were two close-up photographs of two different men, both of them bearded. Erikson could tell from the date stamps that the pictures had been taken within the past day and could guess from their surroundings that they were born of individuals nearby. The man on the right-hand side of the screen had a thick, bushy beard, a light complexion, and reddish-brown hair. Erikson decided he looked Slavic and given the intel he'd been receiving the last couple weeks, he mentally extrapolated that this was another Chechen.

The man on the left side of the screen, however, the sheriff recognized immediately. Dirty, thin, and mean looking, Conor Johnsen's mugshot leered out at them. Erikson sighed.

"Well I know this one," he said as he looked over to Yale, "and I suppose this other character is, in some way, part of the organization we're trying to dismantle?"

"They both are, Sheriff," Yale said from behind the monitor. He had his hands clasped in front of his mouth again, his stubby fingers resting just under his nose. Yale continued, "The man on your right is Gregor—" Waving his hand dismissively, Yale headed off the sheriff's next question. "His family name is not important."

"What is important," Gunderson chimed in, "is that he is a key part of this plot we are seeking to destroy."

"Okay, fine," Erikson shrugged. He was getting used to the cloak and dagger operations. He didn't like it, but he was getting used to it. "Why am I here then? What role do I play in all of this?"

"We need you to help us pursue, investigate, and destroy Mr. Johnsen's organization," Gunderson stated matter-of-factly as if Erikson's enthusiastic participation were a foregone conclusion.

"Okay," Erikson looked at Gunderson. "Why? What has he done to merit me putting my depleted resources into chasing him around?"

"What do you know of Johnsen?" Yale interrupted hands still in front of his face.

"He's a piece of work, for sure," the sheriff said, nodding. "Runs the local blue-collar gang, they call themselves the Revolutionary Independent Front or RIF, and he's been in and out of county lockup, did a stint in the state prison down in the cities. He's a bit of a criminal jack-of-all-trades. Robbery, gambling, prostitution, the occasional act of revolution carried out by his loyal followers. He holds power in the trailer parks, wherever low-income folks feel they are being oppressed. The elimination of factory jobs is just a ploy to keep them oppressed, and he's the hero that will help them rise above."

"Sounds like you know him pretty well," Gunderson mused as he leaned back in his chair.

"What I don't know," Erikson responded levelly, "is how he plays into this."

Yale cleared his throat a little and glanced over to Gunderson. Yale had warned Gunderson that despite the explosion of violence in his county over the past several weeks, Erikson was a lifelong lawman, and probably would not be too keen on the idea of raiding a private citizen's home on the word of an extra-governmental organization such as Norseman Consulting. Yale had even included that analysis in the dossier on the sheriff that his analysts had worked up.

The brief glance did not go unnoticed by Erikson. He knew he was in over his head. Fighting international terrorism is not something a sheriff in a rural district generally anticipates. But he was also tired of being kept in the dark and on the sidelines. As far as he was concerned, a federal agency contracting a private security company to handle an investigation and conduct law enforcement operations was a gross overstep of federal authority. This made Erikson anxious to get involved in the action if only to ensure that it was being done correctly and following due process.

Not quite believing the words as they came out of his mouth, Erikson broke the uncomfortable silence. "Gentlemen, please," the sheriff spoke tersely. "I understand that you don't want to give me too much information. I understand that my position as an elected official and law enforcement officer—not a soldier or spy or whatever another black bag, secret squirrel shit you have going on here—makes it somewhat nuanced as to what information you are willing to give me." The sheriff paused, and his face contorted into a frown.

"But these dirtbags killed twenty-nine people. Eleven of them were my deputies and my forensics team, all of them were citizens in my jurisdiction." Erikson glared at the two men, his voice level, even harsh. It had a heat to it that neither Gunderson nor Yale had likely expected nor Erikson himself was surprised at its forcefulness.

"So, I want in." Erikson enunciated each word by jabbing his index finger down on the stack of papers in his lap. "No more sleight of hand and parceled out information. If you want my help, if I am going to risk the lives of my deputies, then we have to work together. I need to know the full picture, as it develops, not after."

"Agreed, Sheriff," Gunderson nodded his head emphatically. "That's what we were hoping to hear. From now on, there will be open lines of communication between our two agencies. You and your department will have access to our investigative materials and abilities and will be able to use them for your part of the operation."

74

"Okay, good." Erikson was surprised at the success of his little speech, although a small voice in the back of his head was telling him that this had been Gunderson's plan for the meeting all along.

"And," Gunderson continued, "Norseman Consulting will not conduct any further operations without notifying you directly."

"Great," Erikson said, his face relaxing into an almost-smile. "So, what is the deal with Conor Johnsen and his merry band of criminal underlings?"

"Simple," Yale said brightly. "Johnsen and his RIF are trying to set themselves up as a militia of sorts, stockpiling and making their own weapons and ammunition. Their end goal is to establish a little independent haven for communists in the north. They want the Upper Peninsula, the northernmost part of Minnesota, and pretty much all of North Dakota. They needed a little financial and operational boost and have begun supplementing their income by distributing heroin."

"Johnsen's actually distributing hard drugs now?" This was news to Erikson. His department didn't have any undercover assets and finding snitches within RIF had proven to be difficult. "We always suspected that RIF was, but was never able to prove it concretely."

"Just started," Yale responded with a nod. "Gregor here has been using his contacts within Russian-bloc Europe to get Johnsen and RIF some cheap heroin, which they then sell at an exorbitant markup. In exchange for the heroin, RIF also imports, houses, and arms Gregor's men in the name of revolution."

Erikson shook his head. "Holy shit, Conor, what the hell have you gotten yourself into?"

Gunderson interjected into the conversation. "That's not all, Sheriff. Thanks to the steady supply of drugs, Conor has greatly expanded his influence, and he now has trafficking operations all over Minnesota and North Dakota. Anywhere he can find a 'downtrodden laborer,' RIF is there to ease the pain through narcotics and propaganda."

Yale nodded. "We've seen indicators that they are expanding their recruitment. The Chechen/Iranian influence has pushed them to be more accepting; before, they focused their recruitment on blue-collar whites, but they have started to let anyone in as long as they agree with them."

"Hell, the rebrand is allowing downtrodden laborers all over the state to take up arms and get their narcotics fix all in one," Gunderson snorted.

"Well, RIF has always been heavily concentrated in the industrial housing area." Erikson rubbed the dark stubble on his chin. "I hope you're not suggesting we start clearing the entire industrial area out."

"God, no," Gunderson said emphatically. "The place is too damn large, and the population is too damn concentrated for our teams combined. There are still several thousand innocent people living and working out there."

"We do, however, have several targets in mind." Yale clicked his computer mouse a couple times, pulling up an overhead map of the industrial housing area and surrounding countryside.
Nearly a dozen red circles popped into view on the screen, highlighting structures all around Alexandria. Some of the houses were within the city limits, though most were spread out around the industrial housing area and outlying rural areas.

"Holy shit," Erikson grunted. "RIF has been pretty busy getting this all set up."

"Not just them," Yale said gravely. "Their Iranian benefactors as well."

Gunderson went on. "You can see why we need your help. Unfortunately, what I told you earlier about Norseman Consulting not targeting private American citizens is no longer feasible." Erikson's head turned sharply in Gunderson's direction.
"The reality is, we knew this would probably end up being the case, although we did strive to target the foreign nationals more exclusively." Gunderson shrugged. "However, RIF has become so fully integrated with their foreign partners that separating them no longer makes any operational sense."

Erikson exhaled sharply. He'd already wondered about the operations that Norseman Consulting had been running early on. Many of the dossiers that he'd received were of US citizens, as were the three tech guys that had been unceremoniously dumped next to his deputy's patrol car. Now it seemed the Norseman Consulting assaulters were going to start openly targeting United States citizens.

"I don't know how I feel about this." Erikson wanted justice for his community and his department, but he wanted to do it right.

Gunderson took a deep breath through his nose, exhaling as he spoke. "Sheriff, I can't make this more palatable for you at this point. We have terrorists we need to capture, killers who are out there, right now. We have actionable intelligence and are ready to move."

With an intensity that surprised both Yale and Erikson, Gunderson leaned forward before continuing. "The bottom line is, Sheriff," Gunderson's demeanor was aggressive, and his voice was sharp enough that Erikson could feel himself involuntarily wince, "is that Norseman Consulting has been contracted to accomplish an objective. Out of respect for you and our community, we chose to involve your office. We can proceed without you, but it would be much easier if you helped us out, using some of the deputies we have been training over the past several weeks and hitting these targets with us."

There was a brief silence, which Gunderson terminated by snapping his fingers in Yale's direction, never taking his eyes off the sheriff. Yale opened his top desk drawer and handed Gunderson a thick manila folder, sealed with tape. Slapping the folder down on the coffee table in the center of the room, Gunderson continued. "So, what'll it be?"

"Well," Erikson sighed. It did not look like he was going to get a better option. He picked up the folder. "I guess we are in business."

CHAPTER SIXTEEN

Later that evening, Erikson was sitting on his couch in the living room. Ellen had fallen asleep, her head in his lap as he stroked her chestnut hair. His morning at the Norseman Consulting compound had rattled him deeply, and he had spent the rest of his day trying to process the implications of what he was about to ask his department to do.

The ominous manila folder that Gunderson had given him when he left was sitting on the coffee table, the seal broken but its contents placed back inside. He didn't want to think about it anymore, but even with his wife there sleeping, so lovely and peaceful, his mind would not stop racing.

Erikson swirled his glass, hearing the ice cubes clink but not really processing it as he raised the glass to his lips and took a slow pull of bourbon. Typically, a three-finger glass of bourbon settled his nerves enough to where he could sleep. He was on his fifth glass, and all he had managed to do is make the race in his mind slightly fuzzier.

If he was being honest with himself, he wasn't sure why he was so apprehensive. The Norseman contractors were clearly effective, almost ruthlessly so. *Maybe that's why*, Erikson thought as he took another sip.

They slaughtered those thugs in the farmhouse. Another sip.

Can they be trusted? The glass tipped back again.

Part of him thought that his apprehension stemmed from his desire to control the situation. He had been in law enforcement for his entire adult life and had been running the sheriff's department for nearly six years at this point. He was used to seeing shades of gray, but he knew that there was a right way and a wrong way to go about this. In his mind, he still didn't see the involvement of Norseman Consulting as the "right way."

But why not? Erikson considered his nearly empty glass for a few seconds, screwing up his eyes to focus on the two ice cubes. The bourbon was hitting him now, harder than he had expected.

Truthfully, Erikson knew that he needed help. He was not afraid to admit that to himself or to Ellen, but he was worried that if the Norseman Consulting teams got out of hand, he would be left holding the bag. Getting run out of town. Publicly embarrassed.

Erikson shuddered at the thought. He knew that he could handle the public shame, but it would kill Ellie. She loved their community and couldn't fathom them turning on her. Ellen had been a community college teacher and a piano instructor since they had moved to town, and she was heavily involved in many of the youth programs that ran during the summer months. Erikson and Ellen had not had kids of their own, despite trying many times over. It had broken their hearts, but they had agreed to not stop trying. In the meantime, Ellen had adopted the community's children as her own, and Erikson could see the love she had for them in her eyes.

A final, long pull from the tumbler in his hand and the two cubes of ice hit the side of the glass with a soft clink. Erikson pulled the cup back and set it down on the coffee table. Settling his gaze on the folder again, the sheriff eased the top couple pieces of paper out.

A photograph of a small, dingy trailer home was on top. The next page had an overhead view, and directly under that overhead shot was a report on somebody's observations about the house. RIF was allegedly using the house as a sort of base of operations and storage point for heroin. Erikson had already read the report; at this point, he was just holding the paper and staring blankly at the page.

The report was, in and of itself, impressive, but what let Erikson know that Norseman Consulting had some serious backing in their operation was the final page, which had a single sheet of paper clipped to it, bearing the seal of the Supreme Court of the United States in the upper right-hand corner.

James Gunderson had managed to pull a warrant from the Supreme Court. There were a half a dozen files like this one in the manila folder, each with a corresponding authorization, and there was a thumb drive. The thumb drive contained digital copies of the reports and dossiers on all the players that Norseman's intelligence staff had managed to identify so far.

Erikson's foggy mind became slowly aware that Ellie was stirring in his lap.

"You awake, sweetheart?" he whispered.

"Mmmhmmm" Ellie purred without opening her eyes. "Can we go to bed yet?"

Gerry could not help smiling slightly. Whatever he was going through, she always managed to soften his mood. "Sure, dear."

He put the papers back in their folder, pressing the tape seal down. He sat there for a second or two just enjoying playing with Ellie's hair. Moving slowly, he lifted Ellie's head off his lap and slipped off the couch. Crouching down, he slipped his arms underneath her petite frame, and picked up his wife and carried her to their room.

When he'd tucked Ellie into bed, the sheriff undressed clumsily. After five glasses of bourbon, it was something of a miracle he had managed to carry Ellie back to the room. He was going to feel that in the morning. Grunting with exertion as he at last succeeded in removing a particularly stubborn sock, Gerry sat down on his side of the bed, lay down, kissed Ellie on the forehead, and yawned.

No matter what happens, Erikson thought as his eyes closed, *at least I have her.*

CHAPTER SEVENTEEN

The light was just beginning to creep into the sky, casting pink and orange hues over the horizon as Robert leaned against the side of the van, pulling on a cigarette. He was freezing his ass off despite how much he had bundled up, and Sam wouldn't allow him to smoke in the van. Sam would not let him even start the van.

Mostly, he was just pissed he was sitting with the sniper team, watching the objective from a distance as opposed to getting geared up and getting in on the action. The 9mm bullet that had punched through his trapezius had not caused any permanent damage, but Dufraine had instructed Alex to swap Robert for Alejandro for this mission, just in case.

Exhaling a cloud of gray smoke, Robert was trying to exude an air of nonchalance, but failing miserably. Too fucking cold. He was born and raised in Arizona running around the desert chasing snakes with BB guns as a kid, or tearing around on dirt bikes, and the only time he ever wanted to see the snow was when he was in the mountains skiing.

I would never have taken this fucking job if I knew what winter was like here. Robert sucked the last of his cigarette down in one long pull and flicked the butt out into the street. He strode back to the driver's side of the van as he exhaled the last of his smoke. Yanking the door open, he hopped in and slammed the door behind him.

The van's other two occupants did not acknowledge Robert's reentry at first. One of Yale's surveillance team, a former undercover detective, covered in tattoos named Stuart, was peering through the electromagnetic haze of the dim van, silently observing the video feed on the monitors. Without turning his head, or removing his headphones, Stuart chastised Robert. "Do you really have to slam the door?"

"Fuckin' a, I do!" Robert snapped. "This stakeout shit is stupid boring."

Without turning his head, Stuart spoke in his gravelly tone, frustration borne of hours of silently sitting in the cramped van and watching the target house emanated from his reply. "I am here to conduct surveillance. You are here to drive the fucking van, and shoot your fucking gun, but only if I fucking say so."

Sam had been lying on his back on the padded floor of the van, dozing. He lifted his head slightly, pulling his fleece watch cap up off of his eyes.

"Stay in the van, Rob," he muttered. He had a lot of respect for the assault teams, but they had a hard time sitting still.

"Oh, come on, dude!" Robert was exasperated, but a sharp look from Stuart tempered his anger. The old cop gave him the creeps. "Fine. I'll stay in the van."

"Jesus," Sam said as he rolled over towards his rifle, "this guy's worse than Hondo."

"Right?" Stuart croaked.

"Oh, fuck you guys," Rob said as his two companions started chuckling.

"Archer One-Two, Archer One-One," Melvin called from his position in a house facing the opposite side of the objective. "Any movement on your side?"

"Archer One-One," Sam spoke into the mouthpiece clipped to the lapel of his coat. "No movement since last night."

"Roger," Melvin's voice came over the radio in response. "Kickoff is in twenty mikes."

The atmosphere in the van instantly flooded with tension, like the anxious anticipation that athletes felt before the beginning of a race or game.

"Twenty mikes, copy." Sam set to performing last-minute checks on his rifle, while Robert reached behind the passenger seat and retrieved his B&T carbine.

"About goddamn time," the former Army Ranger grumbled as he ran over his equipment for what felt like the hundredth time, checking the chest rig, ammunition, and helmet that were hanging from straps sewn into the back of the passenger seat of the van.

Stuart said nothing, but quickly press-checked his seemingly ancient Beretta 92 to ensure once and for all that, yes, he had chambered a round before departing the Norseman Consulting compound over twenty-four hours prior. Satisfied, Stuart slid his old pistol back into the leather holster on his hip and refocused his attention on the surveillance monitors.

A scant three hundred meters away, Melvin was sitting in his roost, overlooking the objective. Situated in a rundown neighborhood on the outskirts of the industrial area, the aim is a dilapidated, one-story house in the middle of the street. The intelligence team in the Brain had pinpointed it as a sort of bunkhouse where RIF was lodging some of their foreign guests.

Melvin had branched off from his sniper team and set up a surveillance post in an abandoned two-story house facing the back of the bunkhouse. He had initially hoped that the house still had heat, but it'd been left so long that there wasn't electricity running in the house anymore.

Adjusting his collapsible stool, Melvin situated himself behind his rifle, which was located on a tripod in front of the window. Melvin and Sam had both swapped their heavier Desert Tech SRS bolt-action bullpup rifles for lighter, semi-automatics. Where Sam had chosen an Mk14 EBR style, built off a shortened M1A rifle, Melvin had been so impressed with his Desert Tech SRS sniping rifle, that he'd elected to go with Desert Tech's semi-automatic bullpup in 7.62 NATO, the MDR.

The bullpup allowed him a full powered rifle in a much shorter package and was more than accurate enough at the short ranges they were anticipating. Screwed onto the end of the barrel was a thick black suppressor and mounted to the top of the rifle was a variable power Nightforce scope.

In all actuality, Melvin did not anticipate having to make any shots this time around. Instead, he and his team, bolstered by two intel guys from Yale's shop and an additional security guard he had yanked out of Norseman's site security teams, were just supposed to surveil the objective and cover the assault team when the time came.

"You gentlemen ready?" Melvin said softly. Seated just behind him was a guy who simply went by "Chip," who, like Stuart, was former law enforcement, although Chip had been an FBI special agent just two months prior. He was stoic and simply nodded, never taking his eyes off of the electronic surveillance on the monitors that he had been poring over for the better part of the day.

The other kid in the room made Melvin chuckle a bit. At twenty-four, Port was younger than Melvin by eight years. When the radio call from Norseman headquarters had come out, the kid had almost leaped to his feet and started preparing for a quick extraction. Now, as a bit of time passed, Melvin could tell he was trying to play it cool, but his excitement was almost tangible.

"You good, Port?" Melvin grinned.

"Yeah, man, let's get this thing going." Charles "Port" Davenport shot him a hurried thumbs up. Port had been an Air Force Security Forces Airman in the 820th Security Forces Group before leaving the military in the hopes of finding better employment in the private sector. He had stumbled across Norseman Consulting late one night while scrolling through job opportunities in his dorm room at Moody Air Force Base and had applied on a whim.

After separating from the Air Force, he had pretty much breezed through the Norseman Selection process, and when he finally was put on their full payroll, he was disappointed to be assigned to the company's static security teams. The pay was good, though, and despite the bitter cold of the winter, he had really enjoyed the autumn season in Minnesota and was looking forward to the summer.

At the moment, however, Port was anxious. The two men he was ostensibly protecting were cool as ice, and he was trying hard not to fail on his first operation outside the confines of Norseman Consulting's headquarters. He had been focusing on his part of the mission, which was simple: as Chip had put it, "Go where we say, cover our asses, and when it's time, get us the fuck out of there." Chip had then tossed him the keys to an aging suburban, and they'd left the compound to settle in the perch.

"Archer One-One, Axe One-One," the Bluetooth headsets that each man wore fizzled to life. "Ten mikes, how copy?"

"Archer One-One copies," Melvin responded calmly, settling behind his optic. "Be advised, no new movement since last night. As of the last count, there were seven PAX inside the objective building."

"Roger. Out." The headsets fell silent again.

"These dudes don't have any idea," Chip chuckled. It occurred to Port that the former G-man truly enjoyed this type of work. It didn't really surprise him in retrospect, he just had not been around a whole lot of people who enjoyed their jobs.

Port snort-laughed his agreement and checked to make sure that he had chambered a round into his APC300 carbine.

The two Axe teams were driving to the objective in four vehicles, three of the assaulters per car, each with a driver pulled from the site security teams as Port had been. The assaulters had eschewed their typical winter camouflage for bland, forest green jumpsuits. They wore their plate carriers over the top of these uniforms, and while there were no apparent references to the team being sheriff's deputies, their uniforms had been specifically chosen to give the impression that they were.

Alex was sitting in the passenger seat of a Toyota Camry, directing his driver around to their designated launch position in front of the house. In the back sea were Alejandro and Sean. Following Alex was a car carrying Angelo, Ryan, and Riley.

Sam was to cover the approach of Axe One from the front of the house while Melvin covered Axe Two's approach from the back. The house was much too small to have twelve assaulters inside at once, so Axe Two would establish a cordon and act as a reaction force in case the assault didn't go as planned.

The sun still had not risen over the horizon when the four Norseman vehicles parked in their preplanned spots. "Odin, Axe One-One," Alex's radio call was broadcast in each assaulter's headset, as well as the Archer team members'. "On-site, awaiting final authorization."

"Axe One-One, Odin," Dufraine's voice came over the radio network. "Authorization granted."

"All teams this net," Alex's voice was raised. "GO GO GO!"

With that final radio call, the twelve men opened their doors and strode out into the frigid morning.

CHAPTER EIGHTEEN

On the other side of town, the Sword team was taking a slightly different approach. Their objective was a two-story house in a small neighborhood well outside the city limits. The rural location of this objective had changed the surveillance plan a bit, and because there were no abandoned houses to hole up in, Norseman Consulting's intelligence division had relied much more heavily on electronic and overhead surveillance in the form of drones.

That meant there were no eyes on the ground for almost a full day before the raid was to begin. Archer Two had been recruited to ferry two more of Yale's intelligence "assets" as he called them. Archer Two's team leader, Evan, had been pissed at first. He thought he and his team were about to turn into glorified bus drivers. However, Evan and his teammates, Chris and Steve, were pleasantly surprised.

Because the neighborhood was basically a short strip of buildings on one side of the street with an open field on the other, static surveillance would be painfully obvious. This meant that after a couple minutes of looking at an overhead surveillance feed, Archer Two now had a clear mission.

Conducting what Steve had called "some real splinter cell type shit," Archer Two and their attached G-men had snuck up to the objective house to plant some surveillance equipment. With suppressed pistols tucked under their jackets, the two intelligence operatives had crept all the way to the house and stuck cameras and microphones to several windows on the ground floor.

After sneaking back to their vans, Archer Two listened to their radios while the two intel professionals watched the feeds from their monitors. They had remained in the vans for the night and following day, moving the vans around and driving through the countryside while the cameras and mikes recorded the goings on within the house.

An additional challenge with this objective was that the house was on a dead-end street, midway down the block. Behind the house was the frozen expanse of Lake Carlos. While someone could have driven a truck out on the thick ice, there was nowhere to hide. So as night fell, Archer Two-Two and Two-Three, Chris and Steve, had been deposited at the far end of the street and made to sneak into position.

Archer Two-One remained in the warm van and drove the intel weenies around until he got the radio call that Sword was ten minutes away. Evan smiled to himself. Rank still had its privileges.

"Archer Two-One, Sword One-One," Randall called over the radio as his van bumped and slid over a patch of ice. "Ten mikes."

"Copy, ten mikes." Evan's response sounded in Randall's earpiece. Looking around the van, Randall thought his team looked sufficiently unprofessional.

Despite being a rural neighborhood, the houses surrounding the objective were all relatively close to the target house. Yale's intelligence folks had been able to ascertain through numerous social media postings, complaints to local police, and at least one anonymous letter to the local newspaper, that the neighbors were not happy with the activities at the objective house. The house was a stopover point for gang bangers and drugs, mostly heroin, between Minneapolis and Fargo. RIF ran the drugs, which had probably been provided by their Iranian friends.

Where the Axe assault team had chosen to more or less pose as law enforcement to the casual observer, Sword team had decided to lead any onlookers to believe that a rival gang had hit the drug house. Sword Two was to quietly position themselves on the flanks of the house before the arrival of Sword One, keeping well out of the way of Sword One's impending fire. Sword One took two separate minivans with sliding rear doors. Dressed in jeans, red plaid, and red bandanas to maintain the optics of the rival gang theory. To further this illusion, the men had raided the Norseman Consulting weapons locker and selected a myriad of captured submachine guns, shotguns, and assault rifles.

"Archer One-One, Sword Two-One," Rafael's accented voice came through the radio. "Preparing to disembark."

"Roger Sword Two-One," Evan responded. "Covering your approach."

Chris and Steve clicked their acknowledgment through their radios as two sedans rolled quietly to a stop toward the end of the street away from the surveillance van. The six-man Sword Two team strode quickly out into the cold, their breath sending clouds of wispy fog into the air. Rushing past the van, the men made their way down the street to the target house.

Evan started getting his equipment ready. Like Robert in the surveillance van attached to the Archer One team, Evan was acting as the driver. He had decided to focus more on the managerial aspect of leading his team and was armed with just his Wilson Combat 9mm pistol and his radios. Evan admired and respected Melvin, but he thought he got too involved in the trigger-pulling part of the operations. Evan was much more concerned with making sure that his raid was in sync with Melvin and Axe team.

"Whoa," the older intel professional in the back of the van suddenly started. "We have movement."

"Sword Two-One, Hold!" Evan barked into the radio. "We have movement in the target house."

Turning to the back of the van, Evan hissed, "Talk to me Cheat, what do you see?"

The older G-man, Cheat, nodded his head at the screen as he spoke. "One of these guys just walked down the stairs. It looks like he's starting breakfast."

"Archer Two-One," Chris's voice crackled through the radio. "I can see one tango messing around in the kitchen on the first floor."

"Roger that, Two-Two," Evan's face was impassive, but under his jacket, he was starting to sweat. They hadn't anticipated that anyone in the drug den would be awake before the sun was up. "Continue to monitor and cover Sword's advance."

"Sword Two, continue to advance." Evan put his radio down and rubbed his eyes with his palms as Sword Two's team leader, Rafael, clicked his radio twice to indicate he had heard the order and was moving his team into position. Evan turned to speak to the two intelligence operatives in the back.

Neither of them had given Evan their full names. All he knew about them was that both men had, at one time, worked for the federal government and that the clean-cut black man intently monitoring the video feeds went by "Cheat," and the scraggly white guy went by "Burt." Evan had also been surprised to learn that despite the long, gray hair growing from Burt's head, he was only forty, and Cheat was a full decade older.

"Where the hell did this guy come from?" On the screen, Evan could see the tango, a shirtless man covered in tattoos, futzing around in the kitchen, bobbing his head to the music that was softly playing through the audio feed.

"Upstairs," Burt grunted, making a vague shrugging motion.

"We don't have cameras upstairs." Cheat nodded. "He must be the group chef or something. He's making a shitload of eggs."

"Hasn't cracked a single yolk yet either," Burt said levelly.

Evan glared at them. He didn't see how this was the time for jokes. "How does that matter right now?" he strained.

"It matters, jefe," Burt snapped, briefly adopting a poor imitation of a Mexican accent, "because he is focused on his craft."

"Makes it less likely he'll see Sword Two," Cheat nodded.

"Fine." Evan twisted back to face out of the windshield. "Let's hope you're right," he added as he heard the two operatives chuckling lightly from the back of the van.

"Archer Two-One, Sword One-One." The radio on the dash crackled to life with Randall's voice. "Are we clear to approach?"

Evan snatched up the radio headset. "Sword One-One, you are clear to approach." After a moment, he continued, "Be advised, there is one tango in the kitchen who is up earlier than expected."

"Roger, Archer Two-One," Randall responded. "We are two mikes out, any changes?"

"Negative, Sword One-One," Evan said. "Six tangos on the target building."

Two clicks sounded through the radio.

Evan picked up the radio. "Ninety seconds, gentlemen."

Pairs of clicks sounded through the radio receiver as the individual fire teams sounded out their acknowledgment.

To every operative, whether in the warmth of the van or out in the cold Minnesota morning, the last ninety seconds felt like they took forever to tick down. Then, with thirty seconds left in the countdown, a rusty white panel van turned onto the road and into view of the side mirror of the surveillance van. As Evan reached for the radio, the receiver clicked to life.

"All parties this net, be advised." This time Dufraine's voice barked from the Norseman command center across the radio. "Unknown vehicle just turned down the road to Sword's objective."

"Oh, fuck!" Evan snarled as he toggled the radio. "Roger, Archer Two-One has eyes on."

The van was rolling slowly down the dead-end as Randall stared into the rearview mirror.

Within seconds, Sword One's panel van pulled into view at the end of the street behind the unknown van. "Sword One has eyes on the van." Randall's voice was even on the radio. "Archer Two-One, please advise."

"Sword One, hold at the end of the street." Evan was really starting to sweat now; the unknown white van had slowed to an idling crawl once Sword One's gray Dodge Sprinter turned onto the street. As the white van crept slowly closer, Evan knew they'd been blown. Suddenly, there was a faint screeching noise as the rusty white van came to a complete stop less than twenty-five yards from Evan's surveillance van.

Thinking quickly, Evan shouted into his headset. "Switch to contingency! Sword Two, you have the assault!"

Before Evan heard the clicks acknowledging the change in plans, he listened to the muted crack of Chris's rifle, followed by the spinning tires, roaring engine, and spraying gravel as the driver of the white van stomped on the gas pedal.

CHAPTER NINETEEN

Erikson was surrounded by an aura of anticipation. In the weeks that had transpired since the initial terror attack on Broadway and the sheriff's office, his deputies had grown increasingly anxious for payback, and they were now on the verge of getting their first taste.

The Douglas County SWAT team, along with a dozen sheriff's deputies quietly surrounded a house being used as a stopover point for smuggling in drugs and people. One of the Sheriff's deputies presented the evidence connected this house being there terrorists a stopover point for the terrorists who had carried out the massacre on Broadway.

With minimal prodding and partial access to the dossiers that Norseman Consulting had given the sheriff, the detective had agreed to take credit for the find. Now, the balding man was standing next to the sheriff, wearing a soft ballistic vest concealed under the heavy wool coat he was wearing.

Both men were ostensibly poring over a map, but they conversed in low tones as the DCSO SWAT team commander conducted final planning with his fireteam leaders. "Gerry, you gotta tell me what's going on."

Roland Freeman had known Gerry Erikson since moving from the Minneapolis Police Department seven years prior in the interest of maintaining his status as a detective while having a significantly slower pace of work as he recovered from blowing out both knees during a foot chase. After arriving at the Douglas County Sheriff's Office, he had risen steadily, and rapidly became one of Erikson's most trusted friends and team members.

The sheriff sighed. His desire to keep the extent of Norseman Consulting's involvement more or less a secret was waning, especially now that it conflicted with how much he hated misleading his friend and top detective. "After we get through this morning, I will explain my sources."

Detective Freeman merely nodded as the approaching footsteps of the SWAT commander encroached on their conversation.

"Everything is ready, sir." The SWAT commander swaggered over. A career law enforcement officer, Jon Leroy was nearly the same age as Sheriff Erikson, but where constant desk work and politicking had made Sheriff Erikson somewhat soft around the middle, Deputy

Leroy was fit, with biceps that bulged underneath his forest green uniform shirt.

"Alright, Leroy," Erikson responded as Detective Freeman shut the tailgate to the sheriff's patrol SUV. "Bring the guys around real quick before we kick this off."

The sheriff and his SWAT team had set up in the parking lot of a church just down the street from the target. Erikson had pre-positioned his patrol deputies as an outer cordon at each of the four roads that led out of the target area. The deputies were to take their position as soon as the order came across the radio. The SWAT marksman teams had been in place on rooftops across the street from the building and had reported that they had not yet seen any movement from the house again.

The SWAT deputies, Leroy, and Detective Freeman had recently completed their advanced training with Norseman Consulting, and all of them had gone out and purchased new duty rifles based on the experience.

"Gentlemen, lady," Erikson said, nodding in the direction of Deputy Carlson, who was in charge of SWAT Two. "The plan is simple: breach, clear, and capture any and all personnel inside the house."

None of the SWAT deputies in front of him reacted, so Erikson continued.

"As Detective Freeman said earlier, this house was likely one of the stopover points for the terrorists who carried out the attack on Broadway. I know that tensions are running high, and we're all itching for some payback, but we need to apprehend as many personnel in the house as possible. Without the intel that they can provide, it will be slow going trying to intercept the rest of the people responsible for the attack."

Scanning his audience for any questions, and stealing a glance towards Freeman, Erikson continued.

"I ask you to keep your emotions in check and carry out this out his raid as professionally as I know you all are capable of." The sheriff grinned. "Now let's get it done."

The SWAT deputies nodded silently and rallied to their fireteam leaders. Their plan was simple. There was a series of unmarked Ford Escapes in the church parking lot, with patrol cars and SUVs providing the blocking force. The SWAT team was going to move the target house on foot, knock once, and bust open the door.

The target building was a single-story, prefabricated home with two entrances. The backyard contained a small wooden shed about ten yards from the back door. The back door opened into the kitchen, bathroom, and rear bedroom, and the front door opened into the living room and front two bedrooms and an additional bathroom. SWAT One was to knock on the front door of the house, and SWAT Two on the back door. Once inside, the eight SWAT deputies were to use tasers to subdue the suspects residing in the house.

Erikson was understandably concerned that his SWAT team might adopt a shoot first, ask questions later mentality. They'd been itching for revenge, and they were about to kick off their first counterattack. The sheriff didn't have the heart to tell them that the farmhouse massacre had actually been the first counterattack. Most of the Alexandria community, his deputies and SWAT team included, assumed that it had been the terrorist organization cleaning house. This line of thinking had been supported in public opinion by the fact that nobody had stepped forward to claim credit for the carnage.

The SWAT deputies jogged over to each of their first checkpoints, and Erikson and Freeman got into the sheriff's patrol SUV to manage the operation from the radio.

"SWAT One, in position." The radio on the dashboard barked to life.

"Roger, SWAT One," Erikson responded.

"SWAT Two, in position." Deputy Carlson's voice hissed through the radio.

"Roger, SWAT Two," Erikson said. "SWAT, proceed. Blocking force, wait thirty seconds and then take positions." Looking over at Freeman, Erikson issued another order. "Roland, let the EMTs know that we'll be ready for their ambulances in ninety seconds."

Saying nothing, Freeman pulled out his department issued phone and punched in the number for the ambulance teams standing by.

They sat in silence for the next thirty seconds, until the radio announced that all the blocking cars were in position.

"SWAT One, at final approach."

"SWAT Two, at final approach."

"Overlook One, no movement."

"Overlook Two, no movement."

The SWAT team was holding just out of view of the house, waiting for the sheriff's command to proceed. Erikson rolled down his window and motioned at Deputy Leroy, who was monitoring the radio in his own black Ford Explorer next to the sheriff's white patrol Explorer.

"Leroy," Erikson said as the window rolled down on Leroy's SUV, "you ready?"

"Goddamned right I'm ready," Leroy said, his eyes fixed in the direction of his eight SWAT deputies. Erikson lifted the radio handset to his mouth.

"All teams, GO, GO, GO!"

SWAT One and SWAT Two closed the distance to their entry points at a fast, but controlled jog. As SWAT One crossed the threshold onto the target house's lawn, a light in one of the rear bedrooms flicked on behind the curtain. SWAT Two was near to the back door of the house.

"Heads up, guys," Carlson spoke calmly to her team as they moved to the door. "We have movement in bedroom three."

"This is Overlook Two, movement in bedroom three." The tactical radio in each SWAT deputies' ear fizzled.

"Roger that, Overlook Two, continue to advise." Erikson's voice responded.

The two SWAT teams reached their entry points at nearly identical times.

"SWAT One, set."

"SWAT Two, set," Carlson responded, as she tapped the deputy behind her to signal him to prepare the sledgehammer.

As the deputy started to move forward, the full report of a shotgun blast sounded from the other side of the wall from SWAT Two.

"BREACH!" Carlson shouted, and her breacher swung the sledgehammer to smash the door open.

Simultaneously, SWAT One and SWAT Two burst into the house. SWAT One swept the living room and hooked left into the front bedrooms. SWAT Two swept the kitchen and hooked to the opposite side of the house.

Carlson's team worked fluidly, scanning for additional threats as they cleared the small kitchen, and flowed into the hallway to the rear bedroom.

Shouts of "SHERIFF'S DEPARTMENT!" sounded throughout the house, and Carlson's point man was screaming it down the hallway as they moved forward.

"Door in front," the point man announced to the team.

"Door on the right," the second deputy in the stack announced.

"Set," Carlson tapped the second deputy's shoulder, "GO!"

With the first man covering the door in front of them, and the fourth man acting as the rear guard, the second deputy kicked the door open, revealing a nearly decapitated corpse that appeared to have been unseated from the toilet and flung into the bathtub.

"Clear," the second deputy announced meekly, the sight of the corpse rattled him.

Sounds of SWAT One subduing suspects could be heard in the other two bedrooms. Carlson heard the buzzing of a Taser over the sound of blood pumping in her own ears.

"Alright, next room," she said.

"Set," the point man said, having barely shifted forward to make room for Carlson and the number two man to sweep the bathroom.

Before Carlson could have her point man breach the room, another shotgun blast sounded.

"BREACH!" she yelled, pushing her number two man toward the point man to get out of the hallway. Under her breath, she was uttering a non-stop stream of "goddammitgoddammitgoddammit."

"Shots fired in bedroom three," Carlson's rear guard broadcast over the radio.

The point man put his full body weight behind his shoulder and slammed into the door, bursting into the bedroom. Sweeping into the room, Carlson followed the point man.

"Clear!" the point man shouted, as the rear guard ripped open the closet near the door.

"Clear," the rearguard affirmed after ensuring the closet was devoid of all suspects.

"Clear!" the number two man said, unable to draw his eyes away from the bed.

"SWAT Two is clear," Carlson spoke into her throat-mounted radio. "Two suspects dead."

"SWAT One is clear, three suspects in custody."

"Copy all, make your way out of the house," Erikson's voice sounded in the headsets.

"Yo, dude," the rearguard said to the rest of his team as he looked at the grisly scene laid out on the bed, "what the fuck?"

Lying on the bed with his feet over the edge was a naked dead man with a sawed-off shotgun laid across his stomach. The rear wall of the bedroom had been washed in blood after the man had put the sawed-off ten-gauge in his mouth and pulled the trigger rather than surrender to the SWAT team.

Carlson shrugged. "Don't know, and don't care."

"That's cold, bro."

"SWAT Two," Erikson again, "can you please check the shed on your way out?"

"Roger that," Carlson replied.

"Come on guys, let's check that shed."

Outside of the house, Erikson was directing his detectives, led by Freeman, to comb the house for any evidence of drug or people trafficking. He was elated that they were able to conduct the raid without any shots fired by DCSO SWAT, even though it was looking like one of the suspects blew away his comrade before committing suicide. Erikson was standing out on the sidewalk directing the investigative operations through his SUV mounted radio when Deputy Leroy came running over.

"Sheriff," Leroy called, "you gotta call dispatch right now!"

Erikson looked at his watch, 6:32, and immediately knew that something must have gone wrong, with one of the other simultaneous operations Norseman Consulting were executing in the county.

CHAPTER TWENTY

At almost the exact same time that Erikson's SWAT team was leaving their last checkpoint to breach their target house, Axe team was moving confidently to their positions around their objective.

This was nowhere near coincidental. Both Norseman assault teams wanted to execute their operations at the same time that DCSO SWAT started their own raid. The raids intended to sow as much confusion and discord as possible, and a vital part of that would be the nearly simultaneous raids taking place within the next ninety to one hundred twenty seconds.

"Axe One," Alex called over the radio as they crossed the street toward the front door of the house, "check."

"Axe Two, check." Ted, the fireteam leader, responded as his team approached the house from the alley on the other side.

"Archer One has visual on Axe Two," Melvin's level voice continued. "Negative visual inside the house."

"Archer Two has visual on Axe One," Sam spoke as he shifted his crosshairs onto the large window at the front of the house. "Negative visual inside the house."

Alex and his six assaulters moved quickly across the lawn, their carbine muzzles bristling in all directions as the men scanned the area for threats. Within seconds they were stacked up outside the door, ready to breach, enter, and clear the house.

"Axe One is set." Alex's voice was calm.

"Roger, Axe One," Melvin responded. "Negative movement at this time. All personnel this net, Axe One has the stick."

"Roger Axe One is taking the stick." With that radio call, Melvin relinquished command of the assault to the team actually entering the house.

"Axe One breaching," Alex called out over the radio, prompting his breacher, Shawn, to move to the door with his short ax.

"Axe Two moving to cordon."

"Breach!"

The short, intense series of radio calls culminated in Shawn chopping through the door jamb and slamming the door open. As the door swung open, the point man, Angelo, and the number two man in the stack, Alejandro, each tossed a flashbang into the room. One flashbang went to the left, the other to the right.

As soon as the flashbangs detonated in twin ear-splitting BANGs and blinding flashes of light, Axe One rushed into the room, alternating to the left and right. As Alex swung to the left behind Angelo, he could hear the muted cracks as Alejandro opened fire on a man who was groggily stumbling around in the aftermath of the flashbangs and wielding an old shotgun.

Angelo moved quickly forward as the hallway door burst open and a bearded man came stumbling from the bedroom with his pants halfway on and a pistol in his right hand.

Angelo pressed the trigger three times and sent a trio of subsonic hollow point bullets into the man's face and forehead, dropping him onto the coarse carpet.

"Room on the right!" Angelo called the room that the now-deceased man had stumbled out of.

A sudden blast from inside the room sounded as another occupant fired a shotgun through the plaster wall in the general direction of the Axe assault team.

The flurry of buckshot missed the assault team by a large margin and was answered with a sharp crack and heavy thud as Melvin added his own precision rifle fire into the mix.

"Tango down in the bedroom," Melvin announced. "Room is clear."

Without responding, Angelo moved forward down the hallway. Alex could hear Alejandro's element calling the garage clear as they prepared to rejoin Alex's element in the center of the house.

"Room on the left," Angelo called.

"Covering," Alex said. He moved slightly to the side to cover the hallway as Angelo kicked the door in.

As soon as Angelo's foot slammed the door open, a burst of hastily aimed pistol rounds impacted the door next to him. Angelo moved into the room and the final man in the element, Ryan, followed him in. Both men opened up with their B&T carbines, placing quick, precise shots into their targets, leaving both dead, one on the floor and the other on a cot at the end of the room.

"Clear."

"Clear."

"Ready to move," Alex called into the room.

"Friendlies are coming out!" Angelo called.

Ryan and Angelo exited the room and rejoined the stack behind Alex as Alejandro led his element to hold the main section of the house.

"Room on the left," Alex said, preparing the team to assault the third and final bedroom.

The team pushed forward, intending to hit the door and enter the room in one fluid motion.

Alex made the last few steps into the door as quickly as he could, slamming his boot into the door and shattering the doorjamb, then throwing his body inside. Alex was slightly off balance but recovered in time to line his EOTech reflex sight onto the chest of a man holding a machine pistol sideways and raking the rounds closer to Alex's shoulder.

Alex jerked his trigger as quickly as he could, neglecting to count the rounds, and tracking the bullets across the man's bare chest. With a final spasmodic jerking, the man fell to the ground, sending a few rounds into the floor in front of him.

Ryan entered the room just behind Alex but was not quite fast enough to catch the final target as the man blasted away the window with his shotgun, and then fired a shell toward the assaulters as he dove through the window.

"We got a squirter," Ryan shouted. He rushed to the window, hoping to get a shot at the man as he ran across the lawn.
Before Ryan even had a chance to level his rifle, and before the man made it to the sidewalk, a muffled crack sounded, and the man fell face-first into the frozen ground.

"Got 'em," Sam sounded over the radio.

"Alright, we are all clear," Alex said. "Let's get to cleaning up."

At the moment the assault team had breached the door, Port and Chip had moved to break down their hide site. They packed the sensitive electronic equipment into foam-lined cases and were and ready to move out within two minutes. Port could hear the assault transpiring over his radio headset, and it thrilled him.

As an airman, Port had trained for various operations, and during patrols in Afghanistan, he had been in a handful of firefights, but nothing so quick and brutal as what had gone down in that house. Most of the time, the enemy in Afghanistan had engaged from a distance with sporadic fire. His patrol would return fire, and sometimes they got to call in air and artillery strikes on the suspected enemy positions. They rarely saw their enemy up close. This was a whole different ball game.

Port's excitement carried him, adrenaline pumping, as he packed the Suburban with Chip, leaving enough room in the cargo area for anything Axe team would take out of the objective.

"Port!" Melvin called out as he exited the hide site building, gear in tow. "Drive around and meet Axe at the objective, they need some help cleaning up."

Chip was already waiting in the passenger seat when Port hopped into the Suburban and turned the ignition. Melvin slid his gear into the backseat and slammed the door closed behind him.

"Archer One-One, Axe One-One," Alex called over the radio as Port guided the SUV toward the objective building. "Pull up the alley to load the bodies. We'll put the guy on the front lawn in one of our cars."

"Roger that, Axe One-One," Melvin responded. Port didn't have to be told what to do, he made a quick left turn and drove down the snow-filled alley, past the cordon Axe Two was still holding. As Port pulled up next to the two sedans that Axe Two had driven to the objective, the drivers and Axe One were loading plastic bags with cell phones, laptops, and tablets into one of the trunks.

"How much space do you have?" Alex inquired as soon as Port opened the door.

"Uh, like half the cargo bay," Port replied.
"Alright, help my guys load as many of the bodies as we can." Alex threw his thumb over his shoulder toward the house. "We gotta boogie real quick."

Without another word, Port, Melvin, and Chip got out of the Suburban and jogged over to the house, where they could see the Axe One team had positioned six black plastic body bags near the back door.

The Norseman contractors were able to get three of the bodies in the cargo bay of the Suburban. Two of the remaining three were stuffed into the trunk of Axe Two's Ford Taurus, and the final body was crammed in next to the recovered tech items in the trunk of the last sedan.

"Boss," Angelo shouted from inside the house, "we are clean and clear in here."

"Alright everyone, mount up and let's go," Alex called out over the radio. Melvin started to mount up into the truck when Dufraine's voice came over the tactical radio network.

"Archer One, Axe One." The voice on the other end of the radio felt rushed. Instantly, all the contractors picked up their pace and got into their vehicles to leave.

"Be advised, Archer Two and Sword team need immediate assistance at their location."

CHAPTER TWENTY-ONE

With an ear-splitting CRUNCH, the surveillance van occupied by Evan, Cheat, and Burt was thrown forward several feet as the rusty white van slammed into the rear of their own van. Sitting in the driver's seat, Evan had frantically mashed the accelerator but had only managed to spin the tires on the frozen gravel road before the other van hit.

The assaulters in Sword One exited their own minivans as soon as Evan had broadcast his contingency radio call. They moved with precision and lethal grace that betrayed their professional status. They still had quite a bit of ground to cover before reaching the distressed surveillance van.

Sword One was unable to get viable targets in their sights before several rapid gunshots sounded, causing a flurry of radio traffic over the Norseman Consulting network.

"Shots fired! Cheat's been hit!" Evan's voice sounded frantically over the radio.

Leading Sword One, Randall could feel the combined anxiety of his fireteam as he worked to control their advance toward the van. The team's pace quickened, but they stayed in formation as they closed the distance.

The team had closed to less than fifteen meters when the side and rear doors of the white panel van sprang open. The contractors of Sword One reacted fluidly and in total sync with each other, as a few rapid gunshots were thrown in their vague direction from the van.

One man tried to make a run from the van to the house, firing a pistol as he ran. On the far-right side of the Sword One formation, John raised his MAC-10 submachine gun and let loose a long burst of automatic fire. The volley of .45 ACP slugs slammed into the gangster's right hip, turning him slightly as the remainder of the blast stitched up through his gut and chest and dropped him on the ground in a spasm.

To John's left, Vince had proceeded to empty the magazine of his semi-auto Romanian AKM clone into the passenger side of the panel van. His directed his first few rounds at the heads and shoulders of the two gangsters in the front, which yielded the gory results he had desired but kept firing, remembering the unprofessional illusion they were trying to create.

"Van's clear!" Randall shouted as Vince paused to reload a fresh magazine into his now empty AKM. Randall and Finn were checking the dead gangster in the back of the van, while the team's designated medic, Cooper, went running to the surveillance van.

"Odin, Sword One-One," Randall radioed Dufraine back at the Norseman Consulting headquarters.

"Go ahead, Sword One-One."

"All PAX in van terminated," Randall spoke briskly into the microphone integrated into his electronic ear protection as his team surrounded the surveillance van and wrenched the doors open. "Standby for nine-line casualty report."

"Copy Two-One, standing by."

Cooper had run to the van and dragged Cheat out to lay him on the ground and appraise his wounds. Evan and Burt had started patching Cheat up with the first aid trauma kit that had been prepositioned in the van.

Cheat had been hit twice. One round had punched through the back door and caught him in the gut, about an inch to the right of his belly button and had not exited. The second round had caught him just above the left elbow, severing his brachial artery. Evan and Burt had applied a tourniquet to his upper arm, stemming the blood flow, and had done their best to patch the wound in his belly by securing a bandage impregnated with coagulant onto the entry wound.

Even so, Cooper set to work on Cheat, radioing his condition into Norseman Consulting headquarters. Cooper had been an Air Force Pararescue Jumper, or "PJ," before joining the company, and this is where his particular skill set really shone.

Once the radio call came through that Norseman had scrambled their helicopters to come to pick up Cheat, Evan and Randall began trying to re-establish control of the operation.

"Sword Two-One, status?" Evan called over the radio.

"Fuckin' peachy, man," Rafael's voice came over the radio. "These assholes set the house on fire."

After Evan had made the call, Rafael had kicked his team into the contingency mode that they had planned out in advance. When Chris had taken his shot through the kitchen window, killing the man making eggs, Rafael and his team had taken off at a dead sprint to breach the ground level door of the target house.

Unfortunately, there was only one door for them to infiltrate through, so the six men had to flow through quickly to avoid getting stuck. Alfred was first to the door and used the short-barreled shotgun he usually had strapped to his back to blow the locks out of the door.

If the gunfire sounding from the skirmish at the vans wasn't enough to wake up the residents of the neighborhood and the target house, the shotgun blast at the front door definitely was. Rafael led his team into the house. As Sword Two flowed in, their plan started to click into place.

The ground floor was just an entryway, kitchen, and combined living room

Sword Two cleared the bottom floor relatively quickly as the only target on the floor had been the gang member making eggs in the kitchen. "Ready to move upstairs," Rafael directed his team, and the four contractors stepped to the stairwell.

Almost immediately, the point man, Remy, raised his B&T carbine and ripped four quick shots up the stairs. A pistol gripped Mossberg shotgun clattered down the wooden staircase, followed by a dead gangster. Sword Two sidestepped the bloody corpse and continued up the stairs.

At the top of the stairs, Sword Two was faced with a minor dilemma. Two of the three rooms were to their left, and the last room was to their right. Rafael made the decision to hit the single room to the right first. The door was open, and Rafael and Tony stepped in to clear it while Alfred and Remy stayed outside of the room to pull security.

This room was empty, although the two beds had been slept in recently. There were half-empty pizza boxes and soda bottles strewn about the floor, and a small entertainment system on a desk in the corner. Tony quickly ripped open the closet, revealing some clothes, but no targets.

Satisfied the room was clear, Rafael and Tony started to exit. As the two assaulters left the room to join their teammates, a man in a white wife-beater tank top darted across the hall from the room on the left to the place on the right. Remy lifted his carbine and snapped off a flurry of quick shots, eliciting a grunt and a small splatter of blood on the far wall, but the man made it to the next room.

Almost immediately after, the assaulters could smell smoke emanating from the room the man had darted out of.

"Sword Two-One, status?" Evan called over the radio.

"Fuckin' peachy man," Rafael responded. "These assholes set the house on fire."

"Roger that." Evan's voice was even as he struggled to maintain control of the mission.

Rafael made a quick hand signal to his team, directing them forward to the room that had not been set ablaze. As the team stacked up outside the door, they heard breaking glass.

"Squirter out the front of the house."

One of the gangsters was still in the room where the fire started and had opted to jump out of the window. Archer Two-Two called it on the radio, and Steve took a shot with his suppressed Desert Tech SRS. The gangster had barely made it ten yards before the .300 Norma Magnum round punched through his sternum and blew out his back, dumping him onto the frozen ground.

A second window shattered, this time from inside the room that Rafael and his team were waiting to breach.

As they breached, a shotgun blast tore apart the wall just above the door frame, showering Alfred with wood splinters and plaster. He made it through the door just in time to catch a man in sweatpants and t-shirt jump through the freshly shattered window. A second man was facing Alfred, racking a fresh shell into his sawn-off Remington shotgun. Albert stroked his trigger five times, sending three rounds into the man's chest, one into his left eye, and one just above his right eyebrow. The shots knocked the dead man back into the last man left in the room and showering him with blood. The force of the corpse pulled the last man out the shattered window and down to the ground level, screaming as he fell.

In the ground-level living room, Max and Henry were pulling security when the first man jumped through the second-story window. The man crumpled to the ground but immediately sprang back up. He took off running in unlaced boots and short sleeves, making for the frozen lake as fast as he could go.

"Holy shit!" Henry shouted. "Dude just landed outside!"

Max and Henry moved to the window, readying their carbines for a shot on their squirter as he made his way to the ice. As both assaulters took aim through the window, the bodies from the second floor came thudding to the ground in front of them.

"FUCK!" Henry shouted, adjusting his aim down towards the bodies. He could immediately tell that one of them was dead as the top of his head had been near torn off. The other man tangled up on the ground with the body was gasping for air and trying to reach for a little Bersa semi-automatic pistol that had landed on the ground next to him.

"STOP, DICKHEAD!" Henry roared as Max opened fire on the running man. Emitting a thick, rapid cough from the end of his short-barreled B&T, Max's rounds shattered through the window. The glass caused the first two rounds to go wild but destroyed the entire window. As the window shattered, the gangster on the ground snatched up his pistol, still gasping for air.

Henry snapped three rounds into the gangster's face, silencing him for good.

Max focused, slowing his breathing and lining up his sights on the running man. Despite the fall causing the gangster to limp, he had almost made it the fifty yards to the frozen lake. Max let a half a breath out and stroked the trigger.

The suppressed rifle barked softly, a subsonic round spitting out of the muzzle and impacting with the gangster's upper back. The man spun, fell, and then got back up again, a dark red stain on his shoulder. Max focused again and then squeezed the trigger twice as the red dot from his holographic sight lined up on the man's back again. The first round impacted low in the center of the man's back. The second round hit higher in the back and dropped him dead on the ice.

By this time, Rafael, Alfred, Remy, and Tony had left the top floor of the house and rejoined Max and Henry on the bottom floor.

"Time to go," Rafael shouted. "The fuckin' top floor is on fire."

"Sword One-One, we are exiting now and need to refill immediately."

"Roger that Sword Two-One," Randall's voice crackled over the radio. "Get back to the vans. We gotta strip out the surveillance van. Dust-off is on the way."

"Copy all," Rafael responded. Turning to Sword Two, he added, "Let's get out of here."

Sword Two exited the house at a dead sprint, meeting Archers Two-Two and Two-Three as they rallied back at the vans. Sword One, Evan, and Burt had been busy trying to free the surveillance van from the grille of the attacking panel van.

"Hey, we good?!" Randall shouted over to Evan as the van came free with a screech of metal on metal.

The surveillance van fired up, pulling away from the wreckage. Evan leaned out of the driver's side window. "Yeah man, we're good! Dust-off is here in thirty seconds."

Sure enough, the sounds of helicopter rotors were becoming louder. The Norseman-operated HH-65 "Dolphin" came screaming over the treetops.

Gunderson and Dufraine had opted to use the HH-65 Dolphin helicopters as opposed to the more military UH-1s and HH-60s that they were used to, and in many ways preferred because the Dolphin blended in much better with civilians. This particular helicopter had been painted gray with blue and yellow checkers on the tail, making it look a lot like a life-flight helicopter from the local hospital.

As the pilot squeezed the helicopter into the tight space that Cooper had designated as the landing zone, several members of Sword One lifted Cheat using a collapsible stretcher and hoisted him into the waiting arms of the medical response crew on board the helicopter. Cooper hopped into the bird after Cheat, and the aircraft took off, having been on the ground for a grand total of fifteen seconds.

"Alright everyone, we gotta clear the fuck outta here," Evan barked.

The contractors piled into their vans, taking a quick inventory of their teammates and gear. The three vans took off, exiting the one-way neighborhood and onto the county roads, where they scattered before the siren sounds of approaching fire trucks filled the morning air.

CHAPTER TWENTY-TWO

"I'll keep this short," Sheriff Erikson said as flashbulbs glinted around him, leaving bright purple spots in his vision. "The Douglas County Sheriff's Office, in conjunction with federal assistance, tracked down, and in two separate raids, eliminated part of the terrorist cell responsible for the deadly attacks on Broadway this past January."

There was a hush in the room. No sounds were uttered except the clicking of camera lenses. Erikson looked up from his speech, both hands gripping the sides of the podium with the sheriff's office seal on the front.

When it became clear that the sheriff's speech was finished with that one sentence, the room burst to life. Reporters from all over the state, and some as far away as Chicago, had driven to Alexandria to the small briefing room in the sheriff's department building, and they wanted answers.

Erikson detested this part of the job. He had only chosen to give a small number of press conferences in his short career. As evidenced by his brief speech, Erikson was not a big fan of public appearances and wanted the ordeal to be over as quickly as possible. The Norseman Consulting leadership had encouraged him to hold a press conference, though, especially because it was in direct opposition to the mayoral orders he had received.

Grimacing against the nearly deafening racket, Erikson pointed at a young male reporter. The man jumped up, and the noise ceased to accommodate the reporter's question.

"Sheriff," the young man said, looking down at the notes on his phone, "you said that you, quote, 'tracked down and eliminated part of the terrorist cell,' does this mean that there are more terrorists out there?"

Erikson briefly paused to compile his thoughts, running through the series of prepared responses that he and the Norseman leadership had put together.

"At this time," he replied, "we believe that there are a small number of terrorists still able to operate, albeit at a much-degraded level of effectiveness."

The roar resumed again, more flash bulbs burst, and the sheriff picked another reporter, a middle-aged woman. The woman did not rise from her chair, rather just kept her hand in the air as she read her notes off of her iPhone.

"Sheriff Erikson," her voice had an almost accusatory tone, "are these 'terrorists' who you and your deputies eliminated of a foreign or domestic origin?"

"The men that we have apprehended, or been otherwise able to," Erikson paused as he searched for the correct word, "…uh, conduct reconnaissance on, have been of mixed origins between a domestic communist revolutionary group and what we ascertain to be a version of narco-terrorists."

The deafening roar began anew, the journalists refusing to allow a single second to go by without a question being asked or answered. Sheriff Erikson leaned back from the podium as he raised his hand and pointed at the next reporter, a man with salt and pepper hair who was, unlike most of the others, using pen and paper to take notes.

"Sir," the man shouted, the roar trickling off as he rose to ask his question, "my question has two parts."

Erikson made a circular motion with his hand, bidding the reporter to move forward with his line of questioning.

"First," the man continued, "you say that the authorities carried out two separate raids, one on each side of the industrial housing area; however, there are additional reports of heavy gunfire, followed by a house fire, a life-flight helicopter landing, men with guns, etc., all on the northwest side of Lake Carlos, with several dead bodies left at the scene. Are you saying that the DCSO had nothing to do with that raid?"

The sheriff didn't miss a beat. He'd been waiting for this exact question. "No law enforcement agency that I know of was involved in that particular raid. We think that it was part of the foreign actors' plan to liquidate their domestic contacts."

A renewed burst of energy shot into the room, but the reporter with the notepad remained standing, waiting to ask the rest of his question. Erikson pointed at him again, allowing him to continue.

"Finally, Sheriff," the man said, his pen pressed against the notepad, "in both raids for which you are claiming responsibility, there were several body bags taken away from the scene. Are emotions running too high for this investigation to be conducted objectively? You said yourself that some of these terrorists are American citizens."

"I am immensely proud of the way the men and women of the Douglas County SWAT team handled themselves during the operation." The sheriff straightened up, standing at his full height at the podium. "In both raids, full measures were taken to use non-lethal means."

A falsehood that only Sheriff Erikson knew, but nearly all the reporters suspected. First, there had been the farmhouse massacre that had yet to be claimed, and now here were three separate raids, with a whole new pile of dead bodies. Nevertheless, the sheriff continued. "Unfortunately," he blew out a large breath of air, "in one instance, a suspect murdered another suspect and then took his own life before the deputies were able to subdue and apprehend them."

"In the second instance," Erikson's tone hardened a bit, "the suspects opened fire on the tactical team, leading to their unfortunate destruction."

Almost as soon as his last syllable was uttered, more clamoring arose from the room, and the sheriff had to wave them down for almost a full minute before returning to the microphone.

"There is no more time for questions," he stated directly. "I would, however, like to take a few moments to address the citizens of Douglas County." The room waited as Erikson checked his note card one more time and cleared his throat. "I urge all citizens, near and far, to be constantly vigilant. We believe that there are still a small number of bad actors out there and, while they have had their capabilities severely degraded by the effective response of the various law enforcement agencies, they are still dangerous. If you see suspicious activity, please call the sheriff's department tip line. Thank you."

With that, the sheriff walked off the short stage, out the door, and back up to his office, leaving four of his deputies to herd the mass of journalists out of the building and back into the cold February air.

Across town, the mayor was fuming. She knew that Erikson had mostly adhered to her gag order out of a desire to not rock the boat too much. The sheriff was an elected official, much like her, and answered to the entire county, not just the Mayoral Office of Alexandria, Minnesota. In fact, Mayor Stark had no control over Erikson at all, and that drove her insane. Several of her staffers had been given various boating and traffic citations, including a handful of DUIs that she had tried to have erased, to no avail.

Even so, this had not been a part of her plan, and she was coming face to face with the fact that her plan seemed to be unraveling faster by the day. Even that Italian Prick, Antony, had been unable to tell her what was going on.

Mayor Stark had met Antony at a fundraiser for the fire department. She was shaking hands and snapping selfies with her constituents at the Pork Chop Festival two summers ago when he first introduced himself. He wanted just a minute of her time to talk about an issue that could greatly benefit her community and her interests.

Stark had shaken him off at first, but he persisted, eventually landing an afternoon meeting with her in her home office later that summer. Antony wasted no time, promising substantial contributions to her next campaign. She already had her eye on a senatorial seat when the incumbent retired in a few years.

In addition to monetary benefits, Antony assured Stark he could help her shore up her credentials. He told her that he represented a firm that could help her appear to hit every single item on a Minnesotan's "politician checklist." She agreed to a lengthier meeting later in the week and rushed home to tell her husband about her exciting new prospects.

Now she realized she should have known better than to trust someone who would offer so much and ask for so little, but she'd been blinded by her ambition. Within a few meetings, Antony had started to make his demands known. First, they were simple, his firm wanted small contracts here and there around the city. It didn't take much for her to lean on the right person, and Antony had his contracts.

Within a few short months, his demands became much more complex, even to the point of ominous. Finally, one day it all came to a head when Antony sat down in her office and offered to tell her what his plan was, and to make his last demand.

He had promised her the senator's seat or the governor's mansion, whichever she wanted, and he was going to deliver it to her, but first, he needed one last thing.

At this point, the vast quantities of money that had been flowing into her accounts, both personal and political, had prevented her from balking at whatever this man wanted. She was going to give it to him as long as he could make her governor. "We have one more plan to put into action to make you governor," Antony had explained, "I can't give you many more details other than that."

"Just do it," she told him.

Antony had not told her that his plan included a bloodbath on Broadway, but he assured her the following evening that he was going to deliver the people "responsible" for the act. All she had to do was keep the police out of the way. For the amount of money she was being paid, she begrudgingly agreed.

The concept was simple, in her mind. A shocking terrorist attack, followed by Mayor Stark spearheading the efforts to bring the perpetrators to justice, but being hamstrung by a police force that was simply not up to the task. According to the original plan that Antony had laid out for her, Mayor Stark was supposed to publicly fire the police chief for "incompetence" this week. That was to be followed by an announcement that Antony's firm had been hired to pick up the investigative work.

Now that pain in the ass, Gerry Erikson, was getting in the way. Stark fumed at him, and at her inability to control him. She angrily shut off the television and exhaled slowly. "Goddammit, Gerry," she said to herself, rubbing her temples with the palms of her hands. "Goddammit."

Opening the desk drawer, she pulled out a small prepaid phone and turned it on and dialed a number from memory. Antony was going to have to pull a few strings.

Erikson walked into his office to find Gunderson standing near his desk, pouring a brown liquid into the second of two glass tumblers. The television in his office was turned to the news, presumably the channel his press conference had just finished airing. The muted television flickered slightly as the picture turned from a view outside his office to a news anchor sitting behind a desk.

"Well done, Sheriff." Gunderson turned, handing him a glass of Erikson's favorite bourbon.

"I see you've done your homework." Erikson was still a little unnerved about how much Gunderson had been able to find out about him, and the subtlety of this play was not lost on him.

Gunderson raised his glass. "So I have."

"What are we drinking to?" Erikson raised his glass slightly, staring impassively at Gunderson's grinning face.

"To a successful series of missions," Gunderson replied cheerily.

The two men clinked their glasses, draining them in one long pull. The tumblers returned to Erikson's desk, and Gunderson refilled both with two fingers worth of bourbon.

"For now, we are back in intel gathering mode. Within the next couple hours, we should have some idea as to how the enemy is reacting to the raids," Gunderson said, swishing his glass around and regarding the booze closely.

Erikson looked over the former military man standing in front of him and moved around his desk to take a seat behind the computer. "And what is our next step?"

Gunderson beamed down at him. "Ajay informed me that a call went out from Mayor Stark's burner phone just after your speech; we are tracking the call data right now."

Erikson's eyebrows rose. Perhaps they would be able to figure out who this mysterious puppet master was sooner than expected.

"But for now," Gunderson said, "we will continue to work our way through the cell's infrastructure, and sow as much chaos as we can."

"Not too much chaos, I hope," Erikson responded levelly, intent on sending a message that his concerns were still with the citizens of the county. There was no way he would let Norseman turn this place into a warzone.

"No, sir," Gunderson grinned even wider, "just enough."

With that, the contractor set his glass down, made a two-fingered salute to the sheriff, and walked out the door, leaving Erikson alone with the television.

CHAPTER TWENTY-THREE

The modified sheriff's department Ford Explorer SUV navigated the wide streets of the industrial housing area, its tailpipe throwing a wispy cloud of exhaust into the air. The temperature, while still below freezing, had started to climb back up, a sort of sadistic warm spell to remind the residents of this part of the world that nature was truly inhospitable to human life. The Explorer wound its way through the neighborhoods toward the Finger rising from the middle.

Inside the SUV, Deputies Tyler and Johnson were working through their regular patrol, but even the older, grouchier deputy was focused this morning. They had to be. During their morning roll call, just before loading up, the sheriff had given them all a mandate and a list of addresses to check out.

Deputy Tyler was busy scanning the passenger side of the vehicle, looking forward to their first address. "Alright," the younger deputy spoke softly, "it's this peeling yellow one off to the right here."

Johnson did not slow the Explorer down perceptibly. He just drove past, relying on Tyler's ability to observe and record details as they went.

"See anything?" he asked. The sheriff's mandate was simple. They were looking for safe houses and stash houses that belonged to RIF, and recording any suspicious movement, specifically movement into or out of the homes. Johnson and Tyler's list of addresses had been the longest by far, but all of them were within their usual patrol route. They were on track to finish their first round of drive-by reconnaissance before breaking for lunch.

"A couple of lights on," Deputy Tyler said. "Upper level, but no silhouettes or anything."

So far, the patrol had turned up a few interesting pieces of information. Some of the houses that typically had vehicles parked out front and lights on had appeared to now be vacant. These houses were all on the outskirts of the industrial housing area so far, and the deputies still had to continue their patrol into the center.

Their first pass, a quick drive through the center of the area, had led to them actually locating a few of those vehicles closer to the Finger. Neither deputy was under any illusion as to what that meant.

RIF was conglomerating its operations, centralizing them around the Finger in response to the raids that had occurred.

"Alright, man," Deputy Johnson said, looking out the driver's side of the SUV toward the Finger. "Let's make another pass by the Finger and see what we see."

"Roger," Tyler cracked a grin. "Are you buying lunch afterward?"

Cheat was expected to make a full recovery, although the use of his arm was going to be degraded for some time. Thanks to Cooper's quick and thorough attention, the Norseman Consulting medical staff had merely to stuff Cheat full of antibiotics and extract a single 9mm slug from his back muscle before stitching him back up. He had some physical therapy ahead of him, but he would be alright.

Gunderson, Dufraine, Yale, and the operational team leaders were conversing in Gunderson's large office, poring over documents and maps recovered and processed by Yale's team. Spirits were high. The van that had blown Sword's cover had been full of drugs, indicating that they were merely on their way to make an unscheduled drop-off. Despite the unexpected circumstances at Sword team's raid, they had managed to complete their objective, and the strikes had yielded the results they'd been hoping for. Sheriff Erikson's press conference had created a buzz that Yale's analysts were intercepting. The picture was becoming clearer and more apparent each day.

RIF and their Iranian and Chechen friends were quickly moving large amounts of people and product, centralizing their operations around the Finger. There were still a few "outposts," stash houses and safe houses that the terrorists were using as stopover points, in the countryside, but they expected that one or two more successful raids would flush the remainder to the middle of the industrial housing area, right where Norseman Consulting wanted them.

They still didn't know the identity of the Iranian on the ground which was in charge of the operation, but they knew that he had been moving around from safe house to safe house, an option that was now out of the question.

"Mayor Stark made another call to 'Antony' immediately after the sheriff's press conference." Yale pointed to the phone records. "The call lasted thirty seconds."

"Do we have a picture of this guy yet?" Melvin asked, sifting through a printed stack of photographs.

"Unfortunately, no," Gunderson said without looking up from the stack of emails that Yale's analysts had sorted through and highlighted for their consumption.

Norseman Consulting's considerable intelligence apparatus had no difficulty identifying and categorizing most of the domestic RIF gang members, Chechens, and the Iranians that they had so far been able to snap pictures of, either alive or after one of their raids. Nothing, however, was leading them to the leader of the cell, although this "Antony" character seemed like a good lead.

Gunderson and Dufraine really only wanted to identify the leader of the cell so that they could be sure they eliminated him. The assault plans were already being drawn up for what they anticipated would be their final piece of this particular operation, but they wanted to be sure to stamp out any remaining enemies, especially foreign terrorists.

"What's this mayor's deal?" Randall asked the room. "I mean why would she be so down with all this shit?"

"Money," Alex snorted in reply.

"Our analysts suspect she is some sort of sociopath, hell-bent on becoming as powerful as she can." Yale's face was thoughtful. "We even found evidence that the attack on Broadway was partly her idea."

Randall let out a low whistle. "Psycho bitch."

A sudden alarm went off, and Gunderson's phone lit up. Looking down at the alert, Gunderson muttered a low expletive.

"If you gentlemen would be so kind as to finish up in another office," the Norseman Consulting president moved back behind his desk. "I have a very bored pilot I would like to hire."

Jennifer Stark's black Chevy Tahoe pulled into the parking lot of the Midway Mall. She put the car in park and left the engine running. She had a bit of shopping to do before she conducted one final meeting this evening, and the Herberger's at the mall probably had that last piece of cookware that she needed.

Taking her keys with her, she bent against the cold, holding her scarf against her face. It was only a few steps to the door, but the wind whipping at any exposed skin stung and turned her eyebrows pink. She stamped her boots against the rubber mat, shaking ice and snow off of her feet, and ducked inside.

116

She was only in the store for a few minutes, as Herberger's had the Dutch oven she wanted right near the front door, but check out took a bit longer since the woman in line in front of her fumbled with extracting her store credit card from her purse. Jennifer Stark could barely hold back her contemptuous sneer, but she managed to paste on a smile until she was back in the parking lot.

She had only a few minutes before her meeting.

Unlocking the Tahoe, she clambered in, almost throwing the Dutch oven into the passenger seat. She was about to drive off when a voice sounded behind her.

"What'd you buy?" Antony's thinly accented voice nearly made the mayor jump out of her own skin.

"SHIT!" She rested her head against the steering wheel before turning around. "I was just about to come to meet you, you know."

"I thought we could meet here," Antony responded coolly. Antony, whose real name was Ardashir Khorasani, was an Iranian Intelligence Service, or VAJA, operative, and he had been in charge of observing and handling Mayor Stark longer than she'd known him. He was surprised at how easily she believed him when he told her he was Italian.

"As you are well aware," Khorasani continued without waiting for Stark to reply, "it was not a law enforcement agency that attacked the farmhouse, nor was it a law enforcement agency that took down all three of the safe houses this week."

Stark nodded. She was well aware, and despite the sheriff's insistence that two of the safe houses had been the work of law enforcement, her sources inside the police department and the sheriff's office told her otherwise.

"And it was not," Antony pressed forward, "a rival faction either."

Mayor Stark remained silent. She had nothing to add, and she really wanted Antony to get to the point. This little Italian dickhead sure knew how to take his sweet time.

When the mayor did not respond to Antony's statements, he grinned slightly, flashing a thin row of off-white, crooked teeth. "My firm believes that a private firm is behind this and that Sheriff Erikson is responsible for hiring them, with help from someone named Robert Severson."

Jennifer Stark remained impassive after that revelation, waiting to see if there was more. When she was sure that he was finally done talking, she responded. "What do you mean, a private firm?"

"We believe that Gerry Erikson hired a firm in the aftermath of the Broadway attacks, to take credit for the cleanup." Ardashir and his companions knew that this was not the case, but they also were counting on Mayor Stark's political ambitions to obstruct the rational side of her thought process. The team had had a conversation last night, and with the tightening noose, Mayor Stark was now a liability more than she was an asset. This was a last-ditch effort to get the plan back on track.

"You are telling me," Stark enunciated every word clearly and slowly, "that Gerry Erikson, Sheriff Gerry Erikson, hired out mercenaries to do his own job for him?"

"Yes." Ardashir could see the beginnings of a smile tugging at the corner of her pink lips.

"What company?"

"I will get you the details as soon as I can." Ardashir opened the door to the Tahoe. "Goodnight, Jennifer."

Across the street, in a beat-up white pickup truck, an unassuming man appeared to be texting on his phone. In reality, he was snapping high-resolution pictures of the mayor's Tahoe through a camera mounted behind the busted-out oval on the grille of his truck and controlled by the smartphone in his hand. He had been unable to get a clear picture of the man who had followed the mayor to the mall and then jimmied his way into her vehicle while she was shopping, but as the man stepped out, he made the mistake of looking around just a bit too much.

The man in the truck snapped several pictures in rapid succession, never looking up from his phone. "Bingo," he grinned, then hopped out of his truck and walked into the liquor store behind him. It was time for a celebratory drink.

CHAPTER TWENTY-FOUR

As Ardashir drove away in a dirty white Chevy sedan, he made several twists and turns on his way back to his safe house. These seemingly random turns were actually a professionally conducted surveillance detection route, or SDR, that was designed to lure out and identify any potential pursuers.

The Iranian spy had conducted countless SDRs in his lifetime, although he had never performed one in such a flat, cold environment. Ardashir had operated extensively in Afghanistan when the United States was so heavily bogged down in that never-ending quagmire. He'd been in charge of helping and funding the Taliban and other insurgent forces attack American military and coalition personnel and had been largely responsible for the proliferation of the narcotics trade in the Hindu Kush Mountains.

It was a career he was immensely proud of. His success and contacts within insurgent groups fighting in Afghanistan had gotten him hand-selected for this assignment. There were only a few Iranians actually in Minnesota; the rest of their operation had been either imported Chechen and European muscle or organically recruited gang members and criminals from around the state.

Ardashir made several more turns, taking him through the small downtown area just blocks from where the massacre on Broadway had occurred. He was satisfied he was not being followed, as he had not been followed his entire time in Minnesota, but he continued anyway, using the time to reflect on his success so far.

Ensnaring Jennifer Stark had been almost too easy. Before making contact with her, he was sure they were going to have to either dredge up or even manufacture, some sort of scandal to get her compliance. To his absolute delight, her lax cybersecurity had made it possible to crack into her social media, email, and cell phone. Multiple emails, text messages, and phone calls expressing her desire to move up through the political ranks of the state government, making a stop as governor, and then off to the federal government and a seat in the senate.

She planned to remain committed to her Communist ideals, turning her country's political system inside out from within. Her problem was that she needed money, a lot of it, and she needed supporters.

The Iranian spy approached her and was shocked at how quickly she leaped at the opportunity to gain a significant bankroller without even questioning the source of the cash flow. Ardashir supposed that she didn't want to know to maintain plausible deniability. It was not until they started laying out their plans for kinetic operations on her home soil that she began to balk, but even then, she took only a little bit of convincing.

Combined with her ingrained loathing for the "militarized" police, the vast sums of money that were arriving in her accounts made her an easy target.

This new group was a monkey wrench in Ardashir's carefully laid plans, however, and the fact that they were not part of any government agency gave the man no small amount of anxiety. They had anticipated federal and state responses to their operations and had taken the necessary precautions. Law enforcement agencies were a more-or-less known quantity for someone in Ardashir's line of work. A private firm, however, was nearly impossible to predict, especially considering they did not know which firm they were dealing with.

Ardashir gritted his teeth, rechecked his mirrors, and knew he had to figure out who was messing with his operation.

"What's he doing?" The door to the Brain opened and Norseman Consulting operational staff came flooding in. James Gunderson led the way into the room, taking a position near two analysts sitting at their computers. Dufraine and his assault team leaders formed a half circle behind the analysts and stared intently at the large monitor on the opposite wall. A dusty gray Chevy sedan wove its way through the snow and ice-covered streets of downtown Alexandria.

"Still doing an SDR, Mr. Gunderson," the analyst nearest the Norseman president said, pressing a few keys on his computer to bring up a map of the area on a second monitor.

The second analyst was focused more intently on the computer screen directly in front of her. Her computer was running the photos Chip had taken of the unknown man from Stark's SUV against several databases.

"Okay," the first analyst announced, studying the overhead drone feed of the gray Chevy, "it looks like he's coming to a stop."

"I've got something!" the female analyst shouted excitedly. "A passport and entry visa for one Antony D'Avolio from Italy."

A third monitor, this one to the left of the drone feed, showed a passport photo and work visa next to the man seen entering and exiting Stark's SUV. Next to both of these pictures was a second identification card, same man, with some Middle Eastern writing on it.

"Is that Arabic?" Dufraine squinted up at the monitor, trying to make out the image on the screen.

"Farsi," the young woman corrected. "Say hello to Mr. Ardashir Khorasani, an operative of VAJA."

Gunderson looked up at the screen, then over to Dufraine. The two men shared a look "Shit."

The group continued to stare at the computer screen for another couple of minutes, the mesmerizing rotation of the drone playing out around what appeared to be an Iranian safe house.

Alex and Randall were taking in all the tactical information they could, mentally putting together a quick action plan for assaulting the house. It was a single-story in the middle of a city block. There was a narrow alley running between this house and the one behind it. It had been selected by someone who wanted to blend in and did not want to be taken by surprise.

"Where's Yale?" Gunderson asked the two analysts sitting with them. He could see that Yale's office was empty, and he was surprised that the man was not here to show off what his team had managed to accomplish.

"He's pouring over pictures with Chip somewhere," the male analyst said, eyes still locked on the monitor.

"Alright," Gunderson frowned slightly. "Great job, guys. How much dwell time do we have left on this drone?"

"About ninety minutes," the young man said. "But the launch team is preparing the second drone for takeoff within the next sixty."

"Perfect," Gunderson said, clapping the analyst on his shoulder a bit harder than he'd intended. He turned to Alex and Randall. "I want us inside that house before the sun rises."

The two team leaders nodded sharply, although Randall's eyebrows rose. It was nearing eight in the evening, and they didn't know the layout of the house or the number of people living inside. For all they knew, the house could be wired to explode the moment they stepped through the door.

If Gunderson or Dufraine noticed a slight hesitation in their team leaders, they did not acknowledge it.

"Mr. Khorasani is our top priority," Gunderson stated. "We need him alive and willing to answer a few questions."

Alex and Randall nodded once again. "Now get outta here and get your teams together. We need to get a plan in place and start working it as soon as possible."

The assault team leaders spun on their heels and hustled to the team room.

Even after several hours, the assault plan was pretty fluid. Sword team was to be the primary assault force, with Axe acting as a quick reaction force nearby in case Sword got into any trouble. Randall was not happy. His team had been split into the two fireteams, and each team was driving toward the target building in a different commercial sprinter van. They didn't know the size of the enemy force in the house, they didn't know the layout of the structure, and they had no idea what the Iranian would do to avoid capture.

There had not even been enough time to get a sniper team in place. The assaulters had watched the drone feed of the house and waited until about an hour after the last light in the house turned off. Figuring that the occupants were most likely asleep, Randall called out the go-code, and the men had rushed off to complete their mission.

They were set up much as they had been during the assault on the farmhouse. All the assaulters were wearing their winter camouflage uniforms and carrying their Brugger and Thomet carbines. Night vision goggles adorned every man's helmet, illuminating the night around them with an eerie phosphorescent glow.

"Thirty seconds," the driver of the van called over the radio. Randall gave his men a thumbs up, and he felt his body tense with anticipation.

He was anxious for several reasons, but chief in his mind at the moment was the fact that the houses were too close together to land a helicopter, so their medevac options were limited. While each of his fireteams had excellent combat medics, he always felt reassured when he knew the medevac helicopters were only seconds away.

"Ten seconds," the radio sparked to life, and Sword One readied themselves.

Ardashir Khorasani had been having trouble sleeping ever since the raid on the farmhouse. His cell had sustained heavy losses. He was surprised and unsettled that the Americans had not identified his operatives in the news, and his sources had not turned anything up at all as to who had cut down his men so ruthlessly. At the moment, he was staring his laptop, filtering through a secure messaging application. He took a moment to rub his eyes and sigh. These long nights of staring at his computer until the sun rose were really wearing on him.

The Iranian was thankful that he had been chosen for this mission. It indeed was an honor. But the ground commander was a political appointee, and not much of a real leader. Ardashir wished the man would recognize his own inabilities and let Ardashir run the operation as he saw fit. The buffoon had instead chosen to ensconce himself in that ugly apartment building with a good chunk of their best-trained muscle as bodyguards and micromanaged every portion of the operation.

Ardashir scoffed at this. If the Americans figured out who they were and what they were doing, it wouldn't matter how many bodyguards they had at their disposal, they would all be killed or captured. Ardashir had initially banked on the latter, but the last several operations conducted against his cell had given him cause to believe the former was much more likely.

Rubbing his eyes once more, he clicked through the latest bit of asinine communication from the man who was notionally in charge of this operation. Ardashir checked his watch. 2:34? Time had barely moved since the last time he had checked.

The two Chechens that were living in the house with him were likely asleep already. If he strained his war-battered ears, he could just hear the sound of snoring over the ringing that persisted in his head. Ardashir did not trust the two men's ideology, they claimed to be "freedom fighters," men willing to die for the Islamic cause, but in reality, they were just hired guns, men loyal only to a paycheck. Ardashir knew how ruthless the Chechens could be from his time in Afghanistan, and they unnerved him slightly, but he did appreciate their penchant for violence.

Ardashir turned his attention away from the tasks at hand. None of this needs to be done now, he told himself as he snapped the computer shut and pulled the blankets up. He was about to close his eyes in an attempt to sleep when they snapped wide open.

A faint tinkling had alerted him as if a window had been broken. Ardashir's instincts were immediately engaged, and he reached for the

9mm semi-automatic pistol resting in a paddle holster on the nightstand. Drawing the gun from the holster, the Iranian fumbled around in the dark for his flashlight.

There was a sudden flurry of noise from down the hallway. Ardashir could tell whoever had broken the window was not only in the house but that they had just kicked opened the door to the Chechens' room. A series of muffled pops from that direction let him know that they had just executed his Chechen muscle.

Shit. Ardashir's hand waved around in the dark as he knocked the flashlight off of the nightstand and heard it roll onto the floor. Light footsteps were rapidly moving his way, so the Iranian agent threw himself off his bed and away from his bedroom door. He frantically groped under the bed, finally wrapping his hand around the flashlight just in time for his entry to explode inward.

Bringing his pistol to bear, Ardashir raised his arm, only to be hit with intense pain and extreme tensing of his entire body. Ensuing involuntary spasms caused him to discharge his pistol into the wall near his feet.

Ardashir was vaguely aware of a strange clicking noise. Through the mind-numbing pain, he could see the eerie glow from the night vision goggles on the men standing in front of him, and he could see the wires leading from his chest to the Taser in the first man's hand.

"Hit him again!" the assaulter in the back shouted, and Ardashir was hit by another high-voltage dose. Within a few seconds, he was lying face down, stripped of his pistol and handcuffed. The men in his bedroom yanked him to his feet and placed a hood over his eyes before frog-marching him out into the cold.

"Sword ready for exfil." Roughly thirty seconds after they had breached the front door, Randall and his team were already hustling back to the vans, their Iranian prisoner in tow. In the QRF vans parked down the street, Alex blew a sigh of relief.

Alex could see one of Sword team's assaulters throw their prisoner roughly up into the back of the sprinter van before the six men clambered in. The Axe team leader checked his watch. From arrival to exfiltration, the entire raid had taken less than three minutes.

"Roger, Sword," Alex spoke into his radio. "All teams, let's bounce." The four vans slowly drove off into the night, each taking a different route back to the Norseman Consulting compound.

CHAPTER TWENTY-FIVE

Ardashir's head was killing him. He woke in total darkness and sweating. As his mental faculties came back to him, he hazily recalled the events that had led to this moment. A lot of confusion, some intense pain, a hood being thrown over his head, and then a prick followed by a warm sensation rippling through his body as he slipped into unconsciousness.

He could tell that he had been bound, he was sitting in a chair, and he could not lift his hands. A quick shake of his head told him the hood had been removed. That told him he was sitting in a room that had been totally blacked out, and he waited for his eyes to adjust.

After several minutes, it was clear that his eyes would never adjust to this level of darkness. So, he resigned himself to the darkness, and mentally readied himself for what he was sure would come next.

At least I am not gagged, he thought, taking a deep breath and flexed his fingers and toes to get the blood flowing.

"He's awake," Yale said, looking up from the computer monitor on his desk. The image on the screen was a black and white video feed of the holding room where Ardashir Khorasani was sitting. He was occupying the third holding cell that Norseman Consulting maintained on their premises. The two terrorists captured after the Broadway Massacre, Anwar al Kobani and Jesús Longoria Reyes, were being held in the first and second cells.

"Let him sit a while longer." Chip, one of Norseman Consulting's best interrogators, was sitting on Yale's couch, cleaning and trimming his fingernails with a large folding knife and had barely looked up from his task for the past several minutes.

Yale's large office inside the Brain was occupied by Yale, Chip, and Burt. Cheat was still recovering from his injuries. Although he was expected to make a full recovery, the three men in the room expected Cheat to retire from field work afterwards. Burt and Chip were sitting on the couch next to each other and were discussing their notes for taking a run at interrogating Khorasani.

"I'm going to make some coffee," Burt said as he stood up and stretched then ran a hand over his beard. "Does anyone else want some?"

Chip asked for a cup of coffee, black with one sugar, and Yale asked for a cup of tea, chai if they had it. Burt nodded as he headed to the coffee bar over by the far wall of the Brain.

Ardashir Khorasani, a loyal agent of the Iranian VAJA, had no way of knowing it, but he had been in the holding room for just over six hours. He'd been unconscious for almost the entire time. The sedative that had been administered shortly after he'd been handcuffed and thrown into his captor's van had been measured with extreme precision so that he would wake up in the Norseman holding cell only after the intelligence team had a chance to run down as much information about him as possible. What he did know was that he was uncomfortably warm, and he still couldn't see shit.

He was also a little surprised. All of his training to resist interrogation had been centered on Iranian propaganda and experiences with Taliban or other insurgent forces in the Middle East, so he was expecting significantly more savagery. Ardashir was certain that the tooth pulling and finger mangling would begin shortly. He gritted his teeth and tried to fall back asleep.

The lights in the room kicked on suddenly, hitting Ardashir's retinas and causing him to flinch in pain and squeeze his eyes shut. *Here it comes.* He tensed, preparing for the torture he was sure he was about to endure.

Nothing happened immediately, and Ardashir gradually opened his eyes, blinking against the bright fluorescent light. He could feel his anxiety mounting, but at least he could see what was in the room around him. A simple table, bolted to the ground, was directly in front of him. There was a camera in the corner above him and to his right. Directly in front of him, a windowless metal door with a small slot directly in the center—controlled access to the room. There was no handle on the door, and there were no windows anywhere in the room.

Ardashir sat alone for another several minutes, taking in his sparse surroundings. He thought he could hear footsteps approaching the room. A couple of seconds later, he was sure of it. The footsteps grew closer and closer, then stopped directly in front of the door.

There were several seconds of silence, which felt like an eternity to Ardashir. He could feel himself sweating, anxiety building in his throat.

But the steps resumed and faded further and further away from Ardashir's cell. He knew they were messing with him, but he was starting to grow concerned that it was working. A few seconds later, the overhead light started flickering at irregular intervals. Then he felt the temperature soar, causing him to sweat heavily. After a few minutes of hot air being pumped into the room, the temperature started to fall, plummeting down and causing his teeth to chatter. The temperature cycled like this, and Ardashir began to wonder if the sweat was freezing to his skin.

During an interminably long period of cold, an audible groan escaped Ardashir's lips, and he looked up toward the camera in the corner and shouted at it.

"Come on! Let's get it on!" he screamed in the direction of the camera, attempting to mask his fear in bravado. But nobody answered, and he threw his head back in frustration. He threw his head back too hard and found himself tipping backward. With a sickening crack, Ardashir's head smacked against the bare concrete ground. Lying there, dazed, he began to moan. He was flat on his back, staring up into the flickering light. Over his moans, he could hear the heavy lock on the door chunk back, and the door swing into the room.

A moment later, a man clad all in black with a black balaclava and black goggles covering his face stood over Ardashir. In lightly accented English, the man grunted, "Fuckin' piece of shit," and then walked around behind Ardashir and hefted him and his chair back into the upright position.

As Ardashir was returned to sitting, he came face to face with two other men, dressed in gray sweatshirts and jeans, sitting at the table. Spread out across the table were several manila folders. Ardashir did not see any tools and wondered if maybe torture wasn't on the agenda after all.

"Greetings, Mr. Khorasani," said the larger man at the table, on the right. "Mr. Ardashir Khorasani."

Ardashir said nothing in response but tried to crane his neck around the room to locate the mysterious black-clad man who had hoisted him from the floor. The one with the funny accent. Ardashir could not locate him so he figured that he must have taken up a position directly behind him.

"I guess I should say Agent Ardashir Khorasani," the large man at the table elaborated, "of Iranian intelligence."

Still, Ardashir said nothing, refocusing his attention first on the camera in the upper corner, and then back on the two men at the table. They had begun laying the contents of the folders on the table. Ardashir could see them setting out pictures—him meeting with Mayor Stark, his Iranian identification photos, and pictures of his parents back in Addis Abba.

Ardashir's eyes narrowed as the two men continued to unpack the folders in front of him. "Fuck you!" he snarled and tried to spit, but his mouth was too dry.

"Here's how this is going to go," the second, smaller man said. "We are going to ask you questions, and you are going to answer them. If you don't, you will end up like Anwar al Kobani and Jesús Longoria Reyes."

Ardashir's eyes widened at the sound of those names. He had assumed the two gunmen had managed to get to their friendly contact in Minneapolis and disappear; a plan set in place from the beginning for any survivors of the attack. The next contact from them that Ardashir was expecting was from Africa via email with photos of those two gunmen's bodies tossed into hastily dug graves.

"Yeah, they didn't cooperate." The larger man pulled out two additional photos, eight-by-tens of two bodies lying in pools of blood on concrete floors in rooms that looked like his. "But we didn't need 'em anyway."

"You talk, you live," the smaller man said with a shrug. "Or you don't talk. We shoot you, and have our friends drop a Hellfire missile on your parents' house."

Ardashir adopted a stony expression. He didn't know if they actually knew where his parents lived, or that his two younger siblings, a brother, and a sister, lived with them.

The smaller man pulled out yet another piece of paper and held it up to Ardashir's face. "This address on the top, that's your parents address, correct? And the one below that is the address of your older sister in Tehran?"

"I'm sure we can spare a second Hellfire for her, too," the larger man said casually.

Still, Ardashir said nothing, so the smaller man continued, "Do we have a deal, Agent Khorasani?"

The Iranian glared at his two captors, and slowly shook his head, a small smirk on his face. "No deal, American pigs."

Both men shared a quick look, and both men shrugged slightly.

"You see, Ardashir," the large man said with a smirk of his own, "we don't really need you. We took your laptop from the safe house."

Ardashir still did not react.

"We already have everything we need from you." the large man leaned forward over the metal table. "We are simply giving you a chance to save your own skin, and that of your family."

"We'll let you think about it," the small man said, and the two men gathered their materials back into their folders and. "Just shout at the camera when you want to let us know your decision."

With that, the three men left the room with a heavy clank from the door. The lights went out, and the temperature got gradually warmer again. Ardashir swore he could hear a low buzzing in the darkness, but he could not be totally sure.

"What do we need him for at this point?" Gunderson asked. Dufraine, Yale, and the two interrogators were in Yale's office, watching the video from the first round of interrogations and monitoring the live feed from the cell. Yale had been managing the interrogation and intelligence gathering at this point and was frustrating both Gunderson and Dufraine by parsing out information selectively.

"Names, mostly," Yale answered. "We have a lot of locations, and we now have numbers of personnel at the target locations, including how many foreign actors are in the area—"

"—but we don't know their names," Chip finished Yale's sentence.

"So how likely are we to get these names?" Dufraine asked the intelligence operatives in the room. He was an action man. He liked having plans, but he did not have the patience for this part of their operations, which he begrudgingly admitted was what Yale and his crew were best suited for.

"Well," Burt said thoughtfully while rubbing the stubble on his chin, "he is a true believer in the mission here. He was hand-selected for it."

"But we do know that he thinks the ringleader is a dipshit," Yale added.

Gunderson and Dufraine looked at the other three men with raised eyebrows.

"It's true, we found it in one of his secured chat applications on his phone," Yale responded. "He's been messaging with one of the other Iranians about how stupid he thinks this guy is."

"We also think he will cave to save his family," Chip chimed in. "He's a believer, but he's not necessarily a fanatic. We can leverage that."

"Well, how long until he breaks?" Gunderson said. He had people to report back to.

"It could be a while," Burt responded. "He is very well trained and was likely anticipating a much more physical approach to interrogation. This method takes longer, but it is significantly less messy."

"Well, let me know." Gunderson checked his watch. It was noon, the day after the raid had taken place. "I need some shut eye."

Gunderson and Dufraine left Yale and his team to conduct their business and headed to their respective offices to crash on their couches.

Later that evening, Gunderson was on the phone, waiting for the end-to-end encryption to take hold. When the chime finally announced that he was connected, he waited for several rings before the line on the other end was answered.

"We got names, one, in particular, is of note." There was no response from the other end, so Gunderson continued, "Omid Mokri."

There was a moment of silence, then a curt response. "Thank you. Continue as planned. We will get you any additional intel you need."

The phone clicked off, and Gunderson set it back on the receiver, looking up at Yale as he did so. "That was faster than I thought," he remarked.

"I suppose." Yale shrugged in a manner that was meant to be humble but conveyed a bit of arrogance in its composure. "He's gonna be pissed when he realizes that Kobani and Reyes are alive."

CHAPTER TWENTY-SIX

To say that Omid Mokri was furious was an understatement. He had always known that several people involved in the operation would be killed or captured, but those were supposed to be the hired muscle from Syria, Chechnya, Mexico, and America, not any of his Iranian operatives. He wasn't sure how that idiot Khorasani had gotten himself captured, but he was convinced that his insolent, incompetent subordinate had screwed up somehow.

Mokri was, like the rest of the Iranian agents, handpicked for this operation. What made him different from his subordinates was that the rest of them had been picked based on previous successes operating against Iran's enemies, Mokri had been chosen because his father was a prominent Iranian political figure who had put the pressure on VAJA to select his son.

The adverse side effects of nepotism showed. While most of the Iranians had operated undercover in Western nations before, Mokri had never left Iran before. Since arriving in the US, he'd lived in a constant state of panic and had not left his top-level apartment safe house except to rotate safehouses to avoid detection.

He was good, however, at keeping networks of spies together, and at forging relationships with unsavory people. He found that these abilities were invaluable all over the world, and had helped him recruit massive numbers of mercenaries, thugs, and gangsters to support their cause. The nearly unlimited funds from VAJA selling off pirated oil and heroin bought from Daesh militants in Iraq and Syria didn't hurt, either. Sure, the Syrians and Chechens he had recruited had played under the guise of continuing their jihad against the infidels, but they had only allowed themselves to be recruited by the VAJA operative after being promised cash.

The handful of Mexican gangsters they'd picked up had been Khorasani's idea. He figured that it would help sow confusion with American law enforcement. The hope was that would assume that the whole operation was related to the drug trade, and the misdirection would lead to increased pressure on the United States' southern border and not Iran.

Omid had to hand it to his subordinate, the Mexicans that they had hired for the operation were ruthless, and he had used them, in conjunction with some of the more radical Syrians, to conduct the opening salvo on Broadway.

The RIF organization had been happy to join in, as they'd been promised a large share of drugs, mostly heroin, which they incorrectly assumed came from Mexico. Mokri had used his extensive network, and Khorasani's contacts in Afghanistan, to import the heroin from the war-torn nation.

While Khorasani had proven his worth many times over, he was openly insubordinate toward Mokri's authority, which ground at Mokri's nerves even more now that they were being actively hunted and destroyed by the enemy. The fact that Khorasani had not checked in, and the Chechens that Mokri had assigned to him had been found executed in the safe house, had created an ulcer that the Iranian commander was trying to treat by drinking antacid straight out of the bottle.

Mokri wasn't sure if Khorasani had been killed, captured, or if he had deserted, but he knew that he'd prefer it if Khorasani had been killed. Mokri had spent the last day sending out orders to condense the operation and fallback to locations closer to his safe house via his encrypted messaging app to each of the four Iranian agents left in the operation. He knew he might be overreacting, but also knew that they had started taking losses from this unknown player immediately after the Broadway assault, and that had severely hampered the progress he was expected to report to VAJA headquarters in Tehran.

Surrounding Omid in his top-level apartment in the Spire were dozens of crates filled with assault rifles, ammunition, and explosives. Several members of the operation had taken up residence in different rooms on the top floor. One other VAJA agent lived in the Spire, and he was now busily working towards uncovering information on who had been sabotaging his operation.

All of the other men on the floor were elite Iranian military operators, a half dozen in total, who had been chosen for this mission on account of their fanaticism. Any members of the team with strong accents were kept in rooms one story below him. They could not take any chances of them standing out and raising suspicions with the locals. Most of these men were a means to an end. Mokri, Khorasani, and the rest of the VAJA operatives involved in the operation were not very religious. This operation was not about any religious ideology, no matter how they pitched it to the rest of the team. This was about Iran's position on the global stage.

The Americans had been much too involved in Middle Eastern affairs and had frustrated the Iranian military and economic expansion. Iranian political leadership wanted the Americans to get out and stay out of the Middle East, but to make that happen, the US would need a crisis on their own borders. VAJA's objective was to create some a crisis at home to redirect American attention.

The operation had been going on without a hitch. Mokri's operatives had been successful at bribing politicians, sowing political dissent, perpetuating "hate crimes," and even causing a full-scale riot in Detroit—framed as civilian retaliation for the closing of a manufacturing plant. The operation was far-reaching, but the most crucial part was to be conducted right here, in the heart of rural Minnesota.

Minnesota had been chosen by VAJA analysts for several reasons, the most important of which was that the state had experienced relatively little unrest in the past years, despite the political turmoil surging through the rest of the nation. Minnesota hadn't had a mass killing in recent memory and had never been the victim of a terror attack, though there had been several thwarted attempts.

Mokri's cell was aiming to show the Americans that no matter how insulated, no matter how welcoming or pleasant they were, they were subject to have their daily lives thrown into violent disarray.

In the past several weeks, however, several of his operatives had been killed or captured by law enforcement, which he had expected, and this private organization, which he had not expected. At the rate the covert operators were taking down safe houses, Mokri would be out of muscle in a week, which was well before Mokri wanted to move to the next phase of his plan: escalating violence.

He knew he needed to retaliate somehow, but first, he needed to consolidate.

Working at a makeshift desk constructed from weapons crates and a door taken off of the closet in the second bedroom of the apartment, Mokri pored over maps, photographs, and operation plans for moving forward. He was leaning forward on the desk, with both hands balled in fists to support his weight. He knew what he was going to do.

"Javad, come here," Mokri spoke curtly into his radio, his speech clipped and tight. No reply came through the radio, but the other VAJA operative walked into the room a few seconds later. Javad had been operating in Syria for years and, as a result of a Kurdish sniper's bullet, had a permanent hitch in his step.

"Yes, *Aqa*," Javad said, standing at a loose form of attention. Omid Mokri generated his respect from title only, and that title was tenuously held at best. While maintaining a base level of professionalism, Javad felt no need to treat Mokri with reverence.

"Contact the rest of the cell," Mokri said, still leaning heavily on his fists, "and have them relocated to the phase four safe house locations."

"We aren't even done with the second phase," Javad said flatly. "Phase four is for our end-state operations. We won't be ready until the summer."

"I know which phase is which, Javad!" Mokri slammed a fist on his desk, knocking the radio over. "Our men are getting slaughtered out there, and with Ardashir who-knows-where, we need to act now."

"As you wish." Javad nodded and turned to leave the room.

"One more thing," Omid said, and Javad turned. "Where are we at with this private company that the sheriff hired?"

Javad had found out the company name, the owner, and several of the other clients that Norseman Consulting had done work for in the past couple years, but he had been waiting to reveal his findings until he knew who the most recent employer was. He'd not been able to discover who had hired Norseman Consulting to act against the VAJA operation; all he knew was that, contrary to what Khorasani had told Mayor Stark, it sure wasn't the Douglas County Sheriff's Office. Most of his information was thanks, in no small part, to an email that had been left poorly encrypted he had intercepted between the old Judge and the unknown Federal Agent responsible for putting Norseman Consulting on contract.

Javad hesitated for a minute, weighing whether to lie to Mokri or reveal what he did know before he was fully ready. Gauging that he was close enough to reveal some of his knowledge, and accounting for the fact that Mokri held his immediate future in his hands, the VAJA operative explained.

"The group that has been assaulting our safe houses, including the farmhouse, is a private firm called Norseman Consulting," Javad sighed. He despised Mokri and had already determined that if the operation's ground commander was ever on the verge of blowing the operation, Javad would simply kill him and escape North to Canada.

Omid Mokri looked up at Javad with bloodshot eyes. "Good." There was some relief in his voice. "What about their employer? Is it CIA, FBI, or…?"

"I do not know yet," Javad interrupted. "I have a list of their previous employers, but I do not know, specifically, who hired them this time."

Mokri's head drooped slightly, and he took a deep, shaking breath. To Javad, it seemed as if the man might crack at any moment. Omid is going to be a problem, Javad thought, his face remaining impassive. If the situation called for it, he would not hesitate to put Mokri down, no matter who his father was or what his position might be. Javad was a survivor, and he had no desire to die in this frozen hellscape called Minnesota.

Exhaling sharply through his nose, Mokri lifted his head to address Javad again.

"Give me a list of this Norseman Consulting's contracts," he said. "We can see if there is a target for us to hit there."

"I already have one, Aqa," Javad replied levelly. "A man named Robert Severson, a former judge from this area, has contracted Norseman Consulting through their personal security division."

"Good," Mokri nodded. "Put together an attack plan for Robert Severson."

"Yes, *Aqa*." Javad tilted his head back in reply, preparing yet again to leave the room.

"And let's put together something to retaliate against this sheriff," Mokri said. "Mayor Stark has been able to keep us one step ahead of the police, but the sheriff's department has been a pain in the ass."

Javad just nodded his understanding and left the room, heading back to his own quarters to draw up the requested plans.

CHAPTER TWENTY-SEVEN

Deputies Johnson and Tyler had been driving around in circles through the industrial housing area all morning. It was nearing noon, and food was on both of their minds. Ever since the recent raids on safe houses throughout the county, the sheriff's department and the police department had each dedicated one additional patrol unit, so now three patrol units were covering the area.

"There's nobody out here," Deputy Tyler spoke for the first time in over a half hour. "It reminds me of driving through Mosul back in the day, but with, you know, snow instead of sand."

Johnson grunted, his new default response to Tyler. Despite what his curt responses would suggest, though, Johnson had actually grown to like the younger deputy. Sure, the kid was an idealist, but he was also much more realistic than some of the newer deputies that Johnson had run into over his career. Tyler was eager to see the good in people, but he also acknowledged and handled the dark side of humanity with extreme maturity. Johnson supposed that came from the time the kid spent in the military, but either way, he appreciated it, although he'd never tell Tyler that.

Tyler went back to scanning the empty streets. The neighborhood seemed downright abandoned, but then again it wasn't even noon on a school day in February.

"This is APD six-nine," the radio on the dashboard chirped. "Be advised, we have a positive identification of a wanted person."

Johnson and Tyler turned their attention to the radio on the dash.

"APD six-nine, dispatch," the female dispatcher's voice came through the radio speaker. "Which wanted person do you have positive ID on?"

"Dispatch, we have a positive ID on one Conor Johnsen," the city cop in patrol car sixty-nine responded. "He just left one of the houses of interest in the industrial housing area and is headed inward."

"Copy, six-nine," the dispatcher replied calmly. "All units this station, who is available to assist?"

Tyler snatched up the radio set on the dash. "This is DCSO two-two, we are available to assist."

Johnson and Tyler looked at each other and Tyler grinned. Johnson gave his traditional grunt and began navigating his SUV to

APD six-nines position as the radio announced that the other DCSO patrol was two minutes from APD six-nines location.

Conor Johnsen had been panicking non-stop for the past several days. He was the de facto leader of RIF and was accustomed to a certain level of violence, but it had always been on his terms and to his favor. In the past few days, though, a bunch of his men had been killed by what his benefactors were telling him was an unnamed competing interest. Having this shadowy organization pick his revolutionaries apart and all but destroy his business had rattled him to his core.

Conor didn't really care where their drug supply was coming from. He was told they came from Mexico, which seemed bolstered by the presence of several Mexicans tasked with guarding the stash houses. Conor thought he was on the easy street to getting rich and funding his revolution, but now it was looking more and more likely that he was going to get snatched up by this unnamed competitor.

But now all the Mexicans had been replaced by white guys with funny accents and generic "American" names like Bob and Rick. Conor had actually become quite close with one of the men, someone who he presumed to be in some sort of leadership role based on the respect that the other men showed him. Conor knew him only as "John," and through John, he had figured out that most of these men with the funny accents were from Chechnya. Conor did not know where Chechnya was, but wherever it was, these guys meant business and they scared Conor a little.

For Conor Johnsen, the days following the raids on his safe houses had been entirely about survival. Within minutes of the three safe houses being assaulted, he had been rushed to this old yellow house that was rotting from the inside out in the industrial housing area. Moving safehouses and having his guys slaughtered or imprisoned made him feel like control of his gang was being torn from his grasp. Much of his crew, what was now left of it, had been moved to similarly run-down houses in the area and were surrounded by the men from Chechnya, allegedly to protect them, but Conor was starting to get the feeling that the Chechens were there to liquidate them if that order came down.

If he was being honest with himself, Conor was terrified. Many of the men who had been killed or captured had been his own guys, either from Alexandria or from the Twin Cities area who'd answered the call to rally up in preparation for "revolution." Conor didn't even know most of their names, but the fact that they were being systematically extinguished by some unknown entity unnerved him, to say the least.

Conor was reflecting on what this meant for him personally as he threw what meager belongings he had into a duffel bag. John had come to him just minutes before and told him that everyone had to pack up and move to a new safe house within the next fifteen minutes. Conor tossed his bag over by the door and set about making sure that his sawn-off 12-gauge shotgun, folding stock Kalashnikov rifle, and Taurus .40 caliber pistol were cleaned, oiled, and loaded.

If his time came, Conor Johnsen had no intention of going quietly.

There were eight of them in the house at the moment: four Chechens, Conor, and three of RIF's members, two men, Dean and Gary, and one woman, Liz, who had been founding members of the RIF with Conor. They were getting ready to load their belongings into the trunk of Liz's Pontiac Grand Prix while the Chechens sanitized the safe house, running around wiping surfaces with a commercial cleaning solution.

"Conor, what the fuck is going on?" Liz demanded. Of the four RIF members, Liz was the only one who had a legitimate job on the outside, although she was pretty sure she'd been fired from the truck stop seeing as she hadn't been to work in several days.

"Just shut up, Lizzie," Conor snapped. His nerves were frayed, and he fumbled around with the duffle bag hanging over his shoulder. His shotgun and Kalashnikov protruded from the main compartment, and he'd stuffed his Taurus into his pants.

"Ever since we took the smack from these guys, it's been nothing but trouble," she persisted. Liz's duffle only had one firearm poking out, a 9mm Uzi carbine that she had taken a hacksaw to, cutting the barrel from the legal requirement of sixteen inches down to a nub that barely protruded from the receiver. Tucked into a holster in her right jacket pocket was a small Bersa .380 pistol. "First the farmhouse gets hit, then the safe houses, then we get rousted from our own homes, and now being shuffled around every couple hours?"

The other two RIF members were silent. They agreed with Liz, but they were afraid of Conor. They had once seen him brain one of his dissenters with a crowbar, leaving the man with a permanent speech impediment and learning disability.

"Liz, for God's sake. Let's just get to the next location. John will fill us in."

As if on cue, John appeared in the entryway to the house where the RIF leadership had gathered.

"Are you ready?" he asked in his accented English, his expression blank and motionless. He was carrying a plastic bag full of dirty paper towels. As he spoke, the other three Chechens walked up behind him.

"Yes, but what about the rest of our guys?" Conor asked. RIF still had several dozen members, maybe fifty in total, who were holed up in safe houses scattered across the mostly vacant industrial housing area.

"Other members of our organization are getting them to safety," John lied. John's last instruction from Javad had instructed him to gather up Conor and bring him to the Spire. Most of the other RIF members were going to be left where they were for the time being. "Now let's get moving."

The group of eight moved from the relatively warm confines of the safe house and trudged out to the waiting vehicles with their belongings in tow. Conor and Dean of the other RIF members piled into the Chechen's black Nissan SUV with John and one of his men. Liz and Gary got into her Pontiac and the remaining Chechens crammed into the backseat. With the eight people loaded, they took off toward the Spire.

The two Alexandria police officers had been driving by in an unmarked Ford Explorer when they saw "John" and the other Chechens walk up to the dilapidated yellow house. They had parked down the street, where they took turns observing the house through binoculars.

Within a few minutes of their impromptu stakeout, the officers were able to identify Conor Johnsen and other RIF leadership walk out to Liz's Pontiac and a black SUV. As the small convoy drove off, the APD officers called in the sighting and readied the shotgun and patrol rifle they had stashed in the vehicle.

The two officers knew that backup was a few minutes away, and they opted to follow the two vehicles from afar, keeping the incoming units up to date on their location. They pulled away from the curb, adrenaline pumping.

John's phone started ringing just two minutes after pulling away from the yellow safe house.

"Yeah," he answered the phone. An excited voice, in a language neither Conor nor Dean understood, could be heard faintly on the other end. John's body language indicated that whatever was being said was not good news.

John responded to the phone call with a series of short blasts of coarse language, then mashed the hang up button with his giant finger.

"We are being followed," John said matter-of-factly, with no hint of stress in his voice. "It looks like the police."

"What are we going to do?" Conor asked frantically.

"Leave that to us." The large Chechen smiled at RIF's strung-out leader.

A couple blocks away, Evan, Steve, and Chris were conducting their own patrol, making a note of which of the previously identified safe houses had experienced any changes since the snatching of Ardashir Khorasani two nights prior. The three men from Archer Two were armed only with cameras and their personal pistols, concealed under their sweatshirts. They had donned their soft body armor, which was rated to stop several hits from pistol rounds as powerful as .44 Magnum but would be no match for any rifle round. This was a low-profile surveillance mission, so they were traveling light. Chris was sitting in the back, snapping picture after picture through the tinted windows of their Toyota SUV as they rolled through the industrial housing area.

"Whoa," Steve said from the driver's seat, "did you guys hear that? APD has a visual on Conor Johnsen."

"Sounds like they're going to try to intercept," Evan said from the passenger seat, looking out the window. "Let's try to mosey our way toward them."

Contrary to what the APD patrol had expected, the two-car convoy containing Conor Johnsen and his associates had turned away from the Spire and into an unfinished cul-de-sac, where they eased to a stop in the middle of the street. The APD patrol hung back and waited for their backup to show. The two officers looked at each other and unlatched the shotgun and the patrol carbine from the rack. This was going to get interesting.

"We have an additional tango," Chris said from the backseat.

"I see him," Steve responded, motioning to the old Ford Expedition that was mirroring the path of the APD patrol one block over.

"Where's the backup?" Chris asked.

"DCSO is sixty seconds out," Evan said. "Let's hang back and make sure they don't need us."

"I don't like this," Steve said as he put the Toyota in park three blocks away from the unfolding drama.

John received another phone call, spoke briefly into the phone, and nodded to his driver. The driver put the SUV in gear, then pulled forward before turning toward the side of the road. Liz's Pontiac was mirroring their move, so now the two vehicles had effectively blocked both lanes of traffic in the cul-de-sac.

"When I tell you to, climb out of the side of the SUV facing away from the cops," John directed the RIF members.

Conor gulped and nodded. John and his Chechen partner retrieved short-barreled Kalashnikov rifles out from under their seats, John pulled back his rifle's bolt to check that a round was seated in the chamber while the other Chechen stuffed spare magazines in his jacket pocket.

John caught Conor staring at him and said coolly, "I suggest you do the same."

The first Douglas County Sheriff's Office patrol SUV came screaming onto the scene, lights and sirens blaring. The driver slammed on the brakes, causing the big Ford to fishtail and then slide to a stop facing the barricade formed by the Nissan and the Pontiac. The two deputies jumped out of their doors, leveling their sidearms at the vehicles.

APD six-nine fired their engine back up and started moving forward to join their DCSO comrades in blocking off the cul-de-sac. As the unmarked SUV moved forward, the driver was focused on putting his patrol SUV in the exact spot he wanted, and the passenger was looking for signs of danger coming out of the target vehicles.

Neither man heard the roar of the diesel engine of the Ford Expedition until it was too late.

"Oh, shit!" Deputy Tyler shouted, pointing as the Expedition made impact with the APD SUV. The larger SUV smashed the police vehicle off the road, over the curb and sidewalk, and into a telephone pole. Johnson and Tyler could see the side airbags had deployed on the police SUV, and they could see the men in the front seats of the Expedition readying carbines to fire through their windshield.

Johnson smashed the gas pedal of the Explorer, aiming its nose at the passenger side door of the Expedition as the first gunshots blasted through the Expedition's windshield and into the side of the APD patrol.

Hearing the noise of the collision and subsequent gunfire behind them, the DCSO patrol deputies spun around to see what was happening. As they did so, Conor, Liz, John, and their five compatriots piled out of their vehicles, hefting their weapons and ducking behind their cars as cover.

The first volley stitched the hood and windshield of the sheriff's department SUV. The deputies ducked and made a dash to the far side of the Explorer.

The deputy on the passenger side, fifty-five-year-old deputy named Hanson, almost made it before a round from the cul-de-sac caught him in the left calf. He faltered, then dove behind the SUV, ripped a tourniquet off of his duty belt, and started putting it on his own leg. The deputy who had been driving, Swanson, managed to make it unscathed and was crouched behind the rear wheel of the SUV making frantic radio calls for backup.

The impact of Johnson and Tyler's SUV into the Ford Expedition had been jarring enough to deploy the airbags and daze the occupants of both vehicles, but only momentarily. Tyler and Johnson drew their sidearms with one hand, unbuckling their seatbelts with the other, and began firing through their own windshield. The two deputies emptied all fourteen rounds in their Glock 21 pistols, running the magazines dry nearly simultaneously.

Tyler reloaded his magazine while scanning around the scene in front of him. He'd practiced reloading his handgun under stress by conducting physically strenuous gun-handling drills for hours in his off-duty time, and even shot competitive matches with his duty rig on weekends, so he was able to reload quickly without taking his eyes off the carnage in front of him.

Johnson and Tyler's combined twenty-eight rounds had been enough to lay waste to the glass, doors, and upholstery of the Expedition and Deputy Tyler could see that both men had been killed. Blood and viscera carpeted the interior of the truck, and the two bodies were slumped forward, held in place by the locking mechanisms of their seatbelts.

Quickly assessing the APD patrol, he could see that the occupants of six-nine were also dead, eviscerated by the hailstorm of bullets that had been fired through the windshield of the Expedition. Deputy Tyler found himself outside of the SUV, making radio calls as if he was on autopilot.

"Shots fired, shots fired," Deputy Tyler's voice sounded like it was coming from someone far away. "I need immediate assistance, two APD KIA, two enemy KIA, and two DCSO still in contact!"

As he was making his radio call, Tyler rushed back to the tailgate of the SUV, meeting Johnson as the older deputy pulled out his patrol rifle and chest rig stuffed with rifle magazines and medical supplies. Tyler vaguely noted that Johnson was sporting a steering wheel-shaped bruise in the center of his forehead.

Tyler donned his plate carrier and snatched up his rifle, which he had outfitted with all the upgrades he could possibly want, including a variable power Vortex scope, which he now leveled at the enemy.

Through the optic, Tyler could see that the men behind the cars in the cul-de-sac were about to start a flanking maneuver to surround the distant deputies.

"We gotta move up to the Expedition," he screamed over to Johnson, his ears ringing from the gunfire. "They're about to flank the Deputies' SUV!"

He didn't wait for Johnson to grunt in reply; Tyler just ran forward and slammed his body into the mangled hood of the Expedition. He felt Johnson slam into the rear quarter panel. Looking through his scope, Tyler began to settle his crosshairs on the lone

144

female, who was firing an Uzi over the hood of the Pontiac. He was starting to pull back on the trigger when movement caught his eye.

The Norseman Consulting sniper team had a police scanner in their Toyota SUV, so they knew that the law enforcement officers engaged in the cul-de-sac gun battle were not going to be getting reinforcements for several minutes. A short conference between the three men, armed only with pistols, concluded that while they wouldn't be much help against assault rifles, they couldn't just sit there and do nothing.

Steve had punched the accelerator of the SUV and worked his way around the block so he could approach the cul-de-sac from the same direction as the sheriff's department SUV had. The Toyota 4Runner came to a sliding halt right next to the sheriff's deputies.

Careful not to approach the deputies with their pistols out, the Norseman Consulting contractors dove out of their vehicle, screaming "FRIENDLY." As soon as the panic-stricken deputies realized that they had some sort of backup, Chris slid over to the wounded deputy and began assessing him.

"This guy's gonna be fine!" Chris shouted over the din. "But I need to get him into the 4Runner and out of here so I can pack the wound!" Rounds were impacting the 4Runner now with loud pops.
Evan was crouched next to Swanson, shouting in his ear. "We're with Norseman!"

Deputy Swanson's eyes went wide, he had graduated from the Norseman training program some weeks prior, but he did not recognize these three.

"We're here to help, but you need to let your guys know that we're on your side!" Evan was pointing back at Johnson and Tyler, who had set up on the wrecked Expedition only moments before.

With a nod, Swanson raised his radio and relayed the message. "Hey, they're flanking us!" Steve was crouched behind the engine block of the Toyota with his red-dot equipped CZ P-09 pistol drawn. Evan and Chris drew their own guns and prepared to engage targets.

Tyler settled back into the scope of his rifle, eyeing the cars barricading the cul-de-sac. A radio call had come through letting him know that the new arrivals were Norseman contractors and there to help. Now he and Johnson had to prevent them from being overrun.

There were still eight targets down the street, and Tyler was on pretty much the same elevation as them, so when the thugs dropped behind cover, he could not see them. He dialed the magnification on his scope back slightly to give himself a better field of view and found his first target.

Two men had left the cover of their vehicle, moving at a quick, crouched trot towards the two friendly SUVs, and the remaining six had started pouring bullets into the sheriff's SUV and the 4Runner to cover their compatriots' advance. Tyler quickly settled his crosshairs on the upper chest of one of the two men, and depressed the trigger four times in rapid succession, his custom rifle barely recoiling as he did so.

All four of the rounds struck the man high in his chest, dropping him to the pavement in a splash of blood. Tyler transitioned his aim to the second man, but Johnson's rifle barked next to him, and the second man fell to the pavement.

There was a brief lull in the firefight as the six remaining terrorists in the cul-de-sac tried to figure out what had just happened. Tyler was scanning for a new target through his rifle scope when he noticed the second man who'd been shot was trying to sit up. The deputy swiveled his rifle to get a bead on the wounded man, but a sharp gunshot rang out as the Norseman Contractor behind the 4Runner sent a well-aimed 9mm hollow point through the center of the man's forehead.

Tyler shouted to his partner, "Hey Johnson, you good over there?"

"My head hurts," the older deputy shouted, "but I can still see and shoot."

"Roger that," Tyler responded, focusing his attention on the brown hair that was barely poking out over the top of the dusty Pontiac. The deputy dialed up the magnification and settled his crosshairs just above the Pontiac's hood on the crown of the woman's head and squeezed the trigger.

"What the fuck just happened?" Liz screamed. Two RIF members had just been gunned down in the street. John was still crouched behind the Nissan's engine block and was inserting a fresh magazine into his AK74SU. The Chechen had burned through three magazines firing in full-automatic and was down to his last two magazines. Two of the other three Chechens, armed with identical assault rifles, were down to their last two magazines as well, and the third had cast his rifle aside and was left with only his pistol and two spare magazines.

"There are two cops up the block as well," John said, "and three more just showed up."

"They just executed him," Liz snarled, pointing vaguely in the direction of the second RIF member who had been killed. "Fuckin' pigs. He was wounded and down and they just executed him."

"Liz, we need to focus," Conor's voice cracked as he spoke. Conor was checking the magazine of his Romanian under-folding AKM. It was about half full, so he swapped it for the last full magazine in his jacket pocket and put the partially empty one in the back pocket of his jeans.

"Do we rush them?" Liz asked, still crouched behind her Pontiac.

"No," John bellowed. "We bound out of here."

The three other Chechens nodded their understanding, but Conor and Liz just stared at him blankly, neither one of them knew what he meant by "bound."

"You two and Gregor," John pointed at Liz, Conor, and the closest Chechen to Liz, "will start running when we start shooting. When Gregor turns around to shoot, you will turn around and shoot at the cops. While you shoot, the rest of us will run past you, and then turn around to cover you while you run past us."

The Chechen looked down the line at the remainder of his force.

"Everybody good?"

"Yeah," Liz said, shifting her footing and peaking over the Pontiac to get a look at the cops down the street. "I'm ready whe—"

A single rifle shot rang out, and Conor watched in horror as the back of Liz's head exploded outward, staining the frigid pavement a deep red.

"Holy shit!" Conor screamed. He could hear the Chechen crouching next to her cursing as her body twitched on the frozen ground.

John didn't look bothered by this at all. Conor knew that all of the Chechen mercenaries crouched behind vehicles in the cul-de-sac had experienced combat more intense than this, but he had not, and he was losing his mind. He was sure that they were all going to die, and the Chechens all appeared certain they would manage to get out alive.

"Same plan!" the Chechen leader shouted, and he raised his short rifle just above the hood of the Nissan and started firing steady shots in the direction of the SUV with the sniper. Two of the other Chechens mimicked their leader's movements, firing single shots at the three vehicles to keep the sheriff's deputies pinned down.

As the three Chechens fired at their attackers, Gregor and Conor sprang to their feet and started sprinting away from their cars and towards the nearby woods, with Gregor slightly ahead of Conor. Once they had made it about twenty yards from the barricade of vehicles, Gregor stopped, took a knee, and began firing in the direction they had come from. Conor mimicked his movements as best as he could, dropping to a knee and aiming his rifle toward the totaled Expedition up the street.

The three Chechens still at the barricade turned and ran toward Gregor and Conor, but their running path blocked the fire from the two men, and the volume of fire going toward the sheriff's deputies slackened to nothing.

Evan took advantage of this reduction in fire and leaned out from behind the sheriff's department SUV, firing eight rounds from his 9mm Wilson Combat X9. Taking their cue from Evan, Steve and Swanson also leveled their handguns at the retreating terrorists. Chris used the opportunity to help the wounded deputy and hustle behind the wheel well of the 4Runner so that he could use the onboard medical kit to start patching up the wound in the deputy's calf.

Conor heard the gunfire, and one of the Chechens grunted and fell face first onto the ground, his AK74SU clattering across the pavement. The man did not stir, so Conor started firing over the body at the men behind the vehicles. Gregor was doing the same, and the men behind the vehicles had ducked back to cover.

Conor looked to Gregor, waiting for him to tell him to run, when several rapid rifle shots impacted around Gregor, striking him in the chest, arms, and legs. The man cried out in pain, but Conor did not wait to see if he was okay; he jumped up and ran to join the rest of the Chechens behind him.

Deputy Johnson had just emptied the rest of his magazine at one of the men down the street, dropping the man onto the ground. He'd resumed cover behind the Expedition and was fishing a spare magazine out of the chest rig he had haphazardly thrown over his neck. Tyler was behind the front wheel well of the Expedition, but the covering fire had started to impact around him, making it impossible for him to get accurate shots off with his carbine.

"They're bounding to the forest," Johnson said as he pressed the bolt release on his rifle, sending the bolt forward and chambering a fresh round. There was a large, undeveloped area directly behind the cul-de-sac overgrown with tall marsh grass and trees. If the terrorists managed to make it into the brush, it would be much more dangerous to hunt them down.

Tyler poked his head over the hood of the car. The terrorists had focused their attention on the two closer SUVs, so he had an opportunity to get set up on the hood again. He could hear sirens approaching, but they wouldn't arrive in time to prevent the terrorists from escaping. Taking a deep breath, the deputy lined up his crosshairs on the man closest to the forest and started squeezing the trigger.

His first shots missed. His heart pumping and heavy breathing caused the crosshairs to jump around, but he steadied his aim, and placed three rounds at the base of the man's neck, dropping him dead into the snow. Tyler shifted his aim to the next furthest man, who had his back to him and was running full speed away towards the trees. Four well-placed shots in the center of his back sent him tumbling.

A terrorist in a bright red watch cap was running away, too, limping as he went, but a flurry of shots from Johnson and the men down by the SUVs intercepted him, and he spun into the ground.

Tyler lined up his crosshairs on the last man and recognized their person of interest, Conor Johnsen. Tyler gave him just the slightest amount of lead, and depressed the trigger twice in rapid succession, blowing two rounds through the back of the gang-leader's skull, ending his life in an instant.

Cory Penderson had been in the corner bedroom of his two-story house cleaning his camera equipment on the afternoon he was supposed to be working on a group project at school. He was renting the house with a few of his classmates at the local community college, and he was the only one of the group to be stuck at home due to a case of the flu. When he saw the big, black SUV park directly under his window, and the cops pull out a shotgun, he knew something good was about to go down, so he hastily assembled his camera equipment and began shooting video and pictures.

A student in the law-enforcement program, Cory knew an unmarked cop car when he saw one, and he wanted to record what he saw as much for his own education as for notoriety with his amateur photography and videography blog.

The two windows to his room—one pointed straight out over the top of the unmarked cop car, and the other down the street toward the undeveloped cul-de-sac—gave him a prime view of the events that unfolded. Within minutes of reinforcements arriving, Cory Penderson had uploaded untouched, raw footage and pictures of the event to his blog and shared it on every social media page he could think of.

CHAPTER TWENTY-EIGHT

Sheriff Erikson's head hurt. He had been monitoring to the radio calls as the vicious gunfight in the cul-de-sac transpired, and he had been confined to the DCSO headquarters coordinating the response efforts. The deputies he had sent as backup had arrived after the gunplay was over, and he now had two Alexandria police officers dead, one deputy wounded, ten suspects killed, and three Norseman contractors in the office for questioning and debriefing.

The sheriff suspected his headache was a combination of stress, dehydration, and caffeine overload, but the migraine that had been percolating in his head was not made any better by the video the Penderson kid had posted online. From that video, the Norseman Consulting contractors had been identified through crowdsourced investigative work, and within mere hours, the men's current employer had been identified.

Almost immediately after the revelation of Norseman Consulting's involvement in the shooting, Mayor Stark had jumped in front of a camera. While Erikson had anticipated this, he had not expected that she would accuse him of being the one to hire Norseman Consulting, nor that she would outright ignore the fact that the contractors had assisted the law enforcement officers while they were under fire.

Stark had dragged the deputies through the mud and had accused the sheriff's department supplementing their forces with mercenaries who were, as the media represented them, jackbooted thugs. Erikson himself was under fire for allowing his deputies to use lethal force against the gangsters that had opened fire on them with fully automatic weapons after killing two police officers. It was the same asinine questioning that Erikson had seen follow every high-profile law enforcement shooting throughout his career.

Big news outlets had already started clipping and editing the original Penderson video footage in ways that made their agenda more potent. Many of them were replaying the few seconds of the Norseman Contractor, Steve, shooting the wounded gangster as he tried to get back up off the pavement. Another favorite clip showed Tyler behind his scoped AR-15 firing controlled shots into the thugs as they got up to run away.

Wounded or running away, the Chechens and the RIF gangsters were still active threats. It was a good shoot, no question about it. His deputies had performed admirably under stress, and he was proud of the way they handled themselves. From the accounts of the deputies on the ground, and after reviewing the full video, Erikson could tell that the Norseman contractors had performed admirably and—moreover—legally. They were all licensed to carry firearms on their person, and they came to the aid of people in imminent danger.

So, Erikson found himself standing in his office, staring incredulously at the TV with a throbbing headache and building rage.

The sudden ringing of his desk phone snapped the sheriff out of his mental diatribe, and he snatched the receiver up forcefully.

"Erikson," the sheriff grunted angrily into the phone.
The deputy in charge of debriefing the Norseman contractors was on the other end of the line. "Sir, we are done debriefing the Norseman guys, what should we do?"

"Give them their guns back and let them go," Erikson rubbed his eyes. Both were a bit more dry than usual today.

"Roger that."

Erikson put his phone back on the cradle and checked his watch. It was well after quitting time, and he could barely see straight. Blowing out a deep sigh, the sheriff stood up and walked out the door. "I'm going home," he said to nobody in particular.

A half hour later, Erikson was slugging down a glass of water in the kitchen while Ellen watched him nervously. Ellen watched him as he refilled his glass, unscrewed the top of a pill bottle, and drained a second glass of water to wash down the anti-migraine pills that he hoped would cut his headache down to a more manageable level before he went to bed.

The violence had rattled her, but not nearly as much as seeing her husband's name and department being lambasted in the media. She knew her husband, knew that he wasn't running his sheriff's office as a paramilitary unit. Gerry had told Ellen about the Norseman Consulting contractors performing raids, and she knew that the sheriff had labored over the decision to let them operate unimpeded, much less to provide aid to their operations.

In her mind, it appeared as if Gerry had made the right decision. If these terrorists were going to be shooting up cops and civilians alike with assault rifles, the sheriff's office needed all the help they could get, and it didn't exactly look like the state, or federal governments were stepping up.

Ellen knew her husband well, so she watched without saying a word as he stewed and raged inside. Ellen knew that Gerry was angry about the terrible things the news was saying about his deputies, and about the two police officers who had been killed.

At dinner, they ate quietly. Ellen sat close to him, one hand on Gerry's knee while they ate. After a few bites of chicken and vegetables, Gerry put his hand on Ellen's and squeezed it gently. She smiled at him, and he smiled back, but still, no words were spoken.

After supper, they cleaned the dishes together silently, washing them by hand in the sink and standing so close that their hips were touching. They sat down on the living room couch together with separate books and began reading. Ellen placed her feet in Gerry's lap, and he put his hand on her calf. They sat there; the only noise was the occasional rustle of paper as a page turned.

As they were brushing their teeth later, side-by-side over the vanity sink, Gerry turned to his wife.

"Thank you, Ellie."

She merely smiled at him, her toothbrush protruding out of her foaming mouth. She brushed a few more times before spitting into the sink.

"Of course, Gerry." Ellen Erikson looked at her husband, conveying love and support from her soft, brown eyes.

"It has been a hell of a couple days." His head dipped wearily.

"Yes, it has," a gentle, guiding hand nudged him towards the bedroom. They climbed into bed, and Ellen snuggled into the crook of Gerry's arm.

A few minutes passed before Ellen spoke again. "I'm worried, Gerry."

He shifted slightly to look at her. "What are you worried about, darling?"

Ellen hesitated for a moment, wondering if she should trouble her already heavily burdened husband. "Well," she said slowly, "they were using your name in the news as if you were responsible for Gunderson and his men starting their operations here."

"I'll be fine, Ellie," Gerry squeezed her slightly. "Don't worry about me."

Ellen couldn't help worrying, but she did just stroked his arm in response.

A few minutes later, Gerry's exhaustion caught up to him, and his wife felt him slip into sleep. She did not sleep, instead, lay awake for hours just listening to her husband's breath.

"How did this happen?!" Omid Mokri was in another rage, re-watching the video of the shootout for what must have been the hundredth time. The question was not directed toward anyone in particular, but Javad and one of the Iranian special operators were the only other ones in the room. The operation was falling apart, and Javad knew that Mokri was about to become unhinged.

Losing the five Chechens in the cul-de-sac had been unfortunate enough but losing the local gang leaders was likely to be catastrophic in terms of securing manpower. The Chechens had not been too terribly important, and there were still two dozen of them, and another dozen Syrians camped out in the floor below. If the local RIF gang members tried to walk, they would have to rein them in somehow, and Javad figured that money alone wasn't going to cut it anymore.

For the time being, Javad needed to provide his frazzled boss with a viable option for striking back at the Americans. He'd been working up targeting packages ever since they'd identified their enemy as Norseman Consulting.

Javad could feel the IRGC sergeant, a hatchet-faced man named Hakimi, shooting furtive glances his way. The two of them had been working on setting up two targeting packages all afternoon while the rest of the VAJA operatives had been scrambling to keep their RIF contacts from bailing on the mission.

One of the targeting packages was relatively simple and would even be considered a legitimate target by military standards. The second package targeted a civilian woman and was distasteful, to say the least, and also though Javad wanted to avoid it, he knew that Mokri would latch onto it and would not let go.

"Sir," Javad began cautiously, hoping to steer the conversation in a direction that he was comfortable with. "The mayor is performing her role admirably and has gotten the American media to turn against Erikson and the Douglas County Sheriff's Office."

Mokri merely snorted at him. "What are we doing about this, Javad?" He gestured angrily at the video running on the computer screen in front of him.

"Well," Javad sighed and set the two packages on Mokri's crate-desk. "We have put together two kinetic options for retaliation, both of which would also further our mission here."

The VAJA commander snatched the two folders off his desk and began reading. Mokri had picked up the more legitimate operation first and was quickly scanning through the documents that Javad had printed with the help of Sergeant Hakimi. Mokri's eyes were narrowed, but Javad could still see that they were frantic and darted rapidly around the page.

"Good," the senior Iranian grunted before picking up the next folder. It took him only a few seconds, this targeting package was much smaller than the first, and Mokri grinned as he finished reading through it. "Do this one first," Mokri announced, holding up the other folder. "Then this one," holding up the first folder.

"Very well, sir," Javad said, leaning forward to pick up the folders.

"And," Mokri motioned back to his computer monitor, "find out who took this video, and kill him."

Javad and Sergeant Hakimi nodded their confirmation, then turned to make their preparations. The two men had conducted military and paramilitary operations all over the globe, and they had both worked with some crazy leaders. They'd both seen guys like Mokri before, and each knew what the other was thinking.

If Mokri got any further out of hand, Mokri was going to have to go.

CHAPTER TWENTY-NINE

The next morning dawned cold, crisp, and bright. Ellen Erikson had kissed her husband goodbye and settled in to do some of her own work from their third bedroom turned home office. Her position as a teacher with the local community college afforded her a lot of flexibility, and this morning she was working on grading discussion posts for one of her many online classes.

Ellen's mind was not entirely focused on the sometimes-meandering posts, and she often found herself having to refocus after her attention wandered off to Gerry. The two of them still hadn't talked much about the cul-de-sac gunfight, and the sheriff had left the house this morning looking distracted and angry.

Ellie believed that her husband could handle just about anything that was thrown at him, but she worried that it was only a matter of time before the stress of his job overpowered her ability to support him.

When she'd made it through her first section of discussion posts, Ellen leaned back in her desk chair, stretching to relieve the kink in her neck. In the middle of her deep stretch, the doorbell rang, startling her. Pulling up the home security system that Gerry had installed just after moving into their house, she was confronted by two men in suits standing on the front porch. The camera angle was overhead so she could not see the two men's faces under their knit watch caps, and although they were both wearing suits, there was something about the way the suits fit and the way the men carried themselves that made Ellen faintly suspicious.

The one on the right reached forward to ring the doorbell one more time, and Ellen hauled herself out of her chair, deciding to answer the door cautiously. She padded down the hall in her socks and sweats, praying the men would turn away after she asked them to leave.

Opening the door a crack, Ellen greeted the two men pleasantly. "How can I help you?" She remained mostly hidden behind the large front door. Ellen was not expecting any visitors, but the video camera had led her to wonder if they were detectives or state cops.

Up close with the men, she was definitely not getting a good vibe. Both men looked stern, surly even, and one of them had a thin, scraggly beard. Every instinct she had was telling her to back away from the door and call the police, but the clean-shaven man on the right, the one who had rang the doorbell, gave her a reassuring smile.

"Mrs. Erikson?"

"Yes?"

"We are with the Minnesota State Police," the man gestured to his partner, "and we wanted to know if your husband was around to answer some questions."

Now her instincts were screaming at her. Why would the state cops come to their front door, in the middle of the day, and not go straight to Gerry's office?

"No, he's not here, he's at the office," Ellen responded firmly, trying to suppress the fear that was building inside her throat.

"I see," the clean-shaven man said calmly while reaching into his pocket with his left hand. "Well can I leave a card with you and you can tell him we are on our way to see him?"

Ellen nodded, watching the man's hand as he drew it from his pocket, holding a simple white business card. As he stretched out his arm, the poor fitting suit slipped up, revealing a tattoo on his forearm. Ellen's eyes immediately went wide, the letters RIF tattooed in bold letters across the man's wrist.

She froze for a fraction of a second, then tried to slam the door closed, but the bearded man let out a yell and slammed his body into the door. The door knocked Ellen back into the foyer, but she managed to keep her balance and took off toward the bedroom.

Ellen had left her phone charging on the nightstand. She hoped to get to the bedroom and lock herself in, call 9-1-1 and, more importantly, arm herself with the old 12 Gauge Winchester shotgun that she had stashed in the bedroom.

The two men were hot on her heels, so she dove into the carpeted bedroom. Ellen didn't even try for the phone or the lock, reaching instead under the bed and grabbing hold of the shotgun, bringing it to bear as the clean-shaven man dove to tackle her.

She was not able to get a round off, and he was on top of her, trying to wrestle the shotgun from her. Ellen screamed, biting and kicking the man, and held onto her gun for dear life. She managed to grab hold of the man's nose with her front teeth, causing him to scream out in agony and back off just a bit.

It was just enough space for Ellen to swing the butt of her shotgun hard into the man's skull, throwing him backward. That strike gave her enough room to point her rifle at him and pull the trigger.

Ellen's quick shot had been true, and the low-recoil buckshot had blasted through the clean-shaven man's stomach, leaving him convulsing on the floor in a gory puddle.

But the bearded man tackled her, screaming at her in a foreign language, and attempting to wrestle the shotgun away from her. Mrs. Erikson punched and kicked at the foreign man, trying desperately to get away, but he was much stronger than she was. Despite the man's strength advantage, Ellen managed to land many vicious kicks to the stomach and groin of her assailant, howling like a madwoman the whole time.

Finally overpowering her, the bearded man threw the shotgun to the side and rammed a stun gun into the base of Ellen's neck, shocking her into submission. Still muttering curses, the bearded man grabbed the now stunned Ellen and jabbed a syringe into her throat. Ellen felt a warm sensation wash over her. She could no longer control her arms and legs. Her vision grew blurry, and she felt her attacker grab her by the hair and begin dragging her out of the house.

It wasn't even 10:00 in the morning yet, and Sheriff Erikson was already about to lose his mind. He had called the mayor's office only to be told that she was in a meeting and would call him back later. Erikson knew she was in the office and he knew she was blowing him off. The various state and national media were still running clips of the Penderson kid's video, and the little asshole had actually given an interview to the local television station that had been picked up and was running nationwide.

At least the media outlets were now reporting that the two police officers had been killed and that some foreign terrorists had been the ones to start the shooting. Self-alleged "experts," were spouting off about what had been done right or wrong in this case. A whole lot of them were placing the blame for the killings directly on Sheriff Erikson's shoulders, claiming that the DCSO and APD officers acted rashly, spooking the terrorists and causing the shooting to start.

They were finally reporting on the Broadway Massacre on a national scale now too, and that had somehow become his fault as well. One network even broke the story that one of the gunmen from the Broadway attack was still in a medically induced coma at the county hospital, and under heavy guard.

158

One of his deputies had reported that the networks' cameramen had actually tried to force their way into the hospital ward to get a shot of the unconscious man, only to be foiled by the deputy and two particularly passionate nurses.

What a godawful mess, Erikson thought. The internal investigation of the cul-de-sac shooting had, of course, cleared his deputies of any wrongdoing, and had even gone so far to say that the Norseman contractors had been "invaluable" in ensuring the deputies' survival. Erikson made a mental note to make sure that the deputies, especially Tyler, who the report claimed had the most significant impact on turning the tide against the terrorists, were awarded commendations for their actions.

Erikson looked back up at his television screen and flipped it to the weather to see what the projected snowfall was for the rest of the week. As he studied the projected frigid, snowless temperatures with a slight frown, his personal cell phone rang. Checking the caller ID, he saw Ellen's profile picture grinning back at him, and tapped the answer button before bringing the phone to his ear.

"Hi, Ellie," the sheriff answered, trying to sound upbeat. He knew that his sullenness the previous night could not have been easy on her.

"Listen carefully, Sheriff." The voice on the other end of the phone made his blood run cold.

"Who is this?" Erikson demanded forcefully, even though his heart had leapt into his throat and he could hardly breathe.

"We have your wife, Sheriff," the voice hissed through the phone. "We will call you in twenty-four hours with our demands."

"Who the fuck is this?!" Erikson screamed into the phone. "Where is my wife?!"

"Twenty-four hours, Sheriff."

There was a brief scuffling sound on the phone, and Erikson's throat tightened as he heard the panicked whimpering of his wife softly register over the phone.

"G-Gerry, help me." Ellen's voice was soft, pained.

"I'm coming, baby." Erikson had tears streaming down his face. "You're gonna be okay."

"Twenty. Four. Hours." The hissing, accented voice was back, and the call clicked off before Erikson could respond.

Erikson was running on autopilot now. He was only vaguely aware of the concerned and frightened looks from his deputies as he burst out of his office and ran down the stairs. He was only vaguely aware of scrambling to his patrol SUV. He snapped out of his stupor as he drove, tires sliding over the icy road and into his driveway.

The sheriff leaped out of his vehicle, drawing his Glock 21 service pistol as he neared the front door. The door was closed, but not locked like it should have been. Erikson didn't waste any momentum thinking about it and simply pushed through, his instincts and his emotions screaming at him, grappling for control of his actions.

As he crossed the threshold, Erikson saw an extensive blood trail leading out of the bedroom. A muffled snarl left his lips, and he flew into the bedroom, not stopping to check any of the rooms in the hallway.

The room was empty except for small specks of blood on the floor near the bed and, on the wall near the master bathroom, a massive splash of blood and gore that slid over a hole punched in the drywall and down to the floor. A single spent shotgun shell was near the foot of the bed.

Seeing the shell pulled Erikson's instincts back into control. He was able to rationalize that Ellen would not have been able to talk to him after losing so much blood and that the shotgun blast was probably one that she had dealt to her attackers.

Good girl, Ellie. The rational part of his brain was coming back, and he knew that if he wanted to find her, he was going to have to act quickly. Erikson holstered his pistol and was in the act of pulling out his phone from his pocket when he heard a series of car doors slam. Moving to the window, Erikson parted the blinds to find two sedans had pulled into his driveway, and four men were moving cautiously towards his house, AK74SU assault rifles tucked into their shoulders at the "low-ready" position.

Shit. Erikson was armed with only his pistol. His hunting shotgun was unloaded and in the safe in his closet, and his patrol rifle was locked in the brace of his SUV.

Think, Gerry. Erikson drew his pistol, taking a step back from the window. As he let the blinds drop back into place, he heard the men shouting outside in accented English.

Dammit.

160

An idea sprang to his mind, and he rushed into the bathroom. He threw open the window even as he heard the first man come running up the steps to the front door that Erikson had left open. Climbing awkwardly out the barely large enough window, Erikson sprinted to the shed in his backyard, opening the door and slipping inside before anyone saw him.

Fumbling around in the dim light of the shed, Erikson grabbed hold of the fabric draped over his Arctic Cat snowmobile and carefully drew the tarp off of the machine. He'd always left the keys in the ignition, and he'd always backed the snowmobile into the shed, and now he was glad for it. The sheriff mounted the machine and carefully placed his pistol on the dashboard behind the wind visor. He turned the key. The snowmobile cranked but did not turn over.

The sound of the engine turning must have alerted his attackers because he heard one of them shout and the whole group went quiet. "Come on, come on!" Erikson primed the engine again and then turned the key.

This time, the engine caught and roared to life. Erikson goosed the throttle and crashed through the thin shed door. He came roaring out of the shed, shattered pieces of the door smacking him in the chest and face and came face to face with one of the attackers who had been getting closer to the shed.

Erikson turned sharply, and the man lifted his arms to protect himself from the speeding snowmobile. The other three attackers were standing on the back porch, and all raised their assault rifles and fired.

One of the first rounds impacted the mirror sticking out of the side of the snowmobile, causing the mirror to shatter and Erikson to duck. The rest of the bullets went high and away into the woods as Erikson gassed his snowmobile to full throttle and went speeding off into the frosty morning towards the Norseman Consulting compound.

CHAPTER THIRTY

"Did they make any demands?" Norseman Consulting's chief of intelligence operations, Ajay Yale was quizzing Erikson on the events that had transpired in the moments prior to his arrival at the compound's front gate.

"No, they said they would call back in twenty-four hours," Sheriff Gerry Erikson had not lifted his head from his hands for the past several minutes.

"And they called you from your wife's phone?"

"Yes." Erikson lifted his head, his eyes red-rimmed from a combination of sorrow and rage. "They said they would call back on her phone."

Yale shot a glance over to the technical expert who was hooking the sheriff's phone up to a machine to pull off all the data he could. The technician looked up and flipped Yale a thumbs up.

"Okay, Sheriff," Yale leaned forward off of the desk he had been sitting on. "Damon here is going to pull as much information as he can off your phone, hopefully he can figure out where Ellen is."

Erikson merely looked up at Yale and nodded blankly. The look spooked Yale. The anguish in the sheriff's eyes was beginning to dissipate into full-blown rage. Yale had seen the look before and knew that it was almost never followed by rational, productive behavior. Hoping to pull enough information from the sheriff before he shut down, Yale sat down next to him on the couch.

"Alright, Gerry," Yale produced a pen and pad of paper. "Walk me through what happened from the time you left your house this morning to the time you arrived here."

As Erikson began to walk through the events of the morning, Gunderson and Dufraine walked into Yale's office with Alex, the Axe assault team leader. The three men were there to listen to Erikson's account.

Yale's office had much of the seating taken over by map printouts and other technical data, so they stood silently and scrutinized every detail of Erikson's story. The sheriff's expression grew harder as he recounted discovering the blood and gore inside his home, and his suspicion that his wife had managed to kill one of the kidnappers with her old Winchester.

"Well, Sheriff," Gunderson said softly after Erikson finished his story, "my men are dropping everything to work on this. We'll find her."

"Thank you," Erikson's expression was intense, but his eyes were still red, and his voice was a mere croak.

"In the meantime, why don't you bunk here to wait for the next phone call?" Gunderson offered. "We have some extra rooms available, and that way we'll be able to monitor the phone."

Erikson nodded. He couldn't go back home, and he had nowhere else to go.

Dufraine showed Erikson to a room just around the corner, a converted office that Yale maintained as a bunk room for Brain personnel who stayed too late into the night. Norseman Consulting's operations chief made sure that Erikson had fresh sheets and a toiletry set and showed him where he could shower. The sheriff was silent, grunting or nodding to indicate that he understood.

"Sheriff, there is one more thing," Dufraine said awkwardly. "I hate to do it, but I have to ask you to turn over your service weapon." He fidgeted. "It's just a safety precaution. Company policy, you see."

The sheriff simply nodded and unbuckled his gun belt, turning the entire ensemble over to Dufraine.

"Thank you," Dufraine said, his expression a mixture of discomfort and relief that the sheriff had not argued about handing over his weapon. "Try to get some sleep."

With that, Dufraine closed the door and left the sheriff sitting on the bed, staring numbly at the floor.

"What's next?" Alex asked Dufraine as he reentered Yale's office.

"Well, once Damon can tell us where they're calling from, we can dispatch your team to roll them up and hopefully get Mrs. Erikson back," Dufraine responded.

"We'll go back to our list of safe houses and see if any of them are more likely than others," Gunderson suggested, "but I don't think we'll get much out of them. A lot of the houses were vacated after we snatched up Khorasani."

"Worth a try," Alex nodded. "I'll have Ted get the team spun up."

"I'm going to tell Randall to get Sword spun up on standby as well," Dufraine said. "We'll keep them in reserve in case we need to hit multiple houses at once."

Gunderson was standing quietly at the side and appeared to be deep in thought. Yale was busy queuing up maps and dossiers showing which safe houses they believed to still be active. Dufraine and Alex contacted their assault teams to begin preparing for raids at yet to be determined locations.

"Yale," Gunderson finally spoke, "turn on the television. I want us to monitor the local chatter. The gunfire could not have gone unnoticed in the neighborhood where the Eriksons live."

Yale flicked the remote toward the television, and the muted receiver flashed to life, several different news channels displayed in the split-screen configuration. None of the channels showed anything about the Eriksons, so Gunderson and his team turned towards the maps and began their analysis.

A few hours went by and the Norseman Consulting team was still checking maps and making preparations when Erikson appeared in the frame of the open office door.

"What do you guys have to eat around here?" His voice betrayed his stress.

"That's a good question." Gunderson rubbed his chin thoughtfully. "I'll get some food sent down."

"Thanks," Erikson made as if to leave the men to their task, then paused as his eyes scanned the materials on the table. "Have there been any developments?"

"None so far, Sheriff," Yale said soothingly. "We'll let you know as soon as we know anything."

But Erikson wasn't really listening. He was looking around the room at the maps that were displayed on monitors and spread out on the coffee table and desk.

"Where do you think they took her?"

Yale looked down at the map on his desk. "We would expect them to have moved her somewhere close to your home. Travelling too far at once with a kidnap victim can be risky."

"Aren't these safe houses empty?" Erikson was pointing at the three safe houses closest to his home, all of which had been surveilled by his deputies during their patrols of the area.

"Yes, they are," Gunderson affirmed. "So, we're thinking that they were forced to move her closer to the center of their operation in the industrial housing area."

"What about the homes of the RIF members working with these guys?" Erikson offered.

The Norseman Consulting team looked at one another before Yale responded, "We had been figuring that they wouldn't want to bring her to their actual house, but I guess if one of them lives close it might make sense for them to stage there."

Yale sat back behind his computer and started quickly navigating through his files, searching for the folder containing the dossiers of known RIF members.

"Well, shit," Yale said. "There were three guys who lived relatively close to the sheriff. Only one of them is still active though."

"How do you know the other two are not still active?" Gunderson asked.

Yale spun his monitor around and indicated two dossiers. "Because the good sheriff's deputies greased these two in the cul-de-sac."

"My money is on one of these three houses then," Gunderson said. "We can't rule out the deceased's houses since the vacancy would make for less interference."

Dufraine's voice broke in. His attention was glued to the television screen displaying the news. "Ajay, can you unmute the lower right and make it full screen?"

As everyone in the room turned their attention to the screen, Gerry Erikson's face turned white. A picture of Ellen was displayed with the subtitle "MISSING, PRESUMED DEAD" in bold letters underneath.

"—ocal sources say that several rounds of gunfire were heard from the Erikson residence, and when authorities arrived, there was no sign of either Gerry Erikson or his wife, Ellen. City officials have informed us that Ellen Erikson is presumed dead, and that Gerry Erikson is wanted in connection with the disappearance. He is considered armed, trained, and extremely dangerous."

A picture of Erikson popped up on the screen, his department photo from the sheriff's office, with a bold subtext: "WANTED – EXTREMELY DANGEROUS."

All eyes turned to Erikson, whose face was turning crimson with rage.

"What the FUCK?!"

CHAPTER THIRTY-ONE

It had taken the combined efforts of the Norseman Consulting contractors in the room to calm Sheriff Erikson down. The press release labeling him as his wife's suspected killer had sent the sheriff into a blind rage, and he was halfway out the door before Dufraine had managed to grab his shoulder. Erikson had shaken Dufraine off and continued for the door, hell bent on setting the record straight. The rest of the Norseman team had managed to grab Erikson by the waist and pull the distraught man back onto the couch, and Gunderson, Yale, and Dufraine finally filled Sheriff Erikson in on their intelligence surrounding Mayor Stark and her aspirations.

They detailed her contact with the Iranian agent, Khorasani, who had been posing as an Italian investor and political activist before being captured by Norseman Consulting's assault team. They laid out her aspirations and her revolutionary ideology, referred to as a "long march through the institutions of power," which included her plan for becoming as powerful as possible, through any means. Once she had attained a level of power that was acceptable, Mayor Stark was going to start giving the RIF the land they demanded, along with instituting Communist practices throughout her realm. And, most damningly, they showed him the electronic funds transfers into Stark's accounts, money that was supposedly earmarked for election campaign expenses.

Because she couldn't control the sheriff's department, Stark couldn't count on Erikson and his team to fall into line with her plans. Stark needed a total failure of the law enforcement apparatus, one that she could order into existence with the city cops she controlled but she couldn't order the Sheriff's Department around. The Sheriff's Department were supposed to be painted as total buffoons, and the local populace would scream for Erikson to be replaced. The Iranians wanted to undermine the Americans' sense of safety and security to keep them from wanting to re-enter the world's stage. Stark wanted to use the Iranians to erode the trust that the local populace had in the law enforcement so that she could rebuild it with people she hand-selected, people who shared her revolutionary ideologies.

And now Ellie had fallen victim to it all.

Dufraine and Alex helped the sheriff to his feet and guided him gently into the spare room next to Yale's office. He sat down on his borrowed bed, feeling an immense anguish, and could not help but hear the heavy bolt *clunk* into place as Norseman Consulting locked him in his room for the night.

The events of the past few days had been almost too much for Kurt Michaels. First Connor, Liz, and the Chechens were killed in a shootout with the cops, and then their "Italian" handler, Alfonse, shows up with some extra Chechen muscle, announcing that RIF was now under their full control. Anyone who opposed them had the option of walking away.

Two members of RIF had tried to do just that, but Alfonse had his Chechen muscle shoot them as they walked, killing them with suppressed pistol shots to the back of the head. The vicious little man had then turned back to the gathered RIF members and appointed Kurt their new leader. He would report directly to Alfonse.

Kurt's first task was to dispose of the gang members' bodies. The two men had been supplementary muscle from the Minneapolis chapter of RIF, so few of RIF's members felt much obligation to help with the "burial." Kurt had offered his own efforts. A second member volunteered, and together they managed to cut up and parcel out the two corpses, grind them, and then dump them through the holes of an ice fishing house.

The second task bestowed upon Kurt was kidnapping Ellen Erikson. Alfonse had detailed one of his bodyguards, a Syrian mercenary named Farhad, to accompany the kidnapping effort. Alfonse had secured Liz's house. It was closest to the Erikson residence, and now that Liz was being autopsied in the morgue, they knew the house was empty.

The kidnapping team, led by Kurt's friend Eli, with close oversight from the Syrian and three additional RIF members to serve as a driver and lookout team. It was supposed to be easy, but Farhad and the driver had come back with Eli barely clinging to life from the shotgun blast delivered to his abdomen.

"Fucking beetch had shotgun," Farhad grunted as he heaved Eli's limp body onto Liz's kitchen table. One of the RIF members trained as a medic set about trying to save him, but Kurt could already tell from the massive blood trail that Eli wasn't going to make it, and the unfortunate kidnapper had wheezed his last breath even before Farhad dragged the drugged-up Mrs. Erikson through the front door.

There were six RIF members in the house and the two mercenaries that Alfonse left behind. They all stopped for a brief moment to gaze upon the deceased form of Eli, lying in a bloody pool on the table. The Chechen and Syrian mercenaries had little patience for the delay as they continued to bark out orders. Kurt and the rest of the RIF members had a harder time dealing with the death of yet another friend. This operation had gone too far now, and some RIF were starting to grumble about abandoning ship.

Farhad and the Chechen hauled Mrs. Erikson into the attached garage and bound her to a chair borrowed from the kitchen table. The mercenaries reminded Kurt to call Alfonse to report their success. After Alfonse arrived back at Liz's house from his safehouse in the industrial housing area he hurried into the garage where the mercenaries were awaiting his arrival.

Kurt and the rest of the RIF members in the house were ordered to stay out of the garage. Farhad stood outside the door with his short-barreled Kalashnikov to make sure they did. Out of earshot of their foreign overseers, the RIF members under Kurt were starting to whisper ideas of rebellion. All six of them were armed, albeit not nearly as heavily as either the Chechen or Farhad. Some thought that if they moved quickly to overpower and kill Farhad, they could kill Alfonse and the Chechens and get away from the whole operation clean.

As the newly appointed leader of RIF, Kurt was desperately hoping to keep the peace by talking to his RIF underlings. For several hours into the night after kidnapping Mrs. Erikson, he straddled the line between loyalty to his RIF comrades and his fear of the new self-appointed foreign bosses. Kurt knew that even a successful rebellion now would lead to them getting slaughtered later, and he desperately tried to talk to the RIF members gathered in Liz's house out of their mutinous rumblings.

Around midnight, Alfonse emerged from the garage, small flecks of blood still wet on his sleeves. He swaggered up to Kurt, his two guards flanking him with their AK74SU's slung across their chests. For a moment the room where the six RIF members were gathered grew tense, all could see that the foreign mercenaries had their AK selector levers in the "full-automatic" position and their fingers were awfully close to the triggers. Alfonse also had the butt of his Glock subcompact pistol peeking out of a leather inside-the-waistband holster over his half-untucked white dress shirt.

"Come with me Kurt," Alfonse directed. "I have something for you to do."

Kurt swallowed and followed Alfonse into the garage. Kurt had a strong suspicion that "Alfonse" was not the man's real name, and he no longer believed that the man was the Italian communist radical he claimed to be. Even though Alfonse had announced that RIF's operations now fell under the umbrella of VAJA, Kurt's relative ignorance meant that he did not know who or what that was.

What the new leader of RIF did not know was that Alfonse's real name was Hamid Ahmadi, and that he was well known in the murky world of international espionage and terrorism as someone who enjoyed inflicting torture on his victims. Had Kurt known who this man really was, he would not have followed him into the garage. He would have drawn his old Smith & Wesson pistol and tried to kill him on the spot. It was not that Kurt was averse to violence, or even torture. He had delivered his fair share of violence to his enemies before, but he had always considered himself a gentleman, and deliberately harming a defenseless woman was not something he was willing to do.

As it was, he followed Hamid "Alfonse" Ahmadi into the garage and found himself surrounded by the two Chechen mercenaries. After being unceremoniously relieved of the S&W 39 he'd tucked into his beltline, Kurt was handed a hacksaw.

When the call finally came, Gerry Erikson and Norseman Consulting were ready. Damon and Yale had been trying to locate Ellen Erikson's cell phone by triangulating it off of the cell towers in the area, but they surmised that the phone had been disabled immediately after the first call to Gerry. It was evident that they were operating against professionals and not the more disorganized RIF or any of the hired mercenaries.

Ellen Erikson's phone pinged back on just before the twenty-four-hour deadline, and Norseman Consulting's intelligence team immediately started working to locate the phone. Mere seconds after the phone came back online, Gerry's phone started ringing.

"Hello," he answered gruffly.

"Greetings, Sheriff." It was the same voice from the day before, accented and hissing. Gerry gripped the phone with white knuckles. "Noonan's park. Yellow house. One hour."

The phone clicked off.

170

"Did you get it?" Erikson turned to Damon and Yale.

"Yeah," Yale said grimly, "we got it."

"You were right, Gerry," Gunderson said. He was looking over Damon's shoulder at the computer monitor. "They're using one of the vacant RIF houses."

"Let's go then!" Erikson was beside himself; a white-hot energy was coursing through his body. He was done feeling helpless. Gerry Erikson wanted revenge.

"Hang on, Gerry," Dufraine said quickly. "You are going with Sword team to Noonan's park."

"Why?" Erikson demanded.

"Well, they want you to go there, so they must have left something there," Gunderson responded. "Or they might want to meet."

"Hell, they might even just give you your wife back." Dufraine said optimistically, though nobody in the room believed it. "We'll hit the house where the phone is, you go and see what's up at the park."

Thirty minutes later, Erikson was trudging across the frozen park toward the yellow house near the edge of Noonan's Park. During the winter, the park was a popular place for recreation on account of its shallow pond, which always froze through to the bottom. There were always pick-up hockey games or ice skaters of various skill levels. The presence of the locals at the park brought Erikson partially out his blind rage. With them all around, all Erikson could see was potential collateral damage.

The Norseman contractors were scattered across the park, in plain clothes with their body armor and B&T Universal Service Weapons concealed under their coats. The assault team was intermingled with the hockey spectators in the park, pretending to watch the pickup hockey game and Erikson was trying to block all of this out as he picked his way closer and to the yellow house.

He'd had his service weapon returned to him, but he was not wearing his uniform. The Norseman Consulting team had decided that wearing his sheriff's department uniform would only draw attention at a time when anyone who'd been watching the news might think he was a murderer. Instead of his uniform, Gerry was wearing a borrowed pair of jeans and a thick coat and a facemask that covered everything but his eyes. One of the Norseman Consulting contractors had loaned him a concealment holster for his Glock 21, which was now tucked into his waistband.

He was only yards away from the yellow house now, and Gerry rested his hand under his sweatshirt, firmly gripping the butt of his Glock. He felt himself breathing heavily, adrenaline coursing through his bloodstream and the restriction of the body armor causing his breath to exit in rapid clouds of steam. As he approached, he couldn't see any movement in the house. He made a split-second decision and rushed inside the small yellow house.

It was little more than a shack, just the hollow shell of a building that locals had always just referred to as the yellow house and Gerry could tell he was alone. He stood for a minute, looking around. There was nothing in the house. Just a concrete slab under the angled roof. Gerry fished a small LED flashlight out of his pocket and swept it around the floor.

Still nothing.

He could feel a sense of panic rising. His hands were starting to shake as he swept the light upwards along the walls and around the ceiling. He settled on a beam running across the length of the front wall above eye level and just over the front door. A small brown-wrapped box was nestled on the beam in the corner with permanent marker.

To: Sheriff Erikson

His breath coming in short, sharp gasps, Gerry reached up and pulled down the box. He fumbled with the twine that secured the box and ripped into the brown paper wrapping. He could feel something heavy and soft shuddering in the box in rhythm with the trembling of his hands.

The paper fell away, revealing a plain cardboard box. He cracked opened the box and immediately retched, heaving the contents of his relatively empty stomach on the floor.

Randall was monitoring Gerry's movements inside the yellow house while the rest of the Sword assault team circled the park and communicated to each other via radio earpieces tucked under their winter caps. The men were all a bit jumpier than normal, and Randall couldn't blame them. There were civilians all over the park, and they had been unable to identify anyone as a threat, which meant if there *were* any threats, they'd materialize out of nowhere.

"Alright, eyes up," Randall spoke into his radio. "Erikson is in the house."

Randall watched from a distance as Gerry swept a flashlight around the house and eventually reached up and pulled a brown box down from somewhere.

"Okay he found something," Randall broadcast. "Looks like a cardboard box. Fairly small."

The leader of Sword team had a sudden flash of panic as Erikson tore into the box. If he were in that position, he would have assumed the package contained some sort of bomb and left it for the explosive techs. It was too late now to intervene, and they had opted not to give him a radio in case he actually met with someone from the kidnappers. The prevailing thought had been that the kidnappers would spook if they saw him wearing a radio.

"Shit," one of the contractors said over the radio. "Is he really just going to open it? What if it's a bomb?"

All eyes were transfixed on Erikson now, watching him through the small windows and doors to the yellow house as he opened the mysterious package. Randall watched as Erikson dropped the package and started heaving onto the floor.

"Okay collapse on the house," Randall said urgently.

Sword team moved in quickly. Randall arrived within a couple seconds of John, who'd been closest to the house.

"Aw, Christ," John said. His face had taken on a waxy pallor. Randall peered over the man's shoulder. Inside the box was a left hand with a wedding ring, severed at the wrist.

Randall pulled a cell phone out of his pocket and tapped out a call. "Alex, no-joy here. All they left was her hand. Good luck."

With that, Randall slid the phone back into his pocket and directed his team to get Erikson back to the Norseman Consulting compound.

CHAPTER THIRTY-TWO

Alex hung up the cell phone and put it back in the zippered pocket on the front of his plate carrier. He keyed his radio and called, "GO! GO! GO!"

Axe team had been parked a few blocks away from the target house waiting to hear whether Sword team and Erikson were somehow presented with Mrs. Erikson at Noonan's Park. They'd kept their distance to avoid tipping off the thugs inside, and now they drove to within a block of the house before disembarking.

The plan was for the rapid application of brute force. Anyone holding any sort of weapon inside the house was to be considered expendable. Axe team hadn't had enough time or surveillance capability to come up with a more elegant solution, so they went with the age-old K.I.S.S. philosophy: Keep It Simple, Stupid.

Piling out of their vans, the Axe team members rushed smoothly forward in their winter camouflage uniforms, their suppressed carbines up and at the ready. Axe One set up a hasty cordon to cover Axe Two's breach through the front door.

"Axe One, Set!"

Alex and his team had taken their positions, finding limited cover behind cars or in the ditches along the side of the road, their rifles pointing toward the windows of the house.

Axe Two did not respond. As soon as the fireteam was set, Bryan smashed the front door open with a sledgehammer and Elias and Larry tossed flashbangs through the entrance.

There was a deafening *THWUMP* and a blinding flash of light as the two stun grenades detonated within milliseconds of each other.

The assault team piled through the door less than a second later, sweeping their rifles. Ted was first through the door, and he found a RIF member standing in the foyer, blinking and holding his head with both hands. Seeing a small pistol in the man's right hand, Ted shot him three times in the forehead.

Bryan came in behind Ted and turned toward the left. Finding no targets, he continued moving until he was able to cover the far end of the small house. A man carrying a short Kalashnikov rifle came rushing down the hallway. Bryan raised his rifle and depressed the trigger five times, the muffled gunshots reverberating down the hallway

174

and hitting the man high in his chest. He went spinning down with a gurgle.

A short burst erupted past Bryan and he heard a grunt behind him. A target down the hallway was barely leaning around a corner, firing down the narrow passageway. A few of the rounds had struck Carl in the legs and chest.

Joe grabbed Carl and pulled him back to the relative safety of the entryway as the last of Axe Two made it into the house and prepared to clear the structure. Joe started putting tourniquets on both of Carl's legs. After the tourniquets had been clamped down, Joe dragged Carl out of the house and the van to keep him out of the way while Joe worked on his damaged legs and called in the casualty.

Bryan started firing at the target who had shot Carl. The man ducked back behind the corner, but Bryan tracked his rounds through the flimsy walls of the house and was rewarded with a scream of pain and a lull in the gunfire.

Elias used the lull as an opportunity to push forward, and the rest of Axe Two followed him down the hallway. A man with a shotgun jumped out in front of Elias, who fired instinctively, hitting the man in the chest and face. The dead man discharged his shotgun into the floor before crumpling face-first onto the ground.

A woman in a room just off the narrow hallway used the shotgun wielding thug's death as a distraction and leapt out at Elias with a small Beretta pistol. A couple shots hit Elias in the ceramic plates strapped to his chest, and when as he struggled to keep his balance, she tackled him.

The two of them struggled for a moment before Elias gained the upper hand. He ripped the small Beretta from her hand and tossed it back into the room that Bryan was clearing while Larry covered the hallway above the two grappling on the floor.

Elias pushed his left hand into his attacker's forehead to hold her down, used his right hand to draw his Ka-Bar from the small of his back, and slid the knife it into carotid artery at the base of the woman's neck. He twisted sharply before withdrawing the knife. The woman sputtered and her eyes went wide. She was still twitching when Elias sheathed his knife and got up on one knee to signal that he was okay and ready to move forward.

Larry shouldered past Elias, taking his place at the front of the stack. Bryan and Ted followed, putting Elias at the end of the line.

As they neared the corner at the end of the hall, Larry could see that the hallway opened up into a combination living and dining room, and as he rounded the corner, a flurry of pistol shots snapped past his head. Larry dropped the suppressed muzzle of his carbine a few inches and fired through the couch at where he guessed the man's chest and head would be.

A splattering of blood on the wall confirmed his guess. Larry moved cautiously around the couch, stepping over the body of the man who had shot Carl and putting two insurance rounds in his head.

As Larry cleared the room, Bryan prepared to move forward into the last part of the house. Axe Two was almost to the garage, and they still had not found Mrs. Erikson or her phone. The next room was a small kitchen, and it was empty.

"Door," Bryan announced to the other three men remaining in the stack. When the team was set on the door and prepared to push forward, Elias rushed forward and kicked the door in, prompting Bryan to toss a primed flashbang into the garage.

Several of the windows of garage were too thin to withstand the concussion grenade and they shattered. Axe Two pushed forward, Ted leading the way. The inside of the garage was dim, so Ted triggered the flashlight attached to the rail of his rifle. He swept the light across the garage and located his first target, a bearded man standing off to one side holding an AK74SU.

Ted fired five times, the suppressed *cracks* of his 300-Blackout carbine echoing in the confined space of the garage. The man with the Kalashnikov crumpled to the ground as the powerful rounds destroyed his heart, lungs, and spinal column.

A force that felt like a softball careening at a hundred miles an hour smacked into Ted's chest plate. Through the blinding pain, he was vaguely aware of the gunshot report that accompanied the hit, and he swiveled his attention over to the other corner of the garage.

He could see a man with a pistol in his extended arm over someone in a chair. Ted started to lift his rifle, but he didn't need to. A flurry of suppressed shots smashed into the man's face, knocking him down and spilling the contents of his skull across the floor.

Ted kept sweeping his light around, searching for any more targets. A man was kneeling on the ground with his hands in the air. Larry moved forward carefully with Elias covering him, then kicked the man to the ground and fastened his arms behind him with flex cuffs that had been clipped to his plate carrier. Larry roughly searched the man before announcing that he was clear.

"All clear," Ted spoke into his radio.

"Roger, any sign of Mrs. Erikson?" Alex responded over the radio. He'd been busy outside supervising Carl's medical treatment.

Ted strode forward to the woman tied to the chair. Her chin was resting on her chest and it did not appear as if she was breathing. Ted gently lifted her chin.

"We have Mrs. Erikson," Ted said grimly into his radio. "She didn't make it."

A harsh silence fell across the contractors in the room.

"Alright, well," Alex's voice was professional, but everyone could hear the strain in his voice. "Bring her out and let's get out of here."

"Roger, Axe Two exiting with Mrs. Erikson and one prisoner." Ted made a movement with his fist, and Elias hit the garage door opener mounted to the wall next to the door.

Light flooded into the garage. Ted cut Mrs. Erikson's body loose and hoisted her limp form over his shoulder. Larry and Bryan roughly yanked their prisoner off the cold garage floor and forcefully lead him, head down, out to the van.

As they watched Ted carry Ellen Erikson's body out to the van and laid her gently on the floor, the contractors knew that they'd done all they could, but at some level they felt like they'd failed.

"Thank you, Alex," Gunderson said into his phone, his eyes clenched tight while he pinched the bridge of his nose. "Get here as soon as you can. We'll have emergency medical ready to go for Carl."

He hung up his phone and turned to his two partners in the room. "Ellen Erikson is dead. It appears that whoever cut off her hand last night was not so concerned with keeping her alive. Axe team says it appears she bled out sometime last night or this morning."

"Goddammit," Dufraine cursed. Yale merely nodded meekly.

"Carl was shot in the leg," Gunderson added. "They were able to stabilize him at the scene, but they had to exfil quickly, which means they left a house full of dead bodies."

"Well at least he's going to make it," Dufraine blew out a deep sigh. This operation had not gone the way he'd hoped, but it had been thrown together somewhat haphazardly and things certainly could have been worse.

"They also pulled a prisoner off of the target," Gunderson went on, "and Alex thinks he's one of our Iranian friends."

"Why does he think that?" Yale asked.

"Well, the guy apparently won't say anything, but he's a bit darker than the average RIF gangster, and there is one dead Chechen and one dead Syrian in the safe house," Gunderson stated.

"Interesting," Yale mused. "The last Iranian who had been wrapped up with RIF got his brains blown out on the toilet by RIF during that DCSO raid."

"At least we can ask this guy some questions," Gunderson said. "I do wonder why they took him alive, but I guess we'll find out."

"We're running out of room," Dufraine grunted. It was true, Norseman Consulting only had enough room to hold up to five prisoners in separate cells at any given time. With Longoria-Reyes, al Kobani, Khorasani, and this most recent acquisition, they were just about at capacity.

"Let me worry about that," Gunderson dismissed it with a wave of his hand. "We have other things to focus on."

No sooner had the Norseman Consulting president finished speaking than the automated alarm system on all three men's phones started ringing. Looking down at their phones simultaneously, all three were shocked to see the text displayed on their phones. It was a distress call from the command center at Severson manor. The protective detail was under attack from a large force of unknown hostiles.

"Both assault teams are out of pocket," Yale said. "and Axe has casualties."

Dufraine was already on his phone. "Hey, Nelson, get me twelve guys who are available to act as a QRF. Have them at the motor pool in five minutes." He hung up and started dialing the protective detail responsible for keeping Judge Severson safe.

CHAPTER THIRTY-THREE

Lucas "Fish" Fisher had worked for James Gunderson since almost the beginning. A former Navy SEAL, he had cut his teeth during the early stages of the Global War on Terror and had retired from the Navy after twenty hard years. He was still in great shape but as he inched past forty and closer to fifty, his knees and back were not what they used to be.

The years after the Navy had been spent quietly with his now ex-wife out in San Diego tending bar and surfing. He had convinced himself that he was happy where he was, but he knew all along that he missed the action. His wife had left him suddenly, citing a need to be "free" and taking up with a travelling group of free spirited nutjobs, and rather than plunging into a depression- and alcohol-fueled spiral, he had answered an advertisement for "ex-SOF warriors looking to get back into the action."

That job had been with a different Private Security Contractor and turned out to be to serve as a sort of private militia for a Central American businessman and was, if not totally illegal, totally immoral. Fish had walked away from the interview knowing there was no way he wanted any part of that. He had no desire to get taken prisoner or killed in Guatemala. A few days after he returned home, his phone rang and the voice of Dufraine offered him a position with Norseman Consulting leading a close protective detail in central Minnesota.

He took the job without a second thought and he had been working with Bob Severson ever since.

Fish was in charge of three other personnel that made up former-Judge Severson's protective detail. The elderly man had made some smart investments, and more than a few enemies during his tenure as a state judge, but Fish and his team suspected that what the old man wanted more than protection was company.

The other three men on Judge Severson's detail were Grant "Punch" Anderson, another former SEAL, Rick "Trick" Norman, a former Delta Force operator, and Jared Potts, a former Army Ranger who refused to use a callsign, so the rest of the team just called him "NC" for No Callsign. All four of the men had settled into a comfortable routine with Severson and had grown to genuinely like the friendly old man.

With the spike in violence in Alexandria, Fish had established procedures with Norseman Consulting for a quick reaction force, and the team had practiced getting the judge into a recently built panic room. Severson had taken it all in stride, although he stated—only half joking—that if they were attacked, the ninety-year-old man would prefer to be handed a grenade and "take as many of the sonsabitches with me as I can."

This morning had started the same as any other morning, and Fish and his team were busy taking turns patrolling the grounds, sleeping, or surveying the extensive bank of video monitors. It was mostly boring work, but none of them minded much. They were all a bit older than the average assaulter and site security specialist on Norseman Consulting's payroll, and even though they sometimes wished they could get in on the action they knew their time had come and gone.

Fish was enjoying his morning paper, sitting in the hallway just outside the judge's study in an overstuffed leather chair. Punch was tooling around the grounds on a Polaris snowmobile, making more or less continuous laps around the estate. Trick was catching some sleep, as Fish had relieved him only about an hour before. NC was kicked back in the command center, monitoring the surveillance panel.

"Hey, Fish," NC's voice snapped Fish's attention away from the paper he was reading.

"Go for Fish," the team leader responded, taking his eyes off of the sports news on the page in front of him.

"Some visitors are pulling up, not on the list," NC announced. "Actually, a whole lot of them. Six SUVs and a minivan just passed the scanner."

That got Fish's attention. He rose to his feet and moved into the judge's study. Punching a button on the side of his radio, the team leader sent out a local alarm to the rest of the detail that there might be trouble brewing.

"Alright, Trick, swing by and see what you can," Fish directed as he strode purposefully up to Judge Severson sitting behind his large desk. "Everyone prepare to strong point."

"Is something the matter, Lucas?" Severson peered at Fish over his Apple computer. The retired judge often thought that the younger

180

men charged with protecting him often took his security far too seriously, but he tried to humor them.

"Judge, are you expecting anyone today that would be arriving in multiple vehicles?"

"Oh," Judge Severson frowned. "No, I am not."

"Fish, Punch." Trick's voice was alarmed. "These guys are loaded for bear. I count four to six PAX per vehicle, all armed with rifles."

"Alright all stations, fall back to command center, confirm copy." Fish ordered over the radio, listening to his earpiece as his three teammates sounded their understanding over the radio.

"Judge we need to get to the command center pronto," the retired SEAL quickly rounded the desk and unceremoniously yanked the elderly judge out of his chair. "No argument. This one's for real."

Bob Severson did not argue, nor was he in any position to, as the younger man fairly hauled him out of the office and into the hallway. Outside the house, several car doors slammed, and a snowmobile running at full throttle was sounding across the snow-covered estate.

NC's voice came through Fish's radio earpiece calmly but urgently calling for immediate assistance from Norseman Consulting headquarters. The former SEAL reached the command center to find NC and Trick already in position. Punch came running in seconds later, his B&T MP9 submachine pistol swinging from a single-point sling draped around his neck.

The four contractors pulled the heavily armored door closed behind them, sealing the five men inside. Fish handed a heavy vest with ballistic plates and a heavy ballistic helmet to Judge Severson. The old man looked like he was swimming in the vest, and the helmet nearly fell over his eyes. The protective detailed turned their attention to their own gear. Trick was armed with his H&K USP Expert 9mm pistol and a Benelli M4 shotgun. NC had his pistol on his hip, and a B&T MP9 sitting on the command center desk next to him.

Fish pulled on his own ballistic vest and slung his submachine pistol over it. He performed a quick press check, confirming that a 9mm hollow point was seated in the chamber of the weapon. His pistol, a SIG-Sauer P226 TacOps, was holstered on his hip.

NC was glued to the screens. The men outside had dismounted their vehicles and fanned out in front of the manor's front door. This gave the former Ranger an opportunity to count their numbers. "Severson Manor to Norseman Actual," he kept his voice level and clear. "Count twenty-eight men, all with long-arms. So far there has been no attempt at entry."

"Copy Severson Manor. Preparing QRF. Standby for reinforcements."

"Copy, will hold," NC responded, never taking his eyes off of the monitors.

The intruders still hadn't moved toward the house, but a twenty-ninth man had emerged from the middle SUV parked in the large driveway. He was waving around a large pistol, and had a long tube strapped over his back.

"Oh shit, get a load of this," the Ranger said, turning to the other three Special Forces vets.

All of the men had seen those tubes before. A simple, cheap weapon, the RPG-7 was just a simple tube designed to hurl a shaped projectile that would punch through an armored vehicle.

"The command center can withstand a few hits from that," Fish stated matter-of-factly. The command center was designed to survive even if the entire house burned down around it. It was sealed hermetically, with its own air source, power, and fire suppression system. They even had a bathroom that could also serve as a sick little booby trap by storing the excrement and expelling it via a pressurized tube into the faces of the assailants if worse came to worst. While Fish knew all of this, he had no way of knowing if the command center really would withstand multiple direct hits from an RPG-7.

NC made another radio call to the Norseman Consulting headquarters informing them of the most recent development. As he received confirmation that the QRF was departing the compound in five minutes, the man waving the pistol barked out a command, and the exterior of the manor erupted in gunfire.

"Snowmobile at ten o'clock," the heavily accented English sounded through the radio on Farook's belt. The veteran IRGC sergeant was riding in the middle SUV as his strike force approached the Severson manor. He was more than pleased with this assignment. The kidnapping that Hamid had been tasked with was a bit too distasteful for a soldier like him. Farook preferred targets with an actual military significance. Not revenge attacks on innocent women.

This old judge, however, was the bankroll behind their privately contracted enemies, and even had four of their elite soldiers as his guards. Farook had no problem motivating his combined force of Syrians, Chechens, and RIF gangsters for this mission. The Syrians and Chechens were itching for an opportunity to kill Rangers and SEALs, and RIF wanted revenge for all the jail time their members had served at the hands of the capitalist judge.

Lifting the radio to his lips, Farook directed the car in the front: "Ignore it, focus on the house."

"Pulling up now." The first SUV had arrived in front of the house. Farook grinned as he pulled the large Coonan .357 Magnum pistol out of the holster strapped to his thigh. The Iranian racked the slide on the pistol, ensuring that one of the high-powered cartridges slammed home before he returned it to its holster. Farook then turned and pulled the RPG launcher from the cargo bay.

Farook stayed in the SUV for a few more minutes, checking over his RPG rockets while his team took up their positions in front of the house. When he was ready, he opened his door, slung the tube launcher and satchel of rockets over his shoulder, and drew his Coonan.

With the exception of the rifles and shotguns that the RIF gangsters had brought with them and the Coonan in Farook's hand, all of the weaponry facing the Severson manor had been smuggled into the country. Mokri had wanted to take advantage of the US's notoriously lax gun laws to purchase firearms once they were already in country, but Khorasani had managed to explain that even in the US, buying guns left a paper trail. They also pointed out that the weapons they were going to be getting were only semi-automatic, and many of the operatives participating in the mission agreed that they needed the capability to fire on fully automatic. As it was, the foreign terrorists were now armed with the AK74SU assault rifle that was infamously known as the "Krinkov" around the world. All of the terrorists had chest rigs holding thirty and forty round magazines stuffed with 5.45x39mm ammunition, and all of them had a ninety-five-round drum loaded into their Krinkovs for the first volley.

Many of the RIF gangsters were armed with AR15 and AK platform rifles, and four of them had drum magazines loaded into their rifles, but they'd been instructed to hold their fire until after the foreign fighters had emptied their drums into the house so as to cover their reload.

Farook waved his pistol over his head, screaming to his strike force, "Ready!"

The men took up their final positions pointing toward the house. "Aim!"

Selector levers on eighteen Krinkovs snapped into the full-automatic position.

"FIRE!"

Farook's command was drowned out as a barrage of fully automatic rifle fire tore into the front of the manor.

The storm of bullets ripping through the front of the house had no effect on the men cocooned inside the armored command center. None of the high velocity rifle rounds had even made it all the way to the center of the house where the reinforced room lay.

A few of the interior video cameras had been hit, knocking them out of commission. But by some miracle, the exterior cameras were still in action, allowing NC to report details of the attack to HQ. The barrage ended and the men in the room watched the terrorists reload with the magazines in their chest rigs.

"A bit more professional than I had hoped," Fish stated grimly. The fact that the attackers had one element cover the other element while they reloaded indicated to him that they had some level of training. They were now watching the men clear the outside of the house. Their movements were impressive and efficient. "Some of those guys even reloaded out of their pockets and left the ammo on their rigs alone. They came prepared for that initial barrage of suppressing fire."

Trick snorted in reply, keeping his Benelli shotgun aimed roughly in the direction of the command center's door.

"I'm not gonna worry too much until that RPG is right outside our front door," Punch said grimly, standing between Judge Severson and the door, his MP9's folding stock tucked into his shoulder, his support hand firmly clamped on the foregrip of the submachine pistol.

"Here they come, guys," NC said, slipping his submachine pistol's sling over his neck and resting the weapon in his lap. "Get ready."

The terrorists started up the front steps cautiously, and it occurred to the men inside that their attackers probably did not know about the command center and intended to clear the entire house. They could see the leader, still waving his pistol and bellowing orders, the

RPG launcher tube still slung over his back. They could also see that their attackers were leaving almost a dozen men behind as a support element.

"Okay," Fish said, "more than likely, they will not be able to breach, but if they do, short controlled bursts, keep up the communication."

"Got it," Trick grunted. "Kill 'em until they stop coming."

"QRF is still ten minutes out," NC said.

CHAPTER THIRTY-FOUR

Farook pushed his men forward up the stairs and into the large manor. He was hoping they'd manage to take at least one man alive and very much wanted to execute a SEAL or a Ranger point blank. The Iranian had fought against the American special operations community, and while he had a begrudging respect for them and their ruthless tactics, their raids had killed many of his trainees, comrades, and friends all over the Middle East.

Though it would have been helpful had Mokri and Javad been able to obtain the exact layout of the manor, Farook assumed that the old judge had installed some sort of panic room, and that his small protective detail had rushed him inside already. That was fine with Farook. He had brought several RPGs, and three of his men had plastic explosives stuffed into the pockets of their winter coats.

The safe room would be no problem.

The RIF communists were outside rearranging the SUVs to form a multi-tiered blockade of the driveway to oppose the quick reaction force they were sure to encounter. Farook was now monitoring his team from the second-floor balcony window, his Coonan pistol clutched in his right hand and his radio held up in front of him in his left.

Farook was listening to his strike force members inside the manor clear the second and third floor. Still no luck finding the safe room, but Farook was confident that they would find it soon. He turned his attention back to the driveway. The communists were almost done. The last car, a minivan, was placed just in front of the entry to the manor, and Farook could see the tiered blockades sweeping down the long driveway, with the communist fighters taking up positions behind the vehicles to wait for the impending attack.

"Farook." His radio sputtered. "We found the safe room."

"Excellent," the IRGC sergeant grinned. "Leave two men there to guard the room and give them with enough explosives to blow the door open."

Farook released the button on his radio for a brief moment before sending out his next radio call.

"Everyone else, take up your positions. The mercenaries will be here soon."

186

As the remainder of his strike force scattered across the manor to their established positions, Farook unslung the tube launcher on his back and used it to smash out the large picture window overlooking the driveway. His assistant strike team leader showed up moments later, carrying his own satchel of rockets, and Farook loaded and primed the RPG-7 before leaning it against the wall.

Pulling a pair of binoculars from the large pocket on the front of his coat, Farook started scanning the woods ringing the manor. All there was to do now was wait.

Port was nervous. Dufraine and Gunderson had hurriedly briefed the ad hoc QRF on the assault at the Severson manor. The team had been pulled from the ranks of the site security specialists that Norseman Consulting hired to protect its gates or the interests of clients, and most of them were still going through the company's extensive selection process to be part of the assault teams.

Nelson, the leader of the operation, was sitting in the passenger seat of the lead van listening to the radio updates from the command center at the manor.

Fully kitted up with ballistic plates and helmet, B&T APC300 carbine, and Beretta M9A3 pistol, Port was nervously checking and rechecking his equipment in the backseat of the lead van. Most of the guys in the QRF were former Army or Marines, Port was pretty sure he was the only Air Force veteran among the dozen men currently bumping along in the back of the minivans. While most of the former Army and Marines in the QRF had performed this type of mission in the Middle East, Port's experience in the Global War on Terror had mostly involved airfield security and some light infantry patrolling.

The man sitting in the middle captain seat in front of Port was loading the belt of his MCR squad automatic weapon, or SAW, a belt-fed machine gun chambered in 300 Blackout as the Norseman Consulting's carbines were loaded with. He was the Squad Automatic Rifleman for Port's squad.

"Alright everyone, listen up!" Nelson barked into his radio. "The assailants at Severson Manor unleashed a barrage of full-auto and are currently picking apart the manor looking for the safe room. They have blockaded the driveway and are using their own vehicles as cover. We will be disembarking out of visual from the front gate and approaching through the woods on foot."

"Shiiiiit." Port leaned back into his seat. "Good thing they had us bring the SAW, eh Jules?" The Air Force veteran was addressing the man in front of him lovingly preparing the MCR in front of him.

"Hey, shut it Zoomie," the contractor in the seat next to Port, an ornery former Marine named Andrew said. "I'm tryin' to focus."
The van road in quiet for a few minutes while Nelson looked at overhead imagery of the Severson Estate on his ruggedized tablet.

"Alright, gents," Nelson said. "Two minutes 'till we un-ass from the vans. We are going to fan out through the woods. Fireteam Charlie will depart to their waypoint, Bravo will wait two minutes and head to theirs. Then Alpha will wait one minute and head to their checkpoint. When all three teams are set, we will suppress the outside blockades, then maneuver to the house and clear to the command center."

Port was assigned with Jules, Andrew, and the driver, Cody, to Fireteam Charlie. Nelson was going to attach himself to Fireteam Bravo, along with four other contractors, and Fireteam Alpha contained the last four contractors in the QRF. They were going to have to book it through the woods to the far end of the estate, between the back of the house and the lake. Alpha had the most ground to cover, and they were expecting to have to do it through pretty deep snow.

"One minute," Nelson spoke into his microphone. "Word from the command center is that the assailants have discovered the bunker and have left two men with explosives outside the front door. The rest of the men have taken up positions overlooking the estate."

"They're waiting for us," Jules smirked, slipping out of his seat and preparing to spring out of the van and into action.

"Farook," the commercially bought radio handset crackled to life. "We heard a car door slam. I think they're here."

"Hold your positions," the strike force leader spoke into his handset. "Let them come to us."

"Of course, Comrade," the man that Farook had appointed as the leader of the RIF fighters responded. The Iranian could tell that the American communist and his gang were looking forward to the impending clash. The fighters crouching behind SUVs in the driveway were self-proclaimed "anti-fascists," which Farook found highly comical. Most of them could not articulate what that meant besides resisting the US government through random acts of violence and coordinated riots.

Farook expected that the majority of them would be dead before the morning was over. They were a speed bump to slow the QRF, nothing more.

The Iranian sergeant continued scanning through the woods, looking for signs that the Norseman response team was approaching.

There. He saw something, a flash of movement deep in the woods. Peering through his binoculars, he could make out the figures of men in white camouflage fatigues partially concealed by the barren trees.

Farook spoke into his radio. "The fascists are approaching through the woods. Be prepared to fire on my signal."

"Fascists?" Farook's assistant in the strike force looked at him with a smirk.

The Iranian smiled back. "Gets 'em all riled up." The two men chuckled as Farook picked up his RPG-7 tube launcher and pointed it out into the woods.

"All stations, we have been compromised. Personnel inside have noticed our presence."

"Fuck," Jules muttered. He was kneeling behind a tree and could see Port crouching in the snow about fifteen yards to his right.

"Be advised," the radio sounded in their headsets, "there is one tango in the top floor with an RPG."

"They brought the big guns." Cody said from a few yards deeper in the woods.

"On my signal, all belt-feds concentrate fire on the picture window above and to the left of the front door."

Port could see the window Nelson was talking about, although at the somewhat extreme upward angle and at a distance of two hundred meters, it was not going to be an easy shot. Jules slowly dropped down to prone, propping the MCR up on its bipod and zeroing in on the window.

"This is Alpha," The Alpha fireteam leader spoke. Port listened to the radio in his ear while he scanned the area, looking for targets. "We have visual on six tangos crouched behind the cars."

"Roger, Alpha, wait for the signal to engage," Nelson commanded. Port could feel Jules tense up next to him, preparing to unleash the full fury of the belt-fed machine gun he was cradling in the socket of his shoulder.

A sudden flash and puff of smoke appeared from the target window, and Jules did not wait for Nelson's signal, unleashing a vicious burst of automatic fire at the Severson manor as the RPG impacted somewhere in the woods in the direction of Fireteam Bravo.

Rounds were snapping past Port's head now and he started returning fire, aiming his carbine at the men behind the wheel well of the van in front of the large main door. He pressed himself up against the large tree next to him, struggling to maintain effective aim from nearly two hundred meters away.

Port's senses were numbing with the firefight, and he was only vaguely aware of Andrew firing to his left, and Cody was even deeper in the woods to his left.

"Alpha clear, moving up the driveway." The radio was loud enough that Port could just hear it over the sound of Jules firing controlled bursts at the window where the RPG had been fired from.

"MOVE FORWARD!" Andrew screamed.

Port heaved himself up off the ground and burst forward with Cody right behind him. He could see rounds impacting the terrorist's van and the front of the manor. He and Cody took a knee simultaneously, snapping their carbines up and scanning for targets.

The van was about seventy-five yards away, and Port could see a leg protruding from the side as a gunman leaned around the corner. Lining his holographic sights up with the leg, Port fired rapidly, shattering the man's leg and causing him to fall face first out onto the driveway. Breathing heavily, Port walked a few more rounds up across the pavement and into the man's face before he could drag himself out of the line of fire.

Jules was still laying down fire on the front of the building, the rounds smacking into the already shot up siding of the house and splintering the underlying wood. Andrew came running up behind Port and slapped him on the back.

Port and Cody got up and started sprinting forward again. They were almost to the van when automatic rifle fire intensified, kicking up snow behind Port as he dove forward and took cover behind the wheel of the van. He looked back to Andrew and saw him aiming over Port's head and firing rapidly.

190

Cody was lying face down about fifteen meters away from Port and the van, a pool of blood spreading underneath him. A wet *thwump* made Port swivel his head and snatch his carbine up to his eye, only to find that the sound was caused by one of the gunmen falling out of the upstairs window after being hit by Andrew's carbine rounds.

There was a sudden lull in the gunfire, and Andrew picked his way forward carefully, motioning to Port to cover his advance.

"Report!" Nelson's voice coughed over the radio.

"Alpha, nearing the top of the driveway, in sight of manor. No casualties."

"Bravo, bells rung by that RPG, but we are all good."

"Charlie," Andrew said, "at the porch door. One KIA."

"Roger, Charlie cover the advance. Moving now."

Andrew turned and motioned to Jules, who had moved up slightly to get a better angle with his MCR. Jules jumped up and ran the last hundred yards to join his teammates in covering Alpha's advance.

"Watch your fires," Andrew directed, scanning the windows of the manor for more targets. "Alpha will be coming up that direction."

Port nodded. He was breathing heavily, his hands shaking.

A few seconds later, Fireteam Bravo emerged from the woods, rushing forward toward the house. Movement down the driveway caught Port's eye and he screamed, "CONTACT!"

Four guys in a motley assortment of winter clothing and carrying camouflage painted rifles were jogging back up the driveway, doubtlessly trying to respond to Fireteam Alpha's advance. Two of the men turned to take cover behind the SUV blockade closest to the manor, while one pointed at Fireteam Bravo, shouting to his comrades and bringing his rifle up. The fourth guy spotted Port and was just opening his mouth to shout when Port shot him, stitching rounds from the man's hip up to his shoulder.

Port swiveled slightly, adjusting his aim and settling his holographic reticle on the side of the next man's chest, snatching the trigger back twice in rapid succession, only to be greeted with his rifle's bolt locking to the rear on an empty magazine.

"Reloading!" Port dropped back behind the van, extracting a magazine from the chest rig on his vest and seating it in the magazine well of his carbine. Andrew had taken up firing while Port reloaded, and by the time Port ran the charging handle on his carbine, Andrew had eliminated the last two men on the driveway.

"Alpha's up." Fireteam Alpha was coming into view of the driveway. Every one of the contractors was sticking to the cover of the vehicles to avoid being shot by a surprise volley from the house and scanning the windows for additional assailants.

"Bravo's up."

"I'm coming to you, Charlie." Nelson's voice was ragged.

"Roger, Charlie's up," Andrew said into the radio. As Nelson crunched through the hard snow to Fireteam Charlie's position, the contractors prepared to breach the back door.

Fireteam Charlie's three surviving contractors and Nelson hustled around the corner, covering the large picture windows on the ground floor. There was no movement inside the house, and Andrew looked over to Nelson as he took the van driver's position in the stack. Nelson spoke into his radio headset: "Charlie, set."

"Alpha, set."

"Bravo, set."

Nelson looked at Andrew and nodded before announcing, "GO! GO! GO!"

Andrew pushed through the unlocked door and started sweeping inside. The rest of the fireteam fanned out into the room after him, suppressed carbines searching for targets.

"Command center lost visual on most of the tangos," Nelson announced as they saw the ground floor kitchen was clear. "They've started shooting out all the cameras."

Port was sweating through his winter uniform, breathing too heavily out of a combination of sheer exertion and adrenaline.

"Why's it so quiet?" Jules whispered. As the SAW gunner, he was the last one in the house. Even though the MCR was almost as light as the B&T carbines that the rest of the team were carrying, the belt-fed machine gun still stood to slow Jules down a bit, plus he was running it unsuppressed, and they didn't want to be totally deafened by the hammering of his automatic fire. Putting him last meant he was the least likely to need to fire, saving the other men the discomfort of withstanding his deafening muzzle blast.

His point jarred the fireteam though as they prepared to enter into the next room, a dining room. The contractors paused for a moment, listening for any hints as to what lay on the other side of the door.

"Alpha in garage, no tangos."

"Bravo is through the front door, two tangos down in the foyer."

"Press!" Nelson hissed over the radio, and as he pushed the next door open, an explosion ripped through the house, followed by immediate bursts of automatic fire.

Farook was extremely pleased with how his men had handled themselves so far. Sure, the communists outside had gotten slaughtered mercilessly almost as soon as the gunfire kicked off, but Farook had expected that. He was fairly confident that his RPG round had landed directly in the middle of a group of American commandos, but he had not stuck around to see the result.

It was a good thing he retreated too, as the exact spot he had been standing in had disintegrated in a hail of bullets a second later. Farook's assistant had caught some fragmentation in the back as they pulled away from the large window, but it had only given him some minor scrapes across the torso.

His men inside had stood their ground perfectly, waiting for the Americans to get close enough. He'd seen one of his men drop a commando before he was hit by return fire and dropped out the shattered window. From his observation, he had identified only about a dozen men from Norseman in the QRF, less than half his number. The communists outside could sustain casualties and Farook's team was still stay way ahead.

The Iranian had started to retreat with half of his remaining force into the center of the manor while directing his troops to take up their secondary positions in preparation for their next ambush. As he was hustling down the hallway, he noticed the cameras. Cursing to himself for not remembering this sooner, he made a quick radio call and his men had raised their pistols and started shooting out all the cameras they could find.

Now Farook and his team could hear the splintering doors coming from the foyer and the garage. Farook raised his radio to his mouth and issued another command to his newly repositioned strike force.

"Wait fifteen seconds and then trigger the ambush." He couldn't help but grin as he and his assistant settled into the room directly in front of the safe room door. On the off chance that any of the mercenary commandos survived the next onslaught, they would surely be making their way down this one-way hallway. Farook, half the strike force, and the two men they had assigned to guard the safe room with the explosives would easily dominate the hallway and massacre any survivors.

If any men survived that, well Farook did not plan on being taken captive. He quickly checked the small pouch sewn into the breast of his shirt, tapping it to ensure his insurance policy was still there. Finally, Farook pulled the small electronic plunger out of his pocket and made sure the wires running up his sleeve were connected.

The mental clock in Farook's head clicked past fifteen seconds, and the explosion from the booby-trapped room near the garage rocked the manor, followed by a barrage of automatic weapons fire from his men lying in ambush.

The Iranian almost laughed. The Americans were no match for his strike force.

Andrew had pushed forward into the kitchen just in time to see the first man in Fireteam Bravo get cut down by rifle fire. Their SAW gunner immediately took a knee, raking a full burst of fire across the balcony where a half dozen men were firing at the contractors on the ground floor. A round slammed into the SAW gunner's thigh, shattering his leg, but he kept on firing. Several more rounds impacted at the base of his neck, causing the man to drop to his back, clutching at the severed artery.

Fireteam Charlie rushed forward, directing their carbine fire at the shooters on the balcony. Jules shouldered the MCR and unleashed with a full belt, emptying the SAW within a few seconds and then letting the machine gun dangle from its sling while he transitioned to his SIG-Sauer P320 X-Carry.

By this time, two of the men on the balcony were clearly dead, and a third was trying to crawl backwards toward the judge's study.

Fireteam Charlie joined Bravo in the foyer, hastily setting security while the two standing members took stock of the Norseman assaulters who had been dropped on the floor. The point man was clearly dead; his whole head had been turned to unrecognizable mush. The SAW gunner with the severed carotid artery had bled out.

"Stack with us," Nelson directed the last two men in Fireteam Bravo. They nodded and quickly joined Nelson in the back.

194

"Lemme reload real quick," Jules said, pulling an unused belt of 300 Blackout rounds off of the dead SAW gunner and quickly replenishing his own SAW.

"Alpha, status." Nelson requested in his radio. There was no response.

"We gotta move," Andrew announced. "At least three of those guys fell back into the study."

"Following you up," Port answered, and the six remaining contractors quickly ascended the stairs, scanning for the men who had escape their fire.

The door to the study had been shot up pretty badly and was not latched. Nelson pulled out a flashbang.

"I got a better idea," Jules said, tapping Port on the shoulder and drawing a fragmentation grenade out of a pouch on his chest rig. Nobody bothered asking him how he had gotten a frag checked out of the Norseman Consulting armory, and they allowed him to shoulder his way forward.

As the point man, Andrew gently pushed the door open, and Jules tossed his frag, giving it enough oomph to make it all the way to the back of the room.

The grenade went off, followed by screaming from inside the room.

Andrew pushed in, carbine up. A man was upright on his knees, screaming in pain as he stared at the remainder of his arms. He evidently had tried to pick up the frag and throw it back when the grenade went off. Port sent a sympathy bullet into the man's head as Andrew snapped four quick rounds into a man standing behind the judge's desk, bleeding profusely from the ears and nose.

Nelson dumped a half magazine into the last man standing, painting the judge's bookshelf red.

"Clear!" The three men in the room turned to leave when a pistol shot snapped past Port's head, burrowing into the wall above the judge's desk. The wounded man who had been dragging himself away from the balcony was lying in the corner by the door. He was trying to get a bead on Port when Nelson dispatched him with a single round to the head.

"Now we are clear," he announced. "Check your fuckin' corners."

"Friendlies coming out!" Andrew shouted as they walked out the door. Jules and the two surviving members of Fireteam Bravo were holding security.

"Alright well that's seven guys we greased up here," Nelson was counting, "and the command center counted twenty-nine."

"I think we got nine or ten outside," Andrew said. "Port and I dumped three guys each, and Charlie said they had smoked a couple more."

"Okay, clear the top floor," Nelson said. "We still have nine or ten to go."

Nelson took a moment to report the proceedings to headquarters, and while Port and the rest of the QRF couldn't hear what was being said by HQ, they could not imagine it would be anything good.

The house was eerily silent.

The QRF leader turned back to his surviving members. "Alright, we press. Chopper is on the way."

Fireteam Bravo's surviving members were now in the front of the stack, and they started forward, preparing to clear the remaining two rooms on the top floor. Both turned out to be empty, and the team started back down.

They were approaching the hallway that led to the command center, and each man was growing increasingly uneasy with each room that turned up empty. As they neared the hallway leading to the antechamber for the command center, the sound of an approaching helicopter could be heard.

After clearing the rooms on the top floor, Port now found himself the point man, and as he rounded the corner leading into the final hallway, a force like a sledgehammer struck him in the chest, knocking the wind out of him and causing him to stumble backwards.
Nelson grabbed the drag handle on the back of Port's plate carrier and yanked him back around the corner. The remaining men dropped flat as small holes exploded through the plaster of the wall.

"Command center," Nelson shouted into his headset, firing rounds back through the wall, "they're all bunched up outside your front door."

Port was gasping for air. He thought he could just make out a hissing noise coming from the direction of the command center, followed by some heavy coughing.

Nelson jumped up, yanked another flashbang out of his vest, primed it, and threw it as hard as he could around the corner and down the hall. The flashbang went off, and Nelson peered around the corner, snapping his carbine from target to target. Port forced himself off the ground and started down the hallway.

He kept firing as he went, working on autopilot. He felt like he was out of his body, watching himself transitioning between targets and running his carbine dry, only peripherally aware that bullets were snapping around him close enough that he could feel the shockwave as they passed. As he entered the antechamber, he drew his M9A3 and started to bring it to bear on one of the few remaining assailants in the antechamber. Port fired his pistol three times, putting two rounds in the man's chest and a final round in his head. As he watched the man crumble to the floor, Port scanned the rest of the room. His heart rate was through the roof, and as he surveyed the wreckage in front of him, the residual tear gas in the hallway caused him to cough, bringing him back from his out of body experience.

There was one man, reaching for a plunger that had been dropped on the floor. The man was shot in both legs and his chest. He didn't see Port, but he had a big pistol loosely held in his limp hand.

"Hey!" Port shouted. "Drop it!"

The man struggled to lift his pistol and Port shot him twice in the head.

CHAPTER THIRTY-FIVE

James Gunderson felt sick to his stomach. The hastily assembled reaction force had managed to accomplish their mission, but at a significant cost. Judge Severson had been extracted from the manor and flown via helicopter to a secluded cabin somewhere in Canada. The judge's security detail insisted on staying with him and refused to accept replacements.

The QRF had managed to kill all of the assailants, but with a total of five contractors dead and two critically wounded. A brick of plastic explosives had killed two of Fireteam Alpha's contractors and put the other two in the hospital. The reports from the men in the field said that the point man had all but evaporated, and the second man had been killed by the overpressure in the garage. The other two had miraculously survived, though they had sustained traumatic brain injuries.

Judge Severson was beside himself that so many good men had perished trying to save him, and Gunderson had instructed his protective detail to never let him out of their sight. Not that they needed telling. The four men had performed their duties precisely, and without their communication with the QRF and the release of the tear-gas countermeasures from the command center, the rest of the QRF likely would have been killed as well.

The deceased assailants had all been searched and their biometric data had been recorded but knowing who had carried out the attack did not help them figure out who had ordered it.

Gunderson wasn't going to worry about why the attack was carried out. He had known when his company was ousted in the news that any of their clients could become targets, and Judge Severson was the only personal protective detail remotely close to Alexandria. As far as Norseman Consulting was concerned, the "why" behind the attack was simply that Judge Severson had hired Norseman Consulting. Gunderson also knew that their headquarters would not be a likely target for their enemies. The security was too tight, and the location too remote. The Norseman president figured that the Iranians would rather draw the Norseman contractors out and try to entrap them, rather than sacrifice all of their men in a frontal assault.

He slumped into the chair behind his desk and took a sip from his water bottle. He eyed the news, checking for any reference to his company and the assault on Severson Manor and wondered, half-heartedly, what to do with the prisoner from Mrs. Erikson's failed rescue operation.

Gerry Erikson had been grieving in his borrowed room for the better part of an hour now. Gunderson had had the unpleasant experience of relaying to the man that his wife had been killed sometime the previous night. He assured Gerry that Ellen had not suffered, though he doubted that was true, and sat with the man while he sobbed. After a while, Gerry had asked to be left alone.

On his way back to the office, Gunderson had swung by the medical bay where his trauma team were busy working on the wounded QRF members and Carl was laid up on a sedative drip after having undergone surgery for his wounded leg. The deceased members of the QRF were in a side room that the medical team was using as a morgue, and one of the nurses was working delicately with Ellen Erikson's corpse.

James stopped for a minute and watched the nurse cleaning Mrs. Erikson, transfixed and saddened by the scene. By all accounts, Ellen Erikson was a quiet, charming woman whose only tie to this ordeal was Gerry Erikson. She didn't deserve the fate she'd been given, but then the world was never fair to anyone, innocent or not.

The nurse suddenly looked up, surprised to see Gunderson standing there.

She said softly, "Doc told me to clean her up so that Mr. Erikson could come say goodbye."

Gunderson nodded, a knot building in his throat, and motioned to the young woman to continue her task. He then strode back to his office, where he now sat wondering what sort of punishment would be fitting for the terrorists captured during this messy ordeal.

The phone on his desk rang shrilly, and Gunderson was greeted by Yale's excited voice on the other end.

"Hey!" The man was breathless. "Khorasani talked."

Ardashir Khorasani was exhausted. He'd been moved to another windowless room with a toilet and cot. Nobody had interacted with him since the Americans had threatened to drone strike his family into oblivion. Three meals a day were slid under the door, mostly a potato and vegetable-based dish. He was actually a bit surprised that they didn't try to feed him pork products. His Iranian trainers had told him that Americans liked to serve Muslims only pork, or even rub pork fat on their clothes during captivity so as to block their passage into heaven.

The Iranian agent was growing more and more worried that his family had been vaporized, and he had no idea how long he had been in the room. The lighting changed at random from uncomfortably bright to pitch dark and back again. Khorasani had been unable to get consistent levels of sleep, as every time the lights flicked on or off, the light fixture made a loud *bang*. An occurrence that Khorasani figured was built into the light to startle him.

The most recent bout of wakefulness had started like any other; the loud lights woke him, and a few minutes later a bowl of potato and vegetable mush was slid through the tiny slot covered by a metal flap on bottom of the door along with a paper cup full of water. He had long given up trying to see through the slot. The metal flap had no gripping surface, and it only opened one way. So Khorasani sat on his cot, eating his food and returning to his religion for the first time since he was a boy, praying for strength. He was sitting on his cot, murmuring faintly remembered Quran passages when the door to his cell swung open and a man clad entirely in black walked in, shouting at Ardashir to get up and face the wall.

Without thinking, the Iranian hurled his bowl of mush at the man, who easily batted it aside with his hand, scattering the contents across the floor. He then lifted a device Ardashir recognized as a Taser and the Iranian heard its click and buzz as his whole body tensed up and he fell off the bed.

The black-clad man was on top of Ardashir in a flash, rolling him over and slamming a knee into his back. Ardashir had his hands wrenched behind his back and flex-cuffed before being hauled up by his much more powerful adversary. He tried to struggle, but the man forced a hood over his head and marched him out of the room.

Khorasani could not see anything under the hood, but the man did not keep him walking for long. He heard a heavy door swing open. He was jostled forward, spun around, and unceremoniously forced into a chair. When the hood was ripped off of his head, he found himself face to face with the two men who had threatened his family earlier in this same interrogation room.

"Greetings, Agent Khorasani," the man on the right said. "Have you been enjoying your stay?"

Ardashir said nothing, glaring at the two men with fire in his eyes.

"Still not in a talking mood I see," said the man on the left. "Well let's take a look at some pictures and see how you feel after."

"There are two things to consider about these pictures," the man on the left continued while the man on the right started laying the photos out side by side on the table. "The first is that we already know who everyone is. The second thing is that if you cooperate, we are authorized to let you free. If you don't cooperate, we are authorized to bury you in a deep hole."

Ardashir still did not respond, but he did look at the pictures being laid out in front of him. There were dozens of them, all men within the operation—and all dead, from the looks of it. The man on the right finished laying out the pictures and withdrew a single sheet of paper with a seal and some typing on it. The man on the left made a motion to the black-clad man standing behind Ardashir, and his hands were cut loose.

"Since we have no evidence that you killed anyone personally," the man on the left continued to do all the talking, "all we ask is that you confirm the identities of each man in the photographs and answer any additional questions we might have."

Khorasani reached out and picked up the letter that had been drawn out of the folder last. He skimmed it. A letter from the Federal Bureau of Investigation granting Ardashir immunity and safe passage out of the country and into Canada. He could barely believe it, his prayers to be guided home had been answered.

Ardashir Khorasani picked up the photographs and started identifying all the faces he could.

He picked his way through the Syrians and Chechens, explaining to the interrogators that some of the men he had only ever known them by their *noms de guerre*. He identified his Iranian colleagues, including the IRGC sergeant who had been killed at the Severson manor, and further explained that the man had been in charge of the IRGC contingent that was guarding the operation's headquarters.

His identification of the RIF communists was less thorough. His job had been to act as Mayor Stark's handler, and so he'd had very little interaction with RIF. Another VAJA operative had been in charge of rallying the RIF members, Hamid Ahmadi. Not pictured.

"Thank you, Ardashir," the man on the right smiled slightly. "Would you like something to drink? Eat maybe?"

"Water," Khorasani said cautiously, then added, "please."

The black-clad man left the room and the three of them sat in silence, looking at each other.

"There is something else we need from you," the man on the left broke the silence. "And then you will be free to go."

Ardashir looked at the men, weighed his options, and nodded sheepishly.

"Who is in charge of the operation, how many men did you bring, and what is the end goal?"

When Khorasani hesitated, the man on the right spoke again. "Remember that your freedom is contingent upon your cooperation." The heavy metal door swung back open and the man in black put a water bottle down in front of Ardashir, who had started to sweat. The Iranian quickly unscrewed the cap and took several long pulls of water, draining the bottle to about half.

Ardashir sighed, he had come this far; there was no turning back now. Either he gained his freedom and tried to disappear in Canada, or these men made him disappear in a whole other fashion.

"Agent Omid Mokri is in charge of the operation." With that, the floodgates were opened, and Ardashir Khorasani proceeded to tell the Norseman Consulting interrogators everything there was to know about the Iranian operation in Central Minnesota.

"Jee-suss-christ," Alex whistled through his teeth as the assault teams pored over the data that the interrogators had pulled out of Khorasani. The briefing room near the armory and locker room was filled with tables holding printouts of maps and building data for the unfinished apartment complex turned Iranian headquarters. Pictures of known targets were laid out on another table with short dossiers detailing each person's history.

"How many guys are we thinking?" Rafael was examining the building's floor-by-floor blueprints.

"Around fifty," Yale said confidently, eliciting a series of low whistles from the contractors gathered around the table. "We think that there's a platoon-sized element of IRGC troopers at the top floor, along with roughly a dozen Chechens and two dozen Syrians."

"What about the RIF guys?" Alex looked up from the dossier he'd been studying. "Can we expect they'll stick around?"

"Well after the attack on the Severson manor, and a few raids," Yale responded, "all but the most hard-core revolutionaries have elected to disperse. Most want to live and fight the establishment another day, it would appear."

"So, numbers-wise, what are we looking at?" Alex reiterated.

"Probably less than a dozen," Yale said thoughtfully before turning to address everyone in the room. "Alright gents listen up. We have intercepted communication traffic between this Omid Mokri and the remainder of his cell. All personnel attached to the operation have been ordered to fall back into the Finger and prepare for the final phase of their plan. Our captured Iranian friends have informed us that the final phase includes a series of bombings and shootings designed to destabilize the area and make it ripe for copy-cat and sympathetic homegrown attacks to spring up."

Yale paused. "When the raid is launched, you will be up against not only domestic communist and anti-government forces, but also highly trained and well-equipped Syrian and Chechen mercenaries backed by a platoon-sized element of IRGC commandos. Our intelligence indicates that this building has been entirely cleared of civilians. However, it was an apartment building so double check your fires for any squatters inside the kill zone."

Gunderson stepped forward now, taking the reins from Yale. "Gentlemen, this is the job we were hired to do. We received final authorization to conduct this raid less than five minutes ago. We must successfully eliminate this threat, otherwise our little chunk of Minnesota could be the steppingstone for the rest of the state to fall into paranoia and chaos."

The Norseman Consulting president looked around at his gathered contractors. "We must not fail."

Gunderson stepped back and allowed Dufraine to take the reins. He pointed out on a map of the area surrounding the spire where the individual teams would set up, how the infiltration would take place, and how much time they would have for exfil. After making sure the objective was clear, Dufraine stepped back and allowed the individual team leaders to establish how they would conduct their portion of the operation, leaving them with one final statement: "We are wheels up as soon as the sun goes down."

Everyone in the room checked the time, glancing at watches, phones and clocks. They had just three hours to prepare.

CHAPTER THIRTY-SIX

"Sir, we need to plan our extraction." Javad was borderline pleading with Mokri now, speaking in Farsi to emphasize the need to go home. All the VAJA agents had been killed or captured now, save for Javad and the commander, and everyone in the operation knew that those who had been captured were as good as dead. The Iranian government would deny the operation, claiming that the captured men had no governmental ties, and subsequently execute everyone who had survived the failed mission.

Mokri was beside himself after the failed attack on the Severson manor. He'd had no doubt that almost thirty fighters would be able to overcome the small protective detail and impromptu QFR. Moreover, he could not figure out how the Americans had located Hamid Ahmadi within twenty-four hours after the kidnapping of Ellen Erikson, and now he had ordered everyone involved with the operation to return to the Spire to prepare for the last phase of the operation. Mokri would never tell Javad or any of the other operatives involved, but he knew he could never go back a failure. He had to win or die trying, because if he failed and went home, all of the men in the operation would be hunted down and executed.

It hadn't taken long. Their operation had taken huge losses in the past couple weeks, and very few of the imported thugs remained intermingled with the anti-government communists from RIF. Within a few hours, the remaining operatives and committed RIF members were gathered at the Spire, finalizing their preparations for the last push of the operation.

Javad did not mind that they had pushed forward with the operation, although he had tried to convince Mokri that they needed to vacate their headquarters, which had surely been compromised by now. The Iranian commander would have none of it confident in their security, and issued the order to start distributing explosives, weapons, and ammunition immediately.

All Javad wanted to do now was go home. He had been in this frozen hellhole for a year and he desperately missed his home. But he knew that he couldn't go home without risking his life if this mission did not succeed.

The last thing that Javad needed to do was plan the Iranians exfiltration out of the country, into Canada, and back home as soon as the bombs were distributed, and the mercenaries were given their marching orders.

Mokri, however, seemed to already consider himself a dead man, and was refusing to comply with the original plan. He insisted he would stay in America to see the mission to its end. Javad thought it might be because the man's father had sent him here and the disgrace of failure would be too much.

Javad found himself pleading with the man to allow him to move forward with the extraction. Mokri had turned his back toward Javad and appeared to be crying. Exasperated, Javad left the weeping commander in disgust. He passed the IRGC sergeant in the hallway.

They made brief eye contact and the IRGC sergeant tapped the handle of his Glock pistol protruding from his holster while raising an eyebrow at the closed door. Javad shook his head and waved the man off.

Not yet. But they both knew the time was coming.

"I still do not see how we have anywhere near enough guys for this," Alex said. They had the basic framework of their plan in place, but they were still hashing out some of the details. "There's fifty guys in the building, and twelve stories to clear."

"Alright what about this," Randall said, pointing to the map. "We go in here. You wait until we say 'go,' then you start from here and work your way towards us."

Alex studied the blueprints for a moment. "What kind of sentries do they have up?"

"The drone feed shows two guys here," Melvin pointed, then ran his finger to another point on the blueprint, "and another couple guys up here."

Evan spoke up. "Archer One and Archer Two can set up here and here." He pointed to spots on the overhead map around the Spire. "That'll give the teams cover at both entry points, as well as the garage if anyone tries to escape."

"We'll even give you Hondo," Melvin said to the assault team leaders with a grin.

"You can have Steve too," Evan offered. "I'm sure the two of them would rather be in on the action."

"And these are some pretty long shots, I'd rather not have Hondo whining in my ear," Melvin added.

"Alright," Alex said reluctantly, "that'll work." Axe's team leader knew better than to nitpick to the point of paralysis. They had a decent enough plan, an objective to complete, and only—Alex checked his watch—an hour left till show time.

"We only have about an hour until we are wheels up," he looked over at Melvin and Evan. "You two better get your gear ready and head out."

The two sniper team leaders nodded in agreement and fist bumped the others on the way out the door. Alex and Randall turned back to the table.

"It has to work," Alex said grimly.

About forty-five minutes later, the Sword and Axe assault teams were in the locker room preparing their equipment. They understood the odds were against them, but they didn't want to dwell on it. There was a quiet intensity in the room, and while the men kept themselves busy, a few of them were joking around to relieve the tension.

"You know," Hondo said, slapping Elias on the back, "when I answered this help wanted ad, I for sure did not think I'd be doing this type of shit."

"What were you expecting, Hondo?" Ted responded, "Guarding a surf shack in Maui?"

"You know man, the same shit all these private contracting companies do." Hondo shrugged. "Guarding pipelines and shit like that."

Ted laughed a little. "Man, I thought I'd gotten too old for this type of operation."

"Shut up, Ted," Larry shouted, "you're not even forty yet."

A couple of the guys laughed, and they quickly finished their gear checks.

"Everyone geared up?" Alex and Randall were back in the room. "We're out of here in five minutes."

In his bunk room, Gerry Erikson sat on the bed, scrolling listlessly through pictures of his wife on his phone. He'd spent a good part of his afternoon sitting next to her in the morgue, apologizing over and over and weeping softly. He'd failed her.

He was halfway through their trip to Itasca State Park the previous summer when he put the phone down. His tears had all been spent, and now there was nothing more that he could do but sit with his own guilt and grief. He was quite certain that Gunderson wouldn't let him leave until everything blew over. There wasn't much to do in the room besides sleep and think, so he leaned back on the bed and stared at the ceiling, counting the minutes as they ticked past.

Gerry was startled by a knock on the door, and he hauled himself up to a sitting position, facing the door.

"It's open," Erikson said sullenly. The door swung open, revealing James Gunderson, holding a dog-eared paperback book and a steaming cup of coffee.

"How are you holding up, Gerry?" Gunderson asked, walking forward. He held out the book and the coffee and Erikson waved both away.

Erikson glared up at him. "How the fuck do you think I'm holding up?"

Gunderson looked down at his feet from the outburst and stood there for a moment, like he did not know how to proceed, so Erikson pushed forward. "Can I leave or what? I've been here for several days now."

"Actually, that's what I wanted to talk to you about," Gunderson sighed. "I need to keep you here for a little while longer. The last part of our operation is about to kick off, and I don't want you released until we can clear everything up."

"So, I'm your prisoner."

Gunderson flushed. "Absolutely not. You're our guest, and we are taking care of you."

Erikson sighed and lay back on the bed again. "Just let me know when I can leave."

The Norseman Consulting president nodded and walked out of the room, leaving the book and cup of coffee on a shelf as he left. Erikson heard the sound of the door latching in place, followed by the heavy *clunk* of the dead bolt.

"Port, you don't have to go on this one," Nelson said gently. "Nobody would blame you. It was a rough one this afternoon."
The surviving QRF members had gotten back to the Norseman Consulting compound and unloaded the body bags containing their dead teammates only a few hours ago. When the call went out for some

208

additional reinforcements to act as a cordon for the impending raid on the Spire, Port had volunteered immediately.

None of the rest of the QRF with the exception of Nelson had volunteered for it, opting instead to pull a shift doing guard duty at the compound. It was technically Port's day off, but he insisted he wanted to go.

"I'm good Nels," Port said, barely looking at the other man. "Besides, you're going, ain't ya?"

"Alright, then," Nelson sighed, clamping his hand around the younger man's shoulder. "Go get into a fresh set of cammies, get a new ballistic plate for your vest, and meet up in the motor pool for the cordon briefing in two hours."

Port nodded and hustled back to his villa, eager to strip off his dirty, bloody uniform and take a quick shower. He had been so busy with unloading the trucks and debriefing from the attack on Severson manor he had been sitting in his torn, bloodied cammies all day. The carbon blowback from his suppressed carbine had clung to his sweaty body, and he felt pretty disgusting.

Most of Norseman Consulting's employees lived on the compound in the villas just down the road from the main briefing room. Port was no different, and he only had to walk about a hundred yards to his own villa.

He fiddled with his keys, opening the door and tossing his rifle on the couch, then stripping out of his dirty plate carrier and uniform. Port threw the uniform in the hamper and walked into the bathroom, where he caught a good look of himself in the mirror.

There was a huge bruise on his pectoral, and he definitely felt that one. That was the first time he'd ever been shot, and it was not an experience he was looking forward to repeating. Port turned on the shower and waited for it to warm up before stepping in. He stood under the warm water in a daze, running through the events at the Severson manor and the cleanup afterwards.

This was also the first time Port had killed anybody. He'd had to return fire in Afghanistan, of course, but the enemies had always been so far away that he never would have been able to tell if he had hit anyone or not. These guys had been close enough that he could see the expressions on their faces as he pulled the trigger.

But it wasn't the guys he killed today that gave him pause. It wasn't even the Norseman guys who had gotten killed. In all truth, Port had not known any of them very well. Picking up their bodies had jarred him some, but he'd loaded friends and strangers into body bags before.

What was troubling him was the sheer exhilaration he'd felt during and after the gunfight. It was totally different than his time in the military, and what scared him about it was how much he liked it. It was the reason he had volunteered to act as part of the cordon force, even though the likelihood of action was really pretty low. Port turned off the water and got out to dry off before pulling a fresh uniform out of his drawers. A few minutes later, he was jogging in full kit back over to the armory to replenish his ammunition and pick up a new ballistic chest plate.

Around the same time Alex and Randall were finalizing their assault plans and the sniper teams had established where they wanted to set up, Nelson was briefing the cordon force. As Port had expected, they weren't anticipating much action. The cordon force was going to be responsible for getting Sword team to the target building on time, and then preparing for the extraction of both teams while ensuring nobody got away from the target building.

When Port entered the motor pool building, Nelson was just gathering the rest of the cordon force. Everyone turned to look at him, and there were more than a few wide eyes. His plate carrier had the unmistakable stain of dried blood on it, and a burnt black hole on his breast, just below his name tape where the .357 Magnum round had punched into his old ballistic plate.

Once Nelson managed to refocus the cordon force's attention, he finished the briefing and directed the contractors to their vehicles. They weren't messing around this time. There were four big, diesel-powered Ford Excursions in a flat gray color with the Norseman Consulting logo on the front doors. The trucks were outfitted with reinforced front and rear bumpers, heavily tinted windows, and armor systems that were, according to Nelson, capable of withstanding considerable damage.

"Gunderson just got these picked up," Nelson warned, "so he wants 'em back."

In addition to the four armored SUVs, there were four Toyota 4Runners, an old Pontiac Sunfire, and a Nissan Sentra. Motioning to the two small sedans, one of the contractors asked lightly, "What's the deal with the lemons? Who has to drive those?"

That elicited a tense laugh from the contractors, and Nelson broke a slight smile.

"Well, Tim," he answered, "that would be whoever is unfortunate enough to be in the wrong place when Archer One and Archer Two need a lift."

As if on cue, Melvin led the two sniper teams through the front door and stated, "Who's driving?"

No hands went up. Finally, an alto voice broke the silence. "I'll drive," said an athletic, blonde woman in the back of the room.

"Thank you Tiff," Nelson said. "Tim why don't you go, too?"

The sniper teams began loading their gear bags into the backseats of their respective sedans.

"Hey, Tim," Tiff said loudly enough for everyone to hear. "Can you drive stick?"

"Uh…"

"Take the Pontiac then." She was not even looking up, stuffing magazines for her SIG Sauer M11 pistol into pouches on her hip. "The Sentra's for real men."

A round of raucous laughter erupted in the motor pool, and Tim's face turned beet red as he snatched up his B&T carbine and tucked it behind the passenger seat of the Sunfire.

The sniper teams piled into the sedans and Tiff led the way out of the large garage. The rest of the cordon team had a few more minutes to kill. The contractors busied themselves checking over their vehicles, ensuring that everything was exactly as they wanted it.

About an hour later, Port climbed into the Excursion he'd been charged with driving and fired up the engine. The Sword assault team packed into their vehicles and took off, engines roaring in the darkness as they tore out of the compound and toward the Spire.

CHAPTER THIRTY-SEVEN

"Sword inbound, five mikes," Melvin's earpiece alerted him to the incoming assault team.

"Roger, Sword," the sniper team leader responded quietly. "Archer teams are in place and ready."

Randall acknowledged the radio transmission and the radios fell silent again. Melvin and Sam were nestled in their hastily selected hide site in a house across from the spire, spread out just enough to provide maximum coverage of the target. Archer One was set up in a vacant apartment in a building roughly eight hundred meters from the Spire, in two separate rooms with enough window space to give them a good visual. They had been observing the guards in front of the Spire for the past hour. The two men were clearly cold and stood close to the front door to get residual heat leaking from the building.

Mike and Evan had set up around eight hundred forty meters away from the building, trying to get the best angle they could at the rooftop of the Spire. Since the building was nine stories taller than anything else in the area, the Archer teams could only see the edges of the roof from their angles. As far as they could tell, there were only three guys they'd be able to take a shot at, and their primary concern would be relaying intelligence. A drone had arrived overhead roughly twenty minutes ago, and the operator reported a single guard patrolling the roof, making a full circle every couple of minutes and armed with some sort of scoped rifle.

On the off chance that the Iranians and their lackeys managed to get past the Norseman assault teams, Sam and Mike had both picked out rifles with a bit more punching power, while Melvin and Evan had stayed with their 300 Norma Magnums. Set up on a tripod in the room next to Melvin, Sam was busy scanning the area through the scope of his Desert Tech HTI in .50BMG. The massive .50 caliber round was more than capable of knocking out any engine block. Mike was armed with another .50BMG rifle, a shortened Barrett M107A1. The massive guns were to be used only in a contingency. They didn't want a stray ricochet launching through an inhabited neighborhood.

"Sword inbound, two mikes." Melvin clicked his radio twice, signaling his acknowledgment and settling behind his rifle.

"In a few short hours," Omid Mokri was speaking to his assembled warriors, "you will embark on one of the most ambitious attacks on American soil since Pearl Harbor."

Javad thought that was a bit exaggerated, but he kept silent, standing passively behind the pacing VAJA commander as he addressed his troops.

"We will crush the American fighting spirit," Mokri was punching his left hand as he enunciated. "We will cause them to cry out to their leaders to withdraw from their bases in our countries to handle the threats at home. We will sow fear and paranoia among their people, cause citizens to turn against one another."

The Iranian commander turned to pace back in the direction he had come from, and the men sitting in the front row could see that his eyes were bloodshot, his expression wild.

"Your charge is not to die," Mokri continued, "but if martyrdom is warranted, then a martyr is what you will become. If such an event occurs, your families will be compensated for generations in not only wealth and power, but in gratitude that you were the cause of America's downfall."

Javad didn't understand the pull of a religious call to action, although he understood the lure of money and power. These men were ruthless mercenaries that had been recruited straight off the battlefields of Iraq, Syria, and Afghanistan. They would have come to America to kill Americans for the price of bullets and a plane ticket. But Javad supposed that even mercenaries liked to pretend they had principles, too.

Mokri's speech went on for an intolerably long time, and Javad found that he had almost totally tuned the man out as he plotted his escape from this miserable, frozen land. The IRGC sergeant Hakimi had become his co-conspirator in the interest of saving the lives of as many of his loyal commandos as he could. Javad was snapped back to the present by Mokri calling his name.

"Javad, the assignments!"

The VAJA agent walked forward with a stack of sealed manila envelopes and addressed a dozen Chechens and two dozen Syrians sitting, kneeling, and standing in Mokri's office and living quarters, spilling out of the room into the hallway from their sheer number.

"These are your assignments." Javad started passing the envelopes around. Each had a man's name on it. "You are to travel alone or in pairs, and then execute the missions in the exact order in which they appear on the orders you've just received. You leave in the morning, so please take tonight to prepare your equipment and prepare your minds."

The VAJA agents dismissed the men, and Hakimi caught Javad's eye. The commando was itching for the opportunity to execute Mokri and exfiltrate the country, but both men knew that they had to ensure at least that their mercenaries' missions were underway before they left.

Mokri was still standing at the front of the room, his hands clasped behind his back.

"A rousing speech, *Aqa*," Javad said to his commander. "I am sure the men will perform their tasks admirably."

"Even so, Javad," Mokri said, "we cannot leave until we are sure of success."

"I agree," Javad nodded gravely.

Mokri looked at him sideways before continuing. "We must also make our preparations. Leave me."

Javad limped back out into the hallway and headed toward his apartment. He nodded at Sergeant Hakimi as he passed. Tomorrow, he mouthed.

The sergeant nodded slightly, a bleak expression on his face.

Alex and his team sat on the tarmac at Norseman Consulting's airfield, the powerful turbine engines of the twin HH-65 Dolphin helicopters idling over his team's heads. The pilots were performing their last pre-flight checks, and Axe team listened on the radios to their Sword counterparts approach the target building on the ground. Alex looked at the thick ropes coiled at his feet and hoped that the deployment system they'd rigged up would work.

When announced that his assault team was just five minutes from the target building, Raven One and Raven Two lifted off, carrying the twelve assaulters into the air and on a meandering route toward the Spire. Alex watched the faces of the men on his team, all locked in their pre-game rituals. Some men were praying, some were talking to each other, telling jokes, and some were just blankly staring into space.

This was more than Alex had hoped for when he agreed to come work for Norseman Consulting. He had retired from the Marines at thirty-eight and had been working as a manager at a hardware store,

214

growing more and more bored by the day. Dufraine had been a commanding officer of his during his younger, more exciting days, and there had been mutual respect grown through service together in tough situations. The old Marine officer had offered him a job, and Alex had not looked back.

A few short years and a couple of low-key security jobs later, here Alex was preparing to lead an assault force on Iranians on American soil.

"Sword inbound, two mikes." Alex's reflective mood was brought to an abrupt end as the two-minute warning came and the helicopter banked, turning a final time to put the assault team on a direct route toward the Spire.

"Sentry walking to your side, Archer One." The drone operator back at Norseman Consulting's headquarters spoke through the radio. "Should have visual in three... two... one..."

Right on cue, the sentry appeared, looking over the unfinished top floor of the Spire. The man turned to walk the next side of the roof, where, if all went as planned, he would be unable to see the approach of Sword team at the front door below.

"Alright, keep watching him," Melvin directed the drone pilot, before switching his attention to Tiff and Tim waiting in their cars below.

"Driver One, Archer One-One," the sniper broadcast while swiveling his bullpup back to the two goons standing post outside the front door. "Initiate on my mark."

"Roger One-One," Tiff's voice came through the radio.

"Archer Two," Melvin addressed his counterparts in the other sniper hide, "prepare to initiate."

Receiving his two clicks, Melvin checked his ballistic calculations one more time, examined the dials on the powerful scope mounted to his rifle, and settled the crosshairs where he wanted them.

Tiff and Tim had been given an additional task. After dropping off the two sniper teams, Tiff headed over to collect Tim in her Sentra, and the two of them hightailed it to the nearest power transformer.

A dented, dark green box protruded from the frozen ground, and they pulled up in front of it and let the car idle as they waited for Melvin's signal. Tiff was monitoring the Spire through a small monocular, and Tim scanned the area around the power station for any potential danger. The chatted as they waited, and learned that they'd both been in the Army, even stationed at the same base for a short time.

Tim was a former infantryman. He'd spent a six-year enlistment in the 1st Infantry Division at Fort Riley in Kansas. After multiple deployments, the Army was drawing down and threatening soldiers with forced separation. Seeing as Tim never really had plans to stay in a full twenty years, he had hopped out ahead of time and started college on the GI Bill.

A terrible job market greeted him post-graduation, as well as some hefty stigma associated with his status as a combat veteran. As he struggled to find gainful employment, he found Norseman Consulting. He quickly discovered he was not alone; most of the crew at Norsemen landed there by scouring the dark recesses of the internet, aka "unemployment hell." He enjoyed the camaraderie with like-minded soldiers and the hard work, but secretly just wanted to get out and live a normal life for a change.

Tiff had been in the Military Police Battalion at Fort Riley, the 97th, and had done a four-year enlistment. After her first deployment to Africa, she sought out moving to one of the Special Operations Cultural Support Teams. After her application was denied, she finished her enlistment and got out, also on the GI Bill. She got a degree in Criminal Justice and Law Enforcement, hoping to leverage her time as a Military Police officer as a way into the Federal Bureau of Investigation. Here, too, her application was denied. She continued to apply to the FBI after taking on work with Norseman Consulting, though, as anyone could guess, her hopes diminished with every rejection.

As the two shifted to trading workout tips—Tiff was a huge fitness buff and the resident CrossFit expert on Norseman's team—four large, gray SUVs went roaring past her.

"There they go," she said excitedly. "Get ready."

Tim unbuckled his seatbelt and cracked his door, allowing the cold air to invade the small sedan.

A sudden movement at the front door caught Tiff's attention, and she quickly broadcast over the radio: "Be advised, two additional personnel just walked out the front door. Looks like a shift change."

The monocular now showed four men standing in the glow of the streetlight in front of the Spire. The SUVs were rapidly closing in on

216

the building. Norseman Consulting couldn't stop their momentum now; they'd have to improvise and move fast.

"Shit," Melvin breathed as he watched the men walk out of the Spire, seeing them at the same time Tiff did. The sniper leader could sense Sam swiveling his big rifle away from the garage and toward the newcomers in front of the building.

"Archer Two-Two, need you to cover the fourth guy," Melvin ordered through the radio. The four snipers called out their respective targets and waited for Melvin to give the signal. The Ford Expeditions carrying the Sword teams were roaring toward the Spire, but the guards seemed unaware of them. They stood under the streetlight eight hundred meters away from Archer One's position, slightly gesturing when they weren't tucking their hands into their armpits. Melvin settled his crosshairs on the chest of the man closest to the door and squeezed the trigger.

The rifle bucked slightly, the suppressed round snapping out of the barrel and rocketing towards its target. At eight hundred meters, the .300 Norma Magnum round was still a pretty flat shooting cartridge, although the suppressor slowed the bullet's velocity slightly. A split second after Melvin fired his cartridge, there was a muffled boom in the room next to him, and Sam launched a .50BMG round at his target.

From their distance, Evan and Mike were able to see the first target crumple. Archer Two quickly depressed their triggers, near-simultaneous rounds screaming downrange and impacting the stunned guards still standing in front of the Spire. A couple of seconds later, the lights in the Spire went out, dousing the building in darkness for a moment before the emergency power kicked on. The Ford Expeditions rolled to a quick stop, and the Sword teams disembarked. The SUVs tore off to take up their blocking positions.

"Go!" Tiff shouted, and Tim jumped out of the idling sedan and ripped open the electrical box. He had no idea what he was looking at, so Tim tossed in the small strip of plastic explosive, dropping the detonating cord behind him as he hopped back in the car, taking cover before depressing the plunger.

A loud bang reverberated, and the power in the Spire, as well as several houses nearby, was cut off. Through her monocular, Tiff had witnessed the elimination of the four guards at the door, and she turned her attention to the guard on the roof.

"Rooftop sentry should be visible by Archer One in two seconds," the drone operator warned Melvin, and the sniper scanned the unfinished rooftop with his rifle. Sure enough, the guard appeared over the edge of the building. Or rather, the glow of his flashlight appeared. Taking careful aim, and re-checking his calculations for the high angle shot, Melvin squeezed the trigger and sent a round through the man's chest.

The sentry dropped the flashlight and crumpled. His corpse plummeted over the edge, twelve stories down, and impacted the ground with a sickening crunch.

"Rooftop clear," the drone operator announced.

Melvin swiveled his rifle back to ground level, searching for any targets that might appear as Sword began their assault through the front door.

Through the windshield of the Expedition, Randall watched the four guards get cut down within seconds of each other just before his teamed rolled up to the building. The twelve Sword team members jumped out of their vehicles and sprinted up to the front door, and the drivers navigated the SUVs to their positions.

The assaulters cut striking figures in the darkness as they rushed forward in their mottled winter camouflage and four-tube night vision devices mounted to their helmets. Moving quickly and smoothly forward, the twelve men entered the dimly lit front lobby of the Spire. Shutting off the power had shrouded the building in relative darkness, save for a few dim, battery-powered emergency lights. The white phosphorescent glow in the night vision cut through the gloom, showing the assaulters they were alone for the time being.

Without a word, the men pushed forward to the stairwell, pushing upward to start clearing the building a floor at a time.

"Why is the power off?!" Omid Mokri demanded frantically.

"I'm not sure," Javad frowned. It was possible that the outage was coincidental, but the VAJA agent no longer believed in coincidences. He moved to look out the window at the front of the building below but stopped just short of pulling black the thick curtain when Sergeant

Hakimi came running into the room in full combat gear, wearing one of the ballistic vests that only the Iranian commandos had been issued. "The Americans are coming," he blurted.

Javad did not wait for Mokri to respond. "Where are they?" he demanded.

"They killed the locals out front and are making their way through the front door right now."

"Okay, send the rest of the RIF contingent to the fifth or sixth floor to slow their advance from above," Javad thought quickly. "Tell them the fascists just killed more of their comrades without provocation."

"And the others?"

"You choose, Sergeant," Javad said. "You're the commando in charge here. I'll work on our escape."

The sergeant ran off with a quick nod, barking orders to his commandos and rousing the Syrian and Chechen mercenaries to gather their arms.

Javad turned back to his boss. Mokri was still behind his desk, his usually olive complexion a waxy white. Omid Mokri had professed to Javad a desire to die for his country, but Javad knew he had never really thought about how that would happen. It appeared to Javad that perhaps Mokri did not want to perish in service to his country after all.

Neither did Javad, and he shouted at Mokri to jar him out of his panic-induced paralysis. "Sir! We have to prepare to evacuate. Where's your gear?"

Mokri jumped out of his chair, knocking it over and running to his bedroom where he hastily threw on his plate carrier and snatched up his rifle, fumbling to load a magazine into the AK74SU.

He emerged after a few seconds, his rifle magazines curving in all different directions from the pouches on his plate carrier, the rifle itself dangling from a nylon sling around his neck. Mokri had a Glock 19 pistol in his hand and was fumbling for the holster on his belt.

"Wait here," Javad directed and hobbled out of the room. Under normal circumstances, Javad knew that Mokri would not tolerate being talked to in such a manner. Javad's field experience was suddenly very appealing.

Javad reappeared a few minutes later, his short-barreled Kalashnikov hanging from his hand and a chest rig loaded with magazines over his jacket. Javad opted for a slick, low-profile plate carrier that he could hide under a thick sweatshirt or winter coat in case he needed to wear it in public.

"Wha-what do we do now?" Mokri stammered. He looked embarrassed at how afraid he was, especially since his battle-hardened subordinates appeared so calm.

"We wait for the commandos to give us the all clear," Javad said with a disdainful look. He was reasonably sure he would find Mokri's cowardice humorous if they survived, but at the moment he just needed to get as many Iranians out of there as possible. "And then we enact our escape plan."

Mokri gulped and started to nod, letting out a small whimper as the first rapid gunshots echoed up from the lower floors, followed by muffled *cuh-ruhmps* as small explosions shook the building.

CHAPTER THIRTY-EIGHT

The layout of the Spire was simple. Eleven finished floors, counting the lobby, two elevators housed in a shaft in the center that went from the underground parking garage to the eleventh finished floor. Stairwells were running up both the north and south sides of the building, all the way to the unfinished twelfth floor. Each level was more or less identical.

Clearing the building would be difficult, though. Fifteen apartments per floor would make for slow going, and they still didn't know how many hostiles they were dealing with.

Cutting the power had given the assault team a definitive advantage. Randall and Sword One pushed up the north stairwell, their night vision goggles guiding them through the dark apartment building. Green, infrared lasers mounted to the top rail of each man's carbine danced across walls and doors as Sword One cleared the second floor.

Sword Two had leapfrogged Sword One and was busy clearing the third floor. So far, no targets had been sighted, but Sword Two was reporting that they could hear footsteps and shouting a floor or two above them. As the assaulters moved through the building and turned up empty apartment after empty apartment, Randall was becoming increasingly anxious.

What he had hoped for was limited, scattered resistance across the building. It seemed more likely now that they were going to meet a concentrated defense on the higher floors. Randall was toying with the idea of moving the operation agenda forward ahead of schedule and contacting Alex, but he determined that he did not need Alex's help just yet. He was just anxious.

"Clear!" Harold called, and the contractors collapsed back into their tactical stack and started up to the next floor, utilizing the south stairwell this time.

"Third floor clear," Rafael announced in Randall's headset. "Moving to the fifth floor."

"Roger. Second floor clear, proceeding to fourth," Randall confirmed as the point man, John, cautiously opened the door to the fourth floor.

Rafael was pushing Sword Two up the stairs from the middle of the stack. His point man, Alfred, had reached the door and chanced a quick look through the narrow, reinforced glass window.

Jerking his head back, Alfred whispered, "Contact, four tangos in the center of the hallway. They've got carbines."

"Which way are they facing?" Rafael whispered back.

"Two are facing this way, and two are facing the south stairwell door. They have some barricade erected, looks like they ripped doors off and threw them up as cover."

Rafael nodded and reached for his radio mouthpiece. "Sword One, Sword Two-One, we have four tangos sighted on the fifth floor. They have erected a barricade. We are about to go loud."

Two clicks sounded through the radio headset, and Rafael motioned to Max and Henry at the back of the stack. The two contractors moved forward and primed flashbangs as Alfred eased the door open.

The door creaked slightly, and the two targets facing the north stairwell opened fire with their AKM carbines, punching holes through the door. One round barely missed Alfred's hand, and he let go of the rapidly disintegrating door, which swung shut.

Max had been able to throw his flashbang before retreating, pitching it as far as he could down the hall. Henry's flashbang, however, pinged off the door and exploded a few feet in, rocking the contractors with the ear-splitting explosion.

The men in the hallway had not stopped firing, even after the first flashbang detonated in front of their barricade. They were now blindly raking their fire across the wall, firing as fast as they could pull their triggers.

Undisciplined and not formally trained, both men ran their rifles dry at the same time. Mimicking what they had seen in movies, which accounted for the vast majority of their tactical training, they both ducked behind the barricade and screamed, "Reloading!"

Alfred didn't have to be told twice. Yanking the door open, the point man strode quickly into the dim hallway, sweeping his B&T carbine up and tracing the green laser sight across the first target he saw. The man was turning around to cover the north stairwell. Alfred stroked the trigger, sending six subsonic 300 Blackout rounds coughing out of his carbine and into the man's chest. The man bent over backward at the waist and crashed down onto the hastily constructed barricade.

Still moving forward, Alfred swiveled his hips and realigned his sights with the next target, who was still facing the south stairwell. He gave the man no chance to turn around, sending a few rounds into his upper back and allowing the recoil of the carbine to lift the muzzle slightly higher with each shot. The last series blew through the back of the man's skull.

By this time, Tony had joined Alfred in the hallway and was searching for targets. He and Alfred spied two muzzles sticking out above the barricade as the two remaining men struggled to reload their AKMs. The contractors leveled their carbines and started punching shots through the wooden barricade.

An eerie spray of blood was illuminated in their night vision goggles. One of the AKMs clattered to the ground, but the other man hopped straight upright, surprising the two contractors. He'd been shot multiple times but had the strength and wherewithal to level his rifle at the assault team, and they snapped several quick rounds into his chest and face, hammering him over and down into the other barricade.

"Clear!" Alfred shouted.

"Check the rooms!" Rafael was in the hallway now. It was occurring to him how narrow the hall felt when they all were standing in it at the same time.

The four dead men in the hallway had been the only ones on the floor. Rafael spoke into his radio, "The fifth floor clear, four tangos down." Looking down at their bodies, he added, "Judging by their weapons and the slogans on their shirts, looks like these were some of those revolutionary types."

"Roger that," Randall replied. "We are moving to the sixth floor now."

Sword Two was already moving to the stairwell to head to the seventh floor. Alfred and Tony performed quick reloads for their carbines, placing their partially spent magazines in the dump pouches bouncing around on their belts. Remy replaced Alfred as the point man, and Rafael fell in behind him.

"Hallway looks clear," John said as he peered through the sixth-floor window.

A series of taps went down the line and then back up to John, and he pulled the door open and moved cautiously forward. Sword Two had taken contact on the floor below them, and it was increasingly likely that they would encounter resistance as they ascended the building.

John moved softly past the first apartment door and took a knee, covering the length of the hallway while his teammates behind him prepared to clear the floor one apartment at a time. Vince jiggled the apartment's doorknob and, finding it locked, rammed his breaching tool into the frame and wrenched the door open.

Finn led the way into the room, with right behind him. The apartment was much the same as the others they had encountered. Single bedroom with a combination living and dining room and a small kitchen attached. This one appeared to have been lived in recently, judging by the small pile of dirty dishes in the kitchen sink.

The contractors padded softly over the cheap carpet, their carbines leading the way into the bedroom. The bedroom appeared empty with only a foam bedroll on the floor, and they moved to check the bathroom.

"Contact in the hallway," John said into his radio. "Someone just poked their head out of a far room and ducked back in."

"Roger," Finn responded, looking at Randall and Vince as they got in position to leave the first apartment. "This room is clear, and we're coming back out."

Finn joined his teammates at the end of their short line, and they left the bedroom to join John, Cooper, and Harold in the hallway. As they left the bedroom and entered the kitchen, the wall directly behind them exploded inward.

The explosion sent chunks of drywall and plaster flying at the contractors, coating Finn's back with white powder. At the end of the hallway leading out of the bedroom, and Vince had the presence of mind to dive in either direction away from the explosion. Finn was still in the hall and could only dive forward.

His head and ears ringing, Finn rolled over on his back in time to see a man coated in white plaster pick his way through the new man-sized hole in the wall. The man was blinking, clearly disorientated from the explosion. He was holding a Ruger Mini-14 in an ugly Tapco chassis with all sorts of tactical accessories hanging off of the rifle's Picatinny rails.

224

Lying supine as he was, Finn was not able to get the same cheek weld on the stock of his rifle as he usually did. Finn twisted his APC300 to get the laser from his aiming module on the man's torso.

The laser danced over the man's hip, and Finn pulled the trigger. The first round smashed the man's pelvis, causing him to yelp and start to topple over. Finn walked subsequent rounds across the man's torso as he fell, giving him two finishing rounds to the face as he hit the ground.

Two more rifles popped around the corner of the hole in the wall, firing blind rounds over Finn's head as he lay on his back in the hallway. The contractor took the opportunity to scoot backward, keeping his carbine pointed at the hole.

"Are you hit?!" Randall screamed over the gunfire in the apartment.

"No!" Finn yelled back, scrambling around the corner next to Vince, who quickly assessed him for any injuries. Vince flashed a quick thumb up, and Finn became aware that there was gunfire out in the hallway as well, drowning out the suppressed shooting of his teammates.

The gunfire coming from the hole had ceased, Finn levered himself up on one knee and peeked around the corner. He quickly pulled his head back. He signaled to Vince, who rose to stand above Finn.

On Finn's signal, the two contractors popped around the corner simultaneously and discharged their carbines with rapid precision, eliminating the two rifle-wielding gunmen that had just climbed through the hole.

Finn and Vince held their positions. The gunfire in the hallway outside the apartment sounded like it was tapering off, although it had not stopped altogether.

Randall was still kneeling behind his corner, using his radio to communicate with Axe team. "Axe One-One, Sword One-One. Heavy contact encountered. You are good to go."

"Roger, Sword One-One," Alex's voice came through over the sound of helicopter rotors in the background. "Coming to your rescue."

"Fuck you, over," Randall replied. Turning toward the door, he shouted at John, "What's going on out there?"

"We're good," John yelled back. The gunfire had all but subsided. "Two tangos down for sure, one popped back into one of the far rooms."

"Alright, we're coming out," Randall called, motioning to Vince and Finn. The three men hustled out into the hallway. Dozens of spent casings littered the floor and Vince slipped on an empty rifle magazine on the floor, nearly losing his footing. He managed to stay upright, and Cooper snickered behind him. Vince kicked a casing backward at Cooper while he moved forward.

"The last guy ducked into the last room on the left," John said, "Tighten it up you two.". Rifles swiveled in that direction, and the team moved forward, covering the upcoming doorways as they went.

A sudden commotion at the end of the hallway caused the assaulters' carbines to swing toward the last room, and a man went running out toward the exit door to the far stairwell. The first three contractors in line fired rapidly, hitting the man in the back. His body slammed into the entrance to the stairwell, pushing it open slightly as he slid down and leaving a bloody streak. He gurgled somewhat and tried to push himself forward. Vince shot once more, silencing him.

"Alright, finish clearing the floor," commanded before speaking into his radio. "Sword Two, hold on seven and wait for Axe's arrival."

"Roger that," Rafael breathed into his microphone.

Sword One set about clearing the remaining apartments, the faint sound of helicopter rotors growing ever louder.

"That's a helicopter," Omid Mokri said needlessly. The Iranian commander had not said a single word since the gunfire had erupted below them a few minutes prior. Javad had been pulling Mokri around behind him as he had been rushing around, planting explosives on the material that they had to leave behind.

Javad notified the IRGC commander of the approaching helicopter via radio and snatched up his AK74SU, which was leaning against a crate. "That's going to have to be good enough," he said.

The Iranian commander nodded, pitching the last two bricks of plastic explosives into the closest open crate. Javad dug through a duffel bag he pulled out of one of the many containers stacked up in the room and withdrew a series of nylon harnesses.

"Put this on," Javad directed Mokri, tossing him one. As the two Iranians slipped into their climbing gear, stowing the loose carabiner clips to ensure they would not interfere with their weapons, the sound of IRGC commandos running past them was drowned out by the roar of the helicopter just above them.

The lead helicopter came to a hover about fifteen feet above the unfinished roof of the Spire. There were too many unknown obstacles on the roof, made Axe One fast rope out of the helicopter. Thick black ropes dropped out of each side of the aircraft, and Alex led the way, sliding down the line and quickly getting his carbine up and scanning for enemy fighters.

After the six members of Axe One were on the roof, the first helicopter banked and left the rooftop, taking up an orbit around the Spire. The second helicopter carrying Axe Two swung into place, duplicating the maneuver.

Alex was facing the south stairwell when he heard someone scream "CONTACT!" followed by a series of rapid, suppressed carbine shots. Those shots were answered with a loud FWOOSH, and Alex heard Angelo scream, "RPG!"

Raven Two's helicopter pilot had spotted the unmistakable form of the RPG-7's tube launcher silhouetted in his night vision goggles. The pilot swept the helicopter in a quick turn to avoid getting struck by the rocket.

Angelo sent several rounds into the Iranian's chest and head as he ran up onto the roof. The bullets smacked into the man's chest plates and caused him to jerk the trigger on the launcher, shooting the RPG off at a shallow angle. The rocket skipped off of a support column jutting out of the unfinished roof and ricocheted off into the night. The man who had fired it now lay in a heap on the stairs.

The quick rotation of Raven Two had startled the last man sliding down the rope and shake him loose. Joe fell the last five feet to the ground but managed to perform a parachute landing fall, cushioning the drop. Despite that, he felt a sharp pang in his ankle, and he lay on his back, staring up into the night as the helicopter veered off.

"You okay?" Ted was leaning over the fallen man with his hand extended. Joe took Axe Two-One's hand and was hauled to his feet with a groan.

"I think I sprained my fuckin' ankle." Joe winced as he gingerly tried to put some weight on his injured left leg. "I can still work, though."

Ted nodded and said, "Okay, get in the back."

"Hey, let's go!" Alex shouted, and Axe One and Axe Two made their way to their assigned stairwells, hustling to assist the Sword teams on the floors below. As soon as Axe Two turned down the stairs, their point man, Bryan, snapped his carbine up and started firing down the stairwell. A gunman had been waiting around the door to ambush the team, but he was unable to see them in the dark before Bryan's night vision goggles illuminated him in a white phosphorus glow.

The lead assaulter's first shots missed the target, chipping concrete and splintering wood, and inspiring the gunman to let loose with a haphazard burst of fire as he dove back behind the door. The rounds smacked harmlessly into the unfinished cinder-block wall of the stairwell, and Bryan kept inching forward, rifle up and ready to engage. Arriving at the still-open door, Bryan peeled around the corner, searching for the man who had escaped his bullets in the stairwell. There was nobody in the hallway, but there were cords all around the floor, crisscrossing and running from apartment to apartment.

Axe Two pushed forward into the hallway, getting ready to clear the top floor. It didn't take long. "All stations, Axe Two-One," Ted spoke, his voice sounding anxious over the radio. "Negative tangos on the top floor. There are multiple crates, almost all rigged with explosives."

"Roger that Axe Two-One." For the first time since the operation began, the Norseman Consulting command team monitoring the operation from the Brain chimed into the proceedings. "Continue as planned and we will re-evaluate upon completion."

"Roger, Axe Two proceeding to the ninth floor," Ted said, sweat pouring down the sides of his face and along his back. Standing this close to a whole floor of explosives was making him more than a little nervous.

"Axe Two-One, Axe One-One," Alex called. "We are set just outside ten. Multiple hostiles in the hallway and rooms."

"Sword One and Sword Two are set on seven and eight," Randall's voice came through the radio.

Axe Two came to a cautious halt at the door to the ninth floor. Quickly assessing their options, Bryan turned and motioned for the breacher to come to the front of the stack. Larry duck walked past the door frame to avoid exposing himself through the narrow window. He tested the door handle by applying slow, steady pressure. Confirming the door was unlocked, Larry nodded at Bryan.

Bryan and Ted nodded back, pulling flashbangs out of the pouches on their plate carriers.

"On my mark," Alex spoke softly in their headsets. "Three... two... one!"

Four doors swung open, and eight flashbangs were simultaneously thrown into four separate hallways. The explosions ripped through the building, and the contractors flowed into the hall to finish their assault.

On the seventh floor, Remy led Sword Two's assault, pushing into the dimly lit hallway with his carbine up. The first target he found was a man leaning out from an apartment on the left, leveling a short Kalashnikov at the stack of Norseman contractors. The man sprayed a quick volley of shots, hitting the wall next to Remy, the bullets chewing up the cheap plaster and climbing into the ceiling.

Remy discharged his rifle nearly a dozen times, punching rounds through the corner of the alcove and hitting the man in the chest, leg, and arms, causing him to flinch and cry out as the bones in his leg shattered and dropped him writhing on the floor.

The rifle fire served as a signal, and five additional men leaned out of their doorways, firing at the contractors as they filled the hallway. Max and Remy pushed further into the hall, giving the four contractors behind them enough room to clear the first two rooms. The two men knelt, snapping quick pairs of shots at the gunmen down the hallway as they poked their heads out, keeping them from taking aimed shots.

Rafael and Alfred quickly breached the first apartment on the right and rapidly cleared the small living room. Shouting to each other that the place was clear, they turned to clear the bedroom at the end of the short hallway. The two contractors turned and started down the hall and were greeted by a tunnel that ran through the walls of every apartment on the floor.

"They spider holed the entire right side of the floor!" Rafael broadcast through the radio.

"We are clear on this side," Henry responded. "Three tangos down."

As Henry's broadcast came through, an AK74SU was nosed around the corner of the tunnel, and a full magazine ripped across the walls and ceiling near Rafael and Alfred.

The two men dropped back, taking cover around opposite corners from the hallway leading to the spider hole.

"We need some help clearing the right side," Rafael called into his radio.

"Roger, coming to you."
A few seconds later, Henry and Tony hustled through the door.

"Remy and Max have it held down out there," Henry said. "I think they got all of them so far."

"Cool," Rafael nodded. "We gotta clear through the tunnel."

Alfred had been leaning out around the corner, observing the tunnel. "Judging by the flashlight beams, there is at least a half-dozen of 'em back there."

The four men got ready, and then pushed themselves up and through the hallway, preparing to squeeze through the tunnel.

The tunnel the gunmen had smashed through the apartment walls was just high and wide enough for an average man to pass through without ducking. It had a lip of leftover wall that extended about five or six inches up from the floor.

Rafael led the way into the tunnel, swiveling to the left in the direction that the rifle rife came from. A small, red-faced man was right next to the edge of the tunnel. The gunman held his gun in both hands and was aiming at the ceiling. Rafael shot him at point-blank range, spraying the wall with blood as the man crumpled to the floor with a gurgle.

As Rafael eliminated the man in the left corner, Alfred rushed forward to cover the other side. The contractor did not pick up his feet enough, though, and he tripped over the ledge rising out of the floor and pitched face-first into the ground.

The fall saved him. A gunman in the opposite corner had fired at the opening to the tunnel just as Alfred came through, but the rounds sailed over his head. Seeing his target fall, the gunman transitioned to Rafael.

At about the same time that Rafael turned, the gunman fired, and Tony followed Alfred through the tunnel. The gunman's burst slammed two rounds into Rafael's back ballistic plate, knocking the wind out of him and pushing him off balance. A third-round smashed

Rafael's right shoulder, nearly ripping his right arm off and causing him to drop his carbine.

Tony put four quick rounds into the gunman's face, snapping his head backward and blowing the back of the man's skull across the wall.

"Rafael is hit!" Tony shouted as Alfred pulled himself to his feet.

The contractors could see their team leader's teeth gritted in pain as he sat against the wall trying to swim out of his carbine's sling with his only working arm.

Henry came through the tunnel last, and while Alfred and Tony held security, he quickly went to work. Ripping into Rafael's own first aid kit on his belt, Henry poured a packet of clotting agent into the bleeding wound and stuffed gauze on top of it before taping a hasty bandage around his arm.

As Henry worked on Rafael, more rounds started cracking past the contractors in the hallway. Remy and Max ducked reflexively and started firing at the new targets that had appeared out of the doorways down the hall.

Two more gunmen materialized inside the next tunnel through to the next apartment, and Tony and Alfred started discharging their carbines through the opening, dropping both assailants in a hail of suppressed gunfire.

Henry was finishing up with Rafael, wrapping the man's right arm up in a sling and positioning the carbine in his left hand.

"Thanks," Rafael groaned. "Fred, you have the stick."

Alfred nodded his acknowledgment, and Rafael gingerly walked back through the tunnel to the first room to get out of the way and prepare for evacuation. The three remaining contractors prepared to clear the rest of the apartments. They could hear gunfire coming from further down the tunnel.

The three men encountered no resistance in the next couple of apartments, but they knew there were at least two gunmen in the last two apartments. Alfred prepared to move through the next to last tunnel, taking care not to trip over the ledge.

There were two men in the next apartment. One was leaning out the door, firing his AK74SU down the hallway at Remy and Max. The second was just rocking a new magazine into his short assault rifle as Alfred strode in.

The second gunman shouted out, and Alfred shot him three times in rapid succession, dropping him onto the carpet. Alfred's carbine locked open on an empty magazine. Sensing that, he let the carbine fall into its sling across his chest and quickly drew his pistol.

Hearing his friend shout and drop to the floor, the first gunman whirled around and aimed his assault rifle at Alfred.

Alfred could see the rifle coming to bear as his pistol cleared its holster. As soon as he had the pistol level, Alfred fired, letting the pistol climb up to his eye level. The 9mm hollow points left the barrel of the pistol at Alfred's waist level, the first bullet smacking into the ground in front of the gunman's knee.

The rest of the rounds walked up and across the gunman's body, causing him to jerk and spasm and fire his carbine erratically. One stray shot hit Alfred in the plates. The contractor felt his breath leave his body, and he knew his ribs were broken. He grimaced and brought his pistol up to eye level, then emptied the rest of his magazine into the gunman's chest and face.

As the gunman's rifle fell out of his hands and he twitched on the floor, Alfred noticed that his pistol was empty. He made a move to reload it, and the pain from the rifle round spasmed across his chest. Alfred managed to extract a pistol magazine from his pouch, and then gingerly holstered the weapon and reloaded his carbine.

"Last room," Alfred wheezed.

"You good?" Henry asked, keeping his carbine pointed at the last tunnel.

"Yeah," Alfred grunted, motioning for Tony to take point.
There was a long, ripping burst of automatic fire from the next room and then the room went silent.

"Tango down," Max called through the radio. "Hallway is clear again."

Tony quickly pushed Henry and Alfred, who was now bringing up the rear and wincing with every jarring step, into the last apartment. The final gunman on the floor had met his end at the hands of Max or Remy in the hallway.

"Last room clear," Tony spoke into the radio. "Sword Two has cleared the seventh floor."

Overhead, the muffled sounds of gunfire could be heard as the remaining teams fought their way through their assigned floors.

CHAPTER THIRTY-NINE

The eighth floor was bristling with gunmen. As Axe team landed on the roof and worked their way to their positions, John had been observing their adversaries as they set up their defenses. Furniture had been dragged into the hallway, impeding the path of Sword One's assault.

John had counted at least ten men so far, all armed with stubby AK74SU assault rifles and strapped with chest rigs loaded down with spare magazines. John was whispering his observations back to his teammates in the stairwell, and they were improvising a plan.

Speed was the key to success, and with the scattered couches, tables, and chairs strewn about the hallway and shooters loaded to the teeth crouched behind them, their speed was going to be hindered considerably. Finally having laid out an agreeable plan, Sword Two settled in and waited for Alex's countdown.

As soon as the signal was given, John threw the door open, and Vince and Finn threw their flashbangs into the hallway. The six contractors flowed in immediately after and started firing into the barricade. All six contractors were in the hall, spent brass flying from their carbines' ejection ports, suppressed rounds ripping splintering wooden chairs and ripping the stuffing out of cheap couches.

There was no return fire. The two gunmen crouched behind the nearest couch had fallen quickly to the furious gunfire coming from the assault team. One of the gunmen lay draped over the sofa, several bullet wounds in his chest. The second had taken a round straight through the center of his throat and dropped down behind the couch, his head barely hanging onto his neck.

Sword Two ceased firing, peering through the jumble of furniture for additional targets. The hallway was quiet, save for the muffled sounds of gunfire on the floors above and below them. Nobody spoke, and John and Vince covered the rest of the hallway as the other four split into teams of two to clear the rooms on either side of the entrance.

Randall's door on the right swung open freely, allowing him and Finn to rush into the apartment quickly. Empty.

The door on the left was locked, prompting Harold to rear back and slam his boot into it, kicking it inward, the strong momentum pulled him into the apartment with Cooper hot on his heels. As soon as

Harold broke through, a hail of bullets split the air between him and Cooper, and the two men turned outward to cover the room.

A lone gunman was firing his AK74SU from the hip, chasing Harold with a full magazine. Cooper snapped the aiming module of his carbine onto the gunman and started pulling the trigger.

The first three rounds smashed into the gunman's thigh, shattering his femur and ripping through his femoral artery. Cooper kept firing, tracing his rounds into the man's hips, gut, and chest. As a former Pararescue Jumper and highly trained medical professional, Cooper knew that his shots had killed the man, even as he squirmed on the floor and screamed in pain.

Cooper shot him in the head, silencing his screams.

"You good, man?" Cooper shouted to Harold over his shoulder.

"Yeah, man," Harold responded. "No extra holes yet."

"Follow me," Cooper said, keeping his rifle trained on the end of the hallway to the bedroom. Harold fell in line behind the former Pararescue operative, and the two of them walked briskly toward the closed door of the bedroom in front of them.

The door creaked open slightly, and the distinctive flash hider at the end of a Krinkov poked through the crack. Before the gunman behind the door was able to fire, Cooper and Harold opened fire and emptied their carbines through the flimsy wood of the door.

The fire from their suppressed B&T carbines splintered the door, ripping through the wood and cutting through the man on the other side. His AK74SU thudded to the carpet, and Harold and Cooper quickly reloaded their carbines, dropping empty magazines onto the floor and chambering new rounds of 300 Blackout.

Moving forward cautiously, the two contractors could hear a scraping sound from the other side of the door. Cooper reached the door and pulled the door open towards the hallway, the shattered wood dangling from the hinges, and curled around the corner. His eyes immediately found the source of the noise. A dark streak traversed the carpet, leading from the dropped Krinkov by the door to an empty bed frame a few feet away from where a bearded man was dragging himself with one arm, trying to get away. His legs lay uselessly behind him, and his left forearm dangled from a thin piece of skin. The gunman was muttering something in a language that neither Cooper nor Harold understood, although both recognized it as Chechen, that strange sounding mix of Russian and Arabic.

Harold raised his rifle and sent a single suppressed round into the back of the gunman's head.

"Let's go," Cooper said, and the two contractors turned and hustled back into the hallway.

Randall and Finn had rejoined Vince and John and taken up positions on either side of the hallway, and the contractors were waiting for Harold and Cooper to come back from clearing the room. The assault teams could hear shuffling and muttering coming from further down the hallway.

As Harold exited the room, the hallway erupted as multiple shooters started raking 5.45x39mm rounds through the furniture barricades. The bullets chewed through the furniture, and a single shot caught Harold in the side of his head, just in front of his ear and right under the lip of his helmet. The contractor went down without a sound as the round exited his head and blew chunks of bone and brain matter all over the back wall of the hallway.

Cooper was right behind Harold, and he watched the man drop without a sound as if someone had just flipped his life switch to "off." The other four contractors in the hallway returned fire, trying to break through the furniture.

As the team medic, Cooper quickly rushed to Harold and dragged him back into the apartment, but he could tell there was nothing that he would be able to do. That shot had all but emptied the man's head.

Cursing loudly, Cooper stood back up and leaned out the door, firing down the hallway at where he thought the gunmen might be hiding. He ran his carbine dry and ducked back into the apartment to reload.

"Moving!" Randall shouted, and Cooper leaned back out. He, Vince, and John covered Randall and Finn as they clambered over the couch in front of them. The two front men got set and fired their carbines down the hallway.

The gunfire in the hallway was slacking off as Sword One's disciplined return fire pushed the gunmen back under cover. Vince and John climbed over the couch and joined Randall and Finn. Cooper remained, covering the hallway behind.

So far, the contractors had not seen any of the gunmen surface above the furniture. They had entrenched themselves in the barricade and were aiming their fire through the cracks. They'd gotten off a lucky shot with Harold, but now the surviving five assaulters of Sword One were pretty pissed off.

They remained disciplined, though, shooting quick pairs at suspected gunmen positions and communicating with each other as they made their way over the next barricade. This one also had a dead gunman lying behind it. He'd been riddled with bullets, likely from Sword One's return fire as well as the fire of his compatriots behind him.

The contractors had their suppressed carbines leveled over the top of the couch. The fire coming from the gunmen had stopped altogether. Sword One strained to hear with their electronic headsets. There was a series of commands barked out, followed by a series of short, rhythmic words chanted in Chechen.

"They're counting down," Finn said.

Directly in front of the couch that Sword One was crouching behind and about five feet in front of them was a pile of wooden chairs in front of another sofa. When the rhythmic countdown came to an end with an enunciated shout, a gunman popped out on either side of the couch, and two gunmen sprang up over the top of the next couch back.

The gunmen depressed their triggers. One of them landed a burst on the wall directly in front of Cooper, spraying him with drywall and causing him to snap back inside the room. The plaster covered the lenses of his night vision goggles, and he had to wipe the tubes off inside the apartment quickly.

Muzzle flashes stabbed through the dark hallway, illuminating the gunmen and impeding their sight. The Norseman contractors took aim.

Finn and John were in the center of the hallway, kneeling behind the couch. Finn put three rounds into one of the gunmen further down the hall, hitting him at the base of the neck. The gunman dropped down behind the couch. John shot the other man with four rounds to the head.

The gunman leaning out to the left was only about five or six feet from where Randall was positioned, and when the gunman let loose with his AK74SU, Randall could feel the rounds scream past him. Randall shot the man high in his chest, dropping him to the floor. The man struggled to get up, and Sword One's team leader shot him through the face.

Vince shot the last man leaning out to the right straight through the bridge of his nose, and then again as he hit the ground. The hallway

236

was quiet. Waiting for a moment, Randall scanned the entrance and then slowly and smoothly rose to stand.

"Moving," he said and strode forward to climb over the couch.

The contractors clambered over the rest of the barricades, putting security rounds into the heads of the fallen gunmen as they made their way to the end of the hallway.

"Last room clear, Sword Two has cleared the seventh floor."

"Sword One has the eighth floor," Randall radioed in. "One KIA. Multiple EKIA."

Axe Two waited outside the south door to the ninth floor, watching the beams from multiple flashlights bounce off the walls and floor of the hallway, under the door, and through the narrow window. Alex called out the count down.

The flashbangs detonated and Axe Two swept into the hallway, following their carbines and spreading out to dominate the narrow space. Five gunmen were standing in the hall, dazed from the explosions, and Axe Two opened fire, their suppressed rounds ripping through the first two gunmen and immediately crumpling them to the floor.

Two gunmen dove into the alcove that housed the opening to the elevator shaft.

Bryan dropped to his belly and took out the final gunman. He heard a lot of shouting in the apartments lining the hallway, followed by a loud series of explosions as the walls around the contractors erupted into the hallway, sending large sections of wood and plaster raining down on their heads.

The contractors were momentarily stunned, but a barrage of incoming gunfire snapped them out of their stupor, and they began returning fire in the general direction of the newly formed gaps in the walls. The dust from the explosions occluded the contractors' night vision devices and reflected the infrared light from their carbine-mounted lights.

Bryan identified a stab of muzzle flash in the dusty gloom and fired. The firing from that hole stopped, and he swiveled around. Alejandro, who had taken Carl's place on Axe Two, was lying on the ground, a large spear of splintered wall stud sticking out of his inner right thigh. The contractor was bleeding profusely, trying to wrap a tourniquet around his leg while his teammates fired their carbines above his head.

The incoming fire was getting closer. Most of the opening salvo had gone high, as the muzzles of the gunmen's stubby AK74SU assault rifles recoiled and trended upward.

Ted felt a burst of fire crack just past his ear. The dust was beginning to settle into the carpet and his vision improved. Behind him, Larry had kicked open the door to the nearest apartment, and he and Joe went in to clear the room. The two contractors could see that they had gotten incredibly lucky. The apartment held a single gunman, who was only about nine feet away from Bryan, but firing his rifle at the wrong angle through a hole in the wall. Joe put three rounds in his chest, and he and Larry spun around to check the rest of the apartment.

The automatic rifle fire was deafening, even through the contractors' electronic headsets. Larry screamed that the room was clear and then pulled a tiny grenade from a pouch on his vest.

Gunderson had managed to secure a limited number of Dutch V40 mini-grenade clones made by a German firm. The diminutive grenade was slightly larger than a golf ball and perfect for confined spaces.

"GRENADE OUT!" Larry screamed for the benefit of his teammates, then hurled the little grenade through the hole and down the hallway before pulling out a second and hurling it at a different angle.

The first grenade exploded three seconds after Larry had pulled the pin and released the grenade spoon. It hit the floor at the end of the hallway and sent small pieces of shrapnel hissing off through the thin plaster walls of the apartments next to it.

The second grenade sailed through the newly opened wall of an apartment across the hallway and hit one of the gunmen square in the head with a thwack before dropping to the floor between his legs and exploding, eviscerating the gunman and severely wounding the man next to him.

The grenades had the desired effect of causing the gunmen to take cover and cease their firing, which allowed the contractors in the hallway to move forward. The grenades had kicked up some dust, which hung in the air with a gloomy aura.

Bryan and Ted crept to the alcove in the center of the hallway, and Elias covered them as they rushed around the corner, preparing to engage the gunmen who had escaped into the alcove earlier. The two gunmen were flat up against the wall, one right after the other, and

238

when Ted and Bryan broke around the corner, they pulled their rifles up. A burst of rifle fire took Bryan in the throat above his plate carrier. The point man dropped to the floor with a spray of blood and a wet gurgle. Ted shot the second man twice above the bridge of the nose, swiveled, and fired a half-dozen rounds at the first gunman, hitting the wall near the gunman's head with the first round and then landing the last five across his face from ear to ear.

Elias was still covering the hallway when a rifle poked out of another hole. He snapped three quick rounds, impacting the wooden handguard of the Kalashnikov and causing it to clatter out of the owner's hands. Elias kept firing, sending suppressed shots through the thin wall until he was rewarded with a thud on the other side.

Ted quickly checked over Bryan, but he could see the man was dead before he'd even hit the ground. He leaned around the corner to see Joe frantically working on Alejandro, who was lying on his back in the hallway.

Larry moved forward in the hallway, joining Ted and Elias in the center. The three men reached the next hole, and Elias threw a flashbang through the opening before Ted kicked open the corresponding door and the three men flowed into the apartment.

One gunman was crouched next to the fridge, aiming at the hole where the flashbang had come from. Before he had the chance to shift his sights to the door, Elias shot him through the chest and hands. The deceased gunman tipped forward, a bloody stain leaking down onto the linoleum in front of the refrigerator. Elias led the way as the three men pushed into the bedroom.

The bedroom contained two dead gunmen, one leaning against the far wall with the crown of his head missing and another lying face-up on the bed, glassy-eyed, with a pool of blood leaking out of his torso.

A third gunman was sitting in the corner, weakly trying to keep his head up. Bubbles of blood were inflating from his nose with every breath from the bullet in his lung. Elias dropped the muzzle of his carbine and shot the man through the top of his head.

The three men turned and left the apartment and encountered Joe in the hallway.

"How's Hondo?" Ted asked.

"His femoral artery got clipped," Joe said dismally. "It's not severed, though, and I think I managed to stop the bleeding, but he has to get attention quick, or he isn't going to make it."

"We gotta finish the floor," Ted said, shaking his head. "Then we'll get him downstairs."

Joe nodded and the four men set towards the remaining apartments on their floor. The next apartment was the recipient of the second grenade thrown by Larry, and they could see the two dead men through the hole in the wall.

The four contractors burst through the door, fanning out. Clear except for the bodies of the gunmen in the bedroom.

Ted led the assaulters back out into the hallway. He turned the corner and spotted a gunman poking his head over the top of a hole in the wall. Ted snapped off a quick series of shots, but he missed, and the gunman ducked back below the lip of the hole. Ted moved forward, allowing the men following him to get through the door frame.

A second gunman ran into the bedroom, and Joe fired rapidly, hammering the gunman in the torso. The gunman spun to the ground. The contractors quickly stacked up on the door to that apartment and prepared to enter. Elias kicked the door and stepped back. The others flowed around him into the room. Joe was first through the door, and he quickly located and dispatched a target with four clean shots. The living room was clear, so the men rushed into the bedroom. Still in the lead, Joe felt a heavy impact on his chest as a round hit his plates and pushed the air out of his lungs.

He returned fire, killing the last gunman in the apartment with a quick blast to the face. Gasping for air, Joe reloaded his rifle.

"You okay, dude?" Elias said, checking Joe over for any extra holes.

Joe nodded, unable to breathe or speak yet. The contractors turned around and hustled out of the room. They only had one more apartment to clear.

It turned out to be empty except for a few gunmen's corpses scattered across the bedroom and living room.

Ted keyed his radio's microphone. "Ninth floor clear," he said urgently. "Need immediate medevac for one, severe leg wound."

"Roger that Axe Two," Dufraine's voice came through the radio. "Raven Two is en route. Link up with cordon outside to get CASEVAC'd."

240

The contractors turned on their heels, running to scoop Alejandro up and carry him down to the waiting medical team. Larry stopped and looked at Bryan's body.

"Leave him," Ted said firmly. "We'll come get him later."

Larry was about to argue but chose to let it go. The contractors were heading down the stairs when Alex's voice came through the radio, calm but urgent. "Be advised. Tenth floor clear, two tangos down. Multiple tangos are rappelling down the elevator shaft to the parking garage. Axe One is in pursuit."

CHAPTER FORTY

As soon as the Americans had landed on the roof and dispatched the RPG-wielding Iranian, his compatriot had run down from the roof to the eleventh floor with Axe Two hot on his heels. The Iranian commando paused only to snap a quick burst of fire up the stairwell at the attacking contractors before sprinting to the opposite stairwell and down to the tenth floor.

"The Americans are coming down from the roof," the commando huffed to the gathered Iranian contingent. "Ahmad is dead."

"No matter," Javad spoke in Farsi to the commandos spread around the tenth floor. "We proceed to the garage and make our escape."

Mokri was starting to recover from his state of shock, and he was aware that he was no longer even considered in charge. Javad and the commando sergeant were directing the operation now, and he had grown suspicious of them and their furtive shared glances. He desperately wanted to survive this nightmare, however, so he allowed them to do what they had to do to get him out of the Spire alive.

One of the heavily armed IRGC commandos had sprung the door to the elevator shaft open, and Javad grabbed Mokri by the shoulder, dragging him to the elevator shaft.

"Hook up," he directed, and the two men latched their rappelling harnesses to the prepositioned ropes in the elevator shaft.

The escape plan had been contrived nearly immediately after setting up the Iranian headquarters on the eleventh floor of the Spire. As soon as the residents had been pushed out of the lower floors, Javad had directed several of the Iranian commandos to disable the elevator, holding it at the eleventh floor.

Javad and Mokri went rappelling down the elevator shaft, followed immediately by the IRGC sergeant and several of the commandos. The VAJA operatives were just touching down when the flashbangs went off on the floors above.

Mokri flinched and glanced upward into the elevator shaft while Javad forced the elevator doors open into the parking garage with the help of an IRGC commando. A muffled flurry of gunfire echoed down the elevator shaft, and the IRGC sergeant shoved Mokri through the open elevator door and into the frigid parking garage.

The remaining Iranian commandos rushed through the garage, running between abandoned cars. One of the IRGC men ran to the large sliding exit door and slammed the big, red button next to it. The rest of the Iranians scrambled to the four black Chevy Suburbans, some men aiming their rifles behind them, holding security and scanning for any pursuing Americans.

As the garage door rose with a frustratingly loud clamor, Javad opened the driver's side door of the second Suburban, stepping halfway in. Omid Mokri made his way to the rear passenger side door of the same SUV, with the IRGC sergeant hot on his heels, barking orders to his commandos.

"You, you, and you! Stay behind us and hold off the Americans!" the sergeant shouted at the last three commandos crouched near the rear of the last Suburban. The men did not respond, merely keeping their stubby Kalashnikov rifles pointed at the elevator shaft and the door to the stairwell.

The sounds of the battle above were muffled but ongoing. Automatic rifle fire and explosions echoed through the Spire and down into the garage.

"How many men do we have left?" Mokri asked Sergeant Hamidi as he took his place in the front passenger seat of the Suburban.

The IRGC commando craned his neck around, counting the commandos from front to rear.

"Eleven."

The commando who had opened the door was kneeling around the corner and looking for targets. As Mokri looked forward through the windshield, the man's head snapped backward, a muzzled crack reverberating from somewhere in the distance.

"Get the fuck in the cars!" Javad screamed at the commandos crouched in the garage, right before a rapid series of shots slammed into the engine block of the first Suburban.

"Garage door opening," Evan called out, crouched in his selected hide site a few feet away from Chris. The other sniper could see the door through the powerful scope mounted to his .50 caliber Barrett sniper rifle, but the callout was not for him. Archer Two-One was notifying the Archer One sniper team and the surrounding cordon forces.

The sniper teams had been scanning the sides of the Spire, trying to find targets through the windows, but the terrorists that had taken sanctuary deep inside the building had drawn all the shades. The snipers had nothing to do but to scan for any targets trying to escape.

The outside Norseman Consulting forces had received a radio call from Axe Two announcing that the commandos had wired the top floor, followed by occasional reports on the ongoing assault, and finally, Axe One's advisement that targets were escaping down the elevator shaft to the garage.

As the garage door rose, the battle inside the Spire was dying down, the assault teams having cleared the floors and radioed in their progress. One of the Expeditions was rolling up to the front door to pick up the wounded contractors.

"Dude on the left," Chris called. The door rose slowly, and part of the man's leg was visible. "I'm looking for vehicles."

Evan swiveled his rifle on the tripod and settled his crosshairs on the leg. "Axe One-One, Archer Two-One," the sniper breathed into his radio. "What is your location?"

"Archer Two-One," Alex huffed. "Axe One is en route to the parking garage. Just crossing the second floor now. ETA thirty seconds."

"Roger," Evan responded. "Let us thin the herd before you bust through."

"Copy, will wait for you," Alex responded and, as the garage door cleared the man's torso, Evan settled his crosshairs on the gunman's chest. Evan rechecked his calculations, made the proper adjustments to the turrets on his scope, and decided the crosshairs slightly higher on the Iranian commando's forehead.

"I see a couple of guys in a Suburban," Chris called out.

"Alright hit the truck on my mark," Evan replied. He waited to get his breathing correct, counted his heartbeats, and then squeezed the trigger on his .300 Norma Magnum SRSA1 bullpup.

The muted shot left the suppressed muzzle with a supersonic crack, finding its mark a split second later.

Chris's rifle boomed rapidly, the large rounds screaming out of the semi-automatic sniper rifle and slamming into the engine block of the first Suburban, walking the rounds up the windshield and then across. He'd fired all ten shots within a matter of seconds. The first four .50 caliber rounds tore the eight-cylinder engine of the Suburban apart.

The last six rounds punched through the windshield and the two men sitting in the front seats, then out the back of the Suburban.

From Archer Two's position, the four Suburbans were lined up in an "L" shape, with the second SUV lined up directly behind the first, and the third and fourth SUVs were curling off to the right toward the back of the garage and the stairway. The two snipers could see the commandos taking cover while still trying to keep their rear security and prevent an ambush from behind.

The snipers noticed that the commandos were not taking random shots in their direction, which either meant that the commandos had not located the snipers' position, that they were better trained than most of the mercenaries Norseman had encountered these last several weeks, or both. Either way, the commandos inside the garage could not be allowed to escape.

Evan lined up his second shot on one of the commandos pulling rear security while Chris reloaded the ten-round magazine of his Barrett. He saw the commando snap his rifle up to his eye and spout off a burst of gunfire. Before Evan could squeeze his trigger, the man rocked backward, struggled to maintain his balance, and toppled onto the concrete face first.

Alex had not wasted a minute on the tenth floor. Their breach had coincided perfectly with the other three assault teams', and when they flowed into the hallway, they were greeted by a single surprised Iranian commando wearing jeans, a white t-shirt, and a plate carrier. He held an AK74SU in his hands. Robert saw the man standing in the elevator alcove first and hammered him with multiple rounds from his short-barreled B&T carbine. The ballistic breastplate the man was wearing could withstand a few rounds, but the repetitive gunfire caused the body armor to fail, bullets eventually penetrating the plates and slicing through the commando's chest.

The man collapsed, dropping to the floor with a clatter as his rifle knocked into his equipment. Robert quickly pushed forward into the hallway, dominating the space and scanning for additional targets. There was nobody there, and the remainder of Axe One followed Robert into the hallway unopposed.

"There's nobody else here," Robert said, even as Shawn and Ryan kicked open the first two doors, clearing the apartments.

"Hey!" Riley shouted, leaning over the open elevator door. "They rappelled down the elevator shaft!"

"Parking garage," Alex said. "Let's go!"

Alex led the way down past the scorched and pockmarked floors. When they'd reached the second floor, Alex heard Archer Two's radio call, and he and his team sprinted past the ground floor, down one more flight of stairs, and came to a sliding halt next to a heavy metal door. The contractors were breathing hard, sweat pooling under their plate carriers.

Alex looked up the dark stairwell behind him, observing the blue-white glow of his team's night vision goggles. There was very little time for the team to gather their thoughts. They could already hear Archer Two's rapid, precise rifle fire clanging into the Suburban in the parking garage.

Axe One-One pulled the door open and rushed through. Angelo, Shawn, and Ryan peeled to the right as they entered; Riley and Robert followed Alex to the left.

The three Iranian commandos had been distracted by the sniper's gunfire and did not see Alex and his team at first. The movement in the stairwell drew their attention too late. One commando ripped off a startling burst of automatic fire from his AK74SU, punching the high-velocity rounds through the cinderblock wall to Alex's left. The lead contractor snapped his carbine up and slammed four shots into the chest plate of the first man, causing him to rock backward. Alex was about to swivel his muzzle over to a second target, but the first commando staggered back up.

A stream of bullets erupted past Alex's shoulder as Riley snapped a series of quick shots, sneaking one over the top of the commando's ballistic vest and into his throat.

The contractors could now see the Iranians scrambling for cover behind dusty, abandoned cars scattered around the parking lot. The two commandos pulling rear security got their rifles into action, firing quick pairs of shots over the roof of an old Volvo they were using as cover. Their shots went wide, missing the contractors by a fraction of an inch.

Shawn's laser aiming module danced over the hood of the blue Volvo, his suppressed carbine spitting rounds into the hood and catching one of the Iranians through his right eye. The commando dropped to his back, screaming out in Farsi and holding his head and face in his hands.

246

His comrade behind the Volvo shouted back into the parking garage, and muzzle flashes barked out into the darkness as the remaining Iranian commandos returned fire from behind cars and support columns.

A 5.45x39 round smacked into Ryan's helmet, destroying the mount to his night vision goggles and sending bright spots across his vision. Additional rounds skipped off the concrete at his feet and zipped past him. Ryan blinked hard several times, trying to clear the spots from his eyes. He could no longer see in the darkness, but he shot in the general direction of muzzle flashes further down the garage.

The second commando behind the Volvo popped up, taking aim at Angelo, who was working his way forward. Shawn managed to get two rounds into the commando's chest plate, causing him to whirl around. Shawn's muzzle rose slightly, and he fired twice more, blasting the commando through the face.

The commando's death spasm caused him to yank down hard on the trigger, sending a final round into the side of the last Suburban. The commando who had been shot in the head had stopped squirming and was trying to stagger to his feet. Lifting his AK74SU in shaking hands, he fired over the hood of the Volvo in the general direction of the attacking contractors.

The muzzle flame stabbed out over the hood of the car as Ryan fired the remainder of his magazine at the space above the muzzle flash, connecting with the wounded Iranian's head and silencing his rifle. Ryan dropped to a knee, turning to shout that he was reloading while reaching for a magazine on his belt.

A scream of pain escaped his lips as a round ripped through his elbow, rendering his arm useless. He instinctively dropped his carbine and started to go for his pistol, but series of rounds punched up his plates, stalling him, then continued up through his throat and into his eye socket. Ryan folded over at the waist, flopping to the ground in a pile, his legs at an awkward angle underneath his body.

Angelo and Shawn kept moving, leaving Ryan's body for later and taking cover behind the Volvo.

Immediately after entering the garage and taking out the first Iranian, Alex, Riley, and Robert had kept pushing forward, using the last Suburban as cover. The three contractors had traded gunfire with the commandos on the left end of the garage, dropping an Iranian as he tried to avoid the heavy fire coming at the third Suburban from Chris's .50 caliber rifle.

Alex left the cover of the Suburban and scrambled sideways to a concrete pillar a few meters away. He was evaluating the situation on the left when one of the Iranians in the second Suburban started shouting at the men in the back.

Suddenly three AK74SUs barked on full-automatic from behind the second Suburban, and the surviving commandos started bounding forward. Axe One's assaulters ducked behind whatever cover they could find as a deluge of gunfire sparked off cars and chipped concrete around them.

Riley peeked out from behind the last Suburban and aimed at one of the commandos crouching behind a Chevy Lumina sedan. The contractor was firing hasty rounds. The series of bullets were ineffective in stopping the Iranians' rush forward.

The man suddenly came apart in Riley's night vision goggles as a massive .50 caliber sniper round impacted the Iranian's shoulder. The great round would have wholly disintegrated the man, but his ballistic vest kept his torso somewhat intact.

Another commando was about to rush to the third Suburban, but seeing his comrade virtually explode made him pause.

That instant of hesitation killed him. With contractors on both sides drawing a bead on him, multiple rounds found their mark high on the man's chest, and he crumpled, blood leaking out of his eviscerated throat.

The rest of the Iranians at the back of the parking garage through a series of multi-colored smoke grenades, filling the space between them and the last functioning Suburban with a thick cloud of red, white, and green smoke.

"MOVING!" Alex shouted, rushing forward to the third Suburban. The other four surviving contractors started peppering the second Suburban and sending an occasional round through the cloud of smoke.

Robert came running up behind Alex, skidding to a halt.

"The glass is bulletproof," he said. A glance around the corner of the wrecked Suburban they were hiding behind confirmed that. The glass had multiple spiderwebbed marks across the windows, but none of the bullets appeared to have punctured it.

248

Another Iranian commando came slamming into the end of the second Suburban, just a few meters away. Alex snapped his carbine up and sent a flurry of rounds through the side of the commando's head. He tipped forward, face planting into the ground.

Sergeant Hamidi and Javad had climbed out of the SUV, against Mokri's protests, to give their surviving commandos enough covering fire so they could reach the sole functioning vehicle left in the garage. Javad and the IRGC sergeant were old hands at this. They were disciplined, firing their stubby rifles over and around the SUV, communicating with each other and with the few surviving commandos.

Mokri had never been under fire. Where Javad and the sergeant were firing quick pairs in semi-automatic mode, Mokri had laid his rifle over the roof of the Suburban and was spraying bullets on full auto, while remaining in the relative safety of the SUV.

"Come to us!" the IRGC sergeant shouted to the commandos remaining. A sudden swell in gunfire rose from the back, and two commandos ran forward. The first commando took a hit, and the sergeant watched the man virtually come apart before his eyes.

The second man appeared to have seen it too, as he stumbled and skidded to a halt, attempting to backpedal out of the sniper's sightline. Javad was busy laying down covering fire, but Mokri was still inside the SUV, reloading his rifle, and he watched the second man drop to the floor in a spray of blood.

"FUCK!" Mokri screamed, running the bolt on his rifle to chamber a fresh round.

"Throw smoke!" the sergeant called back to his men. Three hissing canisters flew out from the back of the garage and spewed a cloud of multi-colored smoke.

"Start the truck," the sergeant directed Javad.

Javad finished his magazine and then clambered into the Suburban through the passenger side door. He pulled the keys off of the carabiner hooked to his belt loop and twisted them in the ignition. The Suburban fired up, and Javad shouted through the open back door. "Ready!"

In truth, Javad was not ready. They still had no idea where the sniper was, if there was more than one, or if the SUV's armoring would withstand the powerful sniper rounds.

One of the commandos came running out of the smoke, alone. He hit the side of the truck at a dead run, and Mokri shouted at him, "Where are the others?"

"Dead!" the commando shouted back, before leaning around the corner of the SUV to send a burst of fire back at their attackers.

Rounds ripped through him, showering Sergeant Hamidi with blood.

"Get in the fucking truck!" Mokri screamed at the sergeant, who dove into the front seat, slamming the door closed

"Drive!" Hamidi shouted at Javad frantically.

"Is it just us?" Javad asked, turning to the sergeant.

Mokri saw the look between the two men. He saw the sergeant move his right arm toward his hip and the pistol start to come out of the holster. He saw the sergeant begin to turn in his seat.

The gunshot startled Javad. Blood sprayed across the passenger side window, and the bullet was buried in the windshield. The sound was deafening. He blinked as salty blood from Sergeant Hamidi's head sprayed in his eyes.

Javad looked at the twitching sergeant, slumped over the dashboard of the Suburban, his lifeless eyes bulging.

A point of hot metal pressed into the base of Javad's skull.

"Detonate the explosives," Mokri snarled into Javad's ear. Javad slowly withdrew a cell phone from his pocket. Holding the phone up so Mokri can see, he accessed the contacts and called the first one, AAAA.

In the command center on the eleventh floor, a cell phone rang momentarily before the plastic explosives scattered around the floor detonated, blowing out the windows and rocking the building. A series of secondary explosions could be heard over the cacophony as crates of ammunition and explosives caught fire and exploded. Within seconds, fire broke out, rapidly spreading across the now vacant floor and licking the sky.

"Drive," Mokri hissed, his freshly fired Glock 17 glued to Javad's neck.

"Truck," Evan shouted to Chris.

He didn't have to; the sniper nestled behind the .50 caliber rifle had been watching the garage door like a hawk.

The Suburban nosed around the wrecked SUV in front of it. Chris settled his crosshairs on the grille and pulled the trigger twice.

The Suburban came to a grinding halt and emitted steam from under the hood.

"Archer Two," Alex's voice came through the radio, "can you hit the driver?"

"We got it Axe One," Evan responded. Chris raised his crosshairs slightly and pulled the trigger once more.

Inside the Suburban, Mokri felt the impacts on the SUV and the shuddering of the engine as the truck slowed to a halt.

"What happened?" he demanded.

"They have some sort of big rifle out there." Javad calmly kept his hands glued to the steering wheel, and he knew it was going to be all over in a few moments. "They disabled the truck."

Mokri looked around the garage through the splintered windows. Four assaulters were approaching the stricken vehicle, their carbines up behind glowing eyes.

"The Americans are coming," Mokri stammered, pressing his pistol harder into Javad's neck. Javad could feel the slide of the gun slip backward slightly against his skin, pushing the Glock out of battery and rendering it temporarily inoperable. He doubted Mokri noticed. Now was his chance. He had a moment in time to turn the table on Mokri, and maybe deal with the Americans.

Javad started to tense, preparing to spin.

The last .50 caliber round pierced the windshield, and slammed into Javad's chest, blowing his head clean off. Surprised, Mokri accidentally pulled the trigger of his pistol, sending the striker forward ineffectually on the out of battery slide.

Within a split second, the back doors were being wrenched open, and a Norseman Contractor ripped Mokri out of the Suburban, knocking his pistol from his hand and slamming him to the ground. Mokri felt the wind rush out of him as his hands were fastened behind his back. He started screaming, but a pair of hands forced a wad of cloth into his mouth, stifling him. The men pulled him upright and draped a hood over his head.

CHAPTER FORTY-ONE

The lock on Gerry Erikson's door clicked, and the door swung open. Gunderson, Dufraine, and Yale stood in the doorway.

"It's over, Gerry," Gunderson said softly. "Our teams assaulted the Spire this evening and eliminated the last of the terrorist cell."

Gerry looked at the three men without sitting up. "I suppose that's good," he said. "What now?"

"Come with us," Dufraine said. "We have something for you."

Erikson hauled himself off the bed, tugging his rumpled white t-shirt down over the waistline of his old uniform pants. He paused for a minute as if deciding whether or not to follow. He sighed and stepped forward.

The four men walked out of the Brain and down the hallway toward the stairwell to the main offices. They walked in silence, their footsteps tapping on the hard tile floors. Instead of going up at the stairwell, they went down, deeper underground.

They came to a heavy metal door, and Dufraine reached forward to unlock it and pushed the door open.
Sitting at the table in the room were three men bound to chairs.

"You recognize him," Yale said, indicating al Kobani. Erikson nodded.

"And this man you probably knew as Antony," Dufraine said, gesturing to the second. The cogs in Gerry's memory clicked into place. He'd seen the man at various events around town, almost always at the Mayor's elbow. "His real name is Ardashir Khorasani," Dufraine continued. "An Iranian intelligence officer who was acting as Mayor Stark's handler. He is the one who planned the massacre on Broadway."
Erikson's eyes snapped from Dufraine back to Khorasani. He was beginning to understand what was happening.

"And this," Gunderson said, "is Omid Mokri, commander of this little terror cell, responsible for planning and coordinating all of their activities," there was a pregnant, weighty pause as Gunderson took a shallow breath, "including kidnapping your wife."

Without taking his eyes off of the three men, Gerry angled his head and inquired, "What about Reyes?"

"Well," Gunderson responded, "the powers that be have decided that it is not in our national interest to publicly announce Iranian involvement in this ordeal." Gunderson rolled his eyes as he spoke.

"So?" Erikson said. His narrow eyes hadn't left Mokri. The Iranian looked defeated, and Gerry even wondered if he might smell a faint trace of urine emanating from the Iranian commander.

"So, Reyes will be exposed as the mastermind," Gunderson shrugged. "It will be reported as an act of domestic terrorism on behalf of communist or socialist or whatever-ist masterminds, and we will all move on from this as if this was the first, and hopefully last, act of revolution in Minnesota.

"A lot did happen though," Gerry turned to look at them bewildered, "A lot of people died." Quieter, almost inaudible he added, "My wife died.".

"I know, Gerry," Gunderson nodded, then checked his watch. "Which is why an anonymous tip was sent to the Alexandria Police Department about thirty minutes ago. About three minutes from now, they will make entry to one of the safe houses, where they will find Reyes hanging, with an incredibly detailed suicide note at his feet taking responsibility for everything that has happened these three weeks."

"What about these guys?" It was more of a demand than a question.

Gunderson shrugged. "There seems to be no more use for them."

The three men lifted their heads at that statement, anger and fear washing over their faces.

"We can't keep them," Gunderson continued, "and the US government has no desire to spend taxpayer money on babysitting their asses in prison."

There was a shuffling behind Gerry, and the Norseman leadership and Alex entered, carrying Gerry's old duty belt with his Glock 21 in the holster.

Dufraine passed the heavy belt over to the sheriff.

"These men are your responsibility now," Gunderson said. "But do try to decide what to do with them soon, I need to clear space in our compound."

With that, the four contractors left the room, letting the door slam shut behind them.

Erikson stood frozen for a moment, dumbly staring at the three terrorists. Al Kobani glared at him with an unwavering rage, as if he was trying to strike Erikson down with the force of his glare alone. Khorasani had his eyes closed, and he was muttering softly and rocking back and forth. Gerry figured that the man was praying. Mokri was whimpering, tears running down his face.

Gerry considered the weight of his duty belt, holding it in his hands in front of him. He swung the belt around, fastening it around his waist. He subconsciously adjusted it, getting it just right on his hips. The weight of the belt felt loose. Erikson had lost weight in the past few days locked up without eating much in the Norseman compound.

He never took his eyes off the three men.

The faces of his deputies flashed before him; then his wife's sweet smile, her gentle eyes. Gerry started to cry, silently asking the apparitions what he should do. He unlatched his holster. When he looked at al Kobani, he saw Tommy, slaughtered in the street all those weeks ago. With Khorasani he saw the faces of his five deputies, cut down that fateful day on Broadway.

And with Mokri, he only saw Ellen. His wife, so exquisite, so innocent. Butchered.

The specters were silent.

Wiping his eyes and running nose with his forearm, he heaved a sigh. The pistol felt heavier in his hand than he'd expected.

"You really think he'll do it?" Alex asked as they climbed the stairs to the main office.

"Yeah," Gunderson said darkly, "I do."

A quick trio of shots sounded behind them. *Blat, blat, blat!*

The contractors stopped and turned slightly. Gunderson sighed.

"Alex, would you please go get the sheriff and ensure that he makes it out without hurting anyone else." Alex nodded and hustled back down the stairs.

"I'll send someone to clean the cell," Gunderson added.

Minutes later, Gunderson sat in his office. The operation was over, the contract was done, but he had work to do. He had men killed and wounded, and at least one wounded man would never return to assaulter duty again. Gunderson had insurance paperwork to fill out,

254

and it would take him several hours to make sure everything was in order. He'd need to approve life insurance payouts for Ryan, Harold, and Bryan. None of the men had families to support, seeing as it was almost a prerequisite that Norseman contractors be unmarried and without dependents to be on the assault teams. However, they did have parents and, in the case of Harold, an estranged ex-wife who was entitled to the payout.

Gunderson flipped on his television and was greeted with a welcome sight.

"Authorities have informed us that the unfinished apartment building known as 'the Spire' caught fire late last evening," the morning news anchor was saying through his impossibly straight teeth and well-maintained mustache. "The fire chief has assured us that there were no injuries. They believe the fire started due to a gas leak and subsequent explosion."

Gunderson smiled ruefully. The public could sleep comfortably knowing that the sounds of pitched battle sounding from the tallest building around were the sounds of a catastrophic, and highly unlikely to be repeated, gas leak.

The Norseman Consulting president sighed, turning back to his paperwork as the news anchor shifted from the inferno in the Spire to a story about an underdog local bowling team placing in the state tournament.

Everything had gone exactly how Gunderson had promised Erikson it would. Reyes and RIF had been blamed for the Broadway Massacre and the subsequent rash of violence, including the kidnapping and murder of Ellen Erikson. The revelation lifted most of the suspicion off the sheriff, although some members of the public, notably the Mayor and her supporters still held conspiratorial grudges against him.

A week after the assault on the Spire, the whole affair began to fade into the backdrop of American and Minnesotan life. Winter athletics tournaments, ice fishing rallies, and the general hustle and bustle of an increasingly connected and disaffected public had pushed the carnage to the back of Alexandria's collective memory. The national news sources were long gone.

Gerry Erikson had buried his wife in a small, private ceremony at the cemetery behind the tiny Lutheran church where Ellen's grandparents were buried. Gerry's in-laws would not even look at him during the ceremony. He had always known that they did not approve of him, but now there was open hatred.

It wasn't as if Gerry didn't blame himself enough already. Ellen's parents could hate him as much as they wanted; they'd never be able to make him hate himself more than he already did.

When the dirt filled her grave, Ellen's family left Gerry standing alone in the cemetery. They held a private visitation for their daughter to which Gerry was not invited.

Gerry was on administrative leave for a few weeks after burying Ellen. Deputy Johnson had taken up the mantle as interim sheriff.

Gerry's way of dealing with grief had mostly consisted of wandering around his house for a few minutes in the morning, followed by a long spell of sitting and drinking coffee. He barely ate, he did not sleep for the first several days, and he had not shaved in weeks. His reddish facial hair flecked with gray had grown outward into a curly beard.

As his leave came to a close, there were a couple of things troubling him beside the death of his wife. The first was that killing the three terrorists in the Norseman Consulting holding cell had not bothered him all that much. He thought he'd at least have nightmares about the point-blank execution, but when he did sleep, he dreamed only of Ellen. Was he some sociopath that just needed to be triggered? What happened to his sense of justice, the desire to do things right no matter the cost?

The second was that Jennifer Stark appeared to have gotten off more or less scot-free. Erikson had watched her press conference on television where she announced the "resolution" of the Broadway Massacre and Reyes' suicide note. Apparently, the terrorist in the hospital had miraculously come out of his coma and corroborated the note, then mysteriously passed away, his heart giving out one night as he slept.

Stark even credited the Alexandria PD for the dismantling and apprehension of the RIF terrorists, which in and of itself did not bother Gerry. He knew the credit had to go to someone, and the men and women in the APD had worked hard alongside the deputies in his own office. He also knew that Stark wasn't about to give him any credit.

No, what grated on Gerry was that the Mayor was receiving over-the-top praise for spearheading the investigation, as if she had been a detective on the street, searching for clues and other things that hadn't even happened. He couldn't fathom the praise. The major networks were mainly spewing repetitious platitudes and press releases that the Mayor had probably written herself.

Erikson had sat languishing over every incorrect detail, every ounce of undeserved praise heaped on Mayor Stark until the news stories just stopped one day.

Something was going on in the Middle East. The stock markets were up, or maybe down. The Russians were up to something, as usual. A random celebrity overdosed. The events in the small Minnesota town faded into oblivion.

But Gerry Erikson was still there, alone in the house he'd once shared with his wife, and his grief was evolving into anger by the day. He stopped watching television and just sat in the dark house, unsleeping and miserable. He felt paralyzed, caught between wanting to do something, anything, and his desire to just be left alone to grieve.

Then, about four days before Gerry's leave was up, a knock on the door roused him from his stupor. He rose slowly, moving too sluggishly to catch whoever was at the door and was greeted instead with an envelope on top of the snow on his front porch.

Erikson looked around and thought he heard the sound of a vehicle echoing down the street. He picked up the envelope and ripped it open on the way back inside.

A notice of investigation into his conduct during the massacre on Broadway and the weeks following.

He stared at the piece of paper, which felt suddenly heavy in his hand. He had anticipated an investigation, but this piece of paper singled him out. His relationship with Norseman Consulting, in particular, was in question. Gerry felt the frustration welling up as he read the article, signed by some lawyer within the state agency responsible for such matters.

Gerry sat down heavily on the couch, rubbing his eyes and reflexively reaching for his remote. The television clicked on.

"...indicated today that Mayor Stark may be considering a gubernatorial run in the next election. This news comes as no surprise after Mayor Stark's excellent handling of the tragedy in Alexandria earlier this winter."

Erikson's head snapped up, indignation welling up inside him. He screamed, throwing the remote at the television screen and causing it to fizzle and distort for a moment before returning to normal.

Gerry found himself standing in his living room, his chest rising and falling with mounting fury. His fists were clenched so hard his nails were on the verge of piercing his skin. He walked toward the kitchen, then turned suddenly and walked back to his room.

He knew what he needed to do.

It took him the rest of his leave to formulate and plot out his course of action. Multiple phone calls and entire days spent reviewing blueprints and schematics had left him exhausted. Now newly galvanized, Gerry found himself getting solid nights of sleep for the first time in weeks.

Standing in his living room on the last night before he was to return to his office, Gerry solemnly splashed the contents of the red jerry can across his couch and coffee table. Walking backward, he spread more of the liquid across the kitchen and living room, emptying the can around the dining chairs. He picked up the second can and continued until his whole house had the pungent smell of gasoline.

He walked out through the garage and got into Ellen's Volkswagen, backing the car out into the street and waiting until his wick caught.

There wasn't much of a wait. The fire spread quickly throughout the house, and Gerry drove away as the smoke billowed into the night behind him.

He reached over to the passenger seat and picked up the old pistol sitting there. A Colt 1911A1 in .45 ACP, it was a former government model and inherited from Gerry's grandfather who had carried it while working as a detective shortly after the Vietnam War. The old warhorse had not been fired in years, but Gerry had pulled it out of his gun safe to clean, oil, and check the pistol before setting off on his mission.

He drove with his knee on the steering wheel while he slid one of the magazines into his pocket and pressed a second into the butt of the pistol. Gerry worked the freshly oiled, worn-in slide, chambering a fat .45 caliber cartridge. He dropped the magazine and slid a loose round in before replacing the magazine in the pistol.

Even though the pistol was the same caliber as his duty weapon and carried fewer rounds, the Colt was much heavier. It was not the most practical piece, at least compared to the newer polymer framed pistols, but this was as close as he had to a family heirloom.

258

Gerry palmed the pistol, feeling the custom grips that his grandfather had made out of the horns of an elk. He checked the sights, dim white dots in the relative darkness of the car. He clicked the safety back on and put the pistol in the large front pocket of his coat.

It took him just a few minutes to reach his destination. He sat and listened to his radio scanner and waited until the fire department had been dispatched to his blazing house, which he was sure would burn to the ground. Gerry had no doubt the investigators would figure out that the fire had been caused by arson, and that he would be the primary suspect.

That didn't matter. He only needed a temporary distraction. The clock on the car's dashboard clicked past midnight, and Gerry left the Volkswagen and walked through the yard to the darkened house in front of him.

His breath throwing steam in front of him, Gerry crept, purposively, toward the back door. His hand was tight around the pistol in his pocket. He withdrew his hunting knife from his jeans pocket and jammed it into the frame next to the flimsy deadbolt of the sliding glass door.

A few seconds of working the knife back and forth and Gerry managed to force the door open with a sharp pop. He moved quickly and quietly into the house and punched the code he had gotten as a favor from Yale into the home security system.

The alarm disabled, Gerry padded silently through the house, his knife back in his pocket, the Colt in his hands. He moved slowly, keeping his footsteps controlled and allowing his eyes to adjust to the darkness.

His target was on the top floor, so Gerry rounded the corner to the staircase. He stepped cautiously on the carpeted steps; the pistol trained upwards as he slowly climbed the stairs. His breathing and pulse quickened as he reached the upstairs.

At the end of the hallway, the door to the master bedroom was cracked, and Gerry could hear soft snoring. He stood there for a moment, fighting to control his breath. Now that he was here, he wasn't sure he wanted to go through with it. He could leave now, face the music for the arson, and subject himself to the investigation. Nobody would ever know.

He pushed the door open and slipped silently inside.

Erikson's conscience was faintly reminding him that he could still leave. But staring at the sleeping couple in front of him, he knew he had crossed the Rubicon. He had to keep going.

He reached over and felt for the light switch, found it, and threw it on, filling the room with light.

The couple in the bed stirred, and the man opened his eyes first and sat upward with a start.

"Holy shit!" Todd Stark gasped. Gerry supposed that he cut a terrifying figure. He had not shaved in weeks, and his curly beard streaked with red and gray made him hard to identify. Plus, the forty-five in his hand must have had the effect that he was hoping for.

Her husband's gasp woke her, and Jennifer Stark snapped upright.

"Gerry, what the fuck are you doing in our house?" She did not see the pistol outright. Her eyes moved from his unkempt hair, his piercing eyes, curly beard, down over the dusty barn coat he was wearing, and then finally settled on the 1911 in his hand.

Her eyes widened, and Todd summoned the courage to shout at Gerry. "Get the fuck out of my house before I call the cops!"

His fearsome façade struck Gerry as almost amusing—a misguided attempt at intimidating the man with nothing left to lose. Erikson raised his pistol, leveling it at Todd Stark. "Shut the fuck up, Todd."

Todd shrank away from the broad muzzle of the Colt in Erikson's hand. Jennifer was shaking, clutching the bed covers up to her neck.

"What do you want, Gerry?" Jennifer asked meekly.

"This," Gerry said, and the pistol barked. Todd's head snapped backward, soaking the headboard in blood, and his body sank into the pillows. Jennifer screamed, and Erikson moved quickly to her side of the bed, leveling the pistol right up to her eye.

"Shut up!" He shouted in her face. The screaming was replaced with a sobbing whimper.

"Do you see how it feels now?" he demanded. "Do you see how it feels to have someone taken from you?"

"He didn't have anything to do with this, Gerry," Jennifer sobbed.

"Neither did she."

The pistol barked again.

Time to go. Gerry bolted out of the house and into the Volkswagen. He drove aimlessly off into the night.

He wound a meandering path around the various lakes in the area, holding his now-defunct badge in his hand, rubbing the metal with his thumb. He didn't know what to do. There was, quite obviously, no going back. He could turn himself in, but he had no desire to go to prison. He could run, but he had nowhere to go.

There is one option, Gerry thought, a solemn realization that he had only one option left. He turned his car around and pushed the Bluetooth buttons on the steering wheel. The sound of his phone ringing through the car's speaker system broke suddenly into the silence. He stopped on the bridge between two lakes at just past one in the morning and rolled down the windows.

"Huh-hello?" the groggy man on the other end of the phone finally answered.

"James," Gerry greeted him while he stared at his badge in his hand.

"What can I do for you, Gerry?" Gunderson answered, the grogginess wearing off.

Gerry tossed his badge out the window and into the frigid water of the channel. "I need a job."

Made in the USA
Monee, IL
21 May 2020